T0076374

"Jiang-Li's last pearl, nothing more than a lighthouse beacon," Dan said.

Nami nodded, not trusting herself to speak yet. The lighthouse had been erected when she was only a child. A beacon of human and fathomfolk friendship, she'd been told every time she'd asked the officials, her teachers, her mother. To stop the ships from damaging one of the last underwater havens. But Nami knew what it really was. The whispers bitter in the abyssal zone of Yonakuni haven. A bargaining chip. As long as they could see the light twinkling in the distance, the humans were reassured that folk were being obedient little neighbours, circling their oversized fish tank. And the folk were helpless. Staring at their hope but never able to use it.

She picked the pearl up, gingerly holding it outstretched in both hands, wanting to bring it close and yet afraid to have it near her. It throbbed, warm to the touch. Her hands were suddenly damp with sweat, and she nearly dropped it. Dan was saying something, but she couldn't hear him past the rush in her ears. Her heart was beating so fast she could feel it straining through her chest to break free. A long moment passed as she waited for something else.

It could have been her.

"Hello, little one," she whispered into the shell.

FATHOMFOLK

Drowned World: Book One

ELIZA CHAN

orbitbooks.net

This book is a work of fiction. Names, characters, places, and incidents are the product of the author's imagination or are used fictitiously. Any resemblance to actual events, locales, or persons, living or dead, is coincidental.

Copyright © 2024 by Eliza Chan
Excerpt from *The Jasad Heir* copyright © 2023 by Sara Hashem
Excerpt from *The Phoenix King* copyright © 2021 by Aparna Verma

Cover design by Ella Garrett
Cover illustration by Kelly Chong
Author photograph by Sandi Hodkinson

Hachette Book Group supports the right to free expression and the value of copyright. The purpose of copyright is to encourage writers and artists to produce the creative works that enrich our culture.

The scanning, uploading, and distribution of this book without permission is a theft of the author's intellectual property. If you would like permission to use material from the book (other than for review purposes), please contact permissions@hbgusa.com. Thank you for your support of the author's rights.

Orbit
Hachette Book Group
1290 Avenue of the Americas
New York, NY 10104
orbitbooks.net

First Edition: February 2024
Simultaneously published in Great Britain by Orbit

Orbit is an imprint of Hachette Book Group.
The Orbit name and logo are registered trademarks of Little, Brown
Book Group Limited.

The publisher is not responsible for websites (or their content)
that are not owned by the publisher.

The Hachette Speakers Bureau provides a wide range of authors for speaking events. To find out more, go to hachettespeakersbureau.com or email HachetteSpeakers@hbgusa.com.

Orbit books may be purchased in bulk for business, educational, or promotional use. For information, please contact your local bookseller or the Hachette Book Group Special Markets Department at special.markets@hbgusa.com.

Library of Congress Control Number: 2023946379

ISBNs: 9780316564922 (trade paperback), 9780316564939 (ebook)

Printed in the United States of America

LSC-C

Printing 2, 2024

To Ken
For giving me a place to call home

Chapter One

A late arrival elbowed past Mira, knocking her out of position. His jaw was tight, and he wrinkled his nose as he met her eye. "Keep in formation, saltie."

Mira fist-palm saluted sarcastically. She had heard it all before; got into fights with pettier human bureaucrats than him. The delegates continued at a snail's pace, ambling as if perusing market stalls on a Tiankawi festival day rather than inspecting a rooftop military parade in the baking midday sun. The wax coat of Mira's border guard uniform was akin to a simmering claypot. If she strained, she could hear the ocean below, but thirty floors up where they stood, the breeze didn't provide much reprieve. Sweat dripped from her forehead and she cricked her neck.

The captain of the kumiho – the city guard, led the politicians down the line. "And this is Mira, newly appointed as captain of the border guard." The older man was de facto Minister of Defence, but he stroked his silver moustache like an indulgent grandfather offering candied lotus seeds. Mira had seen the other side of him. She saluted the delegates, the Minister of Ceremonies and two junior officials.

"Ah, we've heard a lot about you," said the Minister of Ceremonies, a tall middle-aged woman. "Helping out the Minister of Fathomfolk. The siren."

Helping out was not how Mira would have phrased it. It was

more of a partnership really. She pushed a smile into the corners of her mouth. "Half-siren actually. I'm glad to be here today."

"You should be," the man on the left said. "First fathomfolk in the military and now the first to reach captaincy. Integration at its finest." The words were well-meaning enough but she could hear the abacus beads clicking in his head. Not satisfied with putting her name out as a fathomfolk success story, now they wanted to paste billboards all over the city. Mira had refused. It was difficult enough to do her job without her face staring back from every skybridge, walkway and tram platform. "With all due respect, sir, I hope to inspire fathomfolk to join *all* branches." Her emphasis was deliberate. While she was a trailblazer, there were only four other folk in any aspect of government. All on the military side, all in her chinthe border guard rather than the more influential kumiho city guard. Titans forbid that folk get into the offices of agriculture or transport; the glamour and influence they could have . . .

The remaining official who had not spoken simply pinned Mira's captain badge on the front of her coat: the golden liondog namesake of the chinthe. His hand shook, eyes decidedly not meeting hers. He was afraid. Afraid of the siren mutt without a leash. He did well not to flinch. Mira nodded and smiled, went through the motions of small talk the same way she got dressed in the morning: automatically, perfunctorily, with her mind sorting through endless lists and jobs that needed to be done. If she kept pretending it didn't bother her, one day it might be true.

"Did you see the look on his face? Pale as a sail," a voice whispered behind her as the delegates moved on. One of her lieutenants.

"Bollocks, he'd probably forgotten where he was. Doddering fools refuse to retire until they have to be carried out." Lieutenant Tam's baritone carried above the other voices.

Mira allowed herself a half-smile. At least some people had her back.

Despite everything, it had been a good day. Two of her good friends had been promoted and a rusalka had just completed advanced training. The border guards were never invited to the kumiho celebrations in City Hall. The steamed dumplings and free-flowing wine would be missed, but the entitled city guard would not be. They flaunted their ceremonial swords like children's toys. The chinthe only got symbolic daggers, another slight to add to the heap. Mira ran her thumb down the worn hilt of hers.

This group had been with her for nearly as long as her chinthe dagger; patrolling the waters in the southern districts of the sprawling Tiankawi city state. The border guards' jurisdiction was supposedly only around resettlement and trade. But over the decades, the city guard had refused to have anything to do with the folk-concentrated south. The whole region would have fallen into the hands of gangs had it not been for the chinthe.

From the rooftop training ground, sea level was quite a drop. In her younger days, Mira had clambered across buildings, vaulted and scrabbled through various shortcuts. But the long way had its own charm. The city stretched out, monolithic pillars a canopy above the shanty towns below. At low tide the planks of the walkways oozed with muddy water, threatening to warp faster than they could be fixed. At high tide they were completely submerged, beholden to the mercies of the waters that surrounded Tiankawi. Not that this presented a problem for the folk.

Mira's usual after-work haunt was nothing more than a street stall near the port in Seong district. An elderly couple of stallholders seared skewers of spiced tiger prawns and whole fish over coals, bottles of moonshine floating in the water by their feet.

"To the new captain, Mira o' the chinthe, we are not worthy," Lieutenant Tam said with a mock bow.

"Oh piss off." Mira prodded him with the toe of her boot.

"Don't forget about us when you're a lofty council member," he added. Mira rolled her eyes, not wasting her breath on a retort.

"He has a point," said Mikayil, her other lieutenant, his thick eyebrows wiggling at her from an amiable brown face. He wiped his hands neatly on a square of cloth from his pocket.

"They want you for leadership," Lucia agreed. She was one of the newest ensigns, her uniform still pressed every morning and her face free from the worn river lines the others had. She held her sheathed dagger like they'd given her a nugget of gold. Mira remembered that elation. Wished she had a little of it left.

"They want a tick box in the Council; a head-bobbing, arse-kissing recruitment pamphlet. Well, what do you think?" Mira said, posing with her hand on her hip, a caricature of an enrolment notice. They laughed, clinking bottles and turning to talk of other things. Mira took a long swig of the local brew. She wished it was that easy to brush it off inside as well. The faces of the delegates today confirmed what she already knew. All they saw was a half-siren. No matter the uniform she wore, the exams she passed, the ideas she brought to the discussion; they always saw her as fathomfolk first. She'd never lived in an underwater haven – the semi-submerged city was her only home – and yet she'd always be an outsider.

She helped herself to another bottle, raising it until the stallholder auntie nodded in acknowledgement. Heard the merry-making fall silent suddenly.

A group of folk made their way down the walkway. Walking four abreast, they took up all the space. Mira recognised some of them: the whiskers of the ikan keli catfish twins, the swagger of the broad-shouldered kelpie leader in front. Drawbacks: a group of dissident folk who had been openly sceptical of her appointment. They walked with confident purpose, stopping too close to the border guards' celebration for comfort. Mira felt the wariness of her colleagues, drinks being placed down on tables, hands inching towards baston sticks.

"Congratulations are in order, *Captain*," Lynnette, the

Drawback leader said. Sarcasm tugged on the edges of her words. As if she wasn't tall enough, her tousled mohawk added inches to her height, like the crest of a wave.

Mira stood slowly, closing the distance in their heights a little, trying to defuse the situation with a light-heartedness she did not truly feel. "My thanks, you're welcome to join." Eyes glanced over the makeshift seats; nothing more than upturned wooden crates. The table a couple of damp pallets, mildewed around the edges.

The younger catfish twin was staring at Ensign Lucia, baiting her to look away first. He bared his teeth with a sudden hiss, barbed fins fanning down otherwise human-looking forearms. The effect was startling. Disquieting. Lucia toppled off the wooden crate she was sitting on. Only the quick reactions of those beside her prevented her from falling entirely into the water. The folk cackled.

"We've somewhere to be," Lynnette said.

"Another time perhaps." Mira kept her voice steady. Neutral.

The kelpie flexed her generous biceps, the sand god amulet around her neck swinging. "Unlike some, we're busy making a difference for folk in the city."

Mira heard Tam curse quietly behind her, the tension thick. Despite the alcohol, she suddenly felt very sober. Of course, just because she'd been made captain didn't mean all folk approved her appointment. "Should you have any suggestions for change, I'd be glad to hear them."

"Try changing yourself," a whisper from the back of the new group snarked. Loud enough for all to hear. Not enough of an insult to warrant anything really. What was Mira – the first folk captain in the history of the city – going to do? Arrest the most vocal protest group on her first night? The Drawbacks knew it as well, Lynnette seemingly swaggering up to make this exact point.

"Good night, *Captain*. I'm sure our paths will cross again soon."

The Drawbacks did not wait for the response. They jumped,

cannonball-diving and flipping from the walkway into the water on either side with whoops and jeers. Making splashes so big that the border guards were drenched completely.

Saltwater ran down Mira's face and coat as her colleagues swore and stood up around her. She sat back down, taking a sip of her now salty beer. She'd hoped to enjoy her promotion for at least one day, but there would be no such respite.

Mira had almost succeeded in putting the Drawbacks out of her mind by the time she caught the tram. It was mostly empty apart from a drunk sleeping in the corner and a fathomfolk couple talking in whispers by the doors. The carriage lurched forward on the raised rails as it headed towards the central Jingsha district. Here stood the proud buildings at the heart of the city, the steel-boned monuments to humanity's prowess. Built during the Great Bathyal War, when it became clear that fighting between humanity and fathomfolk would not change the rising water levels; before the decades of floods. Built to endure. The rest of the city was made up of scattered semi-submerged neighbourhoods sprawled around Jingsha. Mira herself came from one of those districts, a shanty town really. She'd never thought that one day she'd live in the centre.

When she opened the door to her apartment, it was snowing. A layer of white covered everything as if a flurry had passed through the room. It was like the stories her ama had told, tales set in winter palaces on top of mountains she'd never known. Flakes like tiny flowers drifted towards her and despite herself, she stuck out her tongue. The cold sliver melted and sharpened her senses. She could've stayed there all night, head tilted as if towards the sun, and let it fall on her face. The sound of familiar footsteps made her turn. Her partner Kai stood waiting for her to notice.

"You have no idea how much I love you right now," he said with a smile that spread from his mouth into his warm brown eyes. He soaked the scene in, clearly pleased with himself.

"What did you do, you mad fool?" she said, unable to stop herself from laughing.

He came towards her, hugging her tight and warm. "Congratulations!"

"What, what is all this?" she said again. Insisting this time. She extracted herself briefly, even though she just wanted to bury her nose in his shirt. He smelt of home. Of soup broth and lemongrass soap. Though he was impeccably dressed, his fingers were nonetheless stained with black ink. She took one of his hands, rubbing at the smudges as he talked.

"I have to be impartial, I know. And you didn't want it to be a big deal. But how can I not celebrate this? You made captain!" he said. Mira cupped the side of his jaw, the bristles on his chin tickling her palm. He could still make her heart sing after two years. "So," he continued, turning to plant a gentle kiss on her hand, "we can celebrate your promotion here – at home – with all the fuss I want to lavish on you."

"Yes, but what is *this*?" She gestured around. Now that she had a moment to look, she realised he had covered the furniture with blankets, rendering the sofa and the dining table into soft white mounds. The snow falling around her was real though. It was all Kai. He demonstrated, flicking water into the air and using his waterweaving powers to freeze the droplets as they fell in perfectly defined snowflakes. It hardly looked like he was putting any effort into it, a level of skill that would make any other fathomfolk sweat with exertion. Delicate precision that only someone of his upbringing could achieve.

"You wanted to see snow; you've never been north. Honestly, I want to take you there. I *will* take you there! But for now, this will do."

Despite the cold, Mira felt her skin tingle where it touched his.

Her head spun with his words. Kai was never one to do things by halves. Even after all this time together, he could still surprise her. She wondered if all folk born in the sea havens were like this, but she doubted it. He was pure sincerity and joy.

He presented her with a scroll in both hands, bowing ceremoniously. The lotus-leaf paper was protected by a glass tube. It had become a tradition of theirs to give each other mock documents: salacious newssheets, penalty notices for missed dinners, or strongly worded complaint letters about the quality of lingering glances. His eyes laughed merrily as she struggled with the wax, finally cutting it loose with her ceremonial blade. He'd made a certificate in flowing legalese, a document verifying that she was captain not just of the chinthe, but of all fathomfolk. And beneath it, images brought to life by a couple of deft brushstrokes. Mira leading a parade of dancing, laughing, singing folk along a riverway. His light touch had captured familiar faces, the idiosyncrasies of people they both knew.

"It's, it's . . . " she began.

"I know," he quipped.

She pushed him lightly onto the sofa, the snow puffing up on impact and making them both laugh as she sat across his lap. A tremor ran through her, the whole room swaying. Kai's face was the one clear thing. "Look at me, I'm shaking," she said in a whisper.

"As much as I'd like to take credit, that's an actual earthquake." He put his hands on her hips and anchored her.

The overhead light was swinging but nothing else was out of place. Growing up on the water, Mira barely noticed the minor tremors, but in the imposing towers of Jingsha she felt them more acutely. They waited for it to pass. She piled the fluffy snow on Kai's topknot, dabbing it into his dark facial hair and on his nose. Giddiness bubbled up through her as he shook himself free, the snowflakes flicking onto her face and down the front of her top. And when he complained of cold, she kissed him better; butterfly kisses down his neck and shoulders. Her hands untied his robes to reach down across his smooth skin, her lips caressing the pearlescent smattering of scales on his collarbone, across his torso and down one arm. She loved that he wore his true colours even when in human form. A water dragon, the only one in the whole city state. The notion still took her by surprise now and then. The closest thing to fathomfolk nobility, and here he was, looking up at her with hungry eyes.

He ran his hands across the fabric of her chinthe green uniform, tracing the braiding, rubbing the brass buttons in a way that made Mira involuntarily exhale. *"I'm* supposed to be treating *you*, remember?" he murmured. The coat fell away and his hands ran down her back. Their lips met and she leaned in, pushing her hips, her chest, her mouth into him, pressing close so he could feel the ache that filled her entirely.

"So . . . how do you want to celebrate?" he asked.

Her response required no words.

Chapter Two

No one said it was going to be easy to steal the dragon pearl.

"Hurry up," Nami said, sinking down to the ocean floor beside Dan. He looked up at her, his kappa's beak pursed tight as he glared back. Gills opened and closed in exasperation. He might be her best friend, but he could still snap bones with one bite. She hastily swallowed her next comment.

"Is it . . . supposed to be doing that?" Hong-Gi asked, the jangjamari so nervous that the kelp covering his whole body quivered in the warm eddy. He inclined his head towards the shield generator. The lights had started to pulse in vivid blue waves like bioluminescence. Even Nami could guess that wasn't a good sign.

"It's fine." She was bluffing. She didn't really know the workings of topside machinery, taking only the minimal classes to pass at the Academy. She jabbed randomly at the buttons again. "Besides, you're supposed to be keeping watch!" The fronds of seaweed floated with him through the water as Hong-Gi drifted back to position. Once there, he was undetectable, another rock covered in seaweed and barnacles along the passageway.

In the comfort of their old student dive, the Anemone Club, it had seemed straightforward enough – sneak into the Peace Tower and steal the dragon pearl. Except they weren't stealing – liberating was more accurate. The last unhatched dragon egg, which the humans insisted on rebranding as the Peace Stone, a symbol of the post-war armistice between humans and fathomfolk. To Nami, it was a symbol of betrayal. One that loomed over the underwater haven, a watchtower rather than a lighthouse.

Dan swam back. "It won't open."

The lights were no longer flashing; the blue hue was simply getting stronger, like staring into the sun. A series of pipes ran like fault lines in jagged right angles. Dan had bitten through the outer casing of the shield generator, but inside things weren't any clearer. A mess of welded metal, knotted wires and moving parts. Nami remembered now that she'd failed the practical exam at the Academy spectacularly, and that was merely tinkering with a simple mechanism for a boat. She poked a finger at some wires, feigning a knowledge she did not have. Why didn't they just label things? Humans had to overcomplicate matters. But the other students had assured them it would work. The same students who'd failed to show up tonight, in fact . . .

Not for the first time, Nami wished she was naturally smart, like her older brother Kai. First in his year at the Academy, finished his overseas studies in two years when it should have taken three, and a skilled waterweaver to boot. He'd know exactly what to do – though he wouldn't even be in this situation in the first place. Not that it mattered; he wasn't here to bail her out any more. Kai had been topside for years now, ambassador to the human city state of Tiankawi.

"Just cut it," Dan said, crossing his webbed hands, "I know you can."

"Will you be able to handle any other problems?"

He barked with laughter, the deep sound peculiar from his slight frame. After years of friendship, it still took Nami by surprise. "Let them come."

Nami forced more oxygen through her gills. The water tingled around her, responding to her call. It flowed through her open palm movements as she moulded it. She could feel the energy growing, vibrating between her fingers like nibbling fish. Still she pushed it, forward and back, lifting more of the water with each sweep, magnetising and focusing it between her hands. Waterweaving. A skill all fathomfolk had to some extent, but Nami had two distinct advantages: an endless stream of tutors and the latent power of her dragon form. She pointed one finger at the door and released the water through a controlled jet. Strong enough to cut.

As soon as the crude hole had been etched, Dan kicked it in with his foot. He smacked his beak together in satisfaction, peering up through the darkened doorway.

"After you, princess," he said with a mock bow. She didn't even waste the time retorting, simply glaring until he shrugged, used to her rage. "We're stealing your mother's pearl, and she's practically royalty."

Dan liked to goad her. He had three sisters and was used to giving as good as he got. He'd stepped on a lot of webbed feet and bowed to a lot of rotten fish to get into the same academy, the same classes that Nami had attended, no questions asked. The scholarship student, in a hurry to start earning. They had graduated together a year ago and Dan had been grafting ever since, scraping together money to feed his family. Two months ago, he'd lost his job. The company he worked for folded, out-competed by cheap surface labour.

"Hong-Gi, we're going in!" Nami said. It was impossible to tell which of the seaweed-covered rocks he was until he moved. She almost wished the jangjamari hadn't come. An artless newcomer from the depths of the kelp forest, he'd sponged up the words of the Anemone Club radicals as if parched with thirst. Nami hadn't the heart to dissuade him, thinking him safer in their circle than being led astray by others. Now she was less certain. Too many things had gone wrong already.

A long, narrow corridor dripped with ribbon-like fringing. Before she could register Dan's warning shout, she'd swept a handful of the strands aside. Sudden pain shot up her arm. The innocuous strings wrapped vice-like around her wrist. Tentacles. She looked up to see a bloom of jellyfish. Their translucent bells twinkled blue like starlight, the same as the shield generator. This was what it had alerted.

Her right arm was completely paralysed, red through from hand to shoulder. Too late, her scales hardened over the top, doing nothing more than making her arm hang heavy at her side. She swore under her breath.

"Did you never play with sea jellies growing up?" Dan slapped the tentacles aside with the back of his hand, peering down the densely curtained corridor. The kappa's thick skin was immune to most stings and poisons. A small consolation for not being able to shift into a human-passing form. When Nami didn't answer, he shrugged. "Of course not. Too busy learning three languages and how to arrange seagrass."

It wasn't exactly how her childhood had gone, but there wasn't time to disagree. Dan cut a path through the stinging corridor and they reached a huge open chamber. Other doors led off on the seabed level, but there was only one way up. A series of hand-holds spiralled around the walls of the central room, emerging through the water and continuing towards the lighthouse eyrie above. Nami pulled her paralysed arm in close to her body. Dan was about to make another remark, a sudden brightness in his round eyes as he looked at the handholds then back at her useless limb. Nami gritted her teeth and kicked off before he could start, using her legs to swim towards the surface. Out of the water, the cold penetrated her skin. The spiral staircase continued upwards, nothing more than stones jutting out of the walls.

"You'd better wait here," she said to Hong-Gi. The jangjamari was slow at the best of times, but above water, he was glacial. As conflicted as Nami felt about her human form, it was a lot more practical in circumstances like these.

Many fathomfolk had land forms and water forms, but Dan only had one shape – another reason why fellow students at the Academy had looked down at him. His small stature meant it would be a long and tiring climb.

"I could throw you," Nami said. "A couple of rotations and launch you upwards, boost you with some water arcs?" She tried and failed to keep the merriment from her voice.

"Like I'm some slingshot pebble? Get your head out your arse, I can climb," Dan said, pushing past her. He jumped from stone to stone, webbed hands and feet splayed, adhering to the walls.

"It'd just be like an immense whirlpool spat you out." Nami was provoking him now. It was only fair given his earlier insults.

"I'm already target practice at home for my sisters, never mind you."

"You've plenty of experience then." She heard only an echo of his response. A choice curse word.

As they continued up, her numb arm wiped the mirth from her face. The climb was difficult and the growing height filled her mouth with bile. Landing in the water would be of no consequence, it was hitting the walls on the way down that worried her.

Nearing the top, she could see the beams that held up the flying eaves on the outside. The humans had made their watchtower beautiful. With multiple tiered roofs it was the only structure in the Yonakuni sea haven that broke through the surface of the water.

Only one place left to go. She hesitated a moment. Her mother would never forgive her. But nor would she forgive herself unless she tried. Humans had done this. Their pollution spilled through the oceans, bleaching the coral of the underwater havens into bones. Their mechanised floating cities vomited out waste. And rather than fight them, the Yonakuni elders traded with them!

No wonder people were leaving. Folk swam from the thickest kelp forests and deepest brine lakes for tickets and papers. Endless emigrants desperate to get out of the water. It was only a matter of time before Yonakuni fell like the havens before. That was what the other students had said. It spurred Nami on.

Her hand looked human in its aspect. Pale-skinned and lithe. Weak. She hardened her scales, watching the iridescent silver gleam coat the back of her hand, her nails turning to talons. She pulled the door open.

The room was as extravagant as her mother's finest chambers. Identical windows on each of the eight walls, shutters closed against the afternoon sunlight. Between these and on the supporting pillars were a series of artefacts. Archaic human script Nami did not recognise. Fading woodblock prints depicting humans and fathomfolk. A curved ceremonial sword with a tassel of finely knotted seasilk.

Dan stood in front of one triptych. His height made a difference out of the water; he had to crane his neck to see the image. It showed a mermaid brushing her hair, confident and free, the waves behind caressing her scales. Then swooning in the arms of some human man, a fisherman or a prince or anyone in between. And the last picture . . .

The kappa spat.

The last picture showed the man cradling the body of the mermaid. It didn't matter why she'd died. A sacrifice for him, for their child, for some unwitting sin. The story was always the same.

"Equality above and below the waterline," Nami said, the words curdling in her mouth. She echoed the official line they'd been taught. Her remaining doubts burned away like morning mist in the glare of the sun.

A carved lacquer box intricately decorated with mother-of-pearl serpentine dragons lay atop a central pedestal. Light shone out, warm and joyful, as Nami opened the lid. As the white spots in her vision dissipated, she could see the single pearl, as big as a newborn's head, within the box. It swirled opalescent and as familiar as the scales on her mother's skin.

"Jiang-Li's last pearl, nothing more than a lighthouse beacon," Dan said.

Nami nodded, not trusting herself to speak yet. The lighthouse had been erected when she was only a child. A beacon of human and fathomfolk friendship, she'd been told every time she'd asked the officials, her teachers, her mother. To stop the ships from damaging one of the last underwater havens. But Nami knew what it really was. The whispers bitter in the abyssal zone of Yonakuni haven. A bargaining chip. As long as they could see the light twinkling in the distance, the humans were reassured that folk were being obedient little neighbours, circling their oversized fish tank. And the folk were helpless. Staring at their hope but never able to use it.

She picked the pearl up, gingerly holding it outstretched in both hands, wanting to bring it close and yet afraid to have it near her. It throbbed, warm to the touch. Her hands were suddenly damp with sweat, and she nearly dropped it. Dan was saying something, but she couldn't hear him past the rush in her ears. Her heart was beating so fast she could feel it straining through her chest to break free. A long moment passed as she waited for something else.

It could have been her.

"Hello, little one," she whispered into the shell.

A roar slammed into the back of her head, sending tremors like ice melting down her spine. The surprise made her jump, throwing the pearl into the air. A flash of green hide knocked her off her feet and she dropped to all fours, reflexively transforming her skin to hardened scales. She rolled to one side and countered, pushing past her attacker to catch the falling pearl. It was instinct, the way she'd been taught by the best martial tutors in the haven.

One of the same former tutors faced her now: Sobekki, Protector of the Realm. His crocodile skin was tough, near impenetrable, and he had brought half a dozen guards with him. "You're in trouble," he said, voice emotionless as his weather-beaten face.

There was no way Nami could win against Sobekki in a fair fight. He'd trained her, knew every one of her weak spots, and that was before considering the minor issue of her paralysed arm.

"I outrank you," she said. She put force behind her voice and noted that some of the soldiers wavered in their positions; one even took a step back.

Sobekki said nothing, simply baring his sharp teeth as he took a step forward.

"My mother will—"

"Who do you think sent me?"

Dan chipped in. "She's fighting for her people! That's a lot more than the Senate have done in decades!"

"I'm not arguing with a couple of children. You only see the surface, not the whole issue. Hand over the pearl."

It was the same platitudes they always gave: it's complicated; you'll understand some day. Nami threw the pearl to Dan. Her body lengthened, her argent scales gleaming as spines grew down her back. Antlers curved out from her brow and her eyes dilated to see into every shadow. Her hands turned to full claws and her face to her true self. In dragon form she could reach all corners of the small room. With a whip of her tail, she knocked three of the guards to the ground. Even with one injured arm, she was more steady on her feet.

"I won't hold back," Sobekki warned.

"Bring it, old one," Nami responded as she leapt.

Sobekki sidestepped her easily, grappling her, twisting his whole body in a graceful cartwheel. Nami did not resist, flowing with the move and disentangling herself as she flipped over his head. She landed hard, her foreclaw slipping under her. Two of the other guards were behind her, approaching with caution. She rolled into a knot, moving in a whirlwind of coiled scales, fast and dazzling. One guard lunged, then the other. They aimed for flesh, but she curved her body out of the way, sending them crashing into each other.

Sobekki ran straight at her with a rain of fists. Nami could only dodge so many before the blows struck her head ridge and across the jaw. Her tricks would not work with him. He was not dazzled by the sight of a dragon the way others were. Her whiskers alerted her to his movements, but she couldn't act quickly enough. She growled low, even though the protective spines were surely hurting her former tutor just as much as her. She snapped at him, but Sobekki was faster, much faster. Nami could hear his voice ringing in her head. *Your true form is bigger, but that also makes you a bigger target. Fast, agile opponents will wear you down.*

A strike on her shoulder blades, another to her side, and she felt her body tiring. The waterweaving, the paralysis, the shape-shifting; it had all taken its toll. She shrank herself down, reflexively turning back into human form, but Sobekki had been waiting for that. The barrage continued unabated, leaving Nami shielding her head from the blows. The dragon scale was the only thing keeping her in one piece.

"You hate them, say you're different, and yet here you are, hiding in human form!" Sobekki was usually a person of few words, and Nami knew he was furious. She didn't have the breath to respond. Her ribs ached and she was gasping just trying to dodge his hits.

"I'm nothing like them." The energy to muster a response distracted her. Long enough for Sobekki to punch her in the side of the jaw. Nami tasted bitter iron in her mouth and sank to her knees. A drop of blood dripped down her chin. She felt the pearl watching her, glowing weakly in Dan's hands as he cowered between two guards. Sobekki loomed over her, a sneer across his features. Then, abruptly, sensing perhaps that she was defeated, he turned his back. Prised the pearl out of Dan's grasp and held it up to his eye. His grip, although reverent, nonetheless dented the pearl's surface. She felt it as though he were pressing nails against her temples. She sucked in a breath through her teeth.

"Soft," he said. Then, looking back at Nami, "But not as soft as their sister."

Chapter Three

Serena leaned over the bed and touched her daughter's forehead. The girl was flushed and damp but the worst of the fever seemed to have passed. Still Qiuyue slept like she was a writhing eel, turning and kicking until the covers were all twisted under her arms. Serena prised the blanket free, laying it over her and kissing her cheek.

"Ama," the child said sleepily, turning her head like a flower towards the sun.

"Go back to sleep, my love."

Qiuyue yawned, fighting back the tiredness to open dark brown eyes that were the spitting image of her father's. "Make the faces again, Ama. Then I'll sleep."

Serena looked quickly towards the doorway, checking that her husband was not within sight. Then back down at Qiuyue, watching her daughter smile and clap her hands together in delight. Her sharp ears picked up footsteps in the corridor and she quickly readjusted her countenance. "Remember, our little secret."

"Promise, Ama. Enjoy your party." The girl turned over in bed, soundly asleep within minutes. So different to her brother, who'd been a needy, whiny child. Serena had high hopes.

"Ready?" her husband said from the doorway. The room was dimly lit by the lamp so she couldn't read his face. All the same, she could see the exasperation in his angular shoulders. "She'll be fine, my dear."

Serena's heels clicked on the floor as she crossed the room, shrugged into the coat he held out. "It doesn't get any easier," she said. "I know, I know, we have one of the best nannies in Tiankawi, but still ..." She shook her head, trying to ignore the gnawing worries that she knew were preposterous. The nanny had been given clear instructions, not to disturb Qiuyue's sleep, to reheat the seaweed soup if she was hungry, and above all else, to keep her away from the water. The woman hadn't reacted, a polite nod of assent, even though Serena knew they all thought she was being hysterical. Her son had experienced one little accident in the water, a decade ago, and now she wouldn't let either of her children near the edge.

She pulled herself back to the moment. Samnang looked fine in his kumiho blue, the formal city guard uniform he wore to big events such as this evening's gala. She was glad she'd asked the tailor to take the trousers out – just a couple of centimetres – without her husband noticing. He would congratulate himself on a trim figure, and she wouldn't have to worry about a button popping off and taking someone's eye out.

"Do we really have to go?" she asked for the third time.

Samnang patted her hand indulgently. "Just show our faces, that's all. People will be expecting us."

Serena wrinkled her nose. "We donate our money already, isn't that enough?"

"My darling, you don't have to worry about that. We can afford it. And you're already dressed for the occasion."

She gave in with a shake of her head. It was true that she had put on one of her favourite outfits: a floor-length dress with hand-painted waterlilies on blue silk. Her brown hair had shimmering silver streaks in it now, but she had artfully concealed them under opal and jade hairpins.

Gede was waiting for them at the bottom of the stairs. Her son took after his father. It had been a great disappointment that even paying visits and drinking tea with all the right people had not been enough to get him into the scholar branch of government. He had no head for figures, failed to remember his laws despite the best tutors. Had even been caught with notes in his sleeve during the formal examination. Serena had pulled out every favour to ensure the press didn't catch a whiff of it. Even Samnang had been disappointed. But at least Gede was under his father's wing now – an officer in the city guard – and could be her eyes and ears when her husband was in a less generous mood.

Their city chambers in the Jingsha district were only a short boat ride from the fundraiser. The family helmsman steered the boat precisely into the small pier at the base of the Toro building. Other guests milled on the walkway, stepping from their sampans, red sails raised. It was easy enough to cut a swathe through the crowd. Samnang's reputation, the opulence of their private boat, made it quite clear how far up the social ladder they were. Some scrambled to get out of the way, a few offering fawning greetings or a hand to help Serena navigate puddles on the wooden walkway. She smiled graciously but ignored them all. The finest trees need not worry about the weeds. She took Samnang's hand alone, liking the way he was still gentlemanly about his actions even after two and a half decades of marriage. She was certain he was as in love with her as the day they met. Constantly remarking about how little she had aged, how beautiful she still was. What was the secret? But she would not tell him, simply smiled and ducked her head.

As they strolled towards the lifts, all eyes turned to watch them, the colourful lights of the gala like a beacon on the sixty-eighth floor of the newly built column.

"I really hope they have meat. Roast pork or at least poached chicken," Gede said, stifling a yawn with the back of his hand. "I'm bored of greens."

Serena frowned at him, shaking her head just a little. Her ears popped as they ascended but she ignored the sensation as best she could. "When I was your age it was seaweed every day. Greens and fresh fruit is something you shouldn't take for granted."

"Yes, yes, everything was harder in your day."

"Gede," his father said in mild warning. "You should be thankful you've not had to suffer as your mother once did." He squeezed Serena's hand until the gems from his ring dug into her skin. She loosened his grip, rubbing the back of her neck as she looked up at the numbers ascending on the lift. He meant well, but his interjection stiffened her shoulders even more. Samnang had been born into one of the wealthiest families in the city.

The lift operator slid open the ornate cage doors and they stepped onto the revolving floor. Even though she'd attended a private members' reception here last month, the sensation took some getting used to. Windows gave them a panoramic view of Tiankawi, and the room had been decorated in blue and green. Hundreds of pebbles, sea glass and shells had been threaded through thin wire and artfully twined into waves around the bar and ice sculptures. The familiar red and blue swirls of witchlight were dotted around on plinths and hanging from pendants. The motion of the floor and the static decorations gave the impression of drifting in water. Which was probably the idea.

Some of Samnang's kumiho colleagues in blue came to greet them, palm-fist salutes and short bows exchanged. The trade ambassador from the western city of Dhinduk was with them, the handsy one who liked to push his luck. Serena smiled and made a vague comment about drinks, stepping away before the ambassador could wheedle his way to her side.

She waited for the bartender to mix the cocktails, brushing her hand against the witchlight on the bar. The impression of the waterweaver behind it was like the signature on a painting. A couple came to stand beside her and she snatched her hand back quickly.

"Lady Serena." It was the Yonakunish ambassador, Kai, and his partner, Mira, the recently promoted chinthe captain. They made a stunning couple: young, handsome and full of energy. Serena's eyes immediately darted to their telltale gill marks. It was often the only clear giveaway when fathomfolk were in human form.

Mira pulled her long curly hair over her neck, quite deliberately hiding her gills as she sipped from her glass of wine. Her hair was the sort of black that shimmered with greens, blues and purples, like an oil slick on the surface of water. Instead of her formal border guard uniform, she wore a bottle-green pant suit with a stiff standing collar embroidered with a border of leaping fish in gold thread. Even her fashion choices were adroit. Despite her petite height, the half-siren commanded an aura of attention.

"Ambassador, Captain," Serena acknowledged, raising the glass the bartender offered her and wetting her lips with it. "You must be very excited about this evening's festivities. The event raises a lot of money for the impoverished people in the city."

"Funny," Mira said, "after fees, taxes, paying for this, that and the other, there's never really much left."

"Funny that," Serena agreed. She combed her fingers through a loose strand of hair, a habit when her hands were idle, curling the end around her little finger. Stopped short of chewing on it when she noticed the captain's raised eyebrow. The ambassador offered to help carry the second drink back to her husband. She ignored him, more interested in the spiky half-siren beside him. Her eyes locked on Mira's. "My motto is 'help yourself up'."

Mira glanced over to where Samnang stood at the centre of

a circle of cooing followers. "I can see how you've put that into practice."

Serena smiled. It was so rare that someone had the audacity to spar with her, to push back, that she was – almost – enjoying herself.

Chapter Four

"They're so infuriating," Mira said, taking a large gulp of her drink as Serena sashayed back towards her husband.

"Just birds with clipped wings. Nothing we can't handle," Kai said. He put his drink down, his fingers brushing her hand on the bar. Despite her annoyance, Mira registered the action. Letting her know he was there. That she could twine his fingers between her own if she needed to.

"I know, I know. But I'm the chinthe captain now. I need to navigate this world. Learn to . . . sing their stupid songs." The last word was said through gritted teeth. She could feel a headache coming from the number of times she'd bowed and bitten her tongue already. It was as if her ears were lying to her. The fawning words and saccharine compliments delivered like a slap to the face. Kind acts followed by slander as soon as they left the room. A whole different game here and she was already sick of it.

"Did you know," Kai said, leaning in conspiratorially, "Serena's not from one of the elite families. It was quite a scandal when Samnang married her, a woman with no name or connections."

Mira looked up at him, cocking her head. He shrugged away her unspoken questions. "Before you begin, I'm *not* gossiping. There are factions at play and I'm not just talking about fathomfolk versus humans. Always important to know how the land lies."

"I don't care *how* it lies; I know *where* it lies: deep underneath the sea." She snagged some canapés from a waiter, a steamed dumpling and some sort of unfamiliar leaf. The food was infinitely better in the southern districts compared with here among the tall towers. The company was better too. Kai excepted. She admired the water dragon's profile. His antlers were hidden but his face was breathtakingly handsome all the same. She regretted not taking his hand now, but she dared not voice the lingering sentiment.

How did they eat this crap? She chewed on the hard, grainy leaf and washed it down with the rest of her drink. Only then did she notice that Kai had nibbled only the end of his leaf, depositing the hard exterior on a discreet silver bowl on the waiter's tray. The waiter curled his lip, but glanced away as Mira stared him defiantly in the eye. She tried another one, scraping the soft pulp with her teeth. Still tasted like shit.

"We'll do a circuit, then go," Kai said, putting his arm around her waist. It annoyed her that his presence soothed her. That he seemed to know she yearned to touch him and at the same time was afraid it would make her appear weak. She could do this alone, but it was so much easier, less frustrating, with him as an ally by her side.

"I'd support it, I honestly would, if it did any good."

"Believe me, it has an impact. You don't want to be the spokesperson for fathomfolk, but they will treat you like one anyway. So show them the Mira I love. The person who can light up a room and argue me to the ground."

Mira couldn't help but laugh, embarrassed by his earnest response. She kissed his cheek, a chaste peck. "Only you feel that way, silly."

They mingled with the other guests. The biggest group in the room were the scholar officials from the various offices. She spotted a cluster in gossamer white robes from the Ministry of Ceremonies, and the Minister of Justice himself, silver hair blending into his grey silk tunic. The top families in the city, the ones whose businesses had paid for most of Jingsha's monolithic buildings and infrastructure. None of them lived on the water; the view from the windows tonight was probably as close as they would get to sea level. They would go back to their stilted mansions in the Manshu and Kenabi districts, satisfied they'd done their bit for the less fortunate.

The charity auction started with all the ridiculousness Mira had come to expect. A list of benefactors as long as her arm. People patting each other on the back for their generosity, wiping away imagined tears for the plight of the impoverished folk and humans as they continued to quaff drinks that cost more than an average daily wage. Feathers were in this season, woven into elaborate hairdos, puffed up on shoulder pads and trimming collars and cloaks.

Her mind and eyes wandered as the auctioneer droned on, selling the decadent items to the neighbours of the people who had donated them. The quantities of money spiralled as the drinks continued to flow, amounts that Mira couldn't even imagine. She wandered over to the buffet table, noticing that the crowd had thinned considerably. Perhaps she could persuade Kai they'd stayed for long enough.

A border guard saluted at her side. Mira reluctantly put the plate down as he told her someone wanted to see her. He was familiar, the guard, one of the old captain's favourites.

He led her out of a back door and down two sets of stairs. She should probably have told Kai where she was going but the relief at having something to do, something to work her mind and her limbs away from the goldfish bowl of a revolving restaurant above, made her stomach churn with excitement. Besides, she didn't want to run to her boyfriend with every little problem.

She was ushered into a small room, a private gambling den by the looks of the square velvet-topped table and the white tiled pieces. In the far shadows, illuminated only by a light of her own making, stood the seawitch Cordelia.

"Nope," Mira said, turning back to the door before it closed behind her.

"My old friend, don't be such a bore!"

"I see you enough as it is, and we don't have an appointment tonight."

She heard the seawitch slither across the floor and a creak as she eased herself into a chair. "We can always close the account now if you'd prefer?"

The hairs on Mira's neck prickled and she finally turned. "What do you want?"

Cordelia had sprawled out now, her eight octopus limbs a relaxed russet hue. Her top half was humanoid, but that was just the image she presented. Other fathomfolk had one, perhaps two forms at most. The seawitch had endless faces. No one really knew what she looked like. "Your predecessor and I had a good relationship. I thought I would offer you the same terms. An introductory offer."

Mira had made a bargain with the seawitch once before. A naïve, impetuous decision that had haunted her ever since. Her stomach suddenly felt queasy, the rich food and drink no longer sitting comfortably. "What are you talking about?"

"Dear saltlick, you're captain now. We can have a mutually beneficial arrangement. Protect the border, keep the law."

"Get to the point," Mira snapped. Stuffed her hands deep into her pockets to pretend nonchalance, but also to hide the clammy sweat on her palms. She knew Cordelia was toying with her. The seawitch was enjoying herself, piling the tiles into a tall pillar, positioning the last one off-centre so the whole thing came tumbling down.

"It's a tricky job protecting the border. The settlement vessels, the fishing boats, people on rickety skiffs or simply swimming right up. Who knows how folk get past the border nets? Who smuggles them in? It's a tough job for anyone, and even the chin-the can miss things."

Mira's fists coiled and she stepped forward before she could stop herself. "If you've brought me here to mock and insult me, I'll—"

"We both want what's best for Tiankawi. For you that's making sure these poor fathomfolk refugees, piled onto a double outrigger for months to escape the war in Atlitya, get a proper hearing. A chance to make asylum claims. That's very honourable, Mira. Your mother would be proud."

Mira flinched, cursing the fact she'd let it show. Cordelia had the courtesy to pretend not to notice.

"For me, well it might be making sure a patron gets his goods in a timely fashion. So much red tape at the port, holding up some lovely seasilk from Yonakuni or a shipment of coconut wine from Dhinduk." The seawitch was bringing in less salubrious items than her listed examples, but it was a game they both had to play.

"What are you suggesting?" Mira said. Her voice was almost gone, faint with the weight of what she was being offered.

"I will watch for these poor souls, let you know when they're in Tiankawian waters. Give them a fighting chance for a new start; the same chance your mother had when she swam across the open seas to seek asylum. And in return, every so often you might lose a ledger or forget to check a shipment. Just helping a small business thrive."

Cordelia oozed confidence, a look of complete ease across her features. Mira felt small and insignificant in comparison. Like fish were taking nibbles out of her and she had nowhere to hide. She'd been appointed less than a week and already she was weary of it.

If Cordelia went to the kumiho, to some other chinthe even, those fathomfolk would be deported immediately without so much as a backwards glance. Back to Atlitya, in the midst of a civil war that was tearing the underwater haven apart. The ones desperate enough to make the journey didn't have anything to go back to. Worse still, they were often targeted more intensely for deserting. For refusing a call to service, or running from crippling debts. Their only chance was to get out of the water.

On the other hand, if Mira helped Cordelia, she'd be even more firmly in the seawitch's grasp. More dirt for Cordelia to twist against her. She did the calculations in her head and the answer was grim either way. But she'd seen how Cordelia interacted with her ama and it gave her just a spark of hope.

"No," she said finally. "I can't make that bargain. And I believe that even you have a modicum of empathy."

Cordelia's shoulders went rigid and a ripple of white stripes ran down her limbs. "My dear, empathy is all well and good, but business is business."

Mira stepped in closer, leaning over the table and restacking the white tiles one by one. "One thing crossed my mind, a terrible thought that can't possibly be true. Because we both know you're always within the word of the law."

"Naturally."

"Because if I find out that you're the one smuggling them in. Taking their money and putting them into broken boats. Offering them to the highest bidder . . . Well. We don't have to worry about that. Just a silly notion. You couldn't possibly be doing anything so dreadful." She placed the last white tile on top, the column much more secure than previously.

"What an awful thought."

"Lucky I have no evidence to prove it . . . yet." Mira was playing with fire, most definitely. But it had been one of those nights when sycophancy and false praise had reigned, and the ability to speak truths, to cut the seawitch's smug look to ribbons, made it all worthwhile.

She walked back up the stairs two at a time, at first buoyantly and then, as her lungs began to heave, feeling the lead in her boots. The further she climbed, the more she began to regret her words. Not the choice she had made but how she'd delivered it.

Cordelia would not take this lying down. No, if anything, Mira had done more to antagonise the seawitch tonight than in all their previous years of interaction. She wrapped her hands tightly around the handrail, her knuckles white as she tried to compose herself. Too late to repair things; she would have to deal with that another day.

"There you are," Kai said as she entered the room. The auction had finished and a couple of zither players had taken the stage. He held out a small wooden box, the lid open. Mira looked at it: a single pearl hanging from a gold necklace stared up at her. "I couldn't resist. I know, I know you don't like extravagance but I wanted to treat you. A gift for your promotion. All for a good cause."

She remained silent as he fastened the clasp, felt the bite of the chain at the back of her neck. The pearl nestled below her collarbone, like a single shed tear. Worth more than she made in a month. She pushed the thought away immediately, the guilt bitter on her palate. It lingered, loitering at the back of her mind.

"Well, do you like it?" he asked, his face bright and earnest and all the things she loved about him.

She licked her cracked lips. Words swirled around her head, failing to form themselves into an appropriate response.

"Did something happen?" he said.

Relief flooded through her. She could tell him; they could put their heads together to solve the problem. She took both his hands, breathing in deeply to summon the words.

"Ambassador, an urgent message." A waiter stood with a scroll sealed in glass.

Kai let go of Mira to take it. A protest sat on her lips. *Hold on.*

Listen, we have things to talk about. But instead she exhaled, the moment moving away like ripples in the water. The distance grew.

Kai's gentle brows furrowed as he read. "It's my sister, Nami."

"Anything I can do to help?" Kai had only told her a little about his family. His impetuous little sister always seemed to be stirring.

"Yes. I think there is."

Chapter Five

"Have you quite finished?" the familiar voice said. Nami's mother, Jiang-Li. The water dragon matriarch was draped in a gown with tendrils like ink in water. Around her middle were silver shells, a river of them like a school of fish. Even though clothes meant nothing to fathomfolk – an artifice they had acquired through trade with humans – she made Nami feel underdressed. Even when telling her off, Jiang-Li was beautiful.

"Breakfast in the dawn chamber in an hour." Jiang-Li did not wait for a response. She didn't really have to. Nami had been unceremoniously dumped at her mother's feet by Sobekki and locked in her quarters like a spoilt child for days. She would obey, if only to find out what had happened to Dan and Hong-Gi.

Their underwater rooms were high up in the seamount on which Yonakuni haven was founded; part on the living surface and part in the heart of the rock, with a bridge linking the sections together. Fathomfolk-made housing spiralled around the dormant volcano like a scaffold to the pinnacle. The natural hollows of barrel sponges and honeycomb coral had been coaxed into malleable structures that could accommodate whole families.

Nami hadn't lived here since before her Academy days. Jiang-Li had asked her to move back when she graduated but she had refused, preferring the independence. Drifting, her mother had described it.

"You could at least dress the part," Jiang-Li said an hour later, arching an eyebrow as she poured kelp juice.

"Nothing wrong with what I'm wearing." It was a recurrent argument. Nami could have fine cloth imported from the human cities, or waterweave an illusion of robes to match her status. But she preferred the loose trousers and tunics of her student days. Clothing that seaweed farmers and fisherfolk wore. She'd also cropped her black hair short, shaved at one side, in defiance of her mother's wishes.

"You aren't some selkie or fish spirit. You're a dragon."

"So you keep reminding me," Nami said. She rolled her eyes but her mother wasn't even looking. "Too much of her father's stubbornness" was the usual complaint. It didn't help that she looked like him: thick straight eyebrows and a square jawline. It also didn't help that he had died when she was a child, on a diplomatic mission to Tiankawi.

The dawn chamber was a large circular room of sponge, curved in a bowl. The walls and floor were lined in a thick seagrass meadow. Red corals with long branches spread from floor to ceiling like pillars. Sunlight filtered through the clear waters, shimmering warmth into the sumptuous surroundings. Someone had already laid out a feast upon the algae-covered table. A spread fit for a festival. Wild rice and sea grapes with vinegared fish, lotus root and cuttlefish stew, candied seaweed, taro crisps and fried water spinach. And for dessert, grass jelly cubes in coconut milk, pandan and mung bean cake and a bowl of mango sago pudding. All of Nami's childhood favourites. Only the most skilled chef could prepare and preserve such dishes within the salty waters of the sea. Nami could just about discern the sheen around each plate – a bubble of air expertly waterweaved.

She sat by the low table, exerting just a little of her waterweaving to anchor herself to the ground. She knew the lecture was to come, but if her mother wanted to bribe her with delicacies, she would take them. Each bite burst in her mouth as the enchantment broke and the taste melted against her tongue. The stew was perfectly warm, the seaweed still retaining its crunch.

"When did you start eating like a baleen whale? I was hoping to send the leftovers to your friends. What are their names again?"

"Dan and Hong-Gi," Nami said, the last mouthful sinking like brine at the bottom of the ocean. She was suddenly not hungry any more. "What've you done with them?"

"Done? What do you think happens to people who break and enter, attempt to steal a dragon pearl?" Jiang-Li carefully pulled a jewelled comb from her elaborate braided hairdo, caught a stray curl and tucked it back in. Everything in its proper place.

"This was my idea!"

"Your incompetence is written all over it," Jiang-Li said, her fingers knitting together.

"Then you can release them?"

"No."

"But you released me."

"Do you know how anything works? How ruinous it would be for my own, my only daughter, to be caught in this? Sent to prison like a common criminal?" Jiang-Li made a long noise through gritted teeth. "Your two little friends have no connections, no clout, no money. They're facing long jail sentences."

The waterweaving that kept Nami seated melted away as her concentration fled. She floated back in the water, drifting further away from her mother. "That pearl: that's my sibling. It could've been me!" Her face flushed in anger. Her mother talked about people like they were game pieces.

Jiang-Li rubbed her temples. "You don't know how lucky you are. It's easier to pick fault than make the decisions that truly matter."

I wish it had been you. I should've hatched the other pearl. That was what she was saying. The words Nami always heard like barbs in her back, making her twist and itch and want to scream aloud. The words she dreaded and yet perversely longed to hear just so it was all out in the open. "If Aba was here—"

"Well he isn't." Jiang-Li cut her off. Even Nami could hear the break in her mother's voice. The clenched jaw behind those words. There was so much she'd never been told about her father's departure.

"There must be something you can do for them." Nami thought of adding platitudes, of appealing to Jiang-Li's maternal instincts, but she baulked. Her mother was no fool, and nor was she known for her fond affection. Nami's childhood recollections of her were nothing more than a flurry of robes and querying her grades, Jiang-Li always distant, always busy with the Senate. It was her father who taught her to shape-shift, who took her topside to look at the stars, who kissed her grazed knees and bumped forehead. When he had gone, Kai had taken his place. Anyone but Jiang-Li, the great dragon of Yonakuni.

No, her mother responded to facts, negotiations and professionalism. "I could do some jobs for you. The archives, perhaps? Or looking at the trade agreements?" Nami named the two dullest tasks she could think of, ones her mother had previously proposed after she finished at the Academy.

"You *can* do something for me. We cannot keep up with Tiankawi's pace of industrial advancement. In a decade or two this haven will be redundant, much like Iyoness."

Iyoness had been another underwater haven, far to the north. It had imploded over a decade ago; crumbling away to nothing when pollution destroyed much of its natural resources. They had some Iyonessian refugees in Yonakuni, but most had resettled in Tiankawi. That was the ostensible reason Nami's father had gone on a diplomatic mission: to negotiate with the human cities over what aid could be offered to the ailing underwater realm. He never returned.

"I'm sure I can do some research . . ." said Nami.

"What I need is a solution."

"A solution?"

"Your brother is busy. This amendment of his, if they ratify it, will change everything. He does not need to be distracted. You, on the other hand . . ."

Nami kept her eye-rolling internal. She had read the newssheets singing Kai's praises for the proposed bill to lessen restrictions on folk migrants to the city state. It did indeed sound like important work. Tedious, dull, but nevertheless essential.

Jiang-Li continued. "Human advancements are staggering. They keep the borders open for folk, give them much-needed jobs. But tell me this, my righteous daughter, do we replicate their methods or destroy them?"

"How would I—"

"You have an answer for everything, don't you?"

Nami took a moment to understand what her mother was implying. Surely her brother could . . . But Kai was the Yonakunish ambassador to Tiankawi. He couldn't exactly go snooping around. Her heart pounded in her chest. A mission, a proper mission. She knew fine well her mother was mocking her, throwing her exuberance back in her face. But she would prove the point. Show her that it really wasn't as difficult as they all made out. No more compromise.

She finally looked her mother in the eye, her excitement fading as she saw the hard line of Jiang-Li's lips, the strain in her neck. "There's something else, isn't there?"

"The Senate wanted to throw you in jail. Even I can't shield you from every consequence. Officially you're being exiled to Tiankawi. No diplomatic immunity."

The words rang in Nami's head. Exiled. Every other misdemeanour had been met with a slapped wrist and a shake of the head. Sure, she'd been younger then, and her actions less reckless, but she never thought it would come to this. She was a dragon, after all; her forefathers had built this haven. Just as the thought came into her head, so did the shame at her own arrogance. "What of Dan. And Hong-Gi?"

"Succeed and there may be room for negotiation. In time, people will forget."

In time. That meant Dan, her best friend, and Hong-Gi, barely an adult, would remain in jail. With a mission as vague as the one her mother had delivered, the task could take months. Years. Was it a ruse? She'd never be allowed home and her friends would be locked up for ever. Noise rushed in her ears, and she felt herself floating off the chair again, pushing her feet into the stony sand underfoot.

She could bribe a guard, break in and ... But the notion was preposterous. She'd failed to free the dragon pearl; there was no way she would fare any better in a jailbreak. She could write to Kai, he was always on her side. But even her charming brother couldn't change the minds of the whole Senate.

Then she could go to Tiankawi, and ... and ... Her mind blanked. She had no idea what she could do above the waterline. She'd only ever lived in Yonakuni. Stories about the human city state were as fantastical as child's tales to her. And she would be cuffed, same as every other new arrival. Her waterweaving powers curtailed by the shackle on her wrist. Her tongue was dry in her mouth. Dan always said fear was healthy. Showed that you were alive. And Nami *was* alive. Willing to fight for the things she believed in. No matter the cost.

This was her chance to prove it.

"Well?" Jiang-Li said, swimming now beside her. Her shadow fell long over Nami's head, blocking out the light from the surface.

"Promise to provide for their families: Dan and Hong-Gi's."

"Done," her mother said, so swiftly that Nami realised she had wasted a bargaining chip. "Then it's decided. In two days you'll be going to Tiankawi."

Chapter Six

Serena put the final dish down on the table, making more than a little noise rearranging the plates so that her husband took the hint and packed away his lotus leaf scrolls. He made a low croon of appreciation as he touched her shoulder and took to his chair. She didn't often cook, they had people for that, but occasionally it was worth the effort. Reminded him of the woman he'd fallen in love with.

Qiuyue had her paper-cut sea creatures out, dancing them on sticks across the table. Such an expense. Paper as a child's toy! Too impractical, too delicate, and yet Samnang kept bringing these little gifts home and replacing the ones Qiuyue had dropped out of boats or left in the rain.

"Where's Gede?" Serena asked.

"On duty in Manshu district."

She paused with the serving spoon for a moment before continuing to scoop rice into each of their bowls. The utensil scraped with shrill edges on the porcelain. "You mean out drinking with those feckless friends again?"

Samnang shrugged, putting a choice piece of fish into his daughter's bowl. "He's young. And networking is half the battle, my darling."

"Indeed, but his so-called friends aren't exactly influential in the city. Bottomless rice buckets who smoke fugu all day."

"We were all that age once."

"*You* were never that undisciplined." Her hand instinctively went to the pouch she wore at her hip, to touch the stone through the seasilk. It was as if her whole demeanour softened, her eyes widening as she caught Samnang's. Her voice becoming the gentle lapping of a tide. "You were a force to be reckoned with even then. Knowing exactly what you wanted and how to get it. Why can't our son be more like that?" She appealed to her husband's pride, even as she privately directed Gede to be more canny than his father.

Samnang drained his sweet tea to hide his expression. "He'll get there. Give him time."

Her husband acted like they had all the time in the world. Like the city would come knocking with opportunities if he simply sprawled out on the day bed. Life had been kind to him, after all. But for Serena there was danger in complacency. Others plotted and succeeded while Samnang's old money and old values stagnated. "You know what that jumped-up poster girl Mira was doing at his age? Demanding that the Qilin district be added to the grid."

"A concession to quieten the protesters." Samnang picked at the meal in front of him, placing more food into his daughter's bowl than his own. Qiuyue was oblivious, chasing a sliver of mushroom around the serving dish with her clumsy chopsticks. He did not notice, or did not care, that Gede had no drive. Satisfied with his son's mediocrity.

"She's a menace. To the kumiho, to you."

"She's one little saltie. I'm surprised you're so bothered."

"We spoke at the charity auction." Serena put down her chopsticks and smoothed the wrinkles in her dress with both hands. The feel of the silk calmed her, a material she could never afford growing up. She touched the seasilk pouch again, absent-mindedly. "Quite arrogant. Thinks she's better than the rest of us because she gets her hands dirty."

"I hardly thought the two of you exchanged more than a dozen words!"

"Some people just leave a strong impression." Looking down at her arm, Serena could see the start of a red rash forming on the inside of her elbow. It only happened when she was irritated. She pulled down her sleeve to hide it, a smile fluttering across her lips. "Can't you do anything about her?"

"The chinthe are a mess, have been for decades. I don't need to do a thing." He patted her hand indulgently. "Come, dear, you needn't worry your head over such matters."

Serena nodded, ignoring the scream inside. She scratched at her arm, drawing blood from the skin. Next year was an election year. The position of fenghuang, head of the Council, would be up for nomination. Samnang would have a good shot at the position - and showing he was tough on crime could only help his chances. But of course sheer luck and coincidence had delivered everything to his feet so far. Always in the right place at the right time. The ideas just came to him: his reserved wife had nothing to do with it at all.

"Look at the state of you," Serena said, folding her paper umbrella. She had taken the family boat out, tracking her son down easily. Gede was nothing if not predictable, drinking in one of the most overpriced teahouses in the area. The tables were white marble and the floor cushions embroidered through with gold. He was half under one such table, his friends asleep in piles around him. She nudged at his prone body with her foot. "I won't ask again."

Despite the fumes coming from his breath and clothes, Gede was alert enough to hear the threat in her voice and stumbled to his feet. Once on their boat, he slumped over the side and vomited long and hard. The sour smell drifted in the breeze.

"This is how you spend your time?" Serena said.

"We can't all ..." He made an elaborate gesture over his face and slunk down to the bottom of the boat. He used to like her changing faces, much as Qiuyue did. Used to. Over the years he had started emulating not just his father, but the wealthy fops in Manshu and Kenabi districts. The ones who could trace their families back generations in Tiankawi, whose skills seem to consist solely of drinking and throwing money away. The training Serena had started when he was a pre-teen was met with reluctance now. Half-hearted excuses until she stopped asking altogether.

"Lieutenant at your age is a fine achievement," she said, switching tone and tack altogether. She pretended a great interest in the grain of the wood, stroking a hand down the side of the boat as she watched her son's reaction. He had one arm over his face, head cocked to the side. Flattery worked on both father and son. "And having the self-assurance to brush off the rumours, the terrible things they're saying about you."

That got his attention. He sat upright, bloodshot eyes narrowing to pinpricks. "What've they been saying?"

"Just that you only got to where you are on your father's robes. That even a saltie from the slums can do better than that." He flinched at her words but he wasn't quite there yet. She twisted the dagger. "I mean, it's not like everyone is talking about it. It was only the Minister of Finance's daughter and her friends."

She could almost see the cogs turning in his alcohol-fumed brain. He would probably consider it his own idea by morning. It helped that she had been dropping in comments over the past few weeks about everything Mira had achieved. Gede slumped with each word of praise, vines curling tighter and tighter around him. It would do him some good. At his age Serena had been working two jobs. Just because he could afford to be idle did not mean he should. She had plans for him. For her whole family.

"If only someone could have a word, make sure she knows her

place." Her hand fluttered towards the seasilk pouch, but no, she did not need it this time. He was a good son. She had made certain of it.

Chapter Seven

"You realise, Captain, you're supposed to make some poor sap do these shitty jobs. They call it delegating." Lieutenant Tam handed Mira her usual cup of spiced tea. The sweetness hit her just a second before the warmth and she ignored his jibe. As she continued down the walkway towards their skiff, he tried to get a rise out of her. "I mean, sure, who doesn't want a day out in the slums with the best lieutenant?"

Mira couldn't help herself. "Didn't trust you to show Lucia the ropes."

Tam rolled back in the boat, pretending he had been punched in the gut, melodramatic and loud as Mira started the engine. Lucia hid her laugh in her sleeve, the ensign still uncertain of how she should act around her superiors.

Mira had argued with Kai after the benefit gala. After he'd admitted tentatively that his family didn't know about her. That his sister, due any day now, might be a bit ... surprised. Mira was still welcome at his place. *My place.* Those were the words that now rattled repeatedly in her head and drew out the moisture from her spice-coated mouth. *My.* A slip of the tongue. Perhaps. He'd corrected himself quickly enough. *Our place.* That was what he'd said when she had moved in, but Mira still couldn't shake the feeling she was a guest. Work was, therefore, a welcome distraction.

The engine picked up speed and she held the steering wheel

loosely, navigating the waterways with ease. Her critical eye swept across the cityscape, darting between leaking roofs and boarded-up shopfronts. The heady smell of rotting garbage wafted in their direction every so often. Sometimes it was overwhelming how much needed to be done. Closing her eyes for a brief moment, she tried to soothe the anxiety gnawing at her insides.

"So we're roughing up the new arrivals?"

Mira stiffened. She knew Tam was joking, trying to provoke a reaction, but all the same, it didn't always hit the mark. "Something doesn't add up. This family have just arrived but they keep getting reported. Illegal fishing, counterfeit land visa, pakalot tampering. My gut says there's more to it. The city guard should be handling it, but . . ."

"You don't trust them with it."

Mira's silence said it all. The slums of the Seong district around the main generating engine were mostly rotting stilthouses. Officially not worth repairing. Residents had been offered incentives to move out and the houses had been earmarked for demolition for more than a few years. But rather than decreasing the numbers, the area had become denser, filling with newly arrived folk who couldn't afford the rent elsewhere.

They tied up the boat once the waterways got too narrow. Folk children were already bobbing in the water, diving to pick whelks and clams from the underside of the docks and tossing them into buckets. Swimming was seen as something folk did. A skill that marked them as primitive, just as their gills made them closer kin to fish and molluscs than humanity. Those who inhabited the lofty Jingsha towers did not expect to get their feet wet. Swimming was beneath them. Even those who did live on the water's edge had little time to teach their children. Too busy surviving to show them anything beyond treading water. The few humans that learned to swim were as rare as the sightings of a nautilus.

Gill-less children were scrubbing the molluscs, swinging their feet in the filthy water and chattering away. It wasn't only the folk who lived in squalor. Poverty cared not about gills or fins. Mira tossed a coin to a few of them, picking out the children whose buckets and bodies had a long way to fill out. "Watch our boat and I'll double it when we return," she promised.

"You can swim ahead," Tam said, perfunctorily. As always, Mira refused. The lieutenant had never seen her in the water. Even when they were recruits together in endurance training, she always took the long way round on land.

The smell of drying squid and fermenting fish sauce assailed her, clearing her sinuses of the city smog. Tam and Lucia had already raised neckerchiefs over their lower faces but Mira loved it. The noises were comforting. The chattering of the aunties, the thud of a cleaver as fish were skilfully sliced into parts, the calls of vendors in their narrow canoes, selling everything from straw hats to dulse noodles in crab shells, passing over the purchases using long-handled hooks. To her, it was a childhood song.

"Strictly speaking, this isn't a registered water market; they shouldn't be trading," Lucia pointed out. She rubbed her nose nervously as she found the nerve to speak up.

"Strictly speaking, you're welcome to go after them, chase them through the water and fill out all the paperwork," Mira replied levelly.

Lucia looked over the side. The water here was particularly viscous. It was the heat from the nearby Onseon Engine perhaps, powering most of the city, or just the sheer number of people washing, cooking, fishing in it that gave it a unique soup-like feel. The ensign shook her head and kept her mouth shut.

Mira saw her stumble as they passed a group of pakalot-less folk. Illegal settlers still slipped through the border nets. Folk desperate enough to live off-grid, avoiding public transport and larger shops where they'd surely be reported. The metal bangle signified visa status for fathomfolk, citizenship even, but it was also a leash curtailing their waterweaving abilities. Lucia looked at her captain again, eyes narrowing as neither Mira nor Tam commented. She swallowed her remark.

Nevertheless, the vendors cleared out, smart enough not to push their luck. Others shuffled on too, the emaciated addicts who'd been lounging on rotten planks with track marks up their arms. Samnang had told Mira to keep out of it. The kumiho would find the gangs who supplied the fugu intoxicants and shut them down. If anything, the drug dealing had got worse in the last few years. More brazen than previously.

A neighbour pointed them to the right house and Mira knocked. The door was a couple of planks of rotten wood, hardly concealing the one-room shack within.

"It's the border guards. A moment of your time." She kept her voice friendly but firm.

The planks were slid aside, the family within already lined up in age order. Ready to be interrogated, resigned to being carted off.

"Sit down, we just want to talk," Mira said abruptly. She hated both the fear and the hope she saw glittering there.

The old man spoke first, his whiskers hanging long to his waist. He stammered incoherently, eyes darting between Mira and Tam. He was trying to tell her something, a message he wanted to conceal from her lieutenant.

"I don't speak Yonakunish," she said. Fathomfolk often assumed, saw her gill lines and came to certain conclusions. Kai had been trying to teach her in the evenings, working through kids' primers. Sometimes she heard her ama chattering away to old aunties, the sound of the Yonakunish or Iyonessian words a weird series of clicks and sounds so high her ears could barely discern them. She regretted refusing the lessons as a child, but back then it had seemed unimportant. Her priority to fit in, not stand out.

He switched to stammering Tiankawian, accent thick and words telegraphic. "It was for the waves. The waves," he said, gesturing for emphasis.

Mira looked at Tam for help, but the lieutenant simply shrugged. She'd brought the wrong man for tact. There was one simple way to get to the bottom of this. Before they could react, she pushed past the residents to see what they were trying to conceal.

It was a shrine. Crude clay and shell figures, candles and fresh flowers. Mira turned one of the figures over in her hands. A turtle. Its shell was mother of pearl and its eyes obsidian shards. There was also a whale similarly formed, each with an island on its back. Sand god statues were rare topside in Tiankawi but were still worshipped by those who followed the old beliefs. Titans – behemoths that supposedly dwelled in the deepest oceans – rising to the surface only once every century or two. These were the seemingly immortal creatures that had formed the world centuries before humans and fathomfolk existed. Stories of the titans took on a mythic quality, the lines between lore and living memory blurring entirely. The rare documented sightings were nearly always in pairs. And then, when they had disappeared altogether, they were elevated to godhood.

Lucia peered over her shoulder. "Sleeping titans, right? They're the figureheads in the Boat Races."

"We believe in the old gods, but us, not our children's fault," the mother said, standing protectively in front of her kids. The oldest was cradling the baby in a practised swaying motion.

"It's not illegal," Lucia said. "Worship whoever you want."

They were in human form, but not all shape-shifting was alike. Some folk could not hide all of their marine characteristics; others defiantly chose not to. Mira saw more than her ensign did. The oldest son's half-formed gills, the vitiligo of his mottled brown and grey skin. The mother's silver-grey hair and flawless

complexion had nothing to do with age. She was a baiji, a fathomfolk who could take dolphin shape. Even in human form her
stance was as graceful as a dancer, and Mira knew that between
her shoulder blades there was a blowhole for breathing. The man
who stood beside her was as far from a baiji as Mira was. An
otter-born dratsie perhaps, indicated by his webbed hands and
the thick white whiskers sprouting on his chin and eyebrows.
Fathomfolk for certain, but not the same.

And that was the real story.

"Who do you share this house with?" Mira asked.

"We—" the baiji started. Her partner touched her elbow, shook
his head, fear etched into the lines of his face.

"You can tell me now or waste more of my day. And the more
time I waste, the more pissed off I get." Mira disliked pulling the
authority card and yet it worked at times like these. New arrivals
frightened of being sent back into the brine crumbled before her
uniform. The power of it was instantaneous. The baiji deflated,
sagging into her ill-fitting robes. Mira kept pushing. "What have
you been fishing?"

"Fishing?" The baiji shook her head, not understanding.

"Just for meals, for the kids," the whiskered man said. "They
can't ... you see, they can't. Sometimes we sell a little. Just to
neighbours."

"No selling at the markets? To restaurants?" He shook his head
to each of Mira's questions. Mystified.

The only equipment was a couple of worn nets and a fishing
rod; this was no illegal fishing business. The visa and pakalot
accusations made by neighbours were just as baseless. Mira could
scarcely hear the family's responses, drowned out by the pulsing
vein on her forehead, the one that Kai said was from biting back
her retorts. Her jaw ached from clenching her teeth together. She
thought about the names she'd once been called, the ridicule she
had endured. And her mother, facing it all with a placid smile and

not a word in retaliation. Sometimes it wasn't even humanity. Fathomfolk could be just as cruel.

"I'm moving you. There's a unit you can share in north Qilin."

They seemed not to believe her at first, waiting for the catch. Slowly, hope diffused around the room. They nodded and yammered on and on until Mira could barely extract herself from the house for all the bowing and thanks.

Tam said nothing, waiting until they were out of earshot. "There's no space in Qilin. Hasn't been for months."

"We'll find a space."

"What makes that family so special?" Lucia blurted, unable to contain herself.

"We're not all exactly the same: dratsie, baiji, siren. Humans lump us together. Fathomfolk. Salties. But we're different. We shape-shift or use our waterweaving differently. Distinct. And some think we should remain so. Stay with our own."

The penny dropped. Lucia's mouth hung open. "All of this because they're a mixed-race family?"

"Exactly."

"But you and Kai . . . " Her voice faded away.

A dragon – frigging paragon of virtue – and a half-siren bitch. Mira had heard the comments. The ones they made to her face and the crueller ones said to her back. Centuries of class differences, animosity between havens, instilled prejudice fuelled by humanity's assumed superiority. These were things invisible to humans, to those outside the community that cannibalised its own. How could she explain all of that in a few brief minutes? She couldn't.

She was about to add more when she saw someone at their boat. Gede of the kumiho, Samnang's son.

"At ease," he said with a wave of his hand. Neither Mira nor the others had even attempted a formal fist-palm greeting. After what had just happened, Mira was not in the mood. "Lieutenant? Just happened to be in the area?"

She'd caught him off guard. Gede looked flustered, but launched anyway into a clearly prepared opening. "Even to the kumiho, your rise through the ranks is admirable." He attempted, and failed, to casually lean back against one of the mooring posts, entirely misjudging the height. Mira kept her expression polite, ignoring Tam's loud snort.

"Lucia, be careful. This area is covered in droppings." Tam looked up at the hazy sky as if he'd entirely forgotten the man was there.

Mira had wanted to be a scholar official. She'd diligently studied the laws and regulations needed for the exams, three years in a row, each time apparently failing by a scattering of points despite her confidence, despite scoring near perfect on practice exams. Finally she'd thrown her lot in with the military. Even then the kumiho had not wanted her. City guards only recruited from their own. Rather, that should be, from their parents' and grandparents' recommendations. Without references, without drinks at exclusive dinner parties, no one was getting into the inner circle.

"How's your father?" she asked. Gede's rise in the kumiho had been meteoric. Innate skill and good luck, they called it. In the privacy of her own home, Mira called it something else.

"He's well." Gede pulled at the cuffs of his jacket, making minuscule adjustments to straighten them. "I don't think he, or I, has ever been in this area of the city. It certainly is ... vibrant. Perhaps you can provide a tour while the others get on with the paperwork?"

Here it comes, Mira thought, wiping her hands on her loose trousers. She would humour him, see what the kumiho had up their sleeve.

Gede walked with her a short distance, cutting a fast pace despite being unfamiliar with the walkways. She supposed he hoped she would hurry after him, her shorter legs working to keep up. Instead she slowed right down to a stroll. Stopped to read the

Drawback slogans painted in jagged letters on the wall, to watch naga kids playing chase in the water, to greet old aunties hanging out their laundry. Gede had to wait, tapping his foot impatiently.

"Such a colourful area. Aren't they resourceful to fit so many people in?" Gede gestured up at the ramshackle illegal houses stacked on top of each other like precarious game tiles.

When Mira was a child, she'd lived in such a shanty town, sleeping top to tail with her mother and the other family they split the rent with. She still remembered the red bean soup they shared. Their house had collapsed, crushed when an upstairs neighbour was repairing his roof. Both Mira and her mother had been out. The other family had not been so lucky.

"Most don't have a choice," she said.

"Ah yes. Like when I had to share a cabin with my sister when we went sailing. A whole week."

"Entirely the same thing, yes." She resisted the urge to shake the fool by his lapels. Slap a pakalot on his wrist and watch him fish for his dinner. Titans help her, she had not an ounce of patience left for these privileged idiots. She had to nod politely at those above her, but she'd be damned if she offered Gede the same courtesy. His every word was an unsubtle insult.

"My family summer in the Southern islands. It's a shame really, to leave such a property empty. A four-bedroom villa with its own orangery."

Mira must have made a noise. She hadn't meant to, hadn't meant to give him a single sign of interest, but all the same, an orangery! To own your own tree – no, trees. She'd been a teenager before she had even seen one. Her mother's potted plants were her pride and joy. Even now the living walls in Jingsha made her look up with awe and hope.

"Yes," Gede said, moving closer as if they shared a kinship over this. Two children whispering conspiratorially. "Brimming with green: ferns and orchids! A freshwater pond filled with koi. Birds that wake you in the morning with sweet song. Picking your own ripe fruit." Something in her expression made him pause. Less certain now. "A shame no one is using it."

"Turn it over to the state. We could have four refugee families in there." Her words hardened against the daydream building in her mind. Such a frivolous waste of freshwater on ornamental ponds when rainwater was painstakingly collected for farming and drinking throughout the city.

He looked at her slack-jawed, stiffening like a ghost had walked through him. Then awkwardly he broke into a laugh. "What a benevolent idea, Captain! Perhaps you should take it over. Move your ama from that leaky sampan."

He was certainly concerned about her. "How kind. I'll give it serious consideration." She managed to keep a straight face. About as much consideration as she gave the guano on her boots. She had expected more from Samnang's eldest. A cunning plan, a steady game of machinations. Instead he had ambled along and rubbed a fistful of gold in her face. So brazen to think that in the first month of her hard-won promotion she'd give it all up.

"Did your father put you up to this?" she asked bluntly. Gede paled in horror. It was probably doing damage to his reputation just being out here. Or perhaps elevating him. Slumming it. Mira couldn't keep track of the scandal stories and the social set that followed them.

"I have my own autonomy," he said.

"I hadn't realised."

The meaning of her words sank in. Mira tried to memorise his expression to share with Kai later. While she wasn't one to be spiteful, it was a picture. After a stunned silence, Gede pulled himself straight, salvaging what was left of his pride. "You've been a most gracious tour guide. I thank you for your time."

Mira felt the satisfaction of winning a sparring session, but her elation was short-lived. Gede was not an opponent of any real mettle. She had merely caught a harmless spider in a glass and released it back outside. She at least owed him a touch of civility. "My regards to your father and mother," she said.

Gede paused, the creases in his brow smoothing over. "And my regards to *your* ama. You must worry about her." He made a fist-palm salute and bowed, dramatically low, before leaving.

Was that a threat? A warning? Her throat tightened a little, making it difficult to swallow. Her overactive imagination was seeing menace where perhaps there was only a gauche kumiho puffing himself up. Regardless, she wished she'd punched him in his smug little face.

Chapter Eight

"Your business in Tiankawi?" The guard looked like he'd not smiled a day in his life. A stack of blank lotus leaf paper sat at his elbow but he made no pretence at taking notes.

"Espionage and anarchy." Nami couldn't help it. They'd finally sighted land two days ago and she'd watched Tiankawi inch into view. But now, just as everyone was being let off at the port, she'd been taken aside for extra questioning. Patience frayed, hungry and tired from the long voyage, she found herself resorting to her default. Stubborn defiance.

The crossing had been rough: constant queuing, no shade from the beating sun, singled out by both the border guards and the fathomfolk as someone who shouldn't be there – the precious princess Dan liked to joke about. Except it wasn't funny any more. Not out here where the dulse cakes her mother had given her lasted all of two days. And any kindness was followed up by a demand. She had seen a few fathomfolk – a nymph who would've blown away with a strong breeze, a naga mother with a sick child – being furtively led into a locked room. They exited an hour or so later with supplies in their arms but unable to look the other passengers in the eye. It didn't take a lot to guess what happened in that darkened room.

A week ago, Nami would've stormed in after them. Kicked up a fuss. But the pakalot bit down on her arm in warning when she even thought about it, and like the others, she kept her mouth shut. The pakalot. A mesh metallic bracelet. Or really, a manacle. It hung like a dead weight, rubbing on her wrist. She knew about them, of course everyone knew about them. The only way fathomfolk were allowed into Tiankawi was on a leash. Like livestock. The device prevented them from harming humans, although she didn't understand the intricacies of it. Perhaps something else she could learn on her educational jaunt.

"Is this it?" she'd asked as the first buildings came into view. She'd turned to the long-armed chang-bi standing next to her by the railing. "Tiankawi?" Those within earshot had burst into laughter. Fishing villages. That was all. The buildings were nothing more than wooden shanties, standing on spindly legs that raised them well out of the water. Once the many stilts may have been straight, but now they splayed at twisting angles, in various stages of rot. A few children waved to them from the wooden platforms, human children, sticks at the ready to beat the flies from the fish drying on angled frames. Nami was surprised. She hadn't expected to see humans in poverty. One girl tossed a bucket of entrails into a hatch below her feet. The water came alive with vying silver bass, their bodies slapping against each other as they rose out of the water. Nami found herself leaning over the railing and then, without even meaning to, half climbing over for a closer look. A guard had snapped at her abruptly, waving his stick in her direction. For a moment she had forgotten – she was not free to simply dive in.

It was madness: they made newcomers sit on a ship for weeks when they could swim across. Trust humans to build walls. Erecting border nets had been part of the peace deal. One settlement vessel from the havens a month was the only legal way in.

More and more of the Tiankawi city state had come into view, and Nami realised the extent of her earlier mistake. It must've been ten times the size of Yonakuni haven. So big her mind couldn't take it all in at once. Wooden stilthouses were replaced with stone and steel constructions. Columns rose in the distance, lofty monoliths that made the Peace Tower look like a child's toy.

By the time they'd passed the submerged roofs of old houses, she'd seen two guards pointing in her direction. She'd known then she was in trouble.

"Where're you staying in Tiankawi?" The border guard spat the question like it was a foul taste.

"Might just float along in my sleep." Nami stretched her arms out and clasped them behind her head, rocking back in the chair. He wrote something. She guessed it wasn't a glowing recommendation.

"We don't tolerate rough sleepers here. Do you have a job lined up?"

"Kraken harpooning. Or leviathan fishing. Haven't decided yet." It was just too easy to wind him up.

"You're a real joker, aren't you?"

Nami nodded in acknowledgement. From the window, she could see another tram leaving the station, the busy port thinning. And another. One of the green-coated border guards on the port looked at his watch. The skies were darkening, and eerie yellow lights flickered on, the glow unlike the witchlight Nami was accustomed to. And then no more trams came. Still the questioning continued.

She considered knocking out the guard opposite her. It would be so easy. The pakalot warned her off, making its presence known up through her arm and across her body like a spreading cramp. It was insidious, a parasite leeching at her blood. She panicked, tugging at it. Her breath quickening as she felt the effects. It instantly tightened around her arm, biting into her flesh. Lessons at the Academy had taught her that the more it was resisted, the tighter the noose pulled. Leave it be, think calm thoughts and it would be no more than a loose bangle again. Yet the desire to claw her own arm was overwhelming.

The guard looked down at her wrist, clearly seeing the response written on her face. She had just made things worse, hadn't she?

A knock interrupted them. The door opened and an older man looked at Nami, surprise widening his eyes. "You still with this one?"

"She's an entitled fish fucker. I could detain her for days, you know, the amount of lip she's got."

"It's payday! You really want to be pissing your evening away on this?" the older man said.

The officer laughed and threw his hands up. "You're right, give me two minutes." He shook his head like it was a trivial misunderstanding, stamping Nami's papers and abruptly pushing her out of the room.

Nami hesitated on the empty tram platform. People would know where Kai lived; he was the ambassador to Tiankawi after all. But she was more than capable of looking after herself. She'd done it in Yonakuni; why would Tiankawi be any different?

The water at the port looked nothing like home. Still, she'd been out of the seas for so long that her hesitation only lasted seconds. It was much more appealing than the unnatural lights swaying in glass domes overhead. The metal tracks and wires of the tram line reminded her of the botched Peace Tower incident. It was too much. Too new and unfamiliar to process as tiredness seeped in at the corners of her vision. Topside could wait.

She dived. All her senses immediately improved as the water filtered through her gills, fatigue drawing back. Familiar, and yet ... The water tasted of iron. Sharp and sudden, like waves against a seawall. The metal lingered in her throat despite her trying to swallow it down. She located the source – a hunkered tram crumpled on the seabed. Orange rust bloomed from the doors and around the windows like a creeping disease. A derelict husk, abandoned after a crash some years before. Around the wreck were submerged houses, a whole neighbourhood of them. Algae and seaweed prised fingers through cracks in the walls. Sardines darted in and out of gaping doorways, bodies like silver arrows. Other creatures, nothing more than dark shapes, loomed behind tainted glass. Nami had no desire to investigate further.

A century ago this city, the whole area, was above land. An archipelago nation, yes, but one built firmly on the ground. Tiankawi had been lucky in that respect. After the Great Bathyal War between humanity and the folk, and the rising floodwaters, they already had the infrastructure in place to allow the city state to survive where other settlements failed. Only a handful of human habitats endured: islands, ship-faring nomadic communities and semi-submerged cities like this one.

A cobalt light in the distant water called out to her. She swam towards it, careful to avoid the more precarious submerged ruins. It was a huge witchlight emanating from a stone monument. The swirls of blue faded into a rosy blush at the base, illuminating the statue below. A tidal wave of kelpies was depicted galloping – rearing and frothing at the mouth – pulling a chariot of breakers. A broad-shouldered merman crested the wave, the steady light a torch carried aloft.

Best of all, around the statue was an immense underwater square, bustling with folk perusing a night market. Weight lifted from Nami's shoulders as she drew closer. Weight she had not even realised she carried. Tiankawi felt a little less foreign as she watched aunties haggling over the price of goods.

"Exquisite, isn't it?"

"Pardon?" She turned and stared at the person next to her. In the water, most folk wore their true form rather than the human face they presented topside. The eight suckered arms that made up the stranger's lower body screamed one thing alone. Seawitch. The old adage rang in Nami's ears. They'd always strike a bad bargain with you. This one was tall and so slim that her exposed collarbones and ribs were taut against her brown skin. On her head, her hair took the form of stony coral, sculpted into a dense crown. But it was the suckered limbs that drew the eye. Currently burnished red, they roamed over the cobbled ground and lingered by Nami's feet, one wrapped delicately around her ankle. The suckers gently fixed to her.

"New in town, saltlick?"

Nami hesitated. The seawitch was looking at her with a ferocious intensity, her horizontal slit pupils unnerving. Nami glanced around, looking for someone more approachable. The fathomfolk chatting by the statue were sirens in full glamour, their skin iridescent. They hummed soft melodies to themselves as they combed out their hair, eyes perusing the crowd. Water sprites no bigger than Nami's hand nimbly sank into the seaweed growing between the cobbles, turning their bodies translucent as they darted between people's legs, pockets and bags. A silent O formed on her lips. Unsavoury types, her mother would say. She muttered, backing away from the conversation.

Octopus limbs folded across her midriff, the witch flashed green eyes at her. Were they always green? She could've sworn they were yellow earlier. "Let me treat you to supper. Come out of the cold stream." Despite the light words, there was no accompanying smile, and the limb on Nami's leg tightened its grip. The witch waved, and pieces of flame detached themselves from the monument. Nami blinked and saw for the first time two giant squid, skin rippling in bands of white and red that pulsed down their mantles and fins. Their bodies alone were taller than her, and this was without the incredible reach of their sucker-covered arms and tentacles. The rhythm throbbed and soothed simultaneously, holding her gaze so completely that the next moment she was inside a building and holding a glass bottle in her hand. The mermaid behind the counter was uncorking another.

Nami took a long sip without even thinking, the alcohol burning her palate as it went down. The effects were almost instantaneous. A friendly drink, kind words. She hadn't had anyone to talk to – not really – since Dan and Hong-Gi.

The second sip slipped down her throat as smoothly as a warm current. Where were they anyhow? A homely little establishment. Other customers were dotted around, anchored in hammocks or drifting through the water. Why, the seawitch was like an auntie to them, taking in all these strays. Setting them up in this lovely place! The limpets decorating the stools were charming and the marbled rock tables were better than the finest she had seen in Yonakuni. The seawitch stroked her fingers through the water in a slow rhythm that matched Nami's exuberant exclamations, and was she not gracious, was she not a fine individual to spend her evening listening to the grievances of strangers?

Nami put the half-finished drink down, or at least tried to. The seawitch caught the bottle before it floated off, lodged it in a holder on the counter. There were more empty bottles. Many more. And where was the promised meal?

The seawitch wasn't drinking.

Six bottles by herself? Nami didn't even remember drinking them, not beyond the initial sip, but that'd been so smooth and warm she could definitely . . .

The seawitch slid a seventh bottle across to her.

Nami unanchored herself from the stool, trying to shake the fugue from her head. Something was not right here. There was somewhere else she should be.

"You're in the right place," the seawitch said. "You were looking for me."

"No, that's not true. I . . . I don't even know your name."

The witch laughed, slapping her hands on her lower limbs and moving closer. "Of course you do. I'm Cordelia and you're Nami. We're firm friends."

Nami pressed her fingers on her temples, trying to clear her mind. What was she doing again? She swam back towards the door. "Thanks for the drink. And next time I'm in the area I'll—"

"What's the rush, saltlick?" The seawitch was pulsing now, purple spots appearing on her limbs and billowing across the skin. She raised herself up. At full height, she towered over Nami. "You're pretty, y'know. Smart too. You could work for me. People would pay a fortune for one of your scales, for the smallest of your claws. The stories say you can floor a sand god with a single drop of dragon blood. My, wouldn't that be fun. It'd be better for you than *them*."

Nami had no idea what she was talking about. Her confusion was painted all over her face as the seawitch clapped her hands together in delight, "Oh my dear, you really are fresh off the boat. I'm getting ahead of myself. Forget I said anything. What a tender morsel. We're going to have fun."

Nami had finally backed up to the door and groped for the handle, all the while trying to keep her gaze away from the magnetising swirls flowing down the seawitch's body. The door slid open under her hand and she gratefully slunk out, kicking her legs hard. Her heart beat frantically as she stared at the door, unsure if Cordelia would follow her or not.

Part of her wanted the seawitch to give chase.

She rubbed at her eyes, blinking to see if it would restore her vision. The seabed rose towards her and the buildings leaned more than they had a right to. She swam away from the square, deciding to take her chances elsewhere. But it was late. The witchlight was not evenly spread around the submerged parts of the city, and the further she swam, the darker the night became. Something passed her, brushing her hip before she could move back. She saw only a wisp of a tail, and damn it, her bag was gone! They'd managed to grab her whole satchel without her noticing.

Once again the easy option came unbidden to her mind. Just

ask where he lived. Her brother would surely reward anyone who showed her the way. He would have shelter, somewhere safe to curl up and sleep. He would take care of everything.

Gritting her teeth, she shoved the thought aside and swam on.

Chapter Nine

Cordelia didn't need the light of the sun to know when morning had come. The small shoals of anchovies regrouped, darting through the open archways in her bar. The scrap collectors were out, stooped grandmothers spearing through the flotsam to earn a few coins. And the protesters had set out their banners.

The seawitch stretched her arms overhead. She was late. She'd have to hurry home soon before her husband suspected something. Early on, she had been clever enough to establish reasons for her absences: visiting her parents on the Southern islands; weekend trips with friends; volunteering. He was unimaginative enough not to ask many questions.

"Nahla, everything to plan?"

The mermaid shot upright from where she'd been half asleep behind the bar. "Yes madam, your guards have marked the trail." Her voice shook. Nahla's mother was a hard worker. The daughter was yet to prove herself.

Cordelia stood before the battered old mirror, the edges barnacle-encrusted. Her hands reached up over her face, the pakalot slipping down loosely on her wrist. As long as it was directly unrelated to humans, she could use her powers as she saw fit. She raised ridges on her forehead, drained her green eyes to brown, flattened her nose and elongated her chin. She worked slowly and evenly on her shape-shifting, like moulding a piece of clay. Stiff and unyielding at first, her powers warmed up and the minor adjustments were second nature. It was hard to emulate a real person, harder still when she'd only met him once, many, many years ago. Under scrutiny it would not hold, but a fleeting glance could be convincing. She was careful not to touch her own face. It was disorientating to find features in the wrong place, no matter how many decades of practice she'd had. She pulled her hood up over her newly formed antlers, masking most of her face in shadow. Dragon antlers were thankfully small in comparison to some folk, these ones curving up and back just behind her head. The disguise would be enough to convince a hung-over new arrival.

She swam out of Glashtyn Square, following the subtle signs her squid guard had left. Finally she saw the ripples of the camouflaged sentry by a boarded-up window. Below, in the doorway, curled into a small ball, was the sleeping figure of Nami. Someone ought to warn her about gill rot. One night would not do her harm, but sleeping in the polluted Tiankawian waters without medication had taken its toll on many.

The sleeping figure reminded Cordelia of her own children. Her hand hesitated just a moment, before she shrugged the troublesome feeling from her shoulders. This was business. She shook Nami hard, face right overhead so that it would be the first thing the sleeping dragon would see.

Nami's eyes flew open, hands flailing widely in surprise as she soaked in the features Cordelia had pulled over her own. The girl's father. "Aba?"

"They're coming!" Cordelia kept the words clipped and in Yonakunish, unsure of what the old dragon Alon had sounded like. Appearances were easy, but voices less so.

"Aba, how . . . ?" Nami said, voice thick with sleep. She rubbed at the bridge of her nose and Cordelia turned, swimming away.

"We need to go. Now!" She kicked, consciously making sure her legs were scaled and clawed, not cephalopod limbs. Behind her, she heard clumsy arm movements as Nami launched herself into the water. Cordelia wasted not a moment more in checking. She swam down the tight alleyway between submerged buildings, through an open window and broken roof, back down between bamboo stilts, only pausing to let the girl catch up a little.

She emerged from the water, pulling herself up onto the walkways in the middle of the morning rush in the Old Town. Humans and fathomfolk filled the raised platforms, hurrying to catch trams or morning ferries to work. The seawitch piled through them, ignoring the wince of her pakalot as she shouldered people out of her way. Nami was right behind her, hand at one point tugging at her robes, demanding an explanation. Too close!

But there, right on plan, was the kumiho early patrol, eating rice porridge at a street stall. Cordelia careered into the nearby stalls, leapt over their table, spilling porcelain bowls and spoons all over the place. Then she slammed open the first door she saw and dropped her disguise. The guards belatedly yelled and leapt to their feet, hot soup scalding their laps. Two followed her through the doorway, but Cordelia had pressed herself against the wall, changing her colours so that her body matched the grain of the wood exactly. She tempered her breathing down. There was so much noise outside that the guards gave no more than a perfunctory glance around, picking up the discarded cloak from the floor.

On cue, Nami came barrelling after her. The kumiho grabbed her easily as she peered beyond them, looking this way and that, twisting against their hold. Cordelia watched in fascination as the young dragon struggled, yelling out in Yonakunish. Most could not understand her – probably assumed she was another bottom-feeding addict. The wildness in her bloodshot eyes certainly gave that impression. The trick had worked perfectly.

Lieutenant Gede took charge, twisting Nami's wrist behind her back and reaching for his manacles. It was useful that his breakfast routines were so predictable. That *he* was so predictable. Just then, someone stepped out of the crowd. At nearly six foot tall, with a dark green mohawk, this particular fathomfolk was easily recognisable. Lynnette, the leader of the Drawbacks. An extremist branch of folk protesters, the Drawbacks had been making a lot of commotion of late. Discordant and uncomfortable noise that curdled the ears.

Lynnette's presence was hard to ignore. She demanded attention, even if she occasionally stumbled over her words. Her muscular arms had once pulled a tuk-tuk through the water, and this hard labour was a great leveller with many folk. Honest. Authentic. That was what her admirers called her. Rough. Primitive. Cordelia had heard her critics spit out less endearing terms altogether.

The Drawback leader clasped her hand on Nami's shoulder. Explained that her newly arrived comrade didn't know the rules. And how could she when folk community centres had been decimated? Voluntary organisations made to fill out endless paperwork for grants that never appeared. What was needed was action, and not fetters around wrists for simple errors. Go ahead then, she goaded the kumiho, arrest us all.

The Drawbacks who'd surreptitiously woven in through the watching crowd all fell to their knees, raising their wrists. Gede's throat bobbed up and down with discomfort, looking at the sprawl of folk around him, at the others watching. Muttering. He had not prepared for this. The crowd drew courage from his silence. No harm done, no harm at all. Let her go!

"After all," Lynnette paused for effect, "she's dragon-born."

Nami looked up, clearly surprised that this stranger knew so much about her. She had wisely kept to human form: hiding her antlers, her scales and claws, concealing everything apart from the gill slits at the sides of her neck. The one smart thing she'd done since arriving in the city was unravelled with Lynnette's statement. The crowd were engrossed. Dragon-born! Another pearl come to Tiankawi. Just a simple misunderstanding. Let her go. Hands reached out and touched Nami's clothes, her hands, making a sign of blessing. Gede reluctantly released her arm. "This is your first and only warning."

Before Nami could respond, Lynnette slapped her on the back and pulled her to one side, whispering to a member of her group. Nami was whisked through the crowd, lost in the sea of onlookers.

It had taken longer than expected. Cordelia would have to make up an excuse. She pondered on it as the crowd slowly dispersed. A sea cabbage seller muttered under his breath as he restacked his cart; broken bowls and spilt rice porridge still strewn across the walkway. A shadow loomed at the doorway, eclipsing the narrow shafts of light.

"You're in here, aren't you, shape-shifter?" It was Lynnette. She clearly couldn't pinpoint where Cordelia was concealed, and the frustration was knitted on her brows. Cordelia considered peeling herself away from the wall but then hesitated. This had not been part of the plan. Any interaction risked destroying her cover.

"Next time, tone it down a bit." Lynnette turned and left, letting light back into the room.

The sheer arrogance of the kelpie and her ilk. They had wanted a fortuitous introduction to the newly arrived water dragon, one that set them up as potential allies. An easy enough job for the seawitch. But Cordelia did not believe in their principles, in the Drawbacks' rhetoric of anarchy to free folk from humanity. She helped them because there was profit in chaos. Undermine the Council, distract the guards and make people more desperate. These all furthered her goals also. But that didn't mean civility was done away with. She'd been in the job for longer than most of the Drawbacks had been alive. She was not about to let some upstart with a rehearsed speech dictate the terms of their agreement.

She curled her lower limbs towards herself and then relaxed them. They wanted to sit at the adults' table. So be it. She was more than prepared.

Chapter Ten

Nami was breathless. Head spinning from the alcohol of the night before, from seeing her father's face and then nearly getting arrested. A cheap trick, she realised now. Siren charm could do it - make believable illusions. A seawitch or a decent disguise was enough also. Someone had wanted to get her arrested, led her straight to the city guards like a fish on a line. To tarnish her reputation, her brother's, all dragons - it could be any of those reasons. Thank the titans the kelpie had intervened on her behalf. Her legs shook, prickles running from her feet up her calves and as she noticed, they caved under her. A hand steadied her before her knees hit the slick walkway.

"Just a little further," the stranger said.

Nami registered his words as the warm grip on her waist released. He had a goal in mind, her soft-spoken rescuer. He guided her onto a semi-submerged roof and they finally caught their breath. The washing lines shielded them from view and Nami pulled her knees up to her chest until they stopped trembling. The stranger said nothing, content to wait. He unwrapped a parcel of food and laid it between them as though coaxing a wild bird. Dulse cakes. Nami shovelled one into her mouth. She shouldn't. Not smart to eat food from someone she didn't know. But after the welcome she'd had, she didn't care any more.

"Thanks," she said finally.

He shrugged, pushing his long hair back. Nami picked up a second dulse cake, surreptitiously glancing at him between nibbles. His hair fell in soft auburn locks around a chiselled face. A shadow of stubble graced his angular jaw. His skin was pale and he had green-flecked amber eyes that crinkled with bemusement as they fixed on her own. She glanced away, mortified.

"Who are you?" She winced. Her words sounded accusatory. But her rescuer didn't seem to take offence.

"Firth. I'm one of the Drawbacks."

"Draw ... backs?" Nami only knew the word in reference to tidal waves. When the water pulled back from the shore, as if inhaled before the ocean swelled to a devastating tsunami.

"We fight for folk rights. A voice for our people." Firth's own voice had fire in it, embers beneath a layer of ash. It felt like the Anemone Club meetings back home. Despite the confusion of last night and this morning, his words buoyed her. The folk in Tiankawi were not as apathetic as she'd assumed.

"That kelpie, your leader – she knew I was a dragon. How?"

Firth stretched out his long legs. "The chinthe, the border guard, are looking for you. Seems your brother is worried."

Nami thought about her time on the settlement vessel and spat. "The chinthe know exactly what delayed me. They can go fuck themselves."

Firth's eyes widened for a moment, and then he laughed. A full-bellied sound that sent the nearby seabirds flapping into the sky. Nami had not expected that reaction but she basked in it all the same. For some reason it felt important to win his approval. A warmth sanded away the tight knot in her chest. He leaned over and she caught her breath, but he was only wrapping up the remaining dulse cakes. "I knew I'd like you."

Pretending not to be flustered, Nami looked away and rubbed her eyes. It felt like there was a film on them somehow. Firth watched her for a moment. "See those tall chimneys to the east?"

He pointed at the conical pillars that pierced the skyline in the distance. Half a dozen stood like immense tube-like sea sponges in the wan fog. Nami had been too preoccupied topside before, but now Firth pointed, she realised that what she'd assumed was morning mist lingered everywhere above water. Nor did it have the dew-like feel against her skin. Dense, almost jaundiced fog, it cloyed against her throat. "That's the industrial heart. For all the talk of improvement, the smog continues."

"Is that why the water feels ... thick?"

"Mmm, delicious, isn't it? Industrial waste poisoning us."

"You mean ...?" Nami looked down, still seeing the shadows of fathomfolk swimming beneath them.

"Living underwater is a death sentence. A slow, painful one, but a death sentence all the same. There are some remedies to slow the progress, but gill rot is a real risk."

Nami rubbed at her own gills self-consciously. Did they feel tight and scratchy, or was she just responding to his words? Firth shook his head reassuringly at her unvoiced concerns. It was a foolish fear, of course; other folk had lived here longer than one night. "Then fathomfolk live above water?"

"The few that can afford it. Technically you need papers. More expenses and red tape."

It was a lot to take in. Nami had to look away from his unruffled expression to regain her composure. Thoughts swirled like a whirlpool. She needed a focal point. Something to hold her steady. Queasiness coated her tongue and stomach.

Her eye was drawn to where multiple tram lines congregated, like rivers flowing towards a basin. Imposing, densely packed buildings rose out of the water to touch the sky above. The other buildings they'd passed – brick structures four or five floors tall or precarious stilthouses – were insubstantial in comparison. "Who lives there?"

"That is the Jingsha district, beating heart of Tiankawi! In other words, a steady stream of whaleshit. The decision-makers, people with more money than sense." Firth frowned, his voice biting. His features darkened, a shadow settling over his shoulders briefly before he shook it off. "Oh, and your brother. In the tallest building in the city."

Nami stood so quickly she slipped. Fell with a clumsy stumble into the fetid water. She raised her head out into the air, feeling the cool morning wind caress her damp hair. The silver monolith was only just outlined against the grey, like a dagger with its tip pointed up. There was a network around it, tramlines like an impenetrable wall of thorns. It must have been seventy, no, eighty floors high, and Kai, near the top, looking down.

"Out of water? B-but he's the ambassador? He's meant to be on our side." Nami's voice squeaked high with incredulity. She swallowed some of the poisonous water but no longer cared.

Firth came down off the roof more gracefully. "Oh yes, the good old *ambassador*."

Nami heard the sarcasm dripping through his words. Cocked her head to one side in confusion. "But he *is* the ambassador, isn't he?"

"There're ambassadors from both Atlitya and Muyeres havens. We had one for Iyoness too, for all the good it did. But none of them sit on the Council. None of them get to be Ambassador Kai of Yonakuni, *Minister of Fathomfolk*."

Nami's head reeled. Kai was just the ambassador to their haven. All the other things . . . well, she'd never paid much attention before.

Firth looked at her kindly, like she was clutching at broken shells, trying to glue them back together. "Kai lives in Jingsha, has a vote on the Council and no pakalot on his wrist. Do I have to spell it out?"

No. She couldn't entertain that thought. Her brother was

many things, but disloyal and deceitful he was not. What had happened in the two years he had been here? "I'm here now, I'll remind him."

"It's not that simple."

"It is! Humans did this! And we need to take it back!" The words hung loud and ringing in the biting air. Nami paused, thinking belatedly to look around her. Empty rowing boats drifted to and fro against their lashings, but it was quiet otherwise. She breathed out just as a door opened, the sound of chatter wafting towards them before it swung shut again.

"We're going to get along, Nami. Swimmingly." Firth reached out to help her out of the water. His expression was fierce, his hand gripping hers like she was caught in a vice. The intensity was blistering, and Nami was unsure how she could break it.

Or if she even wanted to.

The roar of an approaching motorboat entered her consciousness. It was not the guards from before, the blue-coated ones who had pulled her arm so tight behind her back that it still ached. It was the more familiar green-coated chinthe guards. The uniforms she'd come to hate during her long journey aboard the settlement vessel.

The boat pulled up next to them, a diminutive woman and a large man at the helm. The woman scowled, eyes trained on Firth as if he were a bad taste in her mouth. She forced a smile over the top, an awful one that barely hid the suspicion, hands raised in fist-palm greeting. "Nami? It is Nami, right?"

How did everyone in this blasted place know who she was? Nami let go of Firth's hand. Her legs shook a little without him to anchor her. She gripped her own thigh, hiding the tremor behind bravado. "So what if I am?"

"Kai sent me. Come, we'll take you to him." The officer reached out a hand.

"Have I done something wrong?"

"What?" The other woman's confusion was genuine at least. "No, we just wanted to make sure you're safe."

Nami let an acerbic laugh cut through the air. "Border guards keeping me safe?" As the bafflement remained on the woman's features, Nami studied her. She couldn't quite put a finger on it. Despite the shabby patchwork of her uniform and the perfunctory ponytail of thick curly hair, something drew the eye. Her features were delicate, beautiful: a long, slim nose and warm amber eyes set against brown skin that was almost golden, a magnetising sheen. Her gill lines, faint as they were, peeked out from beneath her collar. It clicked. "Siren?"

The officer fastened up her collar button. It simply highlighted the curves of her silhouette. "Half-siren."

"By the tides, talk straight," the older chinthe man behind her said. He gestured between the two. "Nami, meet Mira. Mira, Nami. Mira's not any old half-siren. She's your brother's partner."

Chapter Eleven

The lift had golden cage doors that opened simultaneously, horizontal and vertical layers. Inside, it was padded in cushioned blue velvet studded with rhinestones. Mira slid the doors shut as soon as Nami stepped in, muttering something about finishing her shift as she left. The boat ride over had been awkward enough. Nami was thankful that the officer had the sense to give her some space.

She felt her stomach lurch as the lift shot upwards. Braced herself on the walls and tried not to voice the scream inside her. It was a coffin, this little box, squeezing at her lungs, going faster and faster away from the water. The floors whizzed past, doors blurring into doors until she had to shut her eyes and crouch in the corner.

"Nami? Thank the tides!" She looked up as the cage slid open. Kai wrapped his arms around her before she could respond. He was solid. Real. Not like the wild figure of her father she had seen earlier. The hooded presence that could've been just her own hung-over mind playing tricks.

The smell of him was recognisable: citrus and lemongrass as always. But there was something else now. Something unfamiliar. The bloodshot whites of his eyes reminded her of the days when he read to her all night when she couldn't sleep. Even her mind wouldn't have imagined him this dishevelled. Despite the obvious signs of fatigue, his clothes were immaculate: shirt white as foam and mulberry-coloured robes perfectly knotted with a black braided belt. He did not bother to conceal his prominent antlers or the scales that ran from his temples down the side of his face and jawline in human form. Her brother had always been confident in his own skin.

He loosened his grip on her and scanned her face, taking in all the changes since they had last met: the asymmetrical short haircut, the mismatched piercings that ran up one ear, the pakalot rubbing her wrist. Nami waited for it. The anger. Disappointment. Another lecture, another person she'd let down. Instead, he smiled, squeezing her arms warmly. "Have you eaten?"

Amid all her worries, all her determination to not rely on him, Nami had forgotten that he had never been the type to judge. Suddenly, as painful as the blow Sobekki had placed on her jaw, a pang of wistfulness struck her. She missed him. In a hundred small ways that could not be replicated. Missed running to him for advice. Missed the buffer he had been between her and their mother. Missed how he'd left all his Academy books with neatly written comments in the margins to help her with her studies. She had pushed it out of her mind for so long that she had almost forgotten.

"Kai, I'm sorry." She let herself cry for the first time since she'd been exiled. The salty tears washed the city dust from her smarting eyes. It felt good to let it all go, knowing that she was safe in her brother's presence.

"You dolt, you should've told me if you wanted to visit that badly!" he teased, blinking rapidly and clearing his throat. He brought a sleeve to her face and blotted her cheeks like she was a kid again.

"I let everyone down."

"Nonsense. Ama will get over it. Eventually. She always does."

Kai brushed the whole thing off, and suddenly it felt manageable again. A problem they could solve.

They sat together and it was like the years had never gone by. The two of them against the world. Squabbling over the last pineapple pastry and staying up past their bedtime. It was only when Kai elbowed her awake that Nami realised she had dozed off.

"Spare room is upstairs. Sleep." He was insistent.

She wanted to protest, say she wasn't tired at all. But something about Kai's presence made her stop before the instinctual obstinance tumbled from her mouth. She had not slept well since she left Yonakuni. If she was being honest with herself, this was the first time she'd felt able to let her guard down. Kai was here. Everything would be all right. She would nap – just an hour – then they would talk. Work out a plan for Dan and Hong-Gi. It was okay. Nothing had changed between them.

Kai had filled the window ledge with plant pots: samphire, cordgrass and glasswort – plants of the sand dunes and salt marshes. Mira remembered how he'd had vertigo for the first few months after arrival. She'd been terribly unsympathetic, deliberately taking him on tours via the highest skybridges, where the wind could buffet someone off the side. That was before she started to find the whole thing rather endearing.

Tiankawi came to life as the morning inched into afternoon. The trams whizzed in their curved routes. Plenty of boats were out also, from the bathtub boats in the calm waters to larger vessels with chugging engines or rowers making them scuttle like stick insects.

Mira let herself into Kai's apartment after her shift finished. She completed her exercises, tidied the kitchen, watered the plants. Even had time to patch the threadbare elbow of her chinthe coat before she heard Nami stirring upstairs. They'd not left things on the best of terms and she was hoping to rectify that.

It had not been the first meeting Mira had had in mind. First, Kai's sister had gone missing from the settlement vessel, and then, to make matters worse, the guards from the ship had closed ranks, repeating the same story. They'd never seen her. Lying outright to her face. Mira had resisted the urge to sack the lot of them. They reeked of contempt, a problem she'd have to deal with sooner than later. She had not expected to finally find the errant dragon through a kumiho tip-off, and in the company of a Drawback at that. No, this was not the impression she'd hoped to make.

"Something smells wonderful!" Nami called, bare feet padding down the internal spiral stairs. She caught sight of Mira in the kitchen, and the levity fled as her eyes narrowed. "Where's my brother?"

"Kai has meetings. But he promised to meet us for dinner."

Nami gave no response, face an open book of disappointment. Mira busied her hands with the dough she had already prepped, trying not to read too much into it. "He neglected to tell me what you like, so I made a bit of everything."

Nami's stony face didn't change, but at least she sat. Mira filled the awkward silence with prattle as she heated the pan. "My ama's paratha recipe. Passed down for generations, if she's to be believed."

"You're Atlityan?"

No preamble then, straight into scrutiny. The knots in Mira's shoulders twinged in preparation. "No, I'm Tiankawian."

"But where are you from? Originally?"

"Here," Mira said, emphasising her point with the wooden spoon on the counter. "Born here, brought up here, never lived anywhere else. I'm freshwater." It was a term the folk of Tiankawi had come to use. To indicate they had been born in the submerged city, had just as much claim to it as humanity did.

Nami clearly didn't understand. The lines between her brow were furrows, trying to untangle the spool of thread and failing. "But we're saltwater. Fathomfolk. We come from the abyss, we'll return to the seabed."

Mira shrugged. "I've never seen the deep oceans. My life is in Tiankawi." Words rolled around in her mouth, desperate to be voiced. Apologies for the broken mess that Nami had seen on arrival. To say it wasn't a reflection of the city. Except it was. One part of the kaleidoscope. No matter how the mirrors were angled, the shards of glass were still broken.

"That's awful." Nami's eyes were round and tragic.

Mira was tired. It was not so much what Nami said, more the echo of a hundred voices that had come before. Pitying even though she'd never asked for sympathy. A hundred more would surely come after, stretching out into her future with a shake of their heads. Always about what she'd lost rather than what she'd gained.

She half smiled, pouring two cups of spiced tea from the teapot. Nami's gaze had dropped from her face, roving over her neck, her hands and her body as if there was some telltale mark that would expose the truth. The unvoiced questions lingered between them.

"Ask," Mira said curtly. "Ask and be done with it." Nami licked her lips, shocked at the bluntness. It wasn't often that Mira's patience wore thin, but when it went, it threw the door wide open. "Did I seduce him? That's what you want to know, right? How I ensnared the most eligible bachelor in the city?"

"Well ... I mean, you're a siren."

It broke Mira's heart, although she didn't let it show. Tore through the hard shell of her defences like they were nothing more than illusions. She'd gone through it all before, wanted to laugh at people's stupidity. "He's fully shielded against siren glamours. Your brother's an expert waterweaver; do you really think he'd fall for my charms if I used them?"

"But the glow–"

"Stop being a water dragon. Just stop. Stop using your gills underwater. Stop breathing topside. Can you? This is just me! I can't switch it off." Mira felt her exasperation spilling over, leaking from her despite the attempts to keep it together. The hairline fractures expanding and contracting under stress.

"At the square . . ." Nami stammered to a halt, frowning.

Mira understood. Of course there were sirens who leaned into convention. At teahouses or in the submerged Old Town at Glashtyn Square. But how to explain the complex relationships between humanity and the folk; the imbalance of power, the waves of new arrivals and the Nurseries. Not in the first day. Not even the first week. The city had to soak into Nami's pores first.

"Let's go out. Kai asked me to get you some things anyway. You can make your own mind up."

When she'd fallen for Kai, Mira had never factored in his opinionated little sister. But she wanted Nami to like her. Partly because Kai so clearly loved his sister, but mostly because she felt Nami's righteous indignation burning like hot coals. A mirror to Mira's younger self. All the messy mistakes and their far-reaching consequences. She glanced at the dragon. It was going to be a long day.

Chapter Twelve

On the tram, Nami looked like a caged animal: flustered, trying to pull away from any accidental touch, stumbling as the clanking brakes pushed passengers into each other. The packed and towering buildings of Jingsha gave way to the sprawling districts of the south. Now that they were no longer distracted by the criss-crossing of tracks and skybridges, the long drop beneath them became more apparent. Mira spotted the signs: short, sharp breaths, unfocused gaze and shaking legs. Vertigo, just like Kai when he arrived. She only knew what it was like from his descriptions. Growing up in the city, she'd climbed the bamboo scaffolding with the best of them, pilfering low-hanging vegetables from the vertical gardens and the occasional item of clothes from high-rise washing lines.

She grabbed Nami's arm, a pinch hard enough to make the new arrival focus. "Right, fastest route from Jingsha to Webisu," she said jovially.

The dragon looked confused, still swaying a little, her mouth opening and shutting like a goldfish. Mira goaded her with exaggerated exasperation. "The tram map is right there."

The various lines on the mildewed glass-covered map were connected in a spider's web through the central district. Mira had played the same game during long journeys with her mother, even before the newest routes through the folk districts of Seong and

Qilin had been built. The arteries of the city. She could get from one point to another via tram, cable car or boat. Could avoid siren stalkers and late-night drunks; cross the city in less than two hours to sit yet another scholar exam, bring illicit medicines to families in need, or rehouse an abuse victim.

"Jingsha to Webisu," she repeated.

"The ... the middle line for three stops." Nami's tone was clearly incredulous at how this was even a question.

"It's faster to get off one station earlier and take a water tuk-tuk," a voice piped up. It was a little boy, holding his mother's hand. He pulled his scarf tight over his lower face, shrinking away as Nami looked back, but carried on, "The tram takes ages."

Mira nodded in agreement. "Yes, it goes around all the floating gardens." Her words earned her a toothy smile as the boy poked his chin out again. She turned back to Nami. "One day you won't have to look at the map. Until then, Samaga to Palang?"

Nami raised her head to the yellowing map, frowning but engaged. Her eyes roved between the stations, sounding them out under her breath. By the time they arrived, she was standing straight again.

The Qilin district was nowhere near as polished as where Kai lived. The buildings rose out of the waters fifteen to twenty floors high, but they were more like mismatched jigsaw pieces forced together. Piled on top of each other, with salvaged windows and doors. Everything leaned drunkenly against its neighbour. And while the lines that arched from building to building in the rest of the city to power the flickering lights and rumbling lifts were ordered and straight, here they were like a twisted ball of string, shooting out in every direction. The unused lines cut and hanging like tufts from the corners of buildings. Organic. Chaotic.

There was a central area of sorts, an open-air hawkers' market between adjacent buildings. The smells and heat from the various stalls mingled. Piles of sea greens and noodles, bamboo steamers towering high, and fish being grilled over open coals. Folk called out as Mira and Nami passed, waving and shouting for them to come over and eat. *Discount for you only! You've been eating at the other stalls or something? It's been so long. Sit!* Mira didn't let it slow them, apologising with a smile, agreeing *next time uncle, next time.*

They ducked through an open doorway into a seamstress's workshop, mountains of cloth spilling down one corner of the room as two women worked furiously on clanking treadle sewing machines. Mira pointed at Nami and yelled in the universal language of bargaining. Other doorways showed colourful sights inside: a shop full of shoes, piled waist-high, others swaying on hooks from the ceiling by their laces; a bakery, the smell of warm bread filling the air while customers sat on upturned buckets eating steamed buns in two bites; one place just selling cordage, thick hemp rope, thin fishnet string and long chain links, the loops being tightened in place by an older matron with worn pliers. The disparate smells and noises were music to Mira's ears, a certain nostalgia mixed with the satisfaction of leaving Nami so dazed she had no critique or comment for a good couple of hours. Up and down worn metal stairs, and at one point hoisted on a pulley to the otherwise inaccessible workshop of a leathersmith.

Mira was in her element. She knew most of the shopkeepers by name, and the few she didn't, she knew of their parents, grandparents or aunties. She was charming yet firm. Demanded better quality, more items, firmly keeping her money in her pocket until she was satisfied. And along with the discounts, once a deal was agreed, they were given cups of tea, sesame cakes and bowls of boiled peanuts. She accepted them, charmed and thankful despite having been served the same snacks in the three previous shops. She could see the protest forming on Nami's lips, but she shook her head. It would not do to bruise the pride of the Qilin folk. They had very little, but refreshments were part of the bargaining custom. To refuse was to look down on them.

By the sixth shop, she was discreetly depositing the snacks into her bag, protesting good-naturedly about diet and dinner, winking at Nami as they moved on. The leathersmith finished fitting the clasp to the satchel Mira had ordered, while Nami looked up at the sagging ceiling tiles in clear boredom. Suddenly she pointed up. There was water pouring down one wall. Just a small trickle, a hose clipped in place to send a constant drip. The floor was covered in a couple of centimetres of water, something Nami had not realised. Slow on the uptake that one, but she got there eventually.

Mira glanced back at the leathersmith, bent over his workbench with his hide apron covering most of his front. If she looked closely enough, she could see his gills opening and closing slowly, the focused breathing pattern of someone at work. The water underfoot and dampening the walls made it easier for him to breathe topside, connecting him despite the distance from sea level. He wiped a damp sponge across his forehead, his pakalot rattling, and continued with his task.

"Is everyone in Qilin ... fathomfolk?" Nami asked as they hurried through corridors, weaving between people and stacks of products everywhere.

"Mostly. It's one of the largest fathomfolk communities in the city."

"Why don't they live somewhere safer?" she said.

"Where do you suggest? They're lucky enough to have land visas, but most can't afford the rent elsewhere. There aren't a lot of jobs either. The fishing industry is full. People are stuck doing odd jobs: hard labour and tuk-tuk driving. But no one wanted Qilin – look at it!" Mira felt a peculiar satisfaction as she gestured to the flickering witchlights and exposed pipes that dangled precariously overhead. It was a ramshackle mess, but it was *their* ramshackle mess.

"Did Kai tell you to bring me here?"

"Kai?" she said in surprise. "No, he probably expected me to take you to a tailor in Jingsha and put it on his account. *I* wanted to bring you here. This is where I was brought up." After their house had collapsed, Mira and her mother had moved in with a cousin in Qilin. It was here that she really grew up: learning from the various tradespeople; wearing cast-off clothes and passing them on when she outgrew them; scrounging meals from different neighbours each day of the week while her mother worked long shifts at the Onseon Engine, the behemoth power station nearby that still powered the city today. Her father hadn't been around, but she did not lack for parents in the close-knit community.

They had to squeeze past a knot of people holding hand-drawn placards and shouting. Drawbacks again. They were everywhere lately, with their slick and hostile rhetoric. Mira had not expected the surly kelpie Lynnette to rise to the top of the movement, and yet inexplicably she had. Perhaps there was more behind her sullen expression and large biceps. Mira's ears were unable to entirely tune out the chants as she pulled Nami away. She was not convinced by the words. They were hollow as tube sponge coral. Then again, she was not their intended audience. The Drawbacks had made it quite clear they thought she was part of the broken system, in bed with the Council and much more lewd comparisons.

There was no way to get to the tram platform through the throng that had formed. Mira ground to a halt with an exasperated sigh. She had to hail a boat, the human helmsman looking like he might refuse their business until she promised extra coin.

Out in the open waters, away from the press of bodies, Nami blurted out the question that was clearly on her mind. "Who were they? I've ... seen them around."

"The protesters? Fathomfolk unhappy about the state of Tiankawi. They want to tear it down."

"And where's the problem in that?" She leaned forward, her excitement palpable.

"The system is broken. But there's more than one way to fight." The response softened the steel in Nami's demeanour. Mira licked her cracked lips before expanding. "They've the right to protest, the absolute right to speak their mind. But this isn't us against them. That's just a distraction, it always has been. Just like the Nurseries."

Nami was about to ask more, but then she glanced behind Mira's head and the words fell unspoken from her lips. Mira looked back, trying to see it all with a fresh perspective. It was good to recall now and then the sense of wonder. Arching sky-bridges connected the large towers, high above the water level, about twenty floors up. The bridges were alive, dripping with green moss and plants, pink and purple orchids spilling over the sides.

"Are those trees?" Nami asked, pointing.

The helmsman snorted into his collar, so derisively that she turned red.

"Those are our farms," Mira said proudly. Walls of thick greenery sprouted from the sides and roofs of the tall obelisks, in carefully cultivated rows. They were like silent giants, reclaimed by nature. Stare for long enough and she could spot people hanging on bamboo scaffolding as they tended the crops. Birds flew to nest in crevices between long vines. It felt like the earth was slowly taking back the city, consuming it inch by inch in a creeping invasion of fruit and fronds.

The restaurant was halfway up one of the new buildings near Kai's apartment back in the Jingsha district. The architects couldn't go any higher, so instead they went wilder in the designs. This building fanned out as it rose in the water like a glossy heart-shaped monstera leaf, a series of short skybridges running like leaf veins between the sections. Beautiful and impractical, but even Mira had to admit its silhouette against the skyline was magnificent.

Nami and Mira changed in the public washrooms near the restaurant, cleaning the grime of Qilin from their faces and necks. Mira was thankful she'd had the foresight to do so. Her movements were suddenly clumsy, footsteps loud on the cream marble of the foyer as they approached the hostess at the door. Kai was clearly trying to impress his sister, but the luxurious surroundings made Mira shrivel inside. Heads swivelled to appraise her and the ratty bag of purchases from Qilin that knocked against her thigh. The other customers were elaborately dressed. The glint of jewellery blinded her every time someone lifted a glass to their mouth. Carefully manicured hairstyles, heavy make-up and the smell of dusky scents.

Kai was waiting at the table with a harried smile. "I've already ordered, I hope you don't mind. I need to get back after this."

Mira squirmed in her chair. She had long since learned that things in Jingsha were not designed for comfort. The only way to sit was to perch on the very edge as if it would collapse beneath her at any point. Fortunately she was never going to relax in here anyway.

Kai had ordered Yonakunish dishes, Nami's favourites from home, and yet something was odd about each one. The fish stew was not quite sharp, the prawns were sweet rather than spicy, the soup was too salty. And each portion was small and unsatisfying, more like artwork than food, barely touching the sides of her stomach. Mira knew why Kai had ordered before they arrived, because she would've baulked at the price.

The head chef was fathomfolk. A success story. The only one to open an establishment in the upmarket area. Critics had given him glowing reviews. All Kai's society friends raved about the place – the best fathomfolk dishes in the city, incredibly authentic. Mira looked around as she played with her food, doing the mental calculations. Some of the waiting staff were clearly fathomfolk too, by their gill lines and colouring. Shape-shifters, changed into inoffensive human forms. But their table were the only fathomfolk patrons in the whole place. Her hand clamped down on her spoon and suddenly she was no longer hungry.

Nami was fascinated by the whole affair. Craning her neck at the attire of the other customers, getting out of her chair to watch the cooking display in the open kitchen, tapping at the glass tanks that lined the restaurant, filled with brightly coloured fish.

Kai took his sister's absence as an opportunity to lean in, excitement making his words bounce. "They'll hear us. After the Boat Races."

"Your bill?" Mira said.

"Our bill," he corrected. The self-defence bill. As the daughter of a mixed relationship, Mira had seen the power disparity between her parents. Not simply one of gender and prejudice, but also the physical restraints that a pakalot imposed. Folk could not fight back. Could not defend themselves, their families, from a hand raised in violence. The by-product of a control that only considered danger to be in one direction.

Kai had been on board immediately. Clarified Mira's wording, lobbied the scholar officials behind closed doors. The bill was ready, an added self-defence mechanism to the pakalots that would allow folk a modicum of autonomy.

He reached over to squeeze her arm, still waiting for a response.

"It's a good plan," she agreed. Tiankawian goodwill was highest in the week following the races. A city-wide festival really, celebrating an integration that didn't exist the rest of the year.

"This will be the first pebble, the start of something," he promised.

As Nami sat back down, Kai heaped prawns into her bowl. Picked out the hijiki seaweed garnish before transferring some silken noodles too. His sister barely seemed to notice, munching away as she talked about Qilin. But Mira saw it. Saw how he had changed, even in this short time since Nami's arrival. The protective older sibling had kicked in. He swivelled between filling Nami's plate and Mira's, his own bowl mostly empty but his face overflowing.

"Is Sobekki still at the Academy?" he said, resting his head on one hand.

Nami nodded furiously. "And still intimidating first-years with his *impenetrable hide* speech."

Kai leaned over to explain to Mira. "Protector of the Realm and martial skills master at the Academy. At the beginning of term, Sobekki challenges all the first-years to come at him with whatever weapon they choose. Blades, spears – anything. He stops them all. A waterweaving barrier coating his skin."

"It's all a show. He thinks no first-year is really going to shiv him in the ribs." Nami twisted her chopsticks into her bowl, a sly smile on her dipped face.

"Nami, you didn't! Tell me you didn't?" Kai said.

Mira was confused, the conversation flying over her head as if it was in a different language. It partly was, the siblings trying to use Tiankawian words for her benefit but code-switching in and out of their native Yonakunish.

Nami rubbed at her gills and confirmed it. "There's a nick on that hide now, under his armpit."

Kai clapped his hands together, rocking back on his chair. "Oh, this explains Ama's letters. About how you needed to exercise more restraint in lessons."

"Well," Nami said, "that was one of the reasons . . ."

It was a side of Kai that Mira had not seen before. He became almost like a little boy in Nami's presence. Lapping up the stories like sticky treats they shared after bedtime. Living vicariously through her acts of rebellion. On the few occasions he'd talked to her about his childhood, it was about the heavy mantle of being firstborn. Of general customs and laws in the haven, not this irreverent little sister whom he clearly adored.

Mira had been pushing her food around the plate, separating it into two neat piles at opposite sides. She would never feel comfortable at fine restaurants and galas. But here, within the circumference of their small table, the glow of their affectionate chatter warmed her. This, she could manage. This, she could preserve.

She pushed the two piles back together and started to eat.

Chapter Thirteen

Nami had rarely seen anyone in the days she'd been coming to the Tiankawi city library, ploughing through bamboo scrolls and stacks of lotus leaf papers until her head hurt. She rode the trams and cable cars, getting hopelessly lost every time she had to switch lines. It was so damn convoluted, the tram map denser than a kelp forest. One time she found herself at the end of a line, standing on an empty platform by a closed ticket booth swearing to herself. The people on the platform gave her a wide berth, lowering their gaze as if she shouldn't be provoked. No one else had gills.

On another occasion she decided, screw it, she'd swim to the archives. But the waters were never clear, not like back home. An acid tang in her eyes and gills; stilts and pillars, crumbling houses and rusted detritus forced detour after detour until she admitted defeat.

Kai was working, the line of folk outside his office snaking around the building before he even arrived in the morning. Mira was working: complicated shifts and rushing off even on rest days with her meals half eaten. Nami should be working. It was the reason she was here in Tiankawi. To save Dan and Hong-Gi from lengthy jail sentences, her mother had asked her to figure out human technology. See if they could replicate it back home in the haven. Her – the worst scholar in the family. A task that needed a dozen researchers and academics, not one hare-brained exile. It made no sense! Unless Jiang-Li had merely given her busy work: build up a tower of bricks just to knock it down again, over and over. The possibility did cross Nami's mind, sticking there like a splinter beneath the skin.

She put her forehead on the table and let out a loud groan. She was just no good with books. The words all jumbled together and she didn't understand half of what she was reading. It would be much easier if she could just ... hit something. Break something. Challenge someone. Do something that wasn't sitting here in dread silence. She groaned again, exasperation curdling the sound. It echoed up through the vaulted dome of the reading room.

Official information about the Onseon Engine in the Qilin district, the dominant power source in Tiankawi, was a black hole. Other sources – the eddy farms moving in the waves, and the heliacal mills with their mirror-shine rotating blades – had scroll upon bamboo scroll; stacks of lotus leaf news articles, curling photographs in blurry black and white. Everything about Onseon was restricted or redacted. After hours of digging she found only one passing reference: most of the staff had been recruited from the nearby Nurseries.

That word again. The one Mira had briefly mentioned.

Nami looked up. The library's other resident was still asleep. Despite the many workspaces spread across the large reading room, only one was ever used. Constantly occupied as if someone had set up residence. Untidy heaps of lotus leaf papers were stacked like basalt columns to form a screen around the table's edge. Nami had nearly tripped on the glass scroll holders that littered the floor near the table, rolling against the furniture legs. The scrolls themselves were unfurled, held down with a random assortment of rocks, tea-stained cups and even hair combs. As if the reader had grabbed the first thing from their pocket and laid it down regardless.

The clutter remained a constant throughout her visits. Uncleared but not untouched. Things moved when she was away. More scrolls filled an archival trolley; occasionally stacks of papers went down as if a concerted effort was being made to clean up. And sometimes a floral note of ylang-ylang reached her as she dragged the squeaking ladder across the room to put scroll holders back into their diamond cubbyholes. The distant footsteps of the other person or the back of a head as she turned a corner.

But today, she was there. Slumped with her head in her hands, but there. Long brown hair spilled between pale ink-stained hands. If Nami was being honest with herself, that was why she'd groaned so loudly. Perhaps it would trigger an introduction to the person she felt she already knew. Who might be able to give her some answers, as deeply engrossed in history as she clearly was.

Just as she was contemplating her options, the woman's eyes blinked open and stared right at her. Nami held her breath like she'd startled a wild animal. At last! Unfocused, the woman didn't appear to notice her any more than she did the shelves and books surrounding them. Her hands fumbled across the scrolls, knocking some of them to the floor as she finally found the gold-rimmed glasses that had fallen from her nose. Each movement, each sound magnified in Nami's ears like the two of them were beside each other rather than halfway across an expansive hall.

The second time she looked, Nami stared. She couldn't help it. She'd sat for so many days in that library that she had started to conjure up ideas of who the other person could be. A stoop-shouldered elder historian, reedy-voiced and with an extensive knowledge of everything. That was the person she'd imagined. Not a gorgeous woman her own age, with her shirt misbuttoned and a pen tucked behind one ear. A soft round face and a tiny nose that her glasses slid down. Her blue-grey eyes crinkled at the corners, the freckles across her cheeks dancing as she smiled. Nami could not help but smile back. Just as she was about to introduce herself, the other woman covered her mouth. "Oh shit, you shouldn't be here!"

"Wh-what do you mean?" Nami's face fell into a defensive scowl. Her voice was suddenly too loud, her stomach churning empty.

"I didn't lock the door again, did I? Every time! I'm so sorry! Visitors are only allowed by appointment. Write to the Ministry of Justice. Oh, but he'll never answer you. There's a junior official – Tarik, he's called. He'll listen. Just drop my name." The woman threw out words like a loose kite in a gale, turning and twisting as her train of thought grew more distal. Nami could barely understand her beneath the thick Tiankawian accent and the speed at which she rambled.

The woman was waiting for a response, throat bobbing up and down as she swallowed. Nami licked her lips, realising she had not really taken any of it in. "I was just looking for some information."

"Of course, information is key. Knowledge should be shared. Dissected. Understood. The tabulation of oral history: of the city, the havens, the nomadic groups. They think forgetting is for the best. Rewriting the past we are tainted by. Archive it. Which is my job, of course, but here I go once again, mouth running away with me. You really should make an appointment, I'd be more than happy to help." All the while the woman had started cajoling Nami towards the entrance, a gentle but persistent touch on her elbow, a hand briefly clasped in hers.

"But I can come back?"

"It was absolutely lovely to meet you. We must do this again sometime." She gave a lopsided fist-palm salute and tapped at the faded sign on the front door. And then she firmly but politely closed the door in Nami's face. The faded sign stared outwards. *Closed to the public. Entry by appointment only.*

The relative quiet of the library steps was broken only by a soft lapping of water. Ringing sounded in Nami's ears like the woman had physically boxed them with her onslaught of words.

She chuckled under her breath. Since day one, the library doors had been open and she'd never once been challenged. The eccentric librarian had either not noticed or not cared that scrolls and papers were being mysteriously moved around.

She shrugged, hurrying down the stone stairs as a light breeze blew up. Behind her she heard a soft click and the library door swung back open, the sign hidden in the shadows once more.

Chapter Fourteen

Cordelia added a hearty dose of dried seahorse to the bubbling claypot her assistant was stirring. The tendrils of smoke drifted towards her nostrils. A pinch more hoizo and it would be ready. She moved around her apothecary room with familiar ease, lower limbs reaching up to high shelves, others closing drawers and cupboards. It used to be a shop, her grandmother's first business when she moved to Tiankawi. Sold dried goods from teetering scales, and folk remedies from the back room. Here Cordelia learned how to fool customers with counterfeit weights. Just a little, just enough that they never noticed. Slowly her grandmother saved enough to pay off the rent and eventually buy the whole shop. One of the first fathomfolk entrepreneurs above the waterline. But officials had come sniffing. The press talked about the black market and lack of regulation. They dredged up a little boy who had an allergic reaction to something or other. *At death's door*, they shrieked, the human healers lobbying with all their influence. Suddenly fathomfolk needed a licence to practise. Nothing more than bribes really, but ones that required friends in influential places.

Cordelia's family had pulled down the shutters and the apothecary became an invitation-only establishment. Besides, by that point, her mother had diversified, teaching her daughter along the way.

"It's done. Go make space on the back shelves. I'll be bringing back more stock after this," Cordelia instructed the mermaid.

"From Firth?" Nahla blurted. She blushed, playing with her fins self-consciously. Titans below, another one enamoured with the Drawbacks' second-in-command. So easy to read. Wouldn't get far in this business with an earnest expression like that. They were like suckerfish, his admirers – hovering and clinging for scraps of attention. If Nahla were her daughter, she'd warn her of the dangers of such infatuations.

"Clear the shelves," Cordelia repeated, not unkindly. The mermaid straightened her ridiculous grin, dropped her gaze to the floor hastily. Shifted her green-tailed lower half into human legs as she slid off the chair. Plenty of time for her to learn the pitfalls of a pleasing face.

The bell rang on time, as always, as the elderly siren shuffled in. Her long hair was much greyer than Cordelia's and neatly pinned back in a long braid. Her arthritic hands carefully unknotted the fabric-wrapped parcel: a lacquer box of palm sugar sweets and pandan jellies.

"I tell you every month and it's like your ears are blocked, auntie. I don't eat sweets."

"Look at you, all skin and suckers – eat more!" Trishanjali slipped out of her sandals and reached for the teapot with easy familiarity. She managed to squeeze the dregs out of it, shaking her head at Cordelia.

"Must I reiterate the rules? I provide a service. You are the customer. We're not friends, we're not family." Cordelia reclaimed her teapot and put it out of reach. Without preamble, she began the treatment, wrapping herself around the older woman's core, manipulating the muscles in her neck, extending her arms and flexing them, applying pressure where she felt small knots forming. She could taste with the suckers on her lower limbs where the old inflammation was recurring, the smell of light decay around the hardening joints.

Trish was quiet at first, allowing herself to be moved hither and thither. As Cordelia started working on her legs, her voice piped up again. "I met a naga at the water market last month. Handsome fellow, as tall as you and works in construction. Boats."

"Absolutely not," Cordelia said.

Trish pursed her lips in thought, but it didn't keep her quiet for long. "How about a rusalka then? A single mother, seamstress in Qilin with a young son—"

"I do not need a matchmaker."

"That's just what my daughter said! But I said, take the job, befriend the dragon prince, what harm will it do you? You aren't exactly a hatchling, can't afford to be picky at your age."

Cordelia tightened her grip around the old siren's ankle until she winced, a brief respite from the elder's idle prattle. But even then Trish was not afraid, brushing her off like a petulant child. The suckers teased loose, leaving a row of red welts on her thinning skin.

"Drink your medicine." Cordelia washed her hands in a basin at the back of the room. The elderly siren was the bane of her life, and yet a deal had been struck. A very good deal. She hadn't reckoned with Trish's endless ability to talk through silences, cutting through any attempt to intimidate by nattering about recipes and local gossip.

"So you told me to ask him outright about the pearl," Trish began. Cordelia said nothing. She'd made a non-committal noise when the old siren had monologued about the Yonakunish ambassador. Trish shared the information like they were co-conspirators. "They can't create something from nothing. Once the pearl is hatched, there's only one way to re-form it. A dragon has to sacrifice themselves. Not like the wish-granting of the stories. No golden pavilions in my lifetime, I'm afraid."

Cordelia could've told her this but had chosen not to. Let the old dear find out the long way. Trish looked triumphant as she blew on her hot herbal soup. Like so many of the folk in Tiankawi, her features were sun-spotted around the cheeks and forehead. The veins at her neck and jawline had darkened like blackened roots from years submerged in polluted waters. Under her pakalot her skin was pink and scarred. The heat of the medicinal soup brought a warmth to her lined face, a glow of health that was lacking when she'd first arrived. The seawitch folded her arms in satisfaction. People always remembered her for her deals, not for her skills as a healer. And quite frankly she didn't give a damn if Trish lived or died, but she took great pleasure in solving a puzzle.

"How about a stingray?" Trish said. Only the sediment remained at the bottom of her bowl.

"For wh—?" Cordelia started before she could help herself. She decanted the remainder of the soup, wrapped the untouched sweets back up and thrust them into the siren's arms.

"Just tell me your type and I'll stop asking," Trish promised, leaning forward with a sly whisper.

"Did it never occur to you I already have someone?" The exasperation pushed itself between Cordelia's sharp teeth. She had better things to do than discuss her love life with a meddling elder, and yet every time Trish managed to expertly steer the conversation.

"You do!" The triumph was clear in Trish's voice, and Cordelia regretted providing even that modicum of information. She foresaw much future prying now the siren had crowbarred a way in.

"Yes, it's her mirror." Mira swept in through the seawitch's door without so much as a greeting. She took the parcels from her ama, slinging them over her shoulder. Her foul mood dragged in like dirt from the walkways. She had been caught in the monsoon rains and her green coat dripped wet, buttoned so tight at the neck that it threatened to strangle her.

"Hello saltlick, I haven't seen you in … weeks." Cordelia's face was smooth as ice. She waited for the reaction, the telltale flicker of emotion. Mira only knew one of the seawitch's faces, but it was enough to rile her. The officer's foot twitched, shifting her weight, but her features remained impassive. She shrugged, disinclined to answer.

"I didn't bring you up to be so rude. Not even a hello?" Trish chided as her toes felt the floor for her discarded sandals.

"Not for her, she's heartless."

It shouldn't have stung. People had said it before and would say it again. The offhand comment of a half-siren whelp was water off her back. And yet Cordelia felt her cephalopod limbs pulse in a burst of colour, her skin taking on the texture of sea urchin spines. "I have three."

It had been a one-off bargain. Easy profits. No strings, no relationship between them. But Cordelia had not been able to cure Trish's gill rot. Monthly visits were the best she could manage, and by the abyss, at times she would've given over her profits to a human healer to be rid of the pair of them.

"Get out. And remember, Mira, the current terms of our arrangement are coming to an end. It would be a shame if your mother had to find a different healer."

"She is rather good," said Trish, oblivious to the actual conversation. The elder siren had believed without an ounce of incredulity the story Mira had woven. About Cordelia being hired using military connections or some other nonsense.

Mira said nothing, giving a mocking fist-palm salute.

Cordelia left her assistant to clean up. Business was slowing down lately. She might have to consolidate her various ventures if it went on much longer. She'd gone through dry spells before. Ten years ago, when not many folk were knocking at her door, a slip of a thing, a half-siren with the surety of youth, had come to her to strike a bargain. Her mother had gill rot, and she'd do anything to save her. Anything. Willing to bargain away a part of herself and be done with it.

Of course most people chose the water. Mira was not most people. She was angry at those who presumed she was playing the system, had some sort of unfair advantage because of the lilt of her voice. She'd wanted none of it. Determined to compete with humans on their playing field and win.

Cordelia could've told her that things weren't quite so simple. She could have. Then she'd thought about what she could do with a decade of siren song. The ears she could whisper in. And so she'd struck the bargain.

Little did she know that estuary girl would become the highest-ranking folk in the military. In a serious relationship with the Yonakunish ambassador. The unexpected linchpin in so many of Cordelia's plans.

The seawitch touched the ever-present drawstring pouch at her waist. A gemstone imbued with the remaining siren song from their decade-old bargain. She would run out soon. Before the end of the year. Have to lean on Mira once again. But today she was after other fish.

The Drawbacks had come with another offer. Enticing. Their words were getting louder, more oft repeated below the waterline and above. Their rhetoric had become a talking point at every tuk-tuk stand and building site across the city. They would likely do some damage before the whole group imploded, but that was not Cordelia's concern. She didn't pick sides.

It was her own mother's one downfall. The business had been going well, both the legitimate one and the one conducted in alleys and derelict underwater buildings. But then everything with the Iyonessian refugees and the Nurseries had kicked off. Cordelia's mother, like so many others, had tried to intercede on behalf of other folk. Fat lot of good it did her when a protest turned violent and a thrown brick cracked open her skull. It didn't matter who had tossed it, it was her mother's fault for caring. For being in the waters of the Nurseries rather than at home protecting her own.

In the days and weeks that followed, Cordelia took over the business and struck more bargains than she had done in years. Unequal ones that gave her everything and offered very little in return. Desperate times and all. A clean conscience was irrelevant. Times of upheaval were good for business and she'd be damned if she wasted her efforts helping other folk. She'd not make her mother's mistakes.

Passing fathomfolk gave the seawitch a respectful nod or more commonly a wide berth. Cordelia experimented with her colours. The black and white stripes made a panicked naga flip over her own tail. The orange and purple spots made two young selkies shriek in fright as they swam between the vertical beams of stilt-houses above. Interesting.

The unremarkable old house was partially submerged deep within the Seong slums. The windows were boarded up but Cordelia knocked anyway. Had to peer down near her feet to see the kappa who opened the door. She didn't recognise that one. A new recruit.

Upstairs, the water level reached their ankles. Mossy seaweed clagged up the floorboards, making it difficult to cross the room. Lynnette was lying on an old sofa, the foam spilling from the back and sides with a heavy smell of damp. Black mould spread from the corner of the room and had partly reclaimed the dangling pendant light. At a distance it looked as if Lynnette was holding a bamboo flute, but the end was curved, like the bulb of a plant. She held it over the heat of an oil lamp and inhaled deeply.

Lynnette the strong. Cordelia had raised an eyebrow when the kelpie rose to become leader of the Drawbacks. She had a presence, that was for sure. Hardy as a workhorse, she stood on matters like an immovable pillar. Dependable, reliable and, in her own particular way, likeable. Also heavily addicted to the midnight oil.

It was so predictable really. Just a little at first. To help build muscle strength, endurance. Most of the folk working hard physical jobs used it from time to time. But Lynnette had gone further. Monthly, then weekly, then daily. It was never enough. Cordelia occasionally wondered what the kelpie had looked like before the concoction of stimulants had started: barracuda, killer whale, shark, probably even some giant octopus essence mixed in there. It gave her the physique she wanted. But like every bargain, it was not without its side effects: lost sensation in her limbs and unbearable withdrawal if she stopped. One way or another, it would shorten her life.

The kappa was mixing the various components, grinding them together in a small mortar and pestle. Kappas had thick hides. Tough enough to handle most toxins and come out unharmed. Lynnette had found herself a new assistant. A dealer who knew what he was doing.

The kelpie blew out, filling the small room with smoke, and Cordelia had to step back for a moment as her eyes watered. "It's good, this one, better than your last batch." She side-eyed Cordelia. The seawitch didn't rise to it.

"You really ought to cut back, saltlick. It will be the death of you," she said with exaggerated concern.

Lynnette made a reflexive sign to the sand gods with her palms and let a lazy curse fall from her lips between inhalations. "People die from lots of things. Rotting in a Yonakunish prison for one." The kappa froze for a moment, then continued to mix. The Drawbacks had bought him then. Bought his freedom, bought his loyalty. What was it? Addiction? Debt?

"Well, do you have it or not?" Lynnette waved the pipe around in an uncharacteristically soft motion. Her mohawk of green hair had flopped over her face and she looked like a different person in this light.

"My payment?"

"What?" Lynnette responded. She looked confused for a moment before grinning. "Oh yes."

The kappa carefully cleaned up, meticulous with the equipment. Handed the seawitch the knotted rope. Cordelia kept her colours even and subdued as she examined it. It was woven through with the shed tail of her rival, the clione who'd claimed the northern districts as hers. Poached Cordelia's customers by offering nothing more than love charms and herbal teas. Ridiculous. The belief, of course, that clione were more transparent than seawitches. Their diaphanous bodies reminded people of angels when they flapped their wings, unlike Cordelia's more toxic reputation. But here it was, a binding agreement ceding territory to Cordelia. She didn't know how the Drawbacks had managed it. Her eyes flicked involuntarily to Lynnette's broad shoulders, the scabbed calluses on her knuckles. No, she did know how they had managed it, she just liked plausible deniability.

She pulled the heavy bag of raw drugs – dried and sorted into stoppered vials and tinctures – onto the table. The kappa's eyes bulged. A minute ago he would've sworn the seawitch carried nothing, such was her power of camouflage. It still tickled her what she could get away with. He sorted through them silently, holding the bottles up to the dim lamplight.

"There's only one real way to quality-check." Cordelia's glance dropped to the scars on his arms. "But I see you already know that."

"Dan, is it good?" Lynnette's voice was hungry. Not the rehearsed and charismatic words of her public speeches. Palpable in her dilated pupils and the involuntary reach of her hand. She could crush his skull in an instant if she chose to. Dan nodded.

"Little tadpole, you seem to know what you're doing." Cordelia winked. The finger-shaped bruises on the kappa's skin drew her eye.

"Someone has to pay the rent," he said, voice gruff and low. Even though he spoke decent Tiankawian, his accent was unmistakable.

"So many visitors from Yonakuni," Cordelia said, counting them off on her fingers. "A handsome ambassador, his mouthy little sister, and now a drug-dealing kappa. Every day brings new excitement."

Lynnette and Dan said nothing, but a look passed between them and that was enough. The kappa did have something to do with the dragons after all. Cordelia smiled, genuinely excited by the prospect. Things had been getting a little dull lately.

Chapter Fifteen

"What was that about?" Trish asked as she looped her arm through Mira's.

"Nothing ... You feel any better?" Mira's feet wanted to storm ahead – the march of the border guard – but she adjusted her pace, slowing right down to match her ama's hobble. At least Trish no longer winced at each step; the treatment had made some difference.

"I could dive from fifty feet into a somersault and land in a bucket of water. Stop changing the subject. Did you start an argument with Kai again?" Trish prodded her in the arm. Despite the arthritis in her mother's joints, Mira felt the jab more than any practice sparring. She always knew how to cut to the bone.

"You always assume *I* start it?"

"You're very dear to me – my only child, in fact – but I'd like you to move out properly before I've passed over." The honesty made Mira laugh, drawing her temporarily out of the dark mood.

Only last week, Nami had told her what she'd seen in the crossing. The secret room on the settlement vessel used by officers. Lucia had come back from the investigation with the fury of a maelstrom. She had a right to be. Coercing the vulnerable, blackmailing them into thinking they had no choice. There were at least twenty chinthe on each crossing, and a rota. Did they all know about this disgusting little arrangement? And if they did, could she fire them all at once? Better to lance the sore than let it bubble under the skin.

The optimism faltered, falling under the weight of everything. Mira knew when she was drowning in it, could almost sense the tides washing in. Sometimes a day to herself, sleeping and concentrating on swallowing mouthfuls of food, was enough. But since the promotion, since moving in with Kai, since Nami's arrival, it was like the tide was always high. So many issues needed her attention, and she knew that despite her best efforts, something would be missed. The onus of responsibility made it difficult to sleep and the tiredness made it difficult to work. Still the wheel kept spinning.

Her mother's voice was soothing, continuing whether Mira responded or not. When she was a teenager, she'd accused Trish of not listening, of selfishly talking about the first thing that darted into her mouth. Now she understood the chatter as a balm, her mother's siren song one of comfort.

They walked towards the water tuk-tuks, the walkways and boats already filled with street food sellers. Mira scanned the rank, willing to pay extra for a driver who was careful rather than fast. Most were kelpie seahorses, tarbh uisge water bulls or baiji dolphins, already semi-submerged and in their animal forms. Her mother had stopped by one of the stalls, animated as she pored over the display.

Dulse cakes, shaped like conches and scallop shells, horns and limpets. Sunset red in colour, they were tied together like beaded necklaces. Trish held one up, exclaiming at the skill. Mira dipped her finger into the crumbs on the counter, crushing the moist morsels against her skin. They tasted like childhood. Her hands and face sticky with batter. Her parents laughing together.

"We should buy some. It's nearly Tidal Day." That was it. Dressed in her best clothes to visit relatives with strings of dulse cakes. Kicking her legs back and forward on a wooden stool, a metal chair, a sagging sofa as the adults talked overhead.

A memory rose to the surface. Child Mira being bored. Jumping into the water, swimming, leaving her human cousins behind and exulting in her abilities until suddenly she didn't know where she was any more. The light fading and the fins around her all strangers. Spilling hot salt tears between her hands as she curled up like a sea snail until her mother finally found her.

That was around when it had stopped. The visits to relatives – human relatives – who'd learned the hard way that she had powers other than just swimming. The pretence between her parents crumbling and her father leaving them not long after. Preferring his gill-less mistress to his exotic wife and child. For years afterwards, she'd blamed herself. If only she hadn't swum away that day. If only she'd come back sooner. Then they wouldn't have argued, wouldn't have split up.

"I'm going to buy some for your grandparents," Trish decided, her thoughts clearly in the same direction, counting out coins from her purse.

"They aren't even fathomfolk," Mira blurted. Trish's parents had died long ago. Mira hadn't seen her human grandparents in years; refusing to come out for meals through her teenage years, rejecting every overture, because when she saw them, she was reminded that she would never be human enough.

"You know they paid for your training." Trish dropped the information as if commenting on the weather.

"What?"

"They offered to let us stay with them as well, but I had too much pride."

Memories rose in Mira's mind, lapping at the edges of her focus. The smell of her grandfather smoking fish in the early evening. Playing skipping games with her cousins on broken walkways. Dipping a finger in her grandmother's aloe face cream when no one was looking. She had suppressed a lot. Hardened herself against them when her father had left. But truth be told, they'd helped raise her, especially with her mother always at work. She knew more about local Tiankawian customs – the best place to eat shellfish, the annual Boat Races, the shortcuts through Qilin – than she would ever know about Tidal Day.

She prodded one of the dulse cakes, sending it spinning on its line like her own thoughts. "You used to tell me about the great migration upriver to visit your ancestral grounds. About the floating lantern parade as wide as a lake, and the dancing displays of water and light. But they were just that, stories. I never saw any of it. All I had was dulse cakes and sitting on damp sofas."

Trish and the stallholder exchanged meaningful looks. "Things change. There're no rivers any more. It's hard to keep the traditions when there are so few of us, so spread out. That's why we keep celebrating however we can."

Mira was tired of being reminded how different she was. How she had to be the spokesperson for fathomfolk. And yet she was the biggest fraud. She could feel herself spiralling, digging herself down into a pit. Her mother cleared her throat and nodded. "Let's go home."

And for once, on the journey, Trish stayed quiet.

Chapter Sixteen

Kai could not, or would not, answer questions about the Onseon Engine or the Nurseries. It is your task, not mine, he had said cryptically, offering no further explanation. Switching off the lights around the apartment, straightening the chairs under the table, eyes darting between the door and the empty place at the dinner table. Waiting for Mira.

As much as Nami loved being reunited with her brother, things had changed in the few years they'd been apart. Kai had grown more withdrawn, the mask of control nearly always in place. Hands clasped behind his back, a placid smile on his features. But up close, the paint cracked at the edges, more so as she prodded him with uncomfortable questions and demands in the way only siblings could. Nami had grown up – messily, but grown up all the same. She wasn't a kid needing her brother's protection.

The terse letter from her mother was not much help either. Thanking her for the information she had sent. Jiang-Li's slanted handwriting pointedly stating that it was nothing they didn't already know. Nami read between the lines. Not enough to change the sentencing for your friends. Try harder. She had thrown the scroll tube across the room, the glass shattering against the floor.

This had left only one option. Perhaps standing outside the Onseon Engine entrance asking the shift workers for information was not her best plan. She could've gone to one of the nearby hawkers' markets to speak to staff after work. Or applied for a job there herself. Yes, that would've been smart. Instead, she'd loitered outside, matching her steps with the arriving workers, lobbing questions as they pulled themselves out of the water and into the safety of the locked and guarded gate. Steps hastened as her barrage of questions hit them. Stubbornly she kept at it long after she realised no one was going to stop and talk.

She chewed her bottom lip. She could hear her mother's voice ringing in her head, critical as always. *Always rushing in. Always disorganised. Why can't you be more like your brother?* She'd tried, hadn't she? Tried for weeks at the library, only to be thrown out. No. His methods didn't work for her. Reading, preparing, coordinating her life had always been difficult. Even her waterweaving skills hadn't come naturally, every movement jarringly awkward before she forced it into muscle memory.

Disheartened, she headed back to the tram station, looking for an easier route than the convoluted one she'd taken. The map here was older than the others. The newest stations had been handwritten at the end of the line. And a station had been scored out. Practically obliterated with sharp gouges.

The Nurseries.

Her pulse quickened with her steps. The man at the ticket office shook his head, throat bulging up and down. Telling her it was closed, permanently, before slamming the shutters on his booth.

It was something, then. Something they didn't want to talk about. The excitement made her giddy. She closed her eyes against the vertigo as she got on the next tram. It stuttered and screeched as it moved, slamming to a stop at each station. But it sped straight through the Nurseries, the faded sign blurred under layers of graffiti tags.

Nami alighted and doubled back, diving down through the water. Her gills worked hard as her clumsy movements became more confident, avoiding the boats and building struts that filled the submerged half of the city. The sting had lessened, although the water was no cleaner. Building up a tolerance. Or gill rot. Probably both. She passed a small floating market, filled with nothing more than junk scavenged from a shipwreck. Little things were different to back home. Each stall had a sand god shrine at its foot. She remembered them from childhood, bedtime stories about pairs of slumbering monsters beneath the ocean floor. Some of the elder Yonakunish had shrines in their houses, offerings of food to the gods, but the practice was fading out. To think the folk in the most advanced city in the realm were so superstitious.

She swam past the tuk-tuk drivers chewing thick stalks of kelp. Many of the folk appeared to have settled in the semi-derelict submerged buildings. The shells that decorated doorways, the shrines by the front steps and the manicured curtains of long grass made it easy to spot which were occupied. Drawback graffiti marked the abandoned ones. Nami recognised the slogans now, having seen them dotted around the city:

FLOOD THE SYSTEM.

DROWN THEM ALL.

Kun peng youths swam, colourful feathery scales glinting, tumbling and weaving between the omnipresent wooden pillars holding up houses and walkways topside. No matter which way she turned, the vertical poles were everywhere, making swimming more hazardous than it'd ever been in the havens. Bickering taunts carried through the water, reminding her of Dan and his sisters play-fighting in the warm sands. They wouldn't have time for that now.

She stopped short.

At first she didn't know what she was looking at. Metal frames corralled a small neighbourhood. Like trawling nets had become entangled in the deep seas. They formed shapes, boxy shapes like enclosures, although now battered and rusted out of shape. Underwater cages. The bitter iron caught in her throat as though she'd swallowed the twisted metal whole. She turned away, disorientated. Everywhere she looked, the bars swamped her vision. The beating of her heart was loud, so loud the whole sea floor seemed to pulse up to meet her.

They'd caged fathomfolk. That was the hidden truth of the Nurseries.

A hideous creature loomed. Nami flinched back in horror, a yelp escaping her. A monster from her nightmares. Jerking, with unnaturally long fins, it pressed its head towards her in a rush of bubbles. She pushed them away, panicking, before she registered a face beneath the thick body. It was a human in a rubberised outfit. A heavy tank on their back made them look hunchbacked, and the full-face mask distorted their features into a grimace.

The human was carrying a potted plant in their arms, the leaves dancing in the water. Only then did Nami notice the others that had been left by the sides of the cages, decorative seaweeds spreading soft tendrils over the metalwork.

"Who are you?" she blurted.

They made a hand sign, something Nami recognised as *wait*, even though she'd forgotten most of her signing. Humans could not talk while submerged. Folk used gills, leaving their mouths free to voice. To use the clicks and high tone sounds of Yonakunish or one of the other haven languages that carried well in the current. Humans could only use sign. She had learned the basics of it at the Academy. Reverently the stranger put the plant inside one of the cages, movements clumsy. Then they clasped their hands together and bowed for a moment. The silence broken only by the jostling waves.

They both rose to the surface, where a small rowing boat bobbed. There was a surprising lack of buildings above the Nurseries. Even though space was at a premium, the area was clearly avoided. The diver removed their mask.

"I didn't mean to startle you. It's been an age since anyone else visited. I thought it was just me, although occasionally I see the chinthe captain, but not in a long while – months at least. But yes, I'm sorry about that. You let out an awful yell and for a minute I thought you might faint on me."

The woman from the library. So out of context here, it took Nami a moment to recognise her.

The librarian unfolded her smudged, water-stained glasses. Stared until Nami broke the gaze with a fluster. "Oh, we've met before, haven't we? I'm Eun." She smiled as if they were old friends. Patted a spot next to her in the boat as she wrung her wet hair in a long coil.

Nami pulled herself into the boat, excruciatingly aware of how the small vessel dipped with her motion. She sat on the other bench, knees knocking against Eun's, her wet clothes dripping into small puddles beneath her. Her cheeks burning hot as charcoal. Forced her concentration down into waterweaving the moisture from her clothes and skin, teasing it like a loose thread.

Eun nodded but said nothing, rummaging in her satchel. She thrust something into Nami's hands. A long strip of dried mango. "I always carry these for my stepbrother; he's a ravenous one. Real sweet tooth. Also useful if you forget to eat breakfast or lunch. Which happens more often than not, if I'm being perfectly honest."

"I . . . Thank you." Nami had to say something. Redirect before Eun began monologuing again. The librarian beamed. She didn't seem put out by Nami's appearance, nor even inclined to ask what she was doing there. "I'm Nami, by the way."

"Second child of Jiang-Li and Alon, the last dragon family in Yonakuni. Exiled to the city due to undisclosed infractions and currently living with her brother, Kai, the Minister of Fathomfolk and ambassador to Tiankawi." Eun rattled the words off without derision or judgement. Matter of fact. Dipped her head at the end sheepishly. "I read a lot."

"Eun, tell me about the Nurseries."

The woman's face flickered through conflicted emotions. Nami would've settled for a dry academic lecture about the history of the place, but something was holding Eun back. Making her hesitate. She unstrapped the air canisters from her back and fiddled with the complicated valves. Finally, and in a tone much more contemplative than before, "Open wounds do not heal quickly."

She unscrewed a flask of seaweed tea and shared it with Nami. Spoke at length, unhurried and her voice quiet enough that Nami had to lean in, no longer bothered that her knees pushed up against the other woman's.

Two decades ago, the northern haven of Iyoness had fallen, pollution destroying the fathomfolk settlement entirely. Wave upon wave of Iyonessian refugees had arrived in the city. Initially the Nurseries had been a camp to house them. A divided Council argued endlessly about what to do about this surplus of people: turn them away, let the other havens deal with them. Some had skills, but they'd come with children, extra mouths to feed. Without a decision, Iyonessian immigrants absconded, slipping into Tiankawi without a trace. The newssheets were outraged. The citizens followed suit. So the Council decided to take decisive action. Build enclosures. Keep them in check.

Eun's voice cracked as she spoke, her brow clenched as she quoted harsh words, spitting them as far from herself as she could. The next step was a census, trialling pakalots to ensure the refugees were adhering to Tiankawian values. A spate of fathomfolk crimes, apparently. She sighed. "I won't deny it happened. The arrest documents are all there in the archives. But a handful at most. And all folk had to pay the price."

The Nurseries remained open for six years, until public opinion and the work of a Yonakunish envoy closed them down. The population was rehoused across the city. "Most people pretend it never happened. When I was a kid, my mothers took me to visit. Charity work. It left such an impression. Someone had to ensure it wasn't forgotten. To record the stories, maintain the archives for our children and our children's children. It's not going to change what happened, but at least someone will remember." She shook her head and fell silent, eyes trained towards the sun. She had become more succinct as time passed. As she grew more comfortable with Nami and confident of the truths she told.

They said their goodbyes, and it was only after the librarian started rowing away from her, silhouetted against the orange burst of the setting sun, that it occurred to Nami. *A Yonakunish envoy.* That was not Kai. This was almost fifteen years ago. When her father had gone to Tiankawi and never come back. *He'd* been the envoy. It made sense now, what Firth had said about the Yonakunish ambassador having a seat on the Council. Her father had closed down the Nurseries.

The idea flared like a match to a flame inside Nami. Flickering and unsteady as she absorbed it. Glowing brighter as it became more apparent. For so many years she did not know why her father had left them. Hated him for it. She'd never found out what happened. What, if anything, he had achieved.

He had made a difference. This she knew now, and the resentment towards him loosened like unpicking a knot. He had protected the Iyonessian folk just as he said he would.

Chapter Seventeen

Nami couldn't bring herself to go back to Kai's place. Not yet. After that revelation ... How to begin. Not only had the Yonakunish Senate refused to allow Iyonessian refugees into their haven, they'd assured everyone that Tiankawi welcomed them. Like a sleepwalking fool she had bought it. As young as her mother always said she was. Naïve enough to swallow their lies.

She missed Dan's advice more than ever right now. He would know what to say. Swear along with her and put her rage to use. Productive. But Dan was in jail hundreds of miles away. She would send him a letter at least, gifts so he knew she hadn't forgotten. She clenched her fists, her temples pulsing from the tension. Who was she kidding? Like he gave a shit about a care parcel.

All she wanted was a drink to drown the knowledge. Leave it until the morning. Firth had mentioned a place all those weeks back: an underwater hangout that he and his friends frequented. She had earnestly stuck to her task at first, not wanting to waste time. If she was honest, she was also afraid: of the noise and heat and press of people everywhere she went in the city; and that Firth wouldn't even remember who she was. But now courage summoned itself with reckless abandon. It was not a solution, but it was something.

The Barreleye Club was much bigger on the inside. The relative darkness was lit by witchlights that oscillated with the music. Phosphorescence emanated from the water, shimmered with pinpoints of blue. Phytoplankton. Folk were swim-dancing in the middle of the submerged room, light like a paintbrush trailing their movements in the water. A few rubber-suited humans were also dotted around, leaning on ledges carved into the sides of the walls, or sprawling in large alcoves and partially hidden side rooms.

Bars were dotted against the cavernous walls and Nami ordered the first drink that came to mind. She clutched the glass between both hands, practically draining it with one long sip. She was comfortable at clubs with company, but she was underdressed compared to the seasilks and body paint worn by the other folk. It was bewildering to be around so many people and yet so alone.

A new group swept through the entrance and she waved frantically. Iyonessian kelpies, a dozen of them at least in true form, swam in strong gallops across the dance floor. It was different to meeting Firth and Lynnette by themselves. In a herd, it was like the stories, the rush of hooves an explosion of surging waves. She could feel the tide in their movements, pulling and pushing at her with a magnetic force. Dark coats of tawny and black; manes threaded with streaming seaweed, barnacles and tiny fish. The herd split effortlessly around the dancers, like they were islands in the stream.

"Nami?" One of the kelpies swam towards her. A tall stallion with chestnut fur and a white diamond on his forehead looked down at her. His mane was a dense kelp forest drifting in the water.

"Firth?"

He nodded, shifting into his human form. Face shortening as the red mane became his hair and his lustrous coat melted into pale skin. Nami pushed the blush from her cheeks, training her eyes up, looking at the other kelpies, the athletic build of their bodies clear even in human form.

"Come, meet my people." He introduced her, so many names and faces that they blurred together instantaneously. Nami was unexpectedly timid, shrinking down among the boisterous and imposing horses of the sea. Could do nothing more than nod and smile as she stood half behind Firth. He noticed her discomfort and pointed to a quieter bar high up in the roof of the building. In the press of people, he swam close to her, in synchronicity without trying. Close enough that she could feel the heat emanating from his body.

Lanterns were strung up around the bars, firefly squid glittering within glass orbs. Tidal Day lanterns. Was it Tidal Day already? It had already been nearly a month since she left Yonakuni. As Firth handed her a drink, a tremor ran through the water, sending a rippled current through her. She looked up, then to her glass. Eyebrow arched in jest. "What's in this?"

Firth laughed, a sound that she already wanted to hear more of. "An earthquake. We have a lot of them across the city. You'll get used to it."

"I'm totally useless here. Don't know how to take the tram, only just learned about the Nurseries." She gritted her frustration between her teeth.

Firth's smile drooped briefly, melancholy flitting through his features as he stiffened. He ran a hand around the back of his neck. "I lived there. If you can call it living. My brother and I were just kids when we fled Iyoness." He drummed on his glass, eyes examining it with intensity. "I lied about my age. Worked on building sites. Hoping to get him out too. But one day I went back, and he was gone."

Pain emanated from him, a rough oyster shell opening to reveal soft flesh inside. Nami ached from his revelation, heart sore for him. She'd been so lucky. Had always been shielded from the realities other folk lived. The guilt sat like heavy rocks on her shoulders. She inched her hand forward and brushed it against his. They met, fingers clasping with a squeeze. Despite the reason, she was elated at the contact. Giddy.

Firth pointed down at the milling crowd in the water below. More people danced now, more of the skin-suited humans with their tanks of air. "People act like it never happened. That Iyoness never fell. That the Nurseries were just a bad dream." The grip on her hand tightened. "But they did this. Polluting the waters, turning away when the kumiho shake down another folk family."

Nami was complicit in his words. They were not directed at her and yet wasn't she part of the problem? The concessions she'd been offered as dragonkin. The education she took for granted. The fellow students who spouted fine words but didn't appear on the night of the Peace Tower. She doubted they continued the dissent at home. More likely accepted the state of affairs with a shake of their heads.

"Inaction is like gill rot. Insidious spores long before they're visible. We need to wipe it out." His thumb rubbed hard against her palm. Circles that dug deeper into her flesh until she pulled away involuntarily. Firth's eyes unglazed, looking at her with concern. He barely knew his own strength. Determined to keep up with his toughness, Nami pretended it had not hurt. Flashed him a disarming smile. Firth shook his head and pulled away. "I'm sorry. Just ignore me."

"No," Nami said, the spark catching in her throat. She'd ruined everything, even though he had opened up to her. Needed to prove that she felt the same. "I understand. We need to show them – all of them – what it means to be fathomfolk." Words were not enough; they were never her forte. Eloquence and poetry were her brother's sphere. Frustrated, she turned and swam down, not waiting to see if Firth would follow. She'd demonstrate the defiance she'd had in Yonakuni. She wasn't just some ignorant kid from out of town.

As usual, she had acted on impulse, and suddenly Firth's focus was on her. Waiting with anticipation. His lips had parted a little, an unvoiced question lingering there. Nami wrenched her gaze away. So be it. It was Tidal Day after all. That called for a few waves.

She floated to the centre of the dance space. The sequence of moves came naturally. The dance of her mother, and her grand-mother before that. Flowing arms stretching out and to her side, a roll forward and a twist of her legs. She was the rain, falling strong upon the land, filling the wide flood plains and turning them to lakes. She was the river, long and winding, veins through the land. She sang as she danced, a low hum in the back of her throat, glad for once that her parents had drilled the traditions into her. She saw them now, in gold and blue festival clothes, leading the way. The celebration of the water cycle. Boatloads of gifts pulled upstream to their river and lake kin. The firefly squid lanterns that illuminated the way.

The bioluminescence lit up her moves, making swirls in the water. Whispers assailed her on all sides. She kept her eyes half lidded in case she lost her nerve. Firth was beside her now, match-ing her movements. And then others. Kelpies at first, then other folk, a growing ripple that spread through the club. Some with more grace, embellishing the moves with flourishes. The hum of the Tidal Day song grew, rising through the water and reverber-ating like a leviathan's call. The witchlights flickered with the strength of it all.

It was theirs, the Tidal Day dance, the traditions that had come with it. It was theirs and it had died with the rising of the water level. There was nowhere to travel to. No freshwater lakes, no kin, no ancestors. What was there to celebrate? And yet the dance she'd instigated to defy the humans, to show them what they were not, filled the room with more warmth than Tiankawi's waters merited. Folk were talking, holding hands and smiling as they shared stories with a glow of nostalgia.

"Nami, that was ..." Firth spun her around until she made him stop. His smile filled his face and his hands were soft and fierce at the same time. He cupped her cheek before realising what he was doing and pulling away. The water was cold where his hand had been.

"It's who we are," she said falteringly. Her confidence grew as she looked around them. "What we are. Fathomfolk."

He nodded, hesitating before turning her again. Laughing as she tipped and he caught her, hugging her close so that she could feel his heart thudding in his chest. "We'll show them. Together."

Chapter Eighteen

The monthly social took place in an exclusive rooftop garden in the Jingsha district. Low-hanging vines and decorative gourds filled the space sectioned off by discreet bamboo screens. Yellow kitetails and blue-throated songbirds bobbed in their cages warbling songs, creating a backdrop that masked both talk and the noise of the passing trams below.

Serena, the kumiho captain's wife, needed friends within the upper echelons of Tiankawian society. It would be suspicious had she shunned the gossip and the friendliness of the other Council wives and husbands. Besides, information was the best bargaining chip of all.

As always, they'd formed into a hierarchy: Ayumu, married to the Minister of Ceremonies, wielded very little direct power in the city state, but her wife appointed officials across the districts. A word from her could advance or destroy a career. Although she'd never admit it, Ayumu was also the most advanced in age. She sat at the head of the circular table, furthest from the entrance, taking advantage of the natural breeze and shade. Gesturing like a monarch to the others to pour tea and unstack the towering bamboo steamers. Over the years, Serena had progressed from being jostled by the servers in the doorway, the teapot firmly planted in her hands, to getting closer to Ayumu's position. Samnang, as head of the kumiho, was also the Minister of

Defence. The husband of a junior official offered to plump up her floor cushion. Someone filled her cup.

Serena patted her daughter on the back and Qiuyue did not even glance back, skipping her way to the children's table set up in the far corner of the private area. Serena hesitated, seeing Ayumu's son Finnol there also. Qiuyue idolised the boy, might even have a crush on him. It was one of the reasons Serena hadn't yet shared the secret of their heritage with her. But there would always be these friendships. Her daughter needed to put blood and family first.

"Of course the annual fundraiser will happen at our stall at the Boat Races. Last year was the best to date," Ayumu beamed.

"It was a stroke of genius to sell paper folded animals. Who would've thought the children would enjoy them so much," exclaimed one of her fawning followers.

"Indeed. But I don't want to repeat ourselves this year. What will the ordinary people think?"

Serena flinched at her condescension. Glanced surreptitiously around the table for a kindred spirit. Was she the only one to realise the *ordinary people* didn't give a flying fish what the Council husbands and wives were doing in their free time? But no one else reacted. That, or they had better mastery of their expressions than she'd come to expect. She kept her eye on the newest member to the social gathering, the husband of a senior official in the Finance Office. His eyes positively bulged each time someone spoke up, drinking it all in. He'd be easy to lean on.

Ayumu paused as the woman to her right poured three drops of tea into her already overbrimming cup. Yes, paper was out, and so was the influence of the Housing Minister, whose cousin owned the papermill. More politicking happened over tea than in the Council meeting room itself.

Other ideas were put forward. Serena observed, her expression neutral despite her awareness of the machinations beneath the veneer. Two of them were having an affair; money had been lent between various parties; and most wouldn't hesitate to stab her in the back if it meant gaining Ayumu's favour. It really was her sort of party.

"Serena, you've been quiet on the matter. Is there anything you could offer?" It was not a question; rather a demand that she contribute.

Serena clasped her hands in her lap, plastering a genial smile across her features and ducking her head as if embarrassed. "We ... we could sell beauty products? Hair oil and creams for the face. I've a family recipe ..."

A few noses wrinkled. It sounded like a messy job, collecting and filtering the fish oils needed. Someone scoffed that their fathomfolk nanny made bath salts with the kids.

Ayumu quelled the protests, a thoughtful look on her face. "Yes, but what fathomfolk do is quaint. Primitive. We could elevate it. Add a floral scent, a stylish label, and mark up the price ..." Suddenly everyone was sold on the idea. Never mind that Ayumu's brother had a warehouse of fish oil they couldn't sell after a bad investment. Never mind that fathomfolk had been using lotus flowers and anubias to scent oils since her grandmother's day but could secure neither the rental space nor capital. Serena remained silent. It mattered not.

After the bamboo steamers were cleared, she lingered, offering to reveal her ingredients lists for soap and hair oils. Ayumu sent the others away first, too covetous to share. The captain's wife sighed as she folded the list in half, sliding it across the table. She did not even know when Samnang would be home. Such long hours. Ayumu scoffed, outcompeting her even on this front. "You should be thankful he comes home at all! My wife sleeps at her office most days. I'd suspect an affair but she doesn't have time."

Serena made a non-committal noise, the type that people like to read as agreement. Ayumu was more than happy to continue.

Complaining about Pyanis's eccentric daughter from her first marriage, a librarian, would you believe it? She could be climbing the ladder in the Office of Ceremonies, a junior official at the least. Ayumu touched her temples as if the errant girl was committing heinous crimes rather than choosing an obscure profession.

"There's another reshuffle coming, you know. The Minister of Justice will be, eh, invited to take early retirement." She looked over her stack of papers conspiratorially. "That's why my Pyanis is throwing a party for the Boat Races. I helped her hire a room and tomorrow we're going to book the caterers. I'd invite you, but space is limited – you do understand, don't you? I mean, there's always next year."

Of course Serena understood. It was exactly the information she had loitered behind for. She clasped her hands in a fist-palm salute and heartily wished Ayumu the best of luck. Her head was doing the figures even as she made a mournful Qiuyue say goodbye to her friend. The family helmsman hastened to stub out his cigarette, an apology on his lips, but Serena did not have time for his excuses.

"Ama, this isn't the way home."

"No, saltlick, I have a few errands to run."

"Saltlick?" Qiuyue giggled at the unfamiliar endearment as Serena realised her mistake. She glanced at the helmsman, but he was at the tiller, head lowered after his misdemeanour. She'd been sloppy, too engrossed in planning. It must not happen again.

Ayumu had only confirmed the rumours about the Minister of Justice. A position that could secure their family's future. All she needed was an opportunity to show Samnang's strength and influence. The annual Boat Races was such an event, arguably the most important event in Tiankawi's calendar. One that crossed the divide: tail or legs, stilthouse or high-rise, the races were enjoyed across the waterline.

She swept Qiuyue onto her lap, ignoring the protests. Her daughter liked to pretend she was mature now, but after squirming for a minute, she leaned into her mother and bit her thumb.

"We're going to throw a party," Serena whispered, the peach fuzz around her daughter's forehead tickling her nose. She stroked Qiuyue's hair, checking the nape of her neck. But the charm held, of course it held. She checked it every day, made sure the clasp around the pendant was soldered closed. Samnang had not so much as noticed, she was sure, that their son and daughter wore the same pendants, day and night.

"A party? Will there be music and red bean cakes?"

Serena laughed. "Of course: red bean, green bean, any bean you fancy."

"It's not my birthday yet." The girl's logic was indisputable. Parties always had a purpose, even when they pretended otherwise.

"No, it's for the Boat Races."

"But Finnol's mummies are throwing a party for the Boat Races." Qiuyue glanced up at her mother, giving Serena the opportunity to tickle under her chin. She squealed, the peals of laughter giving Serena life. When Qiuyue had finally calmed down, the girl extracted her thumb from her mouth. "Can I invite Finnol?"

"Of course. In fact, I was counting on it."

Serena had no trouble with the caterers. She knew Ayumu would go for her weekly acupuncture treatment after the meeting. A few coins in a scrawny urchin's palm and a promised message to the kappas who treated her. They'd hold Ayumu there, stall her with a complimentary treatment. Then it was just a matter of offering double the fee to the caterers.

The hotel was trickier. A bead of sweat had formed at the manager's brow as he apologised. The largest banquet room had already been reserved. It was not every day that they were offered such a lucrative booking. The Boat Races took place on the borders of Qilin and Khyagur districts in the less affluent south. The fee they were haggling about was probably more than the establishment made in a year. The manager hastened to suggest alternatives. "Might I interest you in one of the smaller suites? A more intimate affair."

"My apologies, I may not have been clear." Serena casually touched her diamond and peridot earrings. She regretted not putting on the matching necklace this morning. "I want to book the whole hotel." His eyes bulged and she could see him running through the calculations. His hand reached under his collar, loosening it. "Of course we'd also need drinks, entertainment, decorations. An event fit for the Fenghuang himself."

"You mean the head of the Council will—"

"I really couldn't disclose that sort of information. I hope you understand." The Fenghuang, figurehead of the Council, would never show his face at the Boat Races. His empty chair was merely a symbol at Council meetings. But the manager didn't need to know that. He'd already forgotten all obligation to Ayumu. Serena smiled, imagining how enraged the other woman would be. There was no turning back from this, no charming her at those monthly socials. But Ayumu had been fawned over for long enough.

It was about time someone else took her seat.

Chapter Nineteen

"Come on!" Firth said, from his place higher up the slope. He pointed towards something beyond Nami's sight. "A little further!"

Nami doubled over, exhausted, catching her breath as the wind buffeted her. Her limbs were used to being buoyed by water, not climbing upwards on rocky terrain in heavy humidity. But Firth had taken the request to show her around Tiankawi seriously. And according to him, the best view was from the Peak Mountain, the only natural structure above water in the city state.

They'd been hiking for hours, the submerged mangrove trees giving way to rough brush. The shrubs became leaner, drier in the rising heat of the midday sun as the cicadas thrummed ceaselessly. Here near the summit, there was nothing. Barren rocks cut like sword strokes. Long shadows zigzagged in front of them. In places it was so steep that someone had left guide ropes staked in place. Nami tried not to look too closely at the frayed ends as she clambered upwards, sweat dampening the creases of her elbows and knees.

Finally Firth scrambled down the few metres between them to offer his hand. A shower of pebbles rattled past Nami's head. She swallowed the mild alarm. It was one thing to walk about on land where the ground was even and flat. She was used to that now. Up here she felt vulnerable, her footing never certain. Thin shoes did little to protect her feet from the jagged edges. But she refused to let it show, slapping away the proffered hand and finding the next stable step on the ascent.

When they reached the top, the view was impressive. They were looking down on the whole cityscape. Even the tallest buildings were lower than their vantage point. Nami could see the clear differences in areas. Jingsha rose like an island of basalt columns from the water. So much condensed into a tight space. Beyond the centre, the city was spread thin. Boats and wooden stilthouses like twigs floating on the water's surface as far as the eye could see. Plumes of smoke and smog from the distant industrial areas. She hadn't even scratched the surface in her explorations, keeping mostly to the folk-populated south.

"Dizzy?" Firth's voice tickled her ear.

"How did you guess?" she admitted. She turned her head a little, enough that she brushed against him. Her outings with Firth were fast becoming a regular weekly occurrence. He never seemed to tire of her, asking about Yonakuni, about her family. Nami would talk until her voice was hoarse, but he would urge her to keep going. Eyes on her as if spellbound by her mundane utterances. They talked until late at night, until a whole week seemed too long to wait.

"We are but tiny sardines in a behemoth shoal." Firth rarely spoke without deliberate purpose. An economy of words that made others sit up and listen. He unpacked his bag, offering his flask. Nami sipped from it, the intimacy of it making her glow. She shared the snacks she'd brought.

"What's on the other side?" she forced herself to ask. Better to focus on geography than the stirring feelings that threatened to sabotage a perfectly good friendship. She nodded her head north, the far side of the Peak.

"Crags, a sharp drop and choppy seas. They tried to build once, carve houses into the mountainside. Too many earthquakes. The work caused landslides."

Nami had seen some of the failed houses on the climb up, piles of broken timbers like a fist had dropped from the sky to smash them to splinters.

"Can you imagine living here, so far from the water?" The audacity of it filled her voice with wonder.

"I would do it. Just to spit on their heads."

Nami laughed, surprised by Firth's spite. But up here, she supposed, they might be the only two people in the world. She liked that about their relationship. She did not have to mince her words. Didn't have to be the well-bred water dragon. She could cuss and talk rubbish and he never looked at her askance. Never berated her to read more books or hold her tongue until she was more mature. She smiled. "You remind me of a friend from home."

"Oh, captain of the guard? A scoundrel and a cad – popular with the ladies and the gents? A dragon? Naga? Imugi?" Firth struck a teasing pose with his hand on his chin, elbow leaning on a knee. The moment was quite ruined as the pebbles beneath him tumbled away and he tripped forward to catch his balance.

Nami cackled. "No, a kappa."

He was brushing the dust from his trousers, but paused at her words and raised an eyebrow. "Thank you?"

She punched him lightly in the arm. It was the kind of thing she did with her brother, not with an attractive kelpie. If she was being honest, she'd done it so she could touch him. Firth didn't seem in the least put out. She hid her mortification with a blustery explanation. "It's a compliment! One of my best friends. Says what he means. Cares for others." She still hadn't sent Dan a message. She'd been too wrapped up in her own misery, while he and Hong-Gi languished in prison. She put down the flask, no longer enjoying the giddy feeling in her stomach.

Her face must have belied her guilt. Firth studied her solemnly. "Come to one of our rallies."

"What?"

"That's what you did back in Yonakuni, right? Stood up when others dared not? Humanity's laws – their lies – hurt all of us. Nothing will change unless we force it."

"But Mira and Kai said—"

Firth made a noise of disgust, rolling his eyes to make it clear what he thought. "Are the luxurious chambers making you soft?"

Nami bit her lip. He was right. The Peace Tower heist was not something Kai would've approved of. What would she have done anyway: used the pearl? Hatched it? She didn't have an answer. Didn't have a plan. If Firth pushed too far, he would realise, and this bothered her even more. Sometime after the Tidal Day dance, his opinion had risen like the morning sun shining overhead. The scrutiny dazzled her; scared her a little too.

While she was mulling things over, he had laid out a small fabric board embroidered with an intricate hexagon design. Lines, squares and right angles formed a beautiful intersecting pattern. "Do you play?"

Nami looked at the cloth board and the shell pieces. Wunlan. A complex strategy game her parents had taught her in childhood. Firth's hand was warm as he handed her pieces over. "You'll forgive the crushing defeat I'm about to serve you." He flexed his fingers and leaned in, intent on the board. For all the quips, he was taking this seriously.

Nami rolled up her sleeves and crossed her legs under her. Exactly the way she'd been taught. Her mother had been a master at wunlan, never simplifying the game for her children. Hardening them to life's bruises. She had also hoped to teach them strategy and forward planning, a message Nami had invariably grown bored of. She would wander off to find snacks when they were playing, leaving Kai and her parents to discuss complex moves.

A few games later, they were tied, although Nami suspected Firth had deliberately let her win. The game was hampered by the pieces sliding from the uneven surface and the wind periodically picking up, howling about their ears as if they'd otherwise forget it. They lost some of the shells, chasing them down the slope for a few breathless minutes before using stones instead. Still they played on. After three games, tactics resurfaced from deep within her memory, like dredging through silt. She moved her counter on from the crossroads, taking a shortcut diagonally across the board. "Ha!"

Her two counters were a team now, moving simultaneously. Double the points if she could get to the end, but double the risk if he caught her. Firth shook the wun pieces between cupped hands, the low rattle a pleasant noise as he scattered them on the board. "Five!" He raced up from behind and had another turn still. Rolled again. Three. He looked up at her as he tapped out each move.

He would win. A ruthless strategy that left no room for manoeuvre. He looked at her with a silent question as she covered her pieces with a cupped hand. A contravention of all rules. "That's definitely cheating."

"Bending the rules," Nami declared. The kelpie stared at her for a long moment, and then grinned back. Leaned forward to move her hand out of the way. Nami resisted, her merriment ringing in the wind as she kept her hand firmly over the board. "A draw, call it a draw!" she yelled.

Her laughter was infectious as they tussled. Firth tried to prise open her clenched fist, obtain the counters that would end the game. His breath was hot on her neck as Nami rolled herself up. Tears of mirth squeezed from her eyes and there was a stitch in her side. He made a triumphant noise as he held aloft the pieces before flopping beside her, breath ragged. The grey sky above them like a canopy. Only then did it register how much they were touching.

Legs entangled and Firth's head leaning on her outstretched arm. Nami felt the rocks press into the small of her back, but she dared not move. Heat radiated from where they were in contact.

Firth whispered her name, his murmur low. If Nami turned towards him, she knew his eyes would be on her, wide and hungry. That he would reach up to cup her face and kiss her. She knew because she wanted it too.

An appreciative whistle broke the tension. They tumbled apart. Nami's body was still burning, hot and frustrated. People were walking up the dirt track. Humans. Five of them, heads wrapped in towel bandannas and empty baskets lashed across their backs. The woman in the front planted her basket down on the ground next to her. She looked Nami up and down, then at Firth, and smiled cruelly. "A free show!"

The others sniggered.

Nami was too flustered to respond. Hating the humans for having stolen the moment. The woman shrugged when neither of them rose to the bait. "We're quarrying today. Area's off limits. Don't want you lovebirds twisting an ankle."

Firth would talk about it, Nami was certain, once they were out of earshot. About what that was, about what it might have been. She trained her eyes on his back as they started the descent, her breathing agitated from more than the steep slope.

Once they had left the workers behind, he grabbed her elbow. Nami's heart beat faster, wondering if he would kiss her now or ask first. She parted her lips slightly, tilting her face up to his. When nothing happened, she opened her eyes. The kelpie wasn't looking at her at all. His focus was back up the slope, excitement clear. "Did you see?"

"Wh-what?"

"Explosives. Lots and lots of explosives."

"Well . . . they're quarrying."

"Yes, a stroke of luck. They abandoned the old mines decades ago – no coal or precious gems to be found. Can you remember what they were wearing?"

"I guess," Nami said.

"Great. This is great. You must be my good-luck talisman!" Firth grinned, planting a kiss on her forehead. Then he was a million miles away, muttering as he continued down the steep, winding path. Nami touched where he had kissed. Her skin tingled, catching his enthusiasm.

That evening, Kai was home before her for once. The apartment smelt of oil from the battered prawns and vegetables he had been making. He was up every few minutes: another condiment, another bowl, had she found where he kept the pickles, how about some chilli flakes on top. He'd always been this way when he was anxious around others. Guests and relatives. So good, so polite, they'd remark. Nary a button or a hair out of place. But not usually with her.

"How was your day?" he asked.

"I went to the Peak."

"Really?" He paused for further information.

"I had a guide." Nami knew he wanted more than that but was far too polite to interrogate her. She concentrated on her empty bowl. How could she explain her relationship with Firth when she didn't know herself? She distracted herself by snagging the remaining piece of pumpkin, regretting that the batter was no longer crispy. Slouched back in the chair and closed her eyes. At least her stomach was satisfied.

"I should be making more time for you."

Nami opened her eyes. "You've work to do. I understand."

"Work, yes, always work." Kai had hardly touched his own food. Half of his rice was still in the bowl, and he'd picked the crispy batter from his prawns.

"Speaking of which, how is the bill?" she ventured. She knew the gist of it, had endured the weekly updates in Yonakuni. The folk back home compared Kai to a sand god. Here was the golden boy ensuring Yonakunish folk were treated fairly, pushing through a significant amendment that would protect their rights.

"Prejudice always remains," he said.

"Humans, eh?"

He put down his chopsticks, resting them neatly atop his bowl. Folded his napkin in half and half again into a precise triangle. "I didn't foresee the pushback from other folk."

The newssheets in Yonakuni never mentioned Mira. Painted it as Kai's idea alone: protection for vulnerable fathomfolk, especially women in jobs that were ... higher risk. The ones who made use of their charms: dulcet-toned sirens, long-haired rusalka or silver-tailed merrow-maids who worked as hostesses in the entertainment district. Flashbacks came unbidden of the folk on the settlement vessel, the harried look as they followed the border guards into the locked room. But what if even that pretence of choice was taken? They could not fight back. The pakalots would shut them down, making them into victims. The new amendment would allow them to resist. A self-defence provision.

Kai explained, it was the Atlityan ambassador who'd been the most vocal opponent. The small southern haven had been in a bloody civil war for months now, its people split between those who wanted to live topside, start building their own city or fleet; and those who refused to abandon the old ways in the collapsing haven.

He picked up the teapot, holding the spout above his cup, and tipped it, a drop of liquid at a time filling his cup. Slow and sure. "Some think there's not enough goodwill to go around. Spend it all on one cause – one that doesn't directly benefit them – and there'll be none left." He tilted the teapot more steeply, draining the contents entirely. It did not quite fill his cup to the brim. "There are others who think it's too slow. They want change now."

He picked up the cup, holding it between finger and thumb above the table. If he let go, the porcelain would smash and the tea would scald everything. He sipped it instead, never showing the discomfort he must feel.

Nami touched the pakalot on her wrist, a queasy feeling lurching in her stomach. If it was her, if things were so bad, she wouldn't wait for Kai and Mira's bill. She would take a hacksaw to the thing, prise it apart with a hammer. Surely it was possible. Surely someone had found a way.

Kai stood up again, straightening a picture frame on the wall, lighting the candles on the side table. Busy hands. Intuitively, he responded to her unasked question. "Yes, others have tried. Pakalots nullified and visas forged: that's the promise from the seawitches and swindlers who make the deals. It rarely works. Most folk end up in debt beyond their means and with lifelong injuries. If they're lucky."

He let the words hang in the air. Rubbed at his chin before continuing. "Three fathomfolk turned up dead last year. All known to the kumiho, histories of abusive relationships. They'd got lost in the system. Mira has never forgiven herself. I have never forgiven myself."

They couldn't rely on the kindness of humans. Or the laws stacked against them. Firth's words rang in her head. Things had to be taken into their own hands. "Then they shouldn't be with humans. No good will come of it!"

"So a dragon shouldn't be with a siren either?"

"That's not what I meant." Nami felt the blood drain from her face and she stumbled to backtrack.

"But it's what you thought." There was no malice in Kai's voice. Instead it was tinged with great weariness. Back home, dragons did not fraternise with sirens. These unwritten rules mattered less to the diaspora freshwater community in Tiankawi. Their similarities more significant than their differences. Her own friendship with Dan wouldn't have raised an eyebrow in the city, and if she took a kelpie as a lover . . . well, no one would say a thing.

She hadn't been thinking, just blurting out the rhetoric she'd heard in Yonakuni – the same traditionalist ideas she railed against. Was the prejudice so deeply etched through her grain? She hunched over, rendering herself small, so tiny that her words would disappear and her brother would forget she'd said them. Then she wouldn't have to apologise. Wouldn't have to admit she'd spoken out of turn. But they were adults now. She straightened herself back up and held the apology on her lips, ready to say it, waiting for the right moment.

The moment passed.

"So what do you need to pass the law?" She tried to fill the chasm of silence between them. At first it seemed Kai wouldn't humour her, but after half a moment, he answered. "Two more Council members' votes. Ratification from the Fenghuang. I'm hoping goodwill after the Boat Races will do it."

Nami swallowed the unvoiced remorse, the lump like a rock scoring at the walls of her throat on the way down.

"Mira's on the Council, isn't she?"

Kai shook his head. "No. She should be, for the amount of work she does. But officially she has no seat. No vote."

"You, Mira – you both know what you want. And you do it, make a difference. Here I am reading about tram signalling and irrigating vertical gardens! Wasting my time." Nami flopped on the sofa, but it was too hard and narrow to have the dramatic effect she'd been expecting. She prodded at the cushion with her index finger.

"People aren't born knowing what to do. They learn. Through experience. Through mistakes."

"You don't," Nami pointed out. "You've always been effortlessly perfect." As soon as the words left her mouth, she realised how insulting they sounded.

Kai sat next to her, cocking his head to one side. "Is that what you think? That I have everything figured out?"

"Well, now that you've said that ... probably not."

"I ... I always wanted to please Mother and Father. And when you were a kid, you looked up to me. I didn't want to disappoint any of you." His voice was very quiet, almost a whisper. It would've been easier if he was shouting. Nami had never considered the burden of being the firstborn. That perhaps beneath the calm surface, fear and chaos lurked somewhere within him too.

She leaned her head against his shoulder. "You know how relieved I would've been to learn you were struggling too? That you weren't perfect?"

"Perfect? Me? You're the one brave enough to defy our mother, to choose what you wanted rather than having it dictated to you."

Nami gave an incredulous whistle. It was a lot to process. She'd learned more about her brother in this one conversation than she had in a lifetime of interactions. "I like this."

"Me too."

"I'm sorry about what I said." She wrung her hands together, blurting the words out before she could take them back. "You and Mira are good for each other. I see that now."

"Thank you." Kai's antlers seemed longer than usual, straighter too as he held his head up high, proud of the compliment. Nami had always been so sparing with praise, brought up in an environment where it did not come naturally. But seeing the impact of it, seeing words of appreciation have an immediate effect on her brother's mood, made her realise that perhaps kindness had its own power too.

Chapter Twenty

Nami scratched at her gills as she trod water. She was beginning to know the city. Sense its moods through the haze of the morning smog and the tremors underfoot. Firth took her to the distant edges of Tiankawi. To submerged warehouses that were actually bars and bars that were actually shelters. He opened her eyes to things that would otherwise have passed her by, made her question what she always took for granted. She no longer noticed the bitterness in the water, but her skin felt itchy and tight.

Her days were spent with Firth, or occasionally trying to find out about the Onseon Engine. The urgency had faded the longer she was here, her mother responding with only dismissal to each of her letters. None of it made a difference to Dan and Hong-Gi's sentences. It was all a lie. The anger of it lay like red-hot coals in her empty hands and Firth handed her the kindling.

Her first Drawback rally! Her heart quickened in anticipation. She looked over her shoulder for her mother or Sobekki to tell her off, but she wasn't in Yonakuni any more. While Kai wouldn't exactly approve, he was also too busy to drag her home for this small act of rebellion.

Glashtyn Square was busier than when she'd first arrived, the floating market active around the perimeter. Nami swam across the square, watching the folk absent-mindedly with one hand firmly on her satchel. She'd learned her lesson. No longer that yearling. Amid the food stalls, baskets of repurposed old fabrics and Boat Race decorations, a small group of fathomfolk were tying a banner to one of the witchlights. She drifted closer for a look, seeing a painted picture of a selkie caught in a net. Slogans supported the self-defence bill: Kai and Mira's bill. A grin spread across Nami's face.

"Join the movement, sister," said one of the chang-bis. Mostly human in appearance, he would not however be mistaken for one, with arms so long they trailed on the seabed and hands big as spades; the chang-bis had a reputation as fisherfolk. The protesters were wearing chains around their necks and wrists. Some were already securing themselves to the kelpie statue at the square's heart.

"You are bad for business." It was the seawitch, Cordelia. In the water, her remark carried further, allowing Nami to locate her halfway across the square as she approached. Her lower eight limbs ballooned as she came to stand by them.

"Folk rights affect us all." The chang-bi's loose chains smacked together as he gesticulated with enthusiasm.

"Wouldn't this be better above water?"

"Simultaneous demonstrations are happening across the city: on the trams and cable cars, in the shopping quarter and outside the exclusive restaurants in Jingsha. We'll make the authorities notice!"

"So you're the dregs, then, far from the press? Not articulate enough? Or was it that face?" The seawitch scoffed in disgust as she locked up her bar.

The chang-bi swam forward in retort, but any response was lost in the rush of bubbles as giant squid appeared at Cordelia's side. One long tentacle whipped out and the protester was shoved back to land on the rough sand.

Cordelia glanced down, a condescending smile on her lips.

Bemused like she'd witnessed a child's tantrum. She seemed to notice Nami for the first time. "Offer's still open, saltlick. You'd be better on my team."

Before Nami could process the words, the seawitch had gone, leaving her with more than just a tang in her mouth. Foul black ink swirled in her wake. The chang-bi rubbed his back as he muttered to himself.

"Are you Drawback?" Nami asked.

The chang-bi positively shook, twitching and looking around surreptitiously. His large hands tugged at the chains around his neck. "No! I don't have a death wish." He refused to be drawn in, returning to his companions but glancing at her.

Firth called her name, the market crowd parting before him as he swam forward. Giddiness gurgled in Nami's stomach. She had to bend her legs to stop herself from floating upwards. It was hard to pretend nonchalance as his rugged face creased into a lopsided grin. To resist the urge to run her hand along the stubble on his jawline. It'd only been two days since they'd last met, and yet it felt much longer. She was used to acting on impulse. Swooping in on anyone she was interested in and dealing with the messy consequences later. She didn't know the rules here. It was bad enough to be laughed at for her thick accent or inability to drink the local moonshine; she'd mastered neither how to haggle nor how to get served at a busy hawker stall. But she could not risk getting this wrong. Afraid to cross a line even though her memory replayed their day at the Peak over and over. Dreaming of other outcomes.

Firth's eyes lingered on her. Roved her body with a possessive intensity. Long enough that Nami ducked her head and broke the tension with an awkward laugh, face reddening. He finally broke the silence. "Come. The rally awaits."

"Where?"

"I know the way." His response was enigmatic, but Nami didn't mind. The Drawbacks were probably being monitored by the city guard. She envisaged safe houses and clandestine meeting places scattered across the city. The subterfuge thrilled her almost as much as the powerful kelpie swimming beside her. It was what she'd always wanted. Not a group of swaggering students making grandiose statements but never acting. The Drawbacks were bold. Dangerous.

They left Glashtyn Square far behind and entered an area unfamiliar to her. Firth led her up the rusty ladder of an abandoned house until they emerged from the water. Dusk was falling across the city and the witchlights made the dark water shimmer like an oil slick. Light rain started to fall. Without missing a beat, Firth skimmed across a window ledge, down three winding corridors, through the kitchen of a small bakery and past a mermaid reading to her children. The young mother stood up, calling out his name, but he simply winked and held his finger to his lips. She sat down again, blue tail sweeping beneath her. They were in and out of the water so often that Nami barely had time to waterweave the rain from her clothes.

Firth stopped abruptly, Nami colliding with his broad back. She mumbled a flustered apology, her hand on his wet top. Conscious now of the water dripping from her hair and down the hollow of her neck. The kelpie turned with a glint in his eye. Nami took the scarf he held out, not understanding at first. Then she saw the water tuk-tuk lashed beside small fishing boats. Looked back at the strip of fabric in her hands.

"You want to blindfold me?"

"Just for the last bit." His eyebrows waggled and Nami suspected he was enjoying this far too much at her expense. "You trust me, right?"

She could not exactly say no. And thinking about it, she did have faith in him. A kindred spirit of sorts. He spoke sense to her. Options she might've shied away from in the havens, but this was Tiankawi. He understood the city better than her.

She handed him the scarf and turned so he could place it around her eyes. His touch was tender as he secured a knot behind her head. His fingers ran across her forehead, releasing locks of her short hair that had got caught. All her other senses were heightened. The headiness of his smell, the touch of his damp top brushing her arms. She exhaled through her lips.

Firth took her hand at first, callused fingers against hers. Then he swore good-naturedly and, without warning, picked her up. Nami's instinct was to kick.

"What was that for?" She heard the pout in his voice.

"You could've warned me. I panicked!" She was flustered, but Firth held her securely in his arms.

"I should've put you in the tuk-tuk first. Wasn't thinking," he mumbled, but all the same, it seemed to take longer than necessary for him to transfer her to the seat of the vehicle.

She listened as he eased the water tuk-tuk forward. Water slapped the sides and she heard the ring of the tram in the distance as it pulled into a station. Finally, just as the questions were about to burst from her, they stopped. The blindfold was whipped from her eyes and she squinted into the light as Firth moored the vehicle. Despite his attempts to befuddle her, she figured they were somewhere near the abandoned Nurseries. She might not be able to pinpoint the exact location, but she was confident they'd not gone as far as the convoluted journey made out. If anything, they'd circled back at times.

The area was largely derelict, if the rust and the boarded-up windows were anything to go by. A sliding hatch in a door opened to Firth's knock and a bleary-eyed face asked for a password.

Firth shrugged and the door was hastily opened. "That's the password?" Nami asked.

"No. But everyone knows me," Firth said with some satisfaction. "Quickly, we're running late."

He took her hand as he weaved through the derelict building.

The floor level was not entirely clear of the tide, knee-high water making it difficult to wade towards the sound of chatter beyond the far door. The meeting had already started.

Nami had tried to organise gatherings back in Yonakuni. Mostly they turned into drunken tangents or hours arguing theories. Never the dynamic protest meetings of her imagination. Finally she would see how things worked. Her whole body pulsed with excitement and the hand gripping Firth's was shaking. He brought it to his chest, stilling her nerves against his own steady heartbeat.

Sixty figures, maybe more, filled the warehouse-sized room. Witchlights were dimmed, casting shadows mostly on the water rather than on faces. What she could see made Nami cry out in joy. Fathomfolk, from a diminutive clione to a ceiling-sweeping imugi sea serpent – many in their true forms. Tails, fins and horns. She brushed past fur and scales, the smell of the sea stronger than it had been her whole time here. There was a mild murmur as the crowd parted to let her and Firth wade nearer the front, his name whispered in fervent tones.

On a makeshift stage, Lynnette was talking. The charm of her first encounter with Nami was replaced by solemnity. Confidence. Her words were stones polished by the tide. On that stage, feet planted, she was a pillar of strength.

"Our lives are hard – they've made it so. Work every hour of the day, too hungry to be angry, too tired to coordinate. But we are the folk. We can withstand a flood, a storm, a tsunami. We are the drawback. The calm before the change. And we will be heard!" She raised a fist into the air, punctuating each word of the sentence.

Feet and tails stamped in the water, the splashes as loud as the accompanying cheers. Lynnette waited for the room to quieten again before continuing. Her voice was magnetising, low enough that Nami had to strain forward, noticing that the whole room did the same.

"Who polluted our seas? Devastated our homes? Curbed our powers?"

The crowd shouted back as one. Nami called with them, hurling her rage forward.

"Humans! Humans did this!" Lynnette said. "Are we going to sit quietly? Plead and beg and hope they'll let us have one tiny amendment? Please, sir, thank you, sir, can I have the scraps from your table, sir? Are we going to wave banners and chain ourselves to statues like whining brats?"

Disgust roared across the room. Nami hardly heard the Drawback leader's words. Just the power. The injustice.

Lynnette's expression was pure triumph, head tilted towards the sky. "They should be scared of us!"

Nami felt the water before she saw it, streaming from behind her legs and up towards the kelpie's. Lynnette pulled it in with waterweaving, her hands cupped to make a whirlpool by her knees. Drawing up clay from a wheel. It widened, asymmetric now and curving sloppily. Nami had to resist helping. It threatened to spill onto them. There was a flash of panic in Lynnette's eyes and she looked in Firth's direction. She was strong but her movements were unstable, a performer spinning too many plates. Unaccustomed to the amount of water she held within her reach. She flung her arms apart, letting the vortex expand in a wide arc. The impact of the water sent Nami staggering back.

As people picked themselves up off the floor, muttering uneasily, Lynnette blundered on as if nothing had happened. Sticking to the script. "They thought they could manacle us, restrain us, collar us like animals. Even animals bite."

A scrawny man was shoved up next to her. Human. Matted hair framed his face and filthy clothes hung off a skeletal frame. He looked uncomfortable in the water, wheezing loudly and his gaze shifting through rheumy eyes. "Y-you said there'd be more?" His grip tightened around a mostly empty bottle.

The Drawback leader beckoned him closer, waiting as he stumbled awkwardly. "First, a little demo."

The human turned to look at the audience, eyes unfocused. His voice was wary. "She didn't mention that. She said there was drink."

"Come at me," Lynnette instructed him, like it was an everyday request.

"What?" The man held up a hand to shade his eyes from the glaring witchlight. Grime was embedded under his fingernails, highlighting the worn lines of his palms.

"Attack me."

"Why would I do that?" he said. His eyes darted out across the crowd, over their heads to where the doorway was.

"Attack me! NOW!"

The human raised a bony fist half-heartedly towards Lynnette's head. The kelpie slammed a shoulder into his chest, an uppercut, a knee to the groin. The man staggered back, falling in the water, gargling as he choked down mouthfuls of it. Lynnette dragged him up by his shirt.

"The power is ours!" she said, victory savage in her voice. She raised her arm, the pakalot neither tightening nor stopping her attack.

She had done it, Nami marvelled. Broken the restrictions of the pakalot even though Kai had said it was impossible. Excitement ran through the room like ripples. The crowd were back onside. This was no small act of self-defence like the proposed bill. This was something bigger. A weapon to wield. Elation rose in Nami as she watched. Lynnette kept punching. Over and over until the man's rags ran red and his face was unrecognisable, a swollen pulp.

The initial euphoria subsided, replaced only by horror. "Stop," Nami whispered to herself, then louder, "Stop!" Her voice did not cut through the crowd, but her body responded and she pushed to the front, still calling. The kelpie stared at her blankly, lapping up the applause of the braying crowd. Nami was nothing more than a mote of dust.

She turned to search for Firth, having lost track of him in the chaos. Surely he could put a stop to this. There. Deep within the throng, unmoving despite the frenzy surrounding him. His arms were folded, face in shadow as he watched. Nami squeezed back through, elbows and fists knocking her as the crowd howled like a savage beast. Tugged at his sleeve. "Talk to her, stop her!"

He shook his head ruefully. "We can't turn back the tide."

The heap of a man, merely rags and bones, crumpled to the ground, Lynnette breathless from the exertion. She roared, punching her pakalot arm in the air. "This is not the master of you!"

The Drawbacks screamed their unanimous approval, the noise ringing in Nami's ears like a foghorn.

Chapter Twenty-One

It was the small things that gave Cordelia pleasure. She admired the scene from the back of the room, where she was camouflaged against the old rusting piping. The speech was eloquent, a lot more than she'd expected from the kelpie fugu addict. Lynnette and the Drawbacks might well ignite a fire of unrest. Cordelia was betting on it. The best deals were always struck when people were desperate.

And then Lynnette went too far.

Cordelia moved on her lower limbs, rising tall although still unseen. She saw the dragon whelp, Nami, intervene. Saw Firth and Lynnette having heated words while the crowd salivated for more. She considered her options, rapidly cycling through them in her head. This was not according to her plan. It wasn't the blood trailing down the man's neck or the sight of his laboured breathing that moved her. It was the contract he had signed earlier in the day. Seawitches did not renege on an agreement. And this one had promised to keep him safe while under her glamour.

She darted forward and grabbed the unconscious man. Camouflage was easy in the dim light of the room, but slipping past the bloodthirsty crowd less so. She kept low, propelling herself between legs and fins with a blast of her siphon. Folk yelled, stumbled on something underfoot, but she moved too quickly for them to see, lifting the man and retreating before they could stop her, her squid guard helping to force a path to the exit.

Hours later, the Drawbacks finally dispersed. Cordelia heard the altercation between Firth and Nami; saw the dragonborn storm out, face a thunderhead. Then quieter voices. Lynnette's heavy steps on the stairs. The kelpie appeared in the attic, her eyes sweeping across the mould-ridden boxes and detritus. Even she couldn't spot the seawitch.

"They've gone," she said finally.

Cordelia dropped her camouflage, a small sense of victory at the Drawback leader's discomfort. "You could've killed him. That was not our agreement."

"Serena, my dear. Oh! Slip of the tongue. Shells knows why I called you that, dear Cordelia," Lynnette said.

Cordelia's stomach plummeted. Son of a bitch. The kelpie's mohawk flopped to the other side. Smug bastard. Her disguise had finally been penetrated.

Well, the Drawbacks were not the only ones with multiple cards up their sleeves. She looked down on the old man, the cuts in his skin flapping like gills. His real gills beginning to show. The glamour was fading. Cordelia's glamour. They had asked for a wretch, someone desperate to make a little money. Plenty of those in the slums. But the glamour, the human appearance, was something she didn't like to do. If word got out, humans would know it was one of her tricks. They would start to wonder which of their neighbours were folk masquerading as human. And if they found her, saw through "Serena", how long before they found her children too? How long before Gede's comrades in the guards fastened a pakalot to his wrist; before little Qiuyue's playmates rejected her; before their own father . . .

She nodded at the injured man. "He needs treatment." The ink sacs under her gills thrummed, tender to the touch. The threat of a broken bargain wasn't just one of pride alone. It affected the very ink that lay dormant in her body, the same ink she signed her deals with. First it would change colour, turning from darkest black and lightening to a jaundiced yellow, showing the world she was a promise-breaker. And then it would seep from their sacs, soaking into her flesh, blinding her eyes and poisoning her skin.

"A worthless bottom-feeder," Lynnette said, cracking the knuckles of her right hand. Dried blood stained her skin.

It had seemed like an opportunity too good to miss: to sow the seeds of chaos just before the Boat Races. But folk or human, she had not expected Lynnette to go quite so far. Had not even thought to bring her healing remedies.

Her mind swivelled to wondering how much longer Gede could cover for her on the surface today. She had no time for these little games. She needed Lynnette out before the extent of her own powers was fully revealed. "I've had enough of your tricks. Your plan at the Boat Races better go perfectly."

"Do you not want to be on the winning side?"

"Side?" Cordelia repeated with a disbelieving scoff. She scratched at her elbow distractedly, her lower limbs pulsing in dark green rings. Lynnette's words were the drone of a buzzing gnat. "Threaten me again and you'll see whose side I'm on." She nodded, and one of her giant squid slipped out from under a crate and wrapped its tentacles around the unconscious man.

"Oh, that wasn't a threat. When I threaten you, you'll know," Lynnette said.

The seawitch considered her words. The Drawbacks knew who she was. Her family. In their position she would squeeze that bargaining chip for all it was worth. "What's the real aim here?"

Lynnette made the sign of the sand gods across her person. "If you have to ask, then it's not for you to know."

Chapter Twenty-Two

There was a festival atmosphere in the water. Lanterns, round as ripe tomatoes, danced on strings draped between buildings. Windsocks shaped like fan-tailed fighting fish streamed over the heads of the children who waved them. People had found a place to watch; every window ledge and roof filled with families. The smell of grilled eel and fishballs on sticks wafted from the enterprising floating stalls. It was the first time Nami had seen humans and fathomfolk intermingling so closely.

Mira's mother, Trish, pointed ahead, as excited as a kid. Mira was on duty at the Boat Races. Kai had official duties to attend to. Nami would probably have given the whole thing a miss with the mood she was in, but the border guard captain had other ideas, and cajoled her into chaperoning her elderly mother. The older siren had scars on her deep brown arms, the skin raised under her pakalot. A history long since healed but not forgotten. Nami caught her eye, looking away in embarrassment as Trish brought the end of her embroidered scarf across her left arm to cover it. She saw Mira mirrored there: the same full lips and crooked smile, Trish's filled with laughter lines and blurred edges, her wavy hair greying and pulled back into a single braid.

Trish had a persuasive manner, and whether it was siren charm or not, Nami didn't care. The idle prattle was like stepping into a light rain shower. Soothing. She felt useful. Wanted. Even if she suspected that Trish leaned into her walking stick and massaged her hip with exaggerated care.

Nami was avoiding Firth. Flashes of Lynnette smashing the man's face to a bloody pulp, Firth not lifting a finger to stop her. She closed her eyes. The sound of a fist cracking against flesh continued to ring in her ears between the chatter and cheers of the Boat Race festivities around her. She shivered.

"Your first Boat Races!" Trish said, glancing back with a smile. She was in bright orange and pink, material tucked and pleated into her waistband, and had brought a gold-threaded headscarf for Nami too. She was breathing heavily, tired from the shallow incline from the tram station. An earthquake rumbled beneath them. Surreptitiously Nami slowed down, masking it with a barrage of questions.

"Ah, it's a good festival," Trish said. "A Tiankawi tradition organised by the merchant families in the city. Before the trams, before the motor-driven vessels. The best rowers in the city state. You know the Fenghuang and the Council used to pay for it all – drinks and food included. Those were the good days."

"So where do we fit in?"

"You think fathomfolk are going to sit and let humans say they're the best on the water?" Trish laughed so hard she started to cough. Spluttered until Nami made her drink from her flask. She continued nonetheless. "There was nothing to stop folk entering boats of their own. Especially when the rowing families went into decline."

She pointed to where Nami could see four colourful boats filled with double ranks of rowers. Each vessel was brightly decked out in one colour, the rowers wearing matching headbands. If that wasn't distinctive enough, each had a different carved figurehead: whale shark and manta ray, turtle and sunfish. The old sand gods.

Nami collided with something. Someone. Distracted, she'd walked right into a city guard. He tipped his hat to her, wishing her good luck for the race. She didn't know how to respond, frozen in confusion by his bizarre amiability, until Trish called out on her behalf, "May the winds be behind you!"

"That was . . . nice?"

"I told you, it's race day!" Trish grinned as if the words explained everything.

Before Nami could ask further, the children's chorus warbling upon a makeshift floating stage stopped. Nami looked up and saw Kai. It was just his back, but she recognised her brother immediately. Hands clasped behind him, standing straight, the topknot hairstyle. He was talking with some humans, making them laugh. One man slapped him jovially on the shoulder. As he turned, Nami realised that Kai was really laying it on, displaying much of his dragon form without altering his size and shape. A sheen of silver ran up his neck and round his temples where his scales were showing. His antlers were exposed, like delicate branches sprouting from his temples.

"Come, let's find somewhere to watch!" Trish said. Nami protested half-heartedly but allowed herself to be swept along with the enthusiasm. The energy of the festival was infecting her. She found herself smiling, waving at youths holding hand-made flags of their favourite teams, and eavesdropping on excited predictions.

Trish haggled with a stallholder grilling mackerel on skewers from her small boat. A couple of coins changed hands and she and Nami were waved to sit on the rear of the vessel. The stallholder scolded them for rocking the boat but gave each a strip of crispy fish skin to eat.

Nami bit into it, expecting the salt seasoning she was accustomed to. Instead it was coated in a sticky sweet sauce. The flavour took her by surprise. Customers had started to form queues in front of the boat: one in the water, fathomfolk bobbing half submerged; the other on the walkway, a line of mostly humans but also some mixed families and friends. The stallholder alternated deftly between the two, alongside turning the skewers and brushing on the sticky sauce.

Nami scanned the water, people-watching, until a pair of piercing eyes held hers. Firth. Only his red hair and eyes above the waterline. His look beckoned her over. Against her better judgement, Nami made an excuse to slip into the water.

"I've been worried about you." Firth reached out to touch her. An invisible barrier held him back, fingertips brushing the water instead. He pulled his arm back in, his long brown coat fanning out around him. Nami ached to reach across the short distance. A chasm had sprung up between them. Like the tremors uncovering cracks beneath their feet. Too wide, too deep to cross.

"Is that man okay? From the rally?" Nami spoke first, her voice no more than a whisper. She was afraid to voice it and even more afraid of the response.

Firth's face was a mask of confusion. He mouthed her question back as if the words made no sense. Like she'd asked if the sky was still blue. His eyes puckered at the corners. "It was a show. He was never in any danger, you know that."

"Of course I did." The response escaped her lips without bidding. Teased out by Firth's sheer incredulity. She shrank down, small and foolish for asking – for having worried for days, the sight of the man's broken face filling her dreams. The sour stench of the braying crowd in her nose. Atop a still surface, her emotions remained fathomless. Incoherent. She was not silver-tongued as her brother. Hesitating, she forced herself to add, "There was a lot of blood."

"A show, no more. Something to get folk talking." Firth bit his lower lip, eyes dropping to look into empty hands. A lost boy, bewildered. "Nami ... I know the kumiho, the chinthe always assume the worst. I thought you were different, I thought you knew why we were doing this." His look was cutting. Like he'd plunged through the ice into glacial waters, the surface cracked and broken as his faith in her.

Nami reached across the gap, squeezing both his hands. "I'm sorry. You're right, I should've trusted you." She pushed every ounce of apology into her touch. Despairing at her ill-thought-out words. Idiot. Of course he was hurt. She should've listened to him, not the worries bouncing around her skull.

By degrees, Firth melted, softening until his hands took her own. Fingers intertwined. He warmed the frost on her fingertips, calming the tremors still running through her chest.

"Just trust me, okay? Like I trust you."

Nami nodded, not daring to speak again in case she ruined the moment, taking only shallow breaths. Firth's hand reached up to pat her head, flicking away a stray lock of hair. His open sleeves dripped seawater on her forehead and lashes, but she laughed them away.

They said their goodbyes and she slipped back to Trish. Took another bite of the skewer. Now that she was prepared for it, the taste was not so peculiar after all. Just different. Different was not bad. Different simply meant looking at things from another angle.

Chapter Twenty-Three

Mira watched Kai from the side of the race-day stage. Nothing like the dragon he was in private, and yet somehow the same. The same gentle insistence and warmth. She loved that he wore his antlers today. He was a magnetising figure in human form, but he was more than that. She imagined his breath on her ear. He was talking to her alone and not the crowd of thousands of Tiankawians. Heat rose to her cheeks and she reminded herself she was here for work.

"Captain." It was Lucia, her hands cupping a large leaf heaped with sticky lotus seed candy.

"I'm on duty."

"I'm not!" Lucia said with a grin. She looked so much younger in her rowing uniform of striped green. "Will you cheer for us?" She pushed the sweets against Mira's folded arms.

Mira paused for a long moment, then gave in. Took one of the sweets and popped it into her mouth. The flavours were filled with childhood nostalgia. "The others have bet on your team. You'd better win or they'll be scrounging dinners off me for the next month."

"Yes, Captain." The ensign winked, giving a clumsy fist-palm salute despite being laden with snacks. Mira remembered how the kids at her school had become luminaries when they were picked for the races. The disappointment when her name was never chosen.

The racing would last all day, starting with the junior events and going on into the early evening, when the betting really started. Already a dozen teams were warming up and waiting to be called, in different-coloured tunics and matching bandannas. They were bantering mocking chants at each other, the good-natured rivalry that their fans would yell across the waters. The smell of steamed buns and grilled shellfish carried from the street vendors, their wares in hanging baskets balanced on either end of bamboo poles.

Mira couldn't relax. She had heard the reports. The rumours flying around Qilin like summer mosquitoes. Lynnette had beaten a man up at a Drawback rally. A human! Without the pakalot so much as pinching her wrist. She didn't know what to believe, but she knew the Drawbacks were planning something. They had been getting bolder of late; their protests had an urgency that wasn't there before. Building to something. She had tried to warn Nami off, but knew fine well that the water dragon was unlikely to heed her words. Foisting her ama on her today was as much to ensure someone level-headed was watching out for her as it was the other way round.

Someone swore and there was a loud crash to one side. A street vendor had dropped his basket and grabbed at the food parcels that were rolling across the platform. One of the rowers reached down to help and the vendor hissed. The hairs on the back of Mira's neck rose with unease. She tried not to overreact. She had a tendency to see shadows and suspicious plots everywhere lately. The vendor looked up, his brown hooded coat rendering his face a shadow. He redoubled his efforts, frantic now that he'd seen her. Trusting her instincts, she cut an indirect path towards him.

Experience told her to keep slow and steady, not fast enough to send him running. She let herself meander as if she were only looking over the teams, smiling confidently, wishing a few luck in passing. All the while her eyes remained on him.

"Captain Mira," a commanding voice said. A hand gripped her shoulder.

Mira whirled, hand on her baston stick. It was Gede. "Shit."

He stopped short at her unconventional greeting, but swiftly removed his hand. Mira turned back, but her mark had gone.

"I'm working," she hissed. Gede flicked a crumb of the lotus sweet from her lapel and held it up on his finger with an arched eyebrow. "What do you want?"

"To invite you to watch the races with us. We've a hotel overlooking the course. And the food is much better than down here." His voice positively dripped with gold.

Mira wondered if she had misheard. Of course Samnang had booked a whole hotel. "Shouldn't you be working? This is technically kumiho jurisdiction."

Gede tutted. "Oh come, the chinthe can handle a few drunks." And even though his words echoed her own sentiments, coming from his mouth she found them hard to swallow.

"I'll take my chances with the street food." She could at least go and examine where the vendor had been, see if there was anything suspicious.

Her mind whizzed ahead and she was making to move when Gede grabbed her elbow. He hissed in her ear so others couldn't hear. "You think opportunities like this come up every day? There'll be Council members, senior officials there, perhaps even the Fenghuang. Your bill ... Are you really so self-important that you'll turn your nose up?"

Part of her recognised the truth in his words. She acknowledged now with great reluctance that networking was part of the game. But she also realised the rules were different for her. What worked for Gede, the human son of a kumiho, would not work for an opinionated half-siren. Especially one without connections or money to fold into her sleeves. If she were an actual Council member, things might be different, but they'd never vote her in. They'd made that abundantly clear.

"I'm working," she repeated. Didn't trust herself to say any more. Stared hard at the hand on her elbow. Her baston was still in her hand and she gripped it until her knuckles turned white.

"We have more in common than you think, Captain. We could be great allies."

He had aimed for a persuasive tone, Mira suspected, but instead it came across as somewhat pleading. Desperate. She shrugged off his grip.

Chapter Twenty-Four

Qiuyue had of course told her friend Finnol about the upcoming party. About sampling all the pastries to test them and listening to the musicians audition. About the ice sculpture her mother had commissioned and the individual gift bags. As instructed, she'd even divulged the name of the couture dressmaker who'd draped "Serena" in a gown of silver and blue damask. Now the little girl twisted at the waist, hands behind her as she watched the fabric of her own pink dress swishing to and fro. Fathomfolk-made, Cordelia noted, although the label and price would say otherwise. The traditional Iyonessian embroidery about the hem a defiant disclosure.

"And Finnol's mummies?" she asked.

Qiuyue was determined to grind crumbs into dust with the toes of her new shoes, bored of the interrogation. "I only saw Auntie Ayumu. She didn't say anything, but she spilled tea on herself."

Cordelia's smile widened as she let her daughter raid the buffet table once more. Children had the guileless ability to piss people off. Her favourite type of messenger.

She'd invited the journalists first. The nosy one from the *Lontar Journal*, the subdued one from the *Manshu Chronicle*. A photographer was harder to find at late notice, but she traded in old debts. Suddenly one became available, even if his hands shook as he set up his equipment.

In the days leading up to the Boat Races, they came knocking at her door one by one – just happened to be in the area – with their unsubtle questions and their baskets of fruit. Fawning compliments and thick paws. The ministers, the senior officials and even the junior officials, casually asking what her plans were for race day. Throwing a party – no, they hadn't heard. Yes, they did happen to be free. Perhaps they would pop by, just for an hour or two. Samnang went from sceptical to a full-on apology. He should have known better.

The Minister of Defence now greeted the new arrivals, deftly handing a glass of sweet plum wine to the Minister of Agriculture and a cup of tea to his husband. The murmured conversation did not carry to Cordelia's ears, but she heard the compliments all the same. "Of course," Samnang waved his hand, "details are important, especially when it comes to friends and allies."

She cringed, her hands straightening the serving spoons on the table. They had spent evenings revising the names, the interests of each important party, but did he have to be so heavy-handed? Might as well take the notes out of his sleeve. She allowed herself to indulge in a sigh before turning, the gracious hostess as ever.

Of course, it was a shame that the Minister of Justice couldn't make it. She'd heard . . . well, no, she wasn't one to gossip, but she'd heard he'd taken a long trip to the Southern islands. His position would indeed be up for election soon.

She worked the room, flowing like a welcome breeze between her guests. Serena, Samnang's beautiful and genial wife. A calming touch here, a rousing comment there. Planting just enough seeds in fertile ground as she topped up their glasses. Samnang would benefit from a challenge, Minister of Defence was all well and good for upholding laws, but to *make* laws – now that was his true calling.

Just as she was scanning the room with a mental list of who was missing, two figures slunk in through the door behind one of the waiting staff. Faces hidden in heavy cloaks, they moved around the perimeter of the room, darting between columns and groups that idled with drinks in hand. Cordelia cut her guest off mid sentence, homing straight in. Grabbed at the hand that darted out towards the lavish buffet table. She twisted the arm around, eliciting a small yell of pain. She was looking for a vial of poison, a hidden blade or other danger. She'd not been expecting the Minister of Ceremonies' two children pilfering black sesame pastries.

Qiuyue squealed, running over to hug Finnol. The boy was not at all embarrassed. He threw back his cloak and let Qiuyue lead him around the party, taking morsels from each of the fine porcelain platters. His chaperoning sister had the decency to look sheepish. Eun pushed her smudged glasses back up and rubbed at the wrist Cordelia finally let go. "Auntie Serena," she said belatedly. Tried for a charming grin, and, in Cordelia's estimation, failed. The young woman spent too much time with books and not enough with people.

Cordelia let her squirm, the silence between them inflating like a paper balloon. Pyanis's daughter from her first marriage didn't often show her face at society events. She much preferred dusty archives and sending in corrections to newssheets. Ayumu frequently complained that her stepdaughter refused to make herself useful, neither taking up a ministry position nor betrothing herself to a political ally.

"Finnol just wouldn't stop harping on about these marvellous pastries that Qiuyue had told him about, and I said, well in fact the best way to decide this is with empirical evidence. But that perhaps his mother would disapprove and therefore a discreet method of entry was for the best. We would definitely appreciate it if you kept our presence here, eh, inconspicuous." Eun fidgeted with the knotted fastenings of her dress. It was an unflattering shape on her, wrinkled and sagging where it should tuck in, tight where it should flow. Pulled from the bottom of her clothing chest with great haste. If she cared to try, the young woman would easily have turned heads. She still did when she was less self-conscious. Cordelia for once agreed with Ayumu's exasperation. A wasted opportunity.

Still, not her problem.

She plastered the widest smile across her features. Her cheeks ached from it. Clapped her hands in delight as her voice rang above the pleasant din of conversation. "Absolutely delighted you could join us. Samnang, come, have you met the Minister of Ceremonies' children? We simply must get a photograph together!"

She pretended not to notice the scowl on Eun's face. Propelled her with a palm against her back into the maw of the gathering.

Chapter Twenty-Five

The children's teams scuttled across a min-
iature race course in their bathtub boats, spinning in the water
much to the amusement of the crowd. The good-natured cheering
was infectious, and Nami found herself joining in. The comedy
teams came next, one group dressed like ibis birds, another in
oddly revealing silk pyjamas resembling kumiho uniforms. She
shared a wry look with Trish at that, both wondering what Mira
would think. Nami grinned as the rowers clashed oars and ridi-
culed each other with bawdy insults.

The light was fading to grey and the lanterns were lit as the
last two races were announced. Nami wrapped the borrowed
scarf around her shoulders, glad she'd taken Trish's advice. The
rowing teams each had a coordinated introductory dance. The
first group wore red and black and climbed into a human pyr-
amid. The yellow team would not be outdone. Fans with long
orange tails dipped and rose like serpents as they ran across the
stage. The blue team had a song, clapping and thigh-slapping to
a beautifully rendered chant. Fathomfolk. Finally the green team
cartwheeled in, backflipping off each other's knees and tumbling
to the floor. The crowd carried Nami in a wave of excitement,
enthusiasm no longer a polite facade.

The boat bobbed precariously as the stallholder raised her fist
and screamed the name of her favourites. The shimmer of the

gong rumbled and oars rose en masse, the sleek boats sliding forward. The crowd roared, pellet drums and wooden rattles adding to the cacophony. The difference in speed and agility compared to the preceding races was stark. The red boat surged ahead, deftly easing around the first buoy in a loop before the rowers dug in, shooting for the second one. The yellow boat was not far behind, the sunfish head pushing forward. Green and blue were behind, slightly less coordinated but putting in a valiant effort nonetheless.

Nami's eyes focused on the lead boats. She could see the drummer beating out a steady rhythm but couldn't hear it above the din. They'd looped gracefully in the opposite direction around the second buoy and headed towards the weaving section.

"Something's wrong." Trish drew her attention to the lagging boats. The green boat was in trouble, the rowers uncoordinated and shouting at each other. Some had stopped rowing altogether. Nami wondered if they'd decided to drop out. Suddenly the person at the helm stood up and jumped into the water. Others did too, an overfilled container spilling at its sides.

The blue boat had stopped. The crew were gesticulating. Started rowing backwards. The other two were too far ahead to even notice the commotion.

"They're sinking!" Trish said, her voice shuddering with horror.

Rowers from the blue boat extended oars, pulling in the floating swimmers as best they could. The green boat was obviously in trouble now, lying low in the water. The few remaining people were panicking. Sitting there shouting in the waterlogged vessel like mewing hatchlings.

Could they not swim?

By the abyss, they couldn't swim.

Nami stood up, the stallholder's boat rocking precariously, and closed her eyes. Let her true dragon form out. The people around her gasped, awestruck. *It's her. Daughter of Yonakuni.*

Dragon.

Pearl.

She ignored them, focusing on the scales she had hidden since her arrival. They grew from her skin like leaves unfurling from a vine. Down her neck and arms; up her jawline and temples. They kept coming, faster now, dazzling in the witchlight until she was nothing but silver and light. Her antlers grew to full length, branching from her forehead like a magnificent crown. Her body stretched like a ribbon, long and slim. It was not a shape for the narrow walkways and stilt-filled submerged spaces of Jingsha, but here there was open water.

The freedom of it made her dizzy. Exhilarated and afraid. Released from the fastenings that pressed against her in human shape. It had been so long since she'd had the chance to be in water dragon form. It felt familiar and yet different – like she had forgotten how to simply be. To exist without thinking about what it meant, what *she* meant. Her spines fanned up instinctively as she shook off the feeling, diving into the water.

The rush of expectation lapped over her head with the cold salt of the sea, and she dipped back under to shut out the noise. Focus. Longer than one of the race boats, she cut across the remaining space fast, her long whiskers helping her to navigate the murky waters. It was deep here, the race location chosen for exactly that reason. Under the froth of the swimmers and oars, it was hard to see what was happening. Some of the rowers had been pulled to safety by the blue team. But there were four, maybe five people still thrashing about on the boat as it plunged below the surface. Nami flicked her tail and slammed her shoulder into the bow, pushing it up. She heard someone gasp for air, wet and gargling, before the weight of the vessel pulled them back under.

She might be longer than the boat, but she did not have the strength to back that up. Couldn't get a good grip. The shape was unwieldy in her dragon form, slipping between her shoulder blades as she tried to curl her tail around the tiller to keep it afloat. It stayed on the surface longer this time, long enough for her to twist her neck around and meet the eyes of two of the humans, tangled beneath oars and splintered hull. She was too big, too clumsy to pull them out. But in human form she was even weaker.

One of the stronger swimmers from the boat had approached the side. "Come on!" But the other rower shook her head, gripping the sides with a white-knuckled hold. The whole thing rocked precariously with the motion. Screams pierced Nami's ears.

She flipped onto her back, using her claws to hold the boat aloft. Splintered wood and oars fell onto her, the hull crumbling precariously. Panicked feet kicked through the broken planks, thudding into her torso. She slipped. The boat was sinking fast. Plummeting into the depths. People flailed. Water filled her mouth. Burned her gills.

Think, dammit! Don't freeze. Don't just watch them drowning. She screamed at herself but her limbs failed to respond. A tiny voice whispered in the back of her mind: isn't this what you wanted? Screw all humans, right?

A piercing arrow of waterweaving shot past her. It formed under a drowning man, focused on the water beneath him. Cushioned his limbs in a bed of bubbles that buoyed him to the surface. She recognised the precision, the signature of the weaving as if it were her own. Kai. Relief poured through her body as she spotted her brother swimming towards them, one hand outstretched to keep the water flowing. Still in human shape, he was much more dexterous.

His familiar presence calmed her panic. Allowed her to fall back into the role of little sister and follow his lead. Kai had thought about this. Realised dragon form was not the best under the circumstances. Absorbed the lessons she had seen as pointless. He had tried to teach her, so many futile times back in

Yonakuni, but she simply would not listen. She was listening now. But perhaps it was too late.

He gestured down, shaking her from her reverie. She dived once more to support the other struggling rowers. Streamed past the first one, slowly enough that they could grasp onto her antlers, before manoeuvring towards the second. The noise of the crowd assailed her as she burst through the waves with the two of them on her back. Relief and cheering.

"Is that everyone?" Kai's gills opened wide from the effort of the sustained waterweaving.

"Lucia, where's Lucia?" someone asked. A woman looked down at the two dragons. "She was carrying Maddox!"

Kai swore and launched himself back into the water, Nami hot on his heels. It was near impossible to see with the silt they'd kicked up. Nami had to rely on her whiskers to feel and smell in the water. The green boat had broken into large pieces, the manta ray figurehead sloping in a slow downwards drift. Nami split away from Kai, fanning to the right of him and snaking through the water, eyes trained down into the depths. She didn't want to see it. Knew what they were looking for, how long the missing pair had been in the water without surfacing, but she didn't want to be the one to find them.

They were hidden initially by the shadows of derelict buildings. Two figures drifting together, arms spread as if enjoying a leisurely float, but the unnaturally opened eyes made Nami shudder. She reached the woman's body first. Her striped green headband had fallen over one eye. As Nami reached out to grab her, something moved. The flip of a tail into the shadow of the building below.

She didn't react fast enough. Didn't think to give chase until it was too late. In any case, she couldn't leave the bodies. As preposterous as the thought was, she couldn't leave them alone. It ... wasn't right.

They brought them to the surface, Nami watching with detachment as the healers tried to breathe life into them, pumped at their chests, touched fingers to their necks. The only way anyone could survive that long was if they had gills. She let the water cover her mouth, concealed the grimace on her lips. Kai tugged at her foreclaw, pulling her back underwater.

They dived in silence to the submerged buildings. As they searched, Nami haltingly explained what she'd seen. Unsurprised when they found nothing. Her brother's face was still. "It was no accident."

She ran through possible reasons in her head. But it was undeniable. The pieces of the hull littering the seabed could not have been caused by wear and tear. It would have been obvious well before the rowers got in, in the several races before the main event. Something had happened during the race, out in the open, in deep water, to puncture the hull so thoroughly.

"Fathomfolk did this." Kai's hands covered his face.

"We wouldn't," Nami objected, although her voice faltered. An act of protest. An act of terror. Lynnette's fist in the man's face at the rally. How far were they willing to go?

"We need to get back. You didn't see anything, Nami."

"You just said—" she started in confusion.

"Without suspects to arrest, you'd be as good as pointing the finger at all folk." Kai swallowed, and suddenly Nami saw the echoes of soft cheeks and an unlined forehead. Her brother as a child solemnly explaining the world's truths to her. "Ourselves included."

"But we rescued them." The echoes of the crowd reverberated in her ears from when she had changed forms to jump into the water. *Dragon. Pearl.* They might as well have said it aloud. Saviour, that was what they meant.

"We set it up to make ourselves look good," Kai said. His eyes held hers, unblinking. She had to break contact first. He didn't believe that, of course he didn't. But now that he'd voiced it, she could see the links. Fathomfolk murderers and rescuers. Too much of a coincidence. Too tidy.

"It's not as if we're all in on it," she said. "That we have one collective will."

"Are they going to believe that? The Council, the families?"

"I . . ." She didn't know what to say. She wanted to say something. Anything. It seemed wrong to keep silent. Duplicitous. But she couldn't argue with his logic. The cold hand of pragmatism between her shoulder blades. She knew he was right. But she also hated that he was. Hated that telling the truth was not the solution. That even her earnest brother had been worn down by the tide.

Chapter Twenty-Six

Mira ran towards the edge of the stage and stared at the two bodies. A young man – no, a boy really, wet hair slick across his face. She blinked, looked away at … Lucia. Her bright-eyed ensign. A few hours ago, she'd had a mouthful of sweets. She fell to her knees beside the healer, took Lucia's hand. If it were not for the dull weight of her, the young woman could have been asleep. Mira tucked her sodden clothes back into place, trying desperately to push back the tears.

"You can swim!" she told her. She had watched Lucia in practice. Timed her holding her breath underwater. She didn't mean it to be an accusation, and yet it was not fair. Her bitterness like an oily film coating her lungs and making her wheeze. Swimming was still rare among humans in the city; perceived as something only folk needed to do.

"She turned back to help," a slight woman said, gesturing at the second body.

Of course she turned back. Lucia had been talking about the races for months: a family tradition. She'd finally been picked for the team. Lifting weights in the break room, wrapping her blistered hands in bandages, mercilessly mocked by the others. It didn't bother her. She had waved them off without a backwards glance, her rucksack bouncing as she trotted to the tram station.

Someone was kneeling beside Mira. Kai. She gazed at him, the familiar planes and contours of his skin unchanged. Unharmed. Paler than usual, but that might just be his grim expression. She squeezed his hand. Thankful.

A rush of clamouring voices hit them. The other rowers. Who would've done this? Who had access to the vessels? Why? The nasal voice of the junior official who'd been commentating. Kumiho and chinthe guards glared at each other, pushing jostling onlookers out of the way. Baston sticks were out, hands were on the hilts of supposedly ceremonial blades. A strangled sound burned in Mira's throat. Her worst fears realised.

She glanced at the glass-fronted building. How long before they looked up from their rice wine? Had they even been watching the races at all? The early moon reflected off the windows, giving nothing away. She closed her eyes. All she wanted was a moment to mourn. It would have to wait.

"Cancel the rest," she said. She wanted to say more. Ask who had sabotaged the boats, if there was any evidence. But people pressed in and it wouldn't be appropriate to voice guesses in public. They needed calm.

Kai nodded, a united front. "Ask everyone to go home. We'll let them know more tomorrow."

The official commentator wavered, the silver head of the microphone clutched in his palm like he would prefer to lob it at the water dragon. He glanced at Mira's uniform, her captain insignia outranking him, and reluctantly made the announcement.

The people murmured, a discontented rumble beneath the surface. The musicians played the traditional end-of-the-evening song and scattered groups started to trail off. Mira spotted Mikayil and a few other chinthe. Signalled to them. They nodded and disappeared into the crowd. They should know. Should have a moment for their comrade. But the need to prevent panic was greater than individual needs.

It was always going to be a bottleneck at the end of the evening.

Some people had come early for good viewing spots. Others had gone to their own celebration first, showing up in full spirits only when the lanterns were lit. The walkways heaved and the lines for taxi boats stretched out long.

"Who sent people away?" a voice called out. Samnang – finally – his wife by his side. His pupils were dilated and his breath sour with alcohol. "The rowers must have seen something. Call them for questioning!"

"They're in shock. With the healers. We need to deal with the crowd first," Mira said.

"Nonsense! You'll let the perpetrators slip away? Not while I'm Defence Minister."

Mira noticed now the gaggle of other Council members, many still holding their drinks. Hems of outfits costing more than her month's salary were held up gingerly against the saltwater sloshing at their feet. A great fatigue settled over her shoulders. Samnang was gesturing, and blue-uniformed kumiho barred a family of selkies from the edge of the walkway. The father pointed at the water, jiggling a crying toddler on his hip, but the guard shoved him back. Next to him a bunyip puffed out his shaggy brown fur in annoyance, making him appear bigger than he actually was as he intervened. They were too far away for Mira to pick up the words, but she could guess from the expression on the bunyip's flat face. Samnang waved at Gede. The young man was more than happy to head towards the healer's tent, cracking his neck and hands as he swaggered.

"With all due respect, Minister Samnang, it's dangerous to keep everyone here. We don't have the numbers. People will panic." Mira spoke as slowly as she could, keeping the emotion in her voice tempered. Inside she was screaming at him. *Don't do this. Don't make it worse.*

"Two humans are dead!" He stepped forward, a whole head taller than her. The reek of his breath made her eyes smart, but she held his eyes without flinching. His voice was loud, the words carrying through the crowd. The ripple of anger and fear passed from one person to the next. *Dead? Did he say dead?* Titans below, he wanted this. The realisation sank through her like heavy stones. The panic, the chaos. One fucking political manoeuvre after another.

"One was my ensign. The chinthe will honour her. But we don't know who caused this. We also don't know if they've planned anything else." Her neck ached from looking up at him. They were technically of equal rank, the captains of the kumiho and the chinthe. But everyone knew that was a falsehood. She had no jurisdiction here. Her captain status didn't mean shit in a face-off with the Defence Minister. Fighting steel with paper.

"Are you threatening my husband?" Serena suddenly chipped in, hand fluttering against her collarbone.

Mira was flustered. She'd been so focused on Samnang she'd hardly noticed the woman until now. "What? No! I was stating my reasons."

The kumiho's wife cowered, shaking as if Mira had struck her a blow. She tugged at Samnang's sleeve like a frightened child. "She knows more than she's letting on."

"Because all fathomfolk are terrorists?" Mira snapped. The words flew from her mouth. She couldn't stop them. Samnang's eyebrows darted upwards in delight. Just what he'd been looking for. A hysterical estuary.

Serena took a small step backwards, looking fearful. Samnang wrapped his arm around her. Mira wanted to scream, but it would simply add to the tableau. Kai attempted to insert himself between them. "You need space to do the excellent investigative work that is required. Lady Serena, perhaps someone could escort you and your daughter home."

Samnang's wife bit her bottom lip a little before glancing around with dawning realisation. Then she grabbed her husband's hand, reticence gone. "Where's Qiuyue?"

Samnang swatted her away like a fly. "I don't know. Probably still at the hotel." He gestured, and one of his guards rushed to bring the microphone over. For a fleeting moment Serena's features darkened, before she pushed her way back towards the building.

"This is Minister of Defence Samnang. Two humans have been brutally murdered today. Deliberately drowned."

Kai grabbed Mira's hand, giving it another tight squeeze. "I'll be at the healers' tent," he whispered as Samnang droned on. He could not speak out against Samnang, not out here under public scrutiny. Not as the ambassador.

"The people responsible are in our midst. No one is to leave the area." Samnang looked satisfied with his proclamation. Revelled in stepping up where others had failed. His glance slid disdainfully towards Mira as he handed back the microphone. But before he could bombard her with insults, everything went downhill.

Chapter Twenty-Seven

The stallholder was packing up, shooing Nami away. "I don't know, she must have left," the woman said, not even looking. A tray of fishballs tipped into the water in her haste. Her metal pans banged together with tangible urgency. Announcements were made over a loudspeaker, but between the stallholder's racket and the thick Tiankawian accent, Nami wasn't sure what it was about.

She could convince herself, almost had, that Trish had got a boat back to Webisu district. After all, the elder siren seemed more than capable of looking after herself. But then her eye caught sight of a familiar object. Trish's walking stick. Still leaning by the back of the boat. She picked it up, a shiver running through her.

"Trish?" she called. It felt idiotic, calling out like a child in the middle of the chaos, but it was the only thing her panicked head could do. She brandished the stick in front of the stallholder. The woman finally stopped what she was doing, giving Nami a sympathetic look. "Look, I don't know. I'm not her minder. If you value your skin, you'll get out of here while you can."

"What do you mean?"

"Weren't you listening? The kumiho has just closed us in. We're all suspects. I for one don't think some Jingsha-born minister is going to give a damn about actual guilt."

Fathomfolk did this. Kai's words reverberated in her skull, hot and accusing. The image of Lynnette's bloody knuckles flashed unbidden. What was she capable of? A cold trickle ran from her neck in a slow snake down her spine that had nothing to do with wet clothing. They couldn't have . . . They wanted equality, that was all. Same as her.

The festival flags were suddenly out of place against the worried faces, hidden under scarves and hoods as people dispersed. Humans and folk alike bundled their children close to them and headed for the walkways and moored boats. A window shutter slammed as a guard shoved a slight man. They were shouting in each other's faces, the gills of the festivalgoer hissing open and closed. Nami edged past them, tentatively calling Trish's name.

"Is that a weapon?" someone said. It was unclear whose voice it was, but the fear was apparent. Even as Nami turned to explain, people shrank back. She held the walking stick up to her face as if it could tell her where Trish was.

The whole city was going in the opposite direction, rippling out towards open water. Overhead, on the skybridges, families were almost running, flags and noisemakers discarded. Someone slammed into Nami. Then another, and another. The walkways were as crowded as a peak-time tram. Bodies. Arms shoving, shoes scraping her heels. She couldn't see, couldn't breathe in the sea of people, the frantic push, buffeting her like driftwood battered against rocks. Her feet couldn't move faster than a shuffle. Panic bobbed in her throat like a fishbone. People were yelling, swearing. The hot breath of strangers on her face, taking up precious air. Someone behind her shoved hard, crushing her. Black spots threatened the edges of her vision.

The voices rose, the sound of panic like a breaking wave. An aching groan and the walkway began to split underfoot. Suddenly the crowd surged forward.

Two nearby kumiho guards barred the way, their ceremonial swords drawn in one hand, bastons in the other as they screamed – *Back, back!* – until their voices were hoarse. But the leading edge could do nothing to stall the stampede. Those behind pushed on, relentless. Captain Samnang's voice blared over the loudspeakers. "Only the guilty run!"

Nami was swept along in the tide. Others fell under a trample of feet. She grabbed at someone's hand, only for it to be ripped away. The crowd carried her closer to the wall of a nearby building, and instinctively she leapt. Anything to be free of the crush. Her right hand missed, but the left caught the edge of a low-swinging sign. Her arm burned, but she ignored it, dragging her body up by sheer will. *Climb*, she commanded her limbs. *Climb.*

Others tried the same, reaching up for window ledges, lamp posts, even washing lines. Anything that would pull them out of the crush. A woman pushed her young son upwards until he hung on the lower rungs of a ladder. She was swept away from under him. Nami averted her eyes. She couldn't watch. Couldn't help.

Clambering onto one of the lower bridges, she took a moment. There. A couple of chinthe officers. She gulped down her misgivings. After all, Mira was the captain. "I need help," she said.

"Out of my face, saltie!" one of them replied. He didn't even meet her eye, staring instead at the exposed gills on her neck. The scales along her cheekbone she had not yet bothered to retract.

"I've lost an elder siren. Just tell Captain Mira, she—"

The guard's face loomed large next to hers, his nose almost on her forehead. "Fish fucker, I could arrest you for that tone!"

"Wh-what tone?" She was genuinely perplexed, holding her hands out.

"Insubordination. You think you can tell me what to do?"

"No, I was just saying that Captain Mira's moth—"

His hand was on his baston stick and Nami realised it didn't matter what she said. His eyes had almost glazed over with the intensity of his hatred. Shouts came from the direction of the tram station, distracting him. The other guard mouthed silently to Nami: *Go.* She stared at him for an uncomprehending second. He gestured with his hands. She didn't wait to be told a third time. Ignoring the cursing and shouts that followed, she ran.

She turned up the collar of her jacket as she took another set of stairs towards the higher tiers. Up here it was less crowded, but people were still worried. Groups of humans stood dithering, waiting as they had been asked to, while others moved purposefully away from the race site. People caught her eye then slid off, everyone suddenly furtive and guilty. Her breath coming thick and fast, on the edge of hyperventilating. Trish. How could she possibly find one elder siren in all of this?

Her distracted ears started to listen to what was being said around her. Flashes of fear and anger sparked the air.

"... had to be salties. Playing dirty, that's what ..."

"And that smooth-talking ambassador? Minister of Fathomfolk, my arse. Relax the pakalots? Make 'em tighter."

"It's worse two bridges over, fighting has broken out."

"Walk, or someone will notice. She was alive when we left her, okay. I'm sure of it."

Nami turned to look, but the people had passed, flowing on so she couldn't find the owner of the last voice. She saw two figures hurrying from her and moved to grab at one of them. A young face turned in panic, already near tears. A lanky boy holding tightly to an older man. He pulled away before she could apologise.

She retraced her steps across the bridge, ears pricking up for the furtive discussion. But it had been one fragment, blurred with the adrenaline of the day. And everyone looked suspicious; half-lidded glances cast in all directions. A crowd was forming on the far side of the bridge, near the closed tram platform. The muttering was different here.

"Trish!" Nami shouted. Ran without thinking.

People shook their heads, huddled to look down at a crumpled heap. Cooing sympathetically from an awkward distance. A mother pulled her children away, gripping them tightly by the hand. Nami wedged her way between the onlookers, forcing a gap to squeeze through. A body was curled up on stone steps. "Trish?" she said. Two human men stood over it.

"What?" asked one, puffing his chest up brashly. Nami recognised the tone from the earlier guard. Looking for a fight. It had not been satisfying enough then, beating up an elder. He loomed over her, a wall of flab more than muscle. She was irritated when she felt herself flinch. "Move on, bottom-feeder!"

The crowd slid back, whispering for the guards and yet mesmerised by the unfolding scene. The other man also stepped up to her, the planks beneath him creaking as the weight of both settled. "Saltie's got water in her ears."

"What did you do?" Nami hissed through her teeth.

"None of your business," snapped the larger man.

"Nothing he didn't deserve."

He. The mass moved, and where she'd expected to see a face, there was just a shaggy mass of kelp. A jangjamari. He lifted an arm, blood trailing from the limb to the pool beneath him. They had dragged him, bloody and broken. Thrown him down the stairs from the upper skybridge.

It was not Trish. It was not Hong-Gi. But it was still a person.

Anger simmered in her veins, and she spat out without thinking, "You'll pay for this."

The men both stared for a long moment, then burst out laughing. Doubled over and pointing, tears squeezed from eyes as they guffawed. The first one patted her on the head before she slapped his hand away. Indulging her like a pet yapping at their feet.

"Why, you—" As she moved forward, the pakalot pinch on her arm tightened. Sharp pain lanced down the limb and she breathed in through her teeth to stop herself from screaming. Her legs buckled under her.

"She thought about it!" said the second man, almost jumping with glee. "Thought about knifing you between the ribs."

"Fucking shark bait." The first man folded his arms, nudged Nami just a little with his foot. Her rage grew. She knew she should think of other things, ways of diplomacy and tact that would stop her pakalot from pulsing thick waves of nausea to her skull. She couldn't. The image of Trishanjali bleeding in a corner somewhere filled her mind. As she pulled herself back up to standing, her vision blurred at the edges.

She gathered water in her fists, in the toecaps of her shoes. One knee to the groin, that was all. One swift blow. She could endure this. Pain was in the mind. All a lie. If she pushed hard enough, she could get past it. Ignore the poker of heat burning her back. She was strong enough.

Her foot shuffled forward. A painfully victorious half-step.

But it burned. Sharp pinpricks travelled down her fingers and burrowed in her palms. Searing heat pressed against her spine. She was on fire. Her whole body ignited. The men's braying faces loomed over her and everything turned black.

Chapter Twenty-Eight

"One at a time!" Mira said. It was like shouting into a whirlpool. Folk kept diving into the water, some not even waiting until they had reached the surface-level walkways but leaping from windows and bridges into narrow channels below. She had enough experience with drunk diving to know someone was going to get injured. They'd be lucky if it was just a few broken bones.

"Captain?" Mikayil said at her side.

"Do you want to get in their way?" she snapped. Samnang's demand that the guards stop people was what had caused panic in the first place. And by the titans, her chinthe didn't have to take orders from him.

"Fighting has broken out."

"Fighting?" He had her attention now.

The grim-faced lieutenant nodded, hands behind his back formally. It must be bad. "Between humans and fathomfolk. On the Thmanbok and Arimo skybridges, behind the Soksan Building as well."

"That's not fighting." Mira touched her wrist, bare of the pakalot that others endured. Mikayil's eyes narrowed. "That's the beginnings of a bloodbath."

They ran all the way to the Arimo bridge. It was over long before they'd even got there. Mira crouched by the first victim.

They'd been pounded to a swollen mess, arm twisted at an unnatural angle. She found a weak pulse. The second and third were much the same. But the last one had been cut across the gills. Blood oozed from the wound. They gasped through their mouth and nose as Mira called for an oxygen canister. Estuary, just like her.

"We're no good tending the wounded," she said as the healers arrived. "Where're the goddamn city guard? Samnang did this."

She tried to shake off her frustration. She needed to think. Her guards were spread thin, communication already sporadic. They had to get to the problem areas before fighting broke out, not after. Her exasperation gave way to sudden clarity. "Get me guards on the roofs of the hotel, the tram station, anywhere with a vantage point and a telephone."

"Commandeer the telephone exchange?" Mikayil got her meaning immediately.

"If we must."

"That's an emergency protocol, Captain." He paused. "The Council haven't authorised it."

Mira turned to look him in the eye. She knew why he was pushing it. Not because he didn't believe in her. The opposite, in fact. They'd trained and worked together for years. She'd been at his sons' birthday parties and spent many a Boat Race Day with him, Tam and their families. He knew full well what she was doing. He was the prudent voice that ensured she'd thought about all consequences.

"If it's a choice between my career and saving lives, you know my decision."

He saluted, no more questions. Mira sent him off immediately, didn't want him around in case she changed her mind.

At the telephone exchange, she dialled in for the Fenghuang's office. The line was engaged. Of course it was. Every official in Tiankawi had probably called, panicked about their own safety.

She filled in a telegram instead, leaving the message in the flustered hands of an operator.

The evening flew by in a flurry of calls and pins in a map, sending chinthe to break up fights, rescue stranded families and tend to injuries. She couldn't directly rebuke Samnang's command, but she ignored his repeated demands for more guards at the waterfront. His hoarse shouts through the crackling loudspeaker system were less and less coherent as the night wore on. It was a futile exercise anyway; even if they could barricade the waterfront by the race site, there were a hundred ways to slip under.

The phone rang. Mira had answered it a hundred times already and yet the ring was still shrill. "Yes?"

"The corner of the old cobbler's."

"I need more than that," she said irritably with her pen in hand, putting a small cross on the location. Two blocks from where she was.

"It's your mother, Captain!"

The telephone was left swinging by its cord as Mira sprinted out of the door.

Noise roared in her ears as she ran on feet too slow, incapable of keeping up with her fears. She screamed for people to get out of her way, careered into a stack of crates and powered through. It was a false alarm. It must be. Trish was with Nami; how could she be in danger with a dragon at her side? She'd assumed they'd got out early. That Nami would stay with her mother. Protect her. An image of Nami's face, contorted in disgust at their first altercation, her feelings about sirens, rose unbidden in Mira's mind.

She slammed into a wall as she turned the corner. There. Her ama's distinctive voice from a walkway three floors up. A mellow alto blasting a defensive siren song. The space between buildings was too narrow for Mira to see. Feet creaked on wooden planks, shadow monsters overhead.

"Get back! On chinthe command!" she shouted up.

Trish called her name. No stairs here and no time to double back. Mira slammed into the cobbler's door. The solid wood smacked her back, unyielding. She screamed her frustration as she turned her attention instead to the slatted windows, kicking at the closest one until the panels splintered and broke. She scrambled through the broken frame, roughly pushing aside the display of shoes and leather. Up the internal stairs, ignoring the cobbler and his family cowering at the back of the shop. Out of the skylight in the attic and onto the green-tiled roof. She slid down it at a crouch, rolling onto the upper walkway.

A thin line of blood trailed down the planks, smeared and scuffed in places by shoes. She could see them in the distance, a huddled group of four or five, glancing back as they walked swiftly, not quite running. They made awkward silhouettes, hunched as if carrying heavy loads. She saw the orange and pink of her mother's favourite festival outfit. An outfit Mira had wrapped round herself as a child, spinning again and again with the bells on her ankles jangling as she waited for her ama to return from work.

She ran.

No direct harm. No waterweaving directed at humans, even without a pakalot on her wrist. That was the law. Yes, she had special dispensation, but without witnesses to confirm her actions, she could lose more than her job. But she had been brought up in this city. Tested its edges her whole life and learned from each paper cut. She knew the loopholes long before they'd removed the shackle.

They were running now, making no pretence of a casual pace. Still they had time to hurl insults. Fish fucker. Bottom-feeder. Slurs she'd heard so often they fell like rain on a pitched roof. Without missing a step, she reached for the throwing knives concealed in the lining of her jacket. Held them between her fingers and aimed. The first hit the hanging laundry rope perfectly, snapping the taut line so that it swung down, scattering clothes on the assailants. One of them was caught in the sheets and Mira sprinted past. No time for questioning.

The second knife missed, embedding itself into the masonry. The third she aimed at the street stall to the side of the walkway. The pierced basket sent vegetables rolling across the path, tripping one runner and thwarting another long enough for Mira to catch up. Neither carried a burden big enough to be a person.

The last two suddenly split up, one turning down the side of some buildings, the other ploughing straight on. Mira hesitated for only a second, her eyes trained on the pink scarf flapping from the one who'd continued straight.

The walkway led down in a series of narrow stairs between buildings towards sea level. A few moored boats bobbed below. If they reached the water ... Mira didn't know. She couldn't be sure if they were human or folk. They'd not used waterweaving against her, but then again, neither had she. Underwater, they'd be gone in a flash.

She looked up, seeing the ubiquitous shop signs hanging precariously between the buildings. They never seemed to take them down, the carcasses of the older signs simply covered by gaudy paint and newer signage. She flicked her remaining knives, one, two, three, at the overhead ropes and pulleys holding up the swinging boards. They cut true, fraying the thick moss-covered rope.

"Stop! Stop or I'll do it!" she warned.

They kept running.

She swore under her breath and released her last knife. As the largest sign was released from its tether, it swayed into the next and the next, and the whole thing came crashing down.

She ran towards it, baston drawn. Ducked under and barrel-rolled into the assailant, throwing them both down the last few steps before they were flattened by the falling signs. The air was crushed from her lungs, but she cared not, dragging the unconscious assailant off her mother. Pushed them aside and ...

She gawked at a stranger's face, a half-grown child. The girl stared back at her for the longest moment, then burst into tears, wrapping her arms around her rescuer. She wore a pretty festival dress, fuchsia pink and embellished with lotus petals. Her clothes indicated she was no street urchin; a child of a councillor perhaps.

Mira resisted the urge to push the girl away. But by the time she looked up, the perpetrator was long gone.

"I want my ama," the child wailed.

So do I.

Mira took a moment to compose herself, to keep the annoyance from her voice. It was not the girl's fault.

"Who are you? Where're your parents?"

The child lifted her tear-stained face from Mira's shoulder, wiping her nose on her arm. "Qiuyue," she said through hiccuped tears. "My aba is Samnang. The best minister in the whole of Tiankawi."

Chapter Twenty-Nine

Nami opened her eyes to an unfamiliar face. Her head ached like it had been split open, but someone had pillowed it against the ground.

"Slowly does it," a voice said. "I've some water here."

Nami drank greedily from the flask. She was in an unfamiliar residence, a tight living space. A small crowd was around her, some looking at her with concern, others preoccupied with what was happening outside. The person tightening the lid back on his flask was human. A dark-skinned older man with more hair on his chin than his head. "You blacked out. The migraines will continue for two or three days but you'll be able to get up and walk. It's normal. But don't try it again any time soon. Folk have been known to burst vessels in their hearts from the strain."

She must've looked at him blankly. He belatedly added, "Your pakalot."

Nami remembered. The mesh bangle on her wrist looked innocuous now, but the angry raw skin beneath belied this. She had not truly believed the extent of its power until now. A bruise had already started to creep up her lower arm. "I need to find her." Her voice sounded distant from her own ears. She pulled herself into a sitting position.

"Whoever it is can wait. There's been a full-scale riot outside."

"What do you know? You're just a human."

Someone took a sharp in-breath and Nami's fugue cleared a little. The group were mainly human. But she recognised the scale pattern of a couple of imugi and the protruding whiskers of an ikan keli. The latter had a makeshift sling around his arm, and she realised many others had also been wounded in the panic.

"You think a knife knows the difference? Or a baston stick to the skull? I've treated folk and humans my whole life. Illness is illness." The man shook his head, looking like he had more to say. "Besides, you were unconscious for hours. Whoever you were looking for—"

"I need to find her," Nami insisted stubbornly. "Her daughter . . . her daughter's in the border guard, she can get help." Her words were rambling, incoherent to this stranger. She stood up, regretting it immediately. Bright rings pulsed behind her eyes, making her head spin. The man said no more; just gave her a sideways glance as he tended to more compliant patients.

It took her several more minutes to move, gingerly pulling herself over to the window. Hands gripped the frame as she gazed at the city outside. The man hadn't been joking. The walkways she had traversed only hours before had been wrecked. Planks splintered, broken glass and ceramic everywhere. And stains. Dark wet blotches. It was like a typhoon had torn through. But now that the crowds had dispersed, she could see so much further than during those frantic, claustrophobic moments of searching. And she did not like what she saw.

"That's the siren captain, isn't it? What's her name, Mara?" said a girl by her elbow. She tapped on the glass.

"Mira." Nami hadn't seen her at first, the devastation immediately in front of her soaking up all of her attention. At the far end of the walkway several levels below them, Mira's petite green-coated figure stood out. Her dark hair had come loose from its ties, streaming in the wind as she knelt. Nami's heart caught in her throat. Trish lay pale and unmoving beside her. Red stained her clothing.

Chapter Thirty

Cordelia slipped a sleeping draught into Qiuyue's seaweed tea. She lay beside her daughter, stroking her long hair until the child had stopped shaking. Finally Qiuyue fell asleep with her thumb in her mouth, the baby hair around her forehead and neck as soft as down.

Cordelia made promises she couldn't keep. Promised never to leave her, never to let her sleep alone, never to let the bad people take her. She'd considered witchcraft, to soften the memory of the trauma a little. But it was already so complicated. She didn't want to risk an extra touch that would send the whole facade tumbling down.

Gede was waiting for his mother in her little study. A softly feminine room with odds and ends of sewing; scattered diaries and notebooks; unfinished watercolour paintings on rolled-up leaves of paper. On closer inspection, the sewing was never quite completed, the notebooks covered in a thin layer of dust and the inkstone dry to the touch. An astute visitor might note that the carved teak chair was well worn, the tea leaves the best in the house and the rug kinked as if constantly caught on something. Fortunately visitors were not invited into Serena's study.

Her son looked agitated, an unusual expression on his thick brows. Nevertheless, he'd brewed the tea the traditional way, pouring hot water over the cups and teapot to keep them warm.

His father had taught him that. Ceremonies were predictable. Controlled. Step by step he knew what to do. It calmed him in a way that made Cordelia doubt sometimes that he was hers. But everyone had their own way of dealing with the masks they wore.

She said nothing, sitting beside her son until he handed her a teacup. She held it in both hands, inhaling the fragrance. Such a fuss over hot leaf water. Too much of Samnang in this one.

"I intercepted a scroll this morning, as predicted," Gede said. "The serving staff assumed it was some love tryst." He scowled. Her son indeed. The idea of relationships was of no interest unless he could figure out an angle. She'd taught him that.

He handed her the glass cylinder, sealed with wax at both ends. The lotus paper scroll within rattled as she held it, breaking the seal with a small hooked knife from her bureau drawer. A black-mail note. She scanned the demands, each one a barb under her skin. Saying nothing, she lit one end on the candle. Gede reached out as if to stop her, then dropped his hand. They watched it wilt to ash. He broke the silence. "What're we going to do?"

"*We* are going to do nothing. *I* will handle this."

"You need to start trusting me." Both hands were clenched on his knees, the rings on his fingers winking at her. The one on his pinkie alone could pay a modest rent for months. She should be glad her children wanted for nothing, but instead she was aggrieved he had not really earned it. That he would not last a day in the world without Samnang's name and her powers to support him. She did this to him. Kept him sheltered and safe, but as a consequence, weak and indolent.

"I will handle it," she repeated. Gede poured more tea, the audible sound of his teeth grinding setting her on edge. A habit he'd acquired when he was not much older than Qiuyue – a dunking from some other lads on a festival day. They'd fetched her, guiltily, when he would not stop crying. When he had wet himself and refused to talk. Did nothing but grind his teeth for days. She told Samnang it was a fever. Spoke to Gede about keeping up a face, an appearance of confidence and belonging. He had asked for her trust then, to let him help. The boy's face still radiated through his adult features, bottom lip quivering. Too soft to be effective.

"Ama, I—"

"They think it'll intimidate me. Get me to follow their plan. But they don't know who they're dealing with." Cordelia had misjudged Lynnette. Thought her nothing more than brawn and bravado without the wit to orchestrate a riot, let alone a kidnapping at the same time. Even after it was clear the Drawbacks knew her identity, Cordelia had assumed they'd target Samnang's political career, not her children.

She patted Gede on the head, the disappointment written so clearly on his face. He was trying, she had to admit. But some things needed an experienced hand. Couldn't be entrusted to others, even if they were blood. She'd find something else for him to cut his teeth on. Something simple.

Samnang was in the training room, thrashing the wooden dummy with his fists and palms as he had done every night since the Boat Race riots. Cordelia sat at the back of the room, folding towels silently until he noticed her.

"Is she sleeping?"

"For now."

"I'll kill the people who did this." He said the same thing every night. As if saying it enough would make it come true.

"I'd rather you sat with her," she said mildly. Samnang used one of the fresh towels to wipe his brow, draping it across his broad shoulders.

"You know I can't."

Cordelia let the silence linger. He had been hands-on with

Gede, revelling in his every milestone. Invested in his career. But with Qiuyue, he was distant. Buying her pretty dresses or paper kites but content for her to remain a painted doll. As if what lay beneath the surface didn't matter as much.

"They're protesting against the city guards again." Cordelia flicked her glance up, catching the grimace on Samnang's face. Petty to poke a festering wound, and yet she did it all the same.

Samnang lined up against the wooden dummy again, his response punctuated by his hands moving between positions. "Peaceful grassroots protests." Sarcasm dripped like candle wax. "Yesterday in Khyagur district, the day before in Qilin. I don't have the officers, and as the damned siren keeps telling me, I've no jurisdiction while they remain peaceful."

"Looting and graffiti. Bands of fathomfolk roaming the walkways and frightening children!" Cordelia let her voice break, squeezing tears to her eyes and allowing them to splash onto her silk dress. A minuscule amount of waterweaving did the trick. If the Drawbacks wanted to blackmail her, she would make their lives harder. Harder to meet, to hold their little rallies and make threats against her family. Lynnette's unsubtle behaviour would be met with an unsubtle response.

Samnang sighed. "Half a dozen minor offences, nothing more."

"They need a permanent curfew. They can't be trusted. Even the chinthe captain – for all this city offered her – went rogue! Commandeered the telephone exchange! She deserves more than suspension for a few weeks." Cordelia pushed her point, reminding him of Mira and how much of a thorn she was in his side. The plan had been for Samnang to take control of the situation, yes, but his lovely wife would have remained at the tiller guiding him through the ensuing panic. Instead, distracted by Qiuyue's absence and without Serena's support, Samnang had just dug deeper and deeper into a trench of his own making.

He came away from his practice. Wiped his hands and brow

methodically before answering. "They attacked her mother. I thought you'd sympathise with that."

"We're nothing alike."

Her husband hesitated but didn't answer, pouring himself some water from the jug on the sideboard.

"Sensible people are avoiding the folk-populated districts. Arresting salties will not win me votes. It's too heavy-handed."

Cordelia made a sound halfway between a laugh and a scream. He was worried about being heavy-handed? Too little too late. It was all he was known for now; might as well lean into it. "It's decisive! Swift action. And what about the arson attacks at Webisu? The property vandalised by fathomfolk. Law-abiding people afraid to sleep in their own beds?"

Samnang looked down at her in confusion. "I haven't had any reports of . . ." His voice trailed off and his eyes narrowed in understanding. Sometimes opportunities arose, other times they had to be made. Cordelia seized the moment with a grip on his forearm, a songlike lilt in her words. "A curfew. Because imagine – what if the rumours are true? Fathomfolk found some way around the pakalots? Just imagine!"

"No one would believe it."

She handed him the bamboo scroll. This week's news. The headlines carved into the slats. Still no arrests for the Boat Race murders. Clean-up after the riots. And Ambassador Kai's new law was still on the table. To be ratified by the Fenghuang later in the week.

"That's quite a story." Samnang sat down with a heavy thud. Looked at his wife like he was unsure if he was impressed or afraid.

"Make the hard choices." Cordelia's voice was like the lullaby she sang to their daughter. She played with the drawstring bag at her waist.

He blinked, eyes heavy suddenly, and gave a slow nod.

She squeezed her husband in an embrace. He couldn't see the flames in her eyes. Certainly there were distinct disadvantages to a Fathomfolk curfew, but she had multiple guises she could wear. Lynnette on the other hand, relied on her reputation, her face, to build momentum for the Drawbacks. Well, they'd see how much popular support the kelpie could garner with a curfew. And tomorrow Cordelia would be calling in some favours. Take out the Drawbacks' funding, raid their safe houses, choke their fugu supply. No one messed with her family and got away with it.

Chapter Thirty-One

North-west, beyond Jingsha, was a region called Webisu that Nami had had little reason to visit before, known mostly for its floating gardens. It was oddly still out here, the noise of the city hidden behind foliage, silhouetted against the grey afternoon sky. Insects thrummed quietly, a deep-throated song against the lapping of water. In the distance, grand two-storey houseboats were moored, connected by raised walkways.

Just west of the houseboats was a less affluent neighbourhood of sampans docked together like an island archipelago. Their curved roofs were like blankets pulled up over sleeping figures. Mismatched planks and fresh paint patched up older vessels, with simple touches denoting care. A manicured tree twisting out of a porcelain pot; a bamboo water feature clacking rhythmically as it pivoted; laundry strung between two sampans, tunics and undershirts flapping in the breeze. People climbed over the prows of the boats, clambering from one vessel to the next. No one had bothered to build walkways here.

Trish peeped from the innards of her sampan, leaning heavily on the frame and favouring her good leg. "You'll be wanting fed?" she said in lieu of a greeting. Nami made her sit back down, as she'd done every day since the Boat Race riots.

For two weeks after Trish came home, she was bedridden and could barely lift her head from the pillow to drink soup. Then, on the third week, she asked for flatbread and critiqued Mira's fruit rojak. That was when they knew she'd be okay. Still, the hacking cough had settled in her chest, making her wheeze at simple tasks like basket weaving. Her leg was broken in two places and would take longer still to heal. She would not be able to walk unaided for months. If she tried to swim, it would only make things worse. It was fortunate sirens were not shape-shifters, because broken bones could get lost in the transformation, the fragments not quite carrying across.

Her abductor had abruptly changed their mind when they had hit a full-scale riot near Qilin. Bands of humans stalked the streets, walkway planks ripped up and being used to smash in windows, pulling down the signage of folk businesses and burning them in a pyre. Whatever her assailant's motives, they weren't risking their life for her. They'd dumped her on the ground and taken flight. It was the mob who had broken her leg, trampling over her to give chase. Her howls of pain drowned out in the frenzy.

Nami visited daily, lingering with baskets of greens and unspoken guilt. Time and time again she tried to apologise. Stumbling over words that felt counterfeit. Trite. Trish patted her hand and said she had rescued the rowers, that was enough. But it wasn't enough.

"You are too late, there's no more puri!" Mira's voice was muffled behind a mouthful of food.

Trish boxed her daughter on the arm brusquely. "Manners!"

Mira swallowed with a grin, ducking out of reach and bustling around the small houseboat with familiar ease. Nami only caught half the words. Mira's accent changed in her mother's presence, gaining an intimacy and distinctive clipped tones. The freshwater dialect. Familiar and yet strange at the same time.

"Spiced tea? I would've prepared a proper meal if you'd bothered to warn me!" Trishanjali waggled a finger at Nami.

"I ate something at a hawker stall," Nami said. Trish let her know her opinion of that with a loud scoff.

Inside, the boat was one open space. The kettle was steaming over the fire at the heart of the room, and there were short stools scattered around. The arched roof held strings of drying herbs, tied in bunches that brushed against her head; jars of spices from sunflower yellow to terracotta brown; and a small birdcage, door missing and currently empty. The beginnings of a woven basket were on the floor, feather-like leaves folded and tucked into place. A bed was on the far side, with a new walking stick propped up against it. Nami's hands tingled from remembering how she had clenched the old stick until her knuckles ached. It had probably ended up on the seabed with everything else destroyed that night.

On the wall there were scrolls: mounted certificates of Mira's accolades, mould speckles creeping in at the edges. Mira noticed her gaze and lovingly brushed one of the frames. "Ama worked double shifts at the Onseon Engine. Earned enough for us to move here when I was sixteen."

"Should've been earlier," Trish corrected. "The paperwork took a whole year. This is luxury in comparison to our first few places." She shuddered, rubbing at her splinted leg at the mere mention, then beckoned to Mira. Her daughter sat beside her, perched on the bed. Trish tutted at the mess of her curls, at the dirt under her nails.

Nami's ears had perked up at the mention of Onseon. In everything that had happened, she had forgotten about her task. It felt irrelevant now. But perhaps Trish could give her more information on the open secret that no one wanted to talk about.

Mira loosened her hair tie so her mother could work the oiled wide-tooth comb through her locks. She closed her eyes under the attention, talking more to herself than the other two. "I'd worked as a runner, in the fish cannery, or doing odd jobs throughout my teens. But my first proper job, one that had a contract and consistently paid me at the end of every month, was as a typist in a ship maintenance firm. I thought I'd made it! That if I worked harder, faster, better than my colleagues I'd get there."

"And?" Nami said.

"They said I had beguiled the one manager who believed I should take credit where it was due. Fired me."

Nami felt the now familiar twist in her throat, the fury that could not be swallowed whole. She gripped her teacup with both hands, clawing at it. "So why aren't you fighting?"

"There's more than one way to win a war." It was Trish who replied, chiding without raising her voice. The sound of the comb hissed into the silence. Loose strands of wavy hair caught in the teeth.

"Ama got ill. It altered my perspective on things." Mira looked down at her hands.

"Just a chest infection!" Trish laughed quietly. "The healers said it was gill rot, but that was rubbish." Now that she mentioned it, Nami could see the telltale silver-black veins around the elder's gills and nape of her neck.

"You could've sought sanctuary in Yonakuni. Atlitya even, before the war."

"I've never been to those places," Mira said.

"You're fathomfolk."

"I'm not *just* fathomfolk." Mira punctuated her words with a finger stabbing down onto the bed.

Nami opened her mouth, but her retort lingered unspoken. It had never occurred to her that Mira would embrace it. Her fathomfolk side gave her gills, waterweaving, her siren abilities. What did humanity give her? Her gaze drifted again to the old scars on Trish's arms.

Mira whistled and from the eaves a small, brightly coloured bird flew down onto her finger. Its oversized red bill pecked ineffectively at her nail. She smiled and let the bird flit onto its cage, sending the bamboo frame swinging.

She flipped her hair out of her mother's hands with a smile of thanks. Tied it up in a rough knot and stood to examine the certificates on the walls. "I started reading. Just to see if I could get my job back, if laws had been broken. Then to learn what our rights were. I spent my days off at the library, until folk started to know me, came to me for advice."

"They called her their little scholar. Long before your brother came along." Trish's pride shone as she looked up at her daughter.

"You're nothing more than a token, someone put in the military so they can pat themselves on the back." Nami knew the words would smart, but she needed to say them all the same.

Mira shrugged. "I know. They let me into the chinthe and not the kumiho. They want to keep me on a short leash. But it's a foot in the door. To change people's attitudes from the inside. Show them we are people too – not monsters, not beasts, just people."

Nami heard the logic of Mira's words and yet still could not accept it. The flames inside her were too bright. The violence she had witnessed at the Boat Race riots said everything about how well things were going. "Your way will take for ever."

"And yours? Tell me, how has that worked out so far?" That silenced her for a moment, her face hot with thoughts she couldn't articulate. Reminded her of Kai's words. *Fathomfolk did this.* Their hands were just as dirty.

A tremor growled under them, the boat bobbing more than usual. Mira and her mother were unfazed. Mira jumped to her feet to catch the few things that slid about the shelves, latching the door shut and waiting for the quake to pass. Cracks were widening beneath them, deeper than anyone could see.

The ensuing silence dragged. Like the air between Mira and Nami had solidified. Trish cut through it with her open hands.

"Enough. As if being boat-bound is not difficult enough, I have to face you two circling sharks. Say your piece."

"I'm an intruder here, I'll go." Nami tried to stand, but the elder's grip was surprisingly strong.

"Sit down, dragon whelp. This is my boat and I say who stays and goes."

Nami hunched over, tensing herself against the barrage of anger she was certain Mira had against her. Rightly so.

Mira bit her thumb, the nail already ragged and the skin raw. "The Council are coming down hard. Proposing a folk curfew. Gatherings, peaceful protests – even a sashiko group was classed as suspicious. Can you imagine? A suspicious sewing club?"

"Some of them are almighty gossips," Trish said, attempting a little humour. Mira did not notice. Continued listing things. "The housing situation is getting worse. And gill rot cases?" She blew out a long, frustrated sigh, hanging her head low.

In the silence that followed, Nami finally worked up the courage to ask, "You aren't mad at me?"

"You?" Mira laughed drily. "The system was broken well before you arrived. They wanted to hurt *me*, to hurt my family. What would you've done? Dropped unconscious from the pakalot?"

Nami had misinterpreted everything. Mira had barely glanced at her because her other problems were bigger. All the same, the comment about her uselessness smarted. She had underestimated the impact of the pakalot restraint. Assumed she could somehow break it when all the other folk had been stupidly tolerating it for decades. Like they didn't have the insight to push back. All she had done was get in the way. Not the outcome she'd imagined. She swallowed her pride. "What can I do?"

Mira shrugged, pulling free of her mother. "Nothing. Just do nothing."

The comment hurt more than the anger Nami had imagined. She was insignificant. No, worse than that. She was a nuisance.

Mira slipped on her chinthe coat, paused with one foot on the neighbour's sampan before swivelling back. "Oh, there is one thing."

The water dragon straightened herself up, ready to take on any task Mira threw at her. "Anything."

"The Drawbacks are dangerous, Nami. Promise me you'll keep away from them."

Nami had a chance to act on those assurances sooner than expected. Unpegging Trish's laundry from the makeshift line lashed between her boat and the next, she sensed him first. Firth's piercing eyes were like witchlights against the setting sun, drawing her in. He stood like he'd always been there, watching her.

"Mira's mother is recovering?"

Nami nodded, hugging an armful of washing against her chest. Afraid that if her hands were free, she would reach for his. Trish was napping, Mira long since gone to work.

"She will recover." She swallowed the lump in her throat, pushing out the next words despite internal turmoil. "The humans who died in the boat ... did the Draw—"

Firth took two steps towards her, crushing the clean sheets between them as he grabbed both her shoulders. Held her until Nami was forced to look up, dazzled by his ferocity. "I have never doubted you. Never asked about your past in Yonakuni. Why must you keep doubting us? What must I do to prove my sincerity?" Firth's eyes shone fiercely. He looked away, blinking furiously until all trace was gone.

Fathomfolk did this. That was what Kai had said. That was what was staring her in the face as the pieces of the boat sank to the ocean floor. No coincidence, no accident could've wrought devastation so thorough. But she'd leapt to the next conclusion. That the Drawbacks, Firth included, were the culprits. After all, other forces could be at play. He was here, risking the wrath of the authorities, of the captain of the chinthe, to speak to her.

"I'm sorry," she said. She meant it. "I believe you. I just don't know about the others. Lynnette could be … hiding things from you."

"I've known Lynnette since we were kids! She just wants what's best for folk. For us." Firth's hand caressed down her shoulders to her elbows, then her wrists. Nami's every sense was heightened by that touch, feeling the small circles his thumbs made on the back of her hands. "But look what they've done. Frightened families, let humanity beat us up and called it a riot, demanded a curfew. We're nothing more than caged animals again."

"Yes," Nami agreed, breathless. She was barely listening to his words now, her focus entirely on the dusky colour of his lips. The ache deep within her chest fluttered with his ministrations. The laundry slipped between her fingers, pooling around her legs and feet.

"Someday soon we'll take action. And I need you beside me, Nami. Will you be there?"

She could drown in Firth's dark pupils. Amber irises like stars flickering in a midnight sky. The kelpie's hands snaked around her waist and pressed against the small of her back, meeting her bare skin.

More than that though. He needed her. When Mira had made it quite clear that Nami was a burden, nothing more than an annoyance. When Nami herself had done nothing to further her aim of freeing Dan and Hong-Gi. When everyone around her treated her like a nestling, to be humoured and occupied but not taken seriously. Only Firth looked at her like she could make a difference. Like together they could burn it all down and start anew, make something better.

He repeated, "Will you be there?"

Nami scarcely knew what he was talking about. Cared even less.

The heat that rose from her core threatened to overwhelm her and she would have said anything. There could only be one response to his question. Branded on her tongue and etched into the very bones of her being. "Yes."

He shone as if satiated, then bent to pick up the forgotten sheets, depositing them back into her arms. Nami was still hungry, her body tingling from his touch. Bewildered at the distance he'd put between them.

"Good girl," the kelpie said. And then he was gone.

Chapter Thirty-Two

Mira swept a knowing eye around the room. Her guards looked as exhausted as she felt. They'd let her come back to work, pending review of her actions during the Boat Race riots. Understaffed across city and border guards, the Council were too busy to reprimand her. All leave had been cancelled and most of the chinthe had been working without rest days.

Mikayil finished his report in a monotone drone. Several guards were yawning, and one had even put their head on the desk. Finally the newest ensign, the one who started the same time as Lucia, returned from his errand, arms laden with tiered metal tins. He shared out the flatbreads, tearing a piece and passing it on. The aroma of spices from the dishes filled the room and the chinthe roused themselves from their stupor.

Mira slipped him some coins with a nod of thanks. The air of quiet satisfaction that followed dispelled some of the fatigue in the room. It also went a long way towards alleviating her guilt for not being with them the last few weeks.

"I didn't see you at Lucia's funeral," Mikayil said.

Mira didn't have an answer. She had been unable to tear herself from her ama's bedside. Afraid that things would change in her absence. She hadn't even dared close her eyes, catching sleep only by accident and always with the lingering weight of shame. She adjusted the white mourning band on her forearm. The other chinthe still wore them too, long past the one-week etiquette period. She didn't have the inclination to make them remove the torn strips of rag.

"We gave her a full chinthe send-off. Promoted her posthumously."

"Good, that's ... good."

Mikayil shook his head ruefully. He was inching around the subject he really wanted to broach, that much was clear. In a hurry, he blurted out. "I'm sorry, Captain, we went back to look for evidence but the kumiho wouldn't let us. Said they were leading. Bragging about curfews and pakalots."

Mira shrugged. Some days it felt manageable. Rebuilding. Planning. On others it was like sand shifting beneath her feet. "If they want a curfew, they need to come out and order one."

"Sooner the salties know their place the better," one of the newer guards interjected. The way the room turned to look caught the speaker by surprise. She back-pedalled. "Just, what you were saying about curfews ... No disrespect, Captain, I mean, I wasn't talking about you."

"Just the other fathomfolk?" Mikayil cut in before Mira could respond.

"Well, the captain isn't really folk, she's half human ..." The guard's voice petered off. The weight of the food sat in Mira's stomach, making her feel sluggish.

"Which half?"

"Begging your pardon?"

Mira stood, pointing at parts of her own body. "Here? Here? This arm? This knee? Which parts are human and which parts fathomfolk? Can you tell me?"

The guard lowered her gaze.

Mira turned back to her lieutenants, changing the subject to defuse the atmosphere. "Mikayil, what's happening with the Drawbacks?"

"They had another rally last week. You were right – timed it to recruit the new arrivals. The ones without work, without prospects but with a lot of misdirected rage."

She and Kai had got benefactors to set up a few fathomfolk community halls. But after all the pomp and ceremony of the first year, the money had dried up. Philanthropists found that other causes garnered more prestige. Disgruntled youths took to using the windows for target practice instead. Other than working at the Onseon Engine, most of the folk didn't have the options, education or connections to get jobs elsewhere.

Not for the first time, Mira wondered whether she would have joined the Drawbacks if they had existed when she was a teenager.

But then Tam, her other lieutenant, walked in and all questions became superfluous. His face was ashen. He had been on the patrol vessel for weeks now, monitoring the smuggling boats that had run circles around the chinthe.

He whispered in her ear. Mira stared at him until he repeated the news word for word. Just when she thought things couldn't get any worse.

By the time they reached the Samaga district depot in the south, it was raining heavily. The lower walkways were completely submerged, and not for the first time, Mira wished she could just swim. Cut through and beneath the city rather than detouring all the way round.

The depot was where the supply ships were berthed, arriving with steel from the upper reaches; outbound vessels loaded with Tiankawi's pickled vegetables and grain, destined for the other flooded cities and artificial islands. They lay dormant like sleeping titans for weeks, sometimes months, until they were filled to capacity. It was not really a surprise that one ship had gone unnoticed.

"Which one?" she said. Even before Tam pointed it out, she felt the shadows reaching out from around the enormous hull. Was there a smell, or was that simply the vomit bubbling into her mouth?

"We didn't know if we should moor it or not. How to get ... them out."

Mira didn't answer, her eyes glued to the vessel. Tiankawi was full of smugglers. Some brought in drugs, precious gems, metals. But the biggest market was always people.

"We stopped twenty vessels. More. Processed asylum claims. Even a family in a coracle. I thought it was under control." Tam's head hung low, his chin practically touching his chest.

Mira knew what he wanted her to say. Pat him on the shoulder and tell him it wasn't his fault. It was a grim inevitability. They couldn't have prevented it. Sooner or later ... Part of her wanted to assure herself also. The words wouldn't come.

They boarded the silent vessel. A strong smell of urine tainted the air. She nodded at the border guards on board, their lower faces covered with scarves, then forced herself to look. The bodies were huddled in groups, entwined under the hatch as if sleeping. The smell gave it away. The undertone of putrid decay like a punch to the face. Exposed skin – faces and necks, arms and legs – was mottled, discoloured grey and blue. She'd only seen it once before, long ago at the Nurseries. Starved of food, of clean water, of air. These people had perished in here, scratching at a hatch that did not open, because they had been abandoned. Had the smugglers already been in the city when they died, their screams unanswered in the city din? Or had it happened en route, a ship of death slipping into harbour?

Time slowed down. Mira's eyes drifted, seeing things in close detail: a trouser leg that had ridden up on one side; matted hair plastered against a forehead; a bare foot, toenails in need of clipping. Her brain was unable to recognise the whole. And then her gaze settled on a small webbed hand on an adult's chest. A child clutching its parent. She couldn't unsee it, the small bodies of the children. Hollowed out. Dry.

She dragged her eyes away and stepped back before she heaved. Mikayil was punching a metal panel behind her, cursing with each strike. Several others were retching over the side.

"Captain?" Tam said. He looked at her through red-rimmed eyes, face blotchy, hands shaking. Mira wanted to lean forward and weep on his shoulder. But the cold voice of reason said that if she fell apart, nothing would get done. She had to push down what she was feeling. Focus on the practicalities.

"Take a minute. Clear your head. We need the coroner. And as many people as they can spare." She let the other chinthe leave, looks of relief on their faces as they stumbled off the deck. Alone with the bodies, she crouched down, still staring into the hatch.

It could have been her. Her mother never talked about how she got to Tiankawi all those years ago, but at a good guess it wasn't legal. Back when they needed the labour, officials shrugged at the lack of papers and opened the door. Now it was different. A booming business with a high price to pay.

She tried to swallow the lump in her throat, but it stuck there, her mouth completely dry. A strong wind blew around her, sweeping down into the open bowels of the boat. She waited for a complaint, a call to close the door. Only silence rang back.

"The trams will be running." Tam opened his umbrella to shelter both of them. The rain drummed on the wax paper like impatient fingers. They had been at the depot all night, the healers too, until Mira finally made the decision that they needed sleep. It would wait, she said firmly to Tam's protests. And then echoed it again, the truth nearly breaking her in two. It would wait.

"Go home, hug your wife. I'm fine." She needed to sort her

own head out. Decided to walk to Kai's. The floating bridge was a long line of boats supporting the planked path on the water. The boats bobbed as she walked across them, wood shining with wetness. Very few people were out, most hurrying on their way to early shifts at work.

Mira understood why people made desperate decisions. She'd made many herself. She thought it was normal. That everyone had to beat their way through life, knuckles raw on closed doors. Blinking through a storm as it rained ceaselessly. Then Kai had come and built a shelter around her. To him it was unremarkable to be dry and warm and loved.

Everything was too easy. Doors to exclusive restaurants were opened, Council members wanted to be friends. Mira was dazzled by the lights and had forgotten there were still people on the outside. Just not her. She'd bought into it, eaten their steamed canapés and been accepted as one of the few, within *their* parameters, *their* notion of what it was to be folk.

The apartment was quiet when she turned her key in the lock. Kai's sleeping form was silhouetted by the dawn light in the bedroom. His long eyelashes fluttered against his cheeks and the rise and fall of his torso was like a low tide. It felt wrong to disturb that.

By degrees he shifted, somehow aware of her presence. A smile spread across his face and he sat up. "You're soaked through," he said in a voice thick with sleep. She'd not remembered to take her coat off, heavy with water and forming puddles on the floor. Kai swaddled her with a thick towel, muffling her protests, patting her hair and face and clothes.

"I walked out to meet you at the tram station last night, but you weren't there. The office said there had been . . . an incident," he said. He didn't push, leaving the words lingering like the loose string on a kite. Mira could catch it, pull it down and reel it in. Sometimes she let it go, watched his questions drifting into the ether.

The corpses floated from her memory and settled around their bedroom. Lying on the floor, on the bed, slumped over the chair. She could smell them again, a smell that would linger no matter how many times she washed.

"Mira?" Kai held her hands.

She licked her cracked lips, opening her mouth to respond. But the words would not come.

They lay in bed, Kai falling into a light sleep, his breath tickling her hair. Despite touching at chest and hip and feet, Mira felt the distance growing between them.

Chapter Thirty-Three

In Yonakuni, hot tea had been rare. Kelp juice or fermented sea grapes were the drinks of choice. But already Nami had started craving sweet tea in the evenings courtesy of Trish's daily routine.

The older siren was an easy-going companion, filling silences with amiable chat, talking aloud to herself about her day's plans. She took some relish in directing Nami to the tasks she couldn't complete independently. The crutches became a pointer and she'd suck air through her teeth in frustration when Nami misunderstood. But all the same, it was a good-hearted sort of annoyance, easy enough to laugh away.

Nami had asked Trish about the Onseon Engine. Hadn't Mira said her mother had worked there once upon a time? But as chatty as she was about all other subjects, Trish wouldn't be drawn. No. That time of her life was closed. She was firm about the matter, face pinched, rubbing her pakalot. Nami didn't push. She felt responsible for Trish now more than ever, and if there were reasons for not talking, she respected them. It was no less frustrating though. She'd accomplished next to nothing since she arrived.

Firth had not returned since his last visit. The touch of his hands was burned onto her skin and yet she didn't know what it meant to him. He wasn't at the Barreleye Club either, the

Drawbacks seemingly having gone to ground since the Boat Race riots. All Nami could do was wash dishes for an elder.

"Can you smell that?" Trish lifted her head, sniffing the air.

"Can't smell a thing over this floral crap." Nami indicated the pot of grey salve she had been using to massage Trish's legs and feet. The tips of her fingers tingled with the menthol oils.

"No. I mean outside."

"A quake?"

"Quakes don't smell. Not like this."

Nami opened the door. The evening skyline was lit orange. It took a moment to realise it wasn't simply a glorious sunset. Flames. Further down the district, the distinct silhouette of more affluent houseboats alight. The wind picked up, blowing the fire across the vessels like a flickering candle.

What was she doing, just staring like a stunned goldfish. Do something. Now. "Cut the boats loose!"

"What?" Trish dragged her eyes away from the scene.

"The boats are moored together – the whole district will burn. Raise the alarm. Now!" Nami didn't give her time to respond. She waterweaved a rudimentary sickle from puddles of rainwater, slashing it across the tether rope. Banging on every prow she passed, she cut as many vessels loose as she could without breaking her pace. Better rudderless and safe than burning together. Belatedly Trish's song pierced the smoke, a warning beacon rising over the crackle of fire.

Nami jumped from boat to boat, across the ramshackle sampans of Trish's neighbourhood toward the more prosperous end of the district. She leapt onto the floating gardens dividing the two areas, hexagonal tiles spinning at her uneven weight. The radiating heat prickled at her skin long before she reached it, like hands thrusting her back.

Flames licked up a couple of grand two-storey houseboats, coating their wooden beams. Thick black smoke plumed from the hulls, the fire struggling to catch on damp planks. But the heat roared nevertheless, a wall of suffocation.

"Is everyone out?" she managed to call, coughing into her elbow. In the narrow stretch of water around the blazing building, a family in their night robes huddled on a rowing boat.

"My dress for the gala, my pearls, the teak chest you gave me..." one woman listed under her breath. Her eyes were glazed; she was clearly stunned by what was happening. Her partner had an arm around her. Beside them a young boy and a woman of Nami's age held hands, leaning together for comfort. "We're okay," the level-headed partner said. But Nami's eyes were trained on the younger woman at her side. Without the glasses and with her hair shoved into a messy ponytail, it had taken a moment. The librarian from the archives. Eun squinted back with a mirror of Nami's astonishment. Nami's stomach gave a peculiar flip as she realised the woman had been here, in the same district, a short walk from Trish's sampan, for all these weeks.

No time for catch-ups. Nami turned her attention back to the fire, pulling at the seawater with her weaving, dragging it up to douse the flames. The volumes she was trying to manipulate were heavy. Reluctant to part from the main body of water. Like dredging sand from the seabed, slipping through her fingers as fast as she could raise it. Still she kept going, sweat mingling with saltwater. The fire lowered its rage, replaced by biting smoke.

The second house took longer. The fire had completely caught hold, refusing to release its grasp on the warped wood. Nami half recognised some of Trish's neighbours beside her. They could've left the wealthier houses to burn. The opposite would probably have been true. Still they came. Armed with buckets and basins, forming chains to pass them to the front. But the flames were not satisfied with these two houseboats alone.

"Why're you stopping? That's my home!" a man said, his dirt-streaked face up close to Nami. The dragon had barely caught her breath. She couldn't do this herself. Could barely see through stinging eyes.

"The fire is spreading. Cut it loose and save the other houses."

"How dare you? You saved the minister's house but not mine?"

Nami looked at him in shock, waiting for someone to interject. The line of people continued to pass buckets like they hadn't heard. A few folk were waterweaving what they could, trickles of water no more than a stream. A crack overhead and a wooden beam broke, collapsing into the roof of the house. Someone yelled a warning and people jumped out of the way. Dived into the water. A burning timber rolled onto one of the floating gardens. Half a dozen people reacted, leaping with buckets and wet sheets, smothering the wild flames before they escaped. A headache pressed in at Nami's temples and her lips were cracked and dry. The heat was unbearable. She was beyond exhausted, doing her best, and yet it still wasn't enough.

It would never be enough.

Her weakness had always been capacity. Sobekki had lectured her back in Yonakuni. While her finesse – her ability to change the shape of the water, change its state – improved with training, her quantities barely did. Her waterweaving was that of a gymnast, and what they needed was a weightlifter.

Exasperated voices appraised her. Found her wanting. Too slow. Too weak. Too indolent. It was unclear if they were inside or outside her head. It didn't really matter. Eyes on her. Watching. Heads shaking. Disappointed. Not like the dragons of legend. Not at all living up to expectations. She was suddenly glad of the smoke. It gave her cover for her smarting eyes. She couldn't do it.

Suddenly there was a torrent of water like someone had opened a sluice. The deluge poured from the cloudless sky, battering the burning houseboat until it nearly capsized. The infuriated man shouted and waved his fists. But it wasn't Nami.

From the water, a familiar kelpie raised his head. He shook

his ruddy mane and jumped onto the floating garden beside her. Firth. Pushing his wet hair back, he stood back to back with her as if she'd been expecting him all along. She could feel his shoulder blades moving against her back, the smell of him comforting. The cool water on his body soaked into her shirt, and despite her questions, despite any reservations, it revitalised her. Propped her up. Firth raised his hands, weaving water into a heavy wave. The floating platform underfoot wobbled and Nami added her own touch. Precision combined with strength. Together, never touching but sensing the other. Quenching the flames.

She had combined waterweaving before: with Kai, with Dan, with other classmates at the Academy. It took time to synchronise, for her to relax her guard. Here it was effortless. They flowed as one. Firth's silhouette rippled in the water, lit by the fire's glow.

The platform slowly stopped spinning and the flames sizzled to smoke. Nami heaved in air through her nose, gulping it greedily as her shoulders rose and fell. The water slipped back into the sea by their feet, pouring over the decks and down barnacled hulls. "You read my every move," Firth said.

"We're a good team," Nami acknowledged, turning towards him.

"Could do anything together." When he said it, Nami believed. Wholeheartedly. His magnetism pulled her in. Like a fast-flowing river pushing her downstream, she didn't want to struggle against it.

"Like start fires?" The same man as before, his arms across his chest. Nami remembered they weren't alone. Tired, soot-covered residents stood around. Buckets dropped at their feet, too exhausted to pick them up.

"What are you suggesting?" Firth's words were pleasant enough, but his low tone had a serrated edge. Body stiffened as he raised himself to his full height, he towered over the other people around them.

"Someone started the fire."

"We just saved you," Nami said incredulously.

"Saved me? You arrived to save the Minister of Ceremonies and her family! Not me."

"I have no idea who she is – why would I set this up?"

The man squared up to her, fury concentrated into a finger that jabbed to punctuate each word. "You, on the night before the pakalot laws are relaxed? You think us fools?"

Head dizzy, Nami had no time to think. Snatched for the first words that came to mind. "I should've left you to burn!" The crowd gasped. Shuffled back.

"You can't reason with them," Firth said quietly into her ear. He tugged her towards the edge of the platform, toward the water. "Come."

But someone touched her hand on the other side. It was Eun, her sleeping clothes crumpled and smoke-stained. The librarian was oddly solemn in demeanour and restrained with her words. "Don't run. They'll use it against you."

Nami wanted to go with Firth. Be with him. Light the brand and set the whole world on fire. But Eun was right. Swimming away was admitting guilt. This she couldn't do. Trish lived here, Mira lived here. She owed it to them. To Kai's reputation and his bill. She would not run, would not hide like she might once have.

Firth gave her one last look. Shook his head as he let go, leaving Nami to the mob. Every fibre of her body screamed that she should follow. She pushed her shoulders back, trying and failing to keep the tremor out of her voice. "Go ahead then. Have me arrested."

Chapter Thirty-Four

The rooftop park was filled with the laughter of children. The rhythmic tapping of a featherball against knee and foot as a group of friends counted and watched the boy in the centre. Three older women moved in the slow motion of set stretches. Cordelia had previously found it peaceful. But today she couldn't ignore the iron grip around her chest as she watched Qiuyue playing. Every so often her daughter would look up through her curtain of hair, checking her mother was still there. Cordelia gave a half-wave, pretending a tranquillity she did not feel. She was monitoring a man at one of the chess tables, setting up the pieces despite lack of a partner. Didn't recognise him. She calculated how far he was from her daughter, how many steps she would need to get there before him. She damn near throttled him when he stood up to adjust his stool.

"I still can't believe it," Ayumu said. Cordelia had ignored the other woman's frantic waving from across the park, pretending to be engrossed until it was no longer an option. "Kidnapping? Right from under your nose. I could never live with myself if that happened to Finnol."

Cordelia forgot for a moment she was still in Serena guise, flashing Ayumu the look that gave seawitches their reputation. The other woman cocked her head in some confusion, hesitating for a second before continuing her ruthless upbraiding. "And I mean, you'd think the Minister of Defence would be able to get to the bottom of it. A bit embarrassing. I can't imagine what Samnang is going through."

"Investigations are progressing." Cordelia responded with deliberate curtness, hoping Ayumu would move on. She wished she could avoid the next statement, but courtesy meant she'd be marked by its omission. "I'm terribly sorry to hear about your house. I hope everyone is all right?"

"Shaken but safe. Arson, can you believe it? If the alarm had been raised any later . . ." Ayumu shuddered at the thought. She had garnered quite a bit of sympathy retelling the story to anyone who cared to listen.

Cordelia's plans to unseat her rival and give credence to the curfew had not quite gone to plan. She clenched her teeth but nodded along genially to Ayumu's continued laments. Samnang had taken her hints – had to under her charms – but how the havens had the dragon whelp got there so fast? And the fucking Drawbacks again. Always messing up her schemes. It was far beyond a coincidence. She would suspect Gede, but her son was too soft to double-cross her. At least, not deliberately.

Ayumu prattled on, interrupting her thoughts. "As it is, we'll have to remodel the whole upper floor. We only had it done a year ago. I always disagreed with Pyanis's decision to live in such a . . . *multicultural* district. I don't care how up and coming it is. Perhaps she'll actually listen to me now and let us move back to Jingsha." Her hand against her forehead, she paused. They both clocked the unusual figure, Mira of the border guards, making a beeline towards them. Ayumu's tone changed entirely. She leaned in, dramatic whisper behind a pale hand. "You know what they've been saying?"

"What?"

"The chinthe captain and the ambassador. Walking around without pakalots. It was bound to happen sooner or later. Can't trust a saltie."

Mira gave a palm-fist salute, but her pinched expression indicated she'd most certainly heard Ayumu's remarks. She swivelled to Cordelia. "I hope your daughter is well?" Her sincerity was annoying. The seawitch waved in the direction of Qiuyue and her friends.

"I didn't know you were a member," Ayumu commented. The monthly fees to the rooftop garden were likely beyond the captain's salary. By the looks of her, Mira could barely afford to dress herself. Her chinthe coat was worn through and patched at the elbows.

"Lady Serena, a word?" Ignoring Ayumu entirely was a brave choice. The chinthe captain was not in the mood for pandering.

"You rescued my daughter; for that you can have all the words in the world," Cordelia said. A true friend would have made an excuse to leave, but Ayumu was not that. Her eyes drank in the whole scene, sketching notes to tell her wife later. If Cordelia made her go, it would look like she was hiding something. No, Lady Serena had nothing to hide.

The count reached twenty-two before the featherball fell to the ground. The children clapped their friend as he wrinkled up his face with frustration. Another girl took up the challenge. Cordelia dragged her gaze away. All she wanted was to scoop up her daughter and take her home. Too many potential threats. Too many sides to protect against. She turned instead to look out at the cable car on its slow ascent between tall buildings.

"Nami, the ambassador's sister, was arrested two nights ago in Webisu. Accused of arson. There's no evidence. I prevail on you to ask Samnang to release her."

"If she's innocent, what need is there to intervene?" Cordelia enjoyed portraying the naïve innocence of Serena's expression. The pretty wife who didn't really know what was going on. Mira blinked but didn't flinch. Clasped her hands behind her back.

"I only ask that you expedite the process. De-escalate negative sentiments towards the folk."

"Serena," Ayumu interjected casually, "I heard that Samnang has proposed a city-wide curfew on fathomfolk."

"Nami saved your house, your family!" Mira's head snapped towards Ayumu, nostrils flared.

"We were already out. And yes, technically she did put the fire out, but I still don't know how she got there so quickly." Ayumu arched an eyebrow, words left unspoken.

Mira looked down at her battered pocket watch, hissing through pursed lips. She didn't have an official seat on the Council, could only put forward suggestions as head of the border guard. She tried Serena again. "I protected your daughter; does that count for nothing?"

"You have my thanks. The matter is not personal, Captain."

"Thanks buys me nothing. Thanks gets me nowhere. And yes, this is *very* personal." She turned on her heel and stormed towards the exit. The Council would agree to the curfew with an easy majority. The arson attacks were simply the final straw.

"What a tragic soul. Such a shame about the whole … siren thing. I mean, even I have to admit she's beautiful. But you can never tell if she's charming me to think that. I'd sleep safer if she had a pakalot," Ayumu mused. Cordelia did not respond. She wouldn't give the woman any more ammunition.

There was a hierarchy with the folk: subtle cliques and divisions, some that spanned centuries. And sirens, while not quite the bottom of the barrel, were down there. Duplicitous. Nearly as bad as seawitches. Dragons, on the other hand … dragons were like kings.

Rumour had it that the only reason Mira was with Kai was influence. Status. That she was using him. Rumour she made no attempt to quell because she was a fool. She thought honesty and integrity prevailed. Cordelia could teach her so much. Train her to war with words, cakes of tea and rich brocade.

It was not Cordelia's problem. If Mira didn't know, then her siren skills were best used by someone who did. People were generally predictable, easy to move as pieces on the board. There had been some setbacks, some unpredictability, especially from the Drawbacks, but Cordelia could manoeuvre things back on track.

"Ama?" Qiuyue said, tugging her skirts once Ayumu had gone. Cordelia caressed her daughter's hair affectionately. "I'm hungry."

"We'll go for food," she promised.

"Your eyes've gone funny again." Cordelia focused for a moment, altering her horizontal pupils back into Serena's hazel eyes.

"If I try really hard, I can make my eyes do that too." Qiuyue gasped as her mother's grip tightened sharply. The girl pulled away, cradling her fingers. A few glances were thrown in their direction and Cordelia kneeled. Qiuyue's lower lip trembled, the response clearly not what she'd hoped for.

Rubbing her daughter's hands between her own, Cordelia smiled. "You are smart, my little bird. Let's go home. I can teach you a few tricks. But it needs to be our secret, okay?"

The promise of subterfuge lit Qiuyue's interest and she nodded fervently, all upset forgotten. The chatter of her stories faded into the background as Cordelia mentally adjusted her plan. There. Just a slight deviation to the schedule. Things were still under control.

Chapter Thirty-Five

"A curfew will keep us safe? Safe?" Mira paced the length of Kai's apartment. "Even his simpering wife. I rescued their daughter, but all she offered me was thanks. As if the folk can live on thanks." Her foot kicked the corner of the table, stopping her runaway train of thought.

Kai had barely looked up, sitting as if he'd spilled from the sofa onto the floor, his tall frame hunched over. Mira's rage fled. Something was wrong. Very wrong. She sat on the floor next to him. Glass cylinders clinked as they rolled under the sofa. The apartment was unruly, like a typhoon had swept through.

"Kai?"

He blinked as if her voice had made him flinch. Turned with a clear effort to look at her.

"The bill," he said finally.

Mira's busying hands froze from straightening the odds and ends on the tabletop. She'd been so wrapped up in her own mess it had slipped her mind.

"They made me sit in the corridor. All morning the Fenghuang saw petitioners for other matters. I dared not move. But it didn't matter. It was already decided long before I arrived."

"What did he . . . ?"

"He nixed it. No change. Full pakalot restrictions. Actually, he wanted to make it worse. Illegal to have meetings of more than ten folk. Ten! Can you imagine? Houses in Seong have more than that." He laughed bitterly, lobbing crumpled paper across the table.

Mira wrapped her arms around him. All her words were insufficient. Gluing her tongue to the roof of her mouth. What could she say that wouldn't sound trite? Saltwater in open wounds. "I'm sorry."

"They say they're trying to prevent further riots. More like provoking them. Tiankawi may be above the waves, but it's not the flawless paradise they pretend it is."

An uncomfortable sensation pressed against Mira's throat. One that had been there for weeks, festering like an infected wound. She still hadn't told him about the ship of the dead. At first it was too raw, too insensitive to those who'd died. And then the moment had passed. She'd added it to the other secrets she kept from him. The ones about a past she was ashamed of.

Kai was the anchor, the pillar she held onto. She didn't know what to say when their roles were reversed. The words of comfort lay leaden on her tongue. "We'll manage. We always do."

"The newssheets are saying *we* incited the Boat Race riots! And the fire in Webisu. You and I, Mira, the pakalot-less savages!"

Mira swivelled till they were facing each other, pressing her forehead against his, hands on his cheeks. Breathed with him in through her nose and out through her lips. Let her hands fall into his. She was close to agreeing. Wallowing with him in the impossibility of the situation. But if Kai lost his optimism, she wasn't sure she could handle it. Had come to rely on his buoying spirit. She needed this for herself as much as him.

"Well then, we'll just have to find the golden shamisen and play it to awaken the sand gods!" She was rewarded with a glance. A reluctant smile at the corners of his mouth.

"Neither of us can play." His index finger stroking her bitten thumbnail.

"The lost library of Old Iyoness – open the forbidden chamber!"

"Mmm ... dangerous curses sound fun." The rough edges in his body softened like melting ice. His arm wrapped around her, pulling her into an embrace.

"We'll auction a dragon pearl to the highest bidder." The words fell before she could reel them back. Swallow them and box herself around the ears. Kai tensed. A joke that would've won her laughter in Qilin, but not here. For a moment, she'd forgotten.

He pulled away.

"I shouldn't have ..."

"No, you shouldn't." If he'd shouted, if he'd sworn at her, Mira could've handled it. But Kai was not the shouting kind. She put her head back on his shoulder, but it had turned to rock.

The blue skies peered at her from the windows, mocking her with their brightness. Like a calm ocean when she knew that outside the air was stifling, hot beyond comfort. And soon the monsoon rains would come and all they would see was grey.

She tried again. "I didn't mean it."

"Haven't you read the papers – they all think it. Just snap my fingers and solve everything."

"That's not what I think." The words from her mouth were like hooks, cutting deeper into his flesh when she only meant to free him. The more she talked, the more he writhed. She leaned forward to kiss him. Show him how she felt. Her lips found his, but he didn't move, staring instead into the distance. "Kai, I'm tired. We're both tired."

"You could change the city, achieve everything you've strived for with one wish. Isn't that what you want?" He undid his robes, exposing his torso as if she would plunge a dagger into it. The heart of him. She kissed him on the chest, a butterfly touch, before pulling his robes closed again.

"I love you. You who organised community centres across the city, who got supplies to the Qilin district. You who believed in me. In us."

"And all our effort for naught." He waved at the sea of scrolls around him. Floundering. Rubbed his eyes.

"I'll make them listen." She had to believe it.

For both of them.

Chapter Thirty-Six

They interrogated Nami. In windowless rooms they asked her the same questions. How did you get to the fire so quickly? What are the Drawbacks planning? How did you sabotage the boat during the races? Over and over again, hoping to trip her up, until the questions became a litany in her head. She was truthful in all her responses, but it mattered not. The kumiho city guards changed, a different face each day, but the questions were the same. Until all she saw was the sea wall of their navy uniforms.

They spat in her food and kicked it across her cell so that the congealed noodles spilled onto the gravel. Woke her every two hours to search her cell, to search her person, as if she had time and inclination to smuggle in contraband when all she could do was fitfully sleep. They clasped extra pakalots to her limbs. A second on her other wrist and one on each ankle – just in case. Her body dragged heavier than it had ever done. Her scales flared and faded with the tension of it, attempting to shield her from a danger they did not understand. They pulled at her attention, like an open wound, tender with even the smallest movement.

And then, finally, the guards ran out of time. Nothing to hold her for. "An administrative error," the lieutenant said as she unfastened the extra pakalots. Neither her smirk nor her tone rendered the excuse believable. But Nami did not have the energy to snap back. Willed her legs to move, one foot in front of the other, in case the kumiho changed their minds.

She was still filled with the stench of the holding cell, the bruises the only thing she could feel in her body. It reminded her of another arrest. One that seemed a thousand years away in time and depth.

Mira lived by their rules. Eun too. Don't give them a reason to hate. To complain. But it was easier on the outside. When someone wasn't aiming a kick at her head. When half a glass of water was all the city guard allowed a day, lest she use it against them. The filthy waters no longer stung her eyes, and despite the murkiness, she could see clearly for the first time.

Firth had left a message with Trish. After passing it on, the elder siren pleaded with Nami to wait, to meet with Mira and Kai first. But she could not do that.

No more waiting.

At the Drawback safe house, Firth was waiting for her. Eyes tracked her as she walked towards him. Ideas had been fermenting in that closed prison cell for days and she finally unstoppered the bottle. The words coated her tongue, corroding with every acrid mouthful. "We helped them and we got blamed. There's no reasoning with them. Despite what Mira says, what my brother says, there's only one way they'll listen. Where do we start?"

"You won't regret it." The kelpie looked at her fiercely, his grip tight. In the chaos she'd felt since arriving, the Drawbacks were clarity. No compromise.

"One condition. I need to know what the abyss is going on with the Onseon Engine. No more vague answers."

His eyes crinkled in an indulgent smile. It annoyed Nami. Filled her with a rush of blood that was a foghorn in her ears.

"I deserve answers." She pushed forward, stepping towards him as he danced back like it was a game. She licked her lips, noticing how his eyes lingered on the movement.

"Of course you do."

"I'm not a child." Another step forward, pressing her point. Firth was up against a wall now, one eyebrow arched as if in challenge.

"You're not." He waited, eyes holding hers, unblinking. Daring her to tilt her face up towards him. She hesitated.

He moved so quickly it was a blur. Nami felt herself spin, and then her body slammed against a hard surface. Her heart was pounding, somewhere between desire and fear, and she was shaking despite herself. The kelpie leaned in, hands pressed up against the wall on either side. Lips swooping down to touch hers. A soft groan escaped her as they kissed. All the frustration she'd felt since their day on the Peak. Her mouth yielded to the caress of his lips. His hands snaked around her waist and pressed against the bare skin at the small of her back.

He confused her. The kiss had taken her by surprise. She forgot there was anything but him and this room and the need, the sudden urgent need that consumed her.

"I shouldn't have done that." His voice was different as he slowly pulled back. Deeper. Breathless. His dilated pupils held hers. The green flecks seemed to dance in amber pools. He rubbed a thumb across her collarbone. "But your defiance – it drives me wild."

Nami was pleased with herself. So pleased that she didn't at first notice the door opening.

"Nami?"

Dan. The kappa left behind in a Yonakunish prison – her friend – stood in the doorway. His eyes darted from Firth to Nami and back again, as she awkwardly untangled herself. She wiped her mouth with the back of her hand, the taste of Firth still lingering there. Blinked as she tried to compose herself, to comprehend that Dan was in Tiankawi.

Seconds ticked by, time during which Nami gaped at her oldest friend. Finally she shook herself into action. A hug masked her wordless shock, but wrapping her arms around him, any thoughts of it being a dream shattered. She would never have imagined him this frail. He'd always been small, but the strength of will, the furious intent more than made up for it. Now he shook in her arms. Insubstantial as a hatchling in downy pin feathers. The shell on his back was flimsy, like it would break under pressure. He smelled faintly of decay. "What – how . . . you're here!" she spluttered.

"I've the Drawbacks to thank for it." Dan's bones were visible between the webbing of his hands and at his collarbones. His cheeks mere hollows. He glanced at Firth.

The kelpie quietly stepped out of the shadows. "Lynnette has contacts."

"What about Hong-Gi? Is he here too?"

"He's free," Firth said. A fleeting look passed between the kappa and the kelpie. Dan bobbed his head in agreement. "He was just a kid, Nami. We should never have involved him."

It had been months since Nami had come to Tiankawi. When she thought back on the Peace Stone incident, she was mostly disappointed. A stunt that had achieved nothing. Had she really wanted to free her unborn sibling or just rattle the cage?

At least Hong-Gi wasn't imprisoned for her foolishness any longer. After just a few days' confinement, Nami had an acute awareness of how much worse it was than she had imagined. Stories of prisoners released after long sentences were grim. Blinded by the sunlight's dazzle and open spaces.

"Thank the titans," she said finally. "It was my idiotic plan." She was truly thankful. She'd found people who believed in the same cause. Been reunited with her friend. Now that she had figured out where she fitted in, things were on the up.

Later, Lynnette slapped her on the back so hard Nami sprayed a mouthful of kombu liqueur on the other Drawbacks. The leader of the rebels was pleased to have her onside. Repeated it several times as she bought another round, sprawling between Firth and Nami on the sagging couch. The submerged back alley bar in Glashtyn Square had no signage out front and drinks were served in an eclectic range of containers, from chipped but ornate three-legged cups to glass jars and coconut shell bowls. The walls of the dive were covered in fake pearls and old bottle caps, a mosaic of debris made beautiful. Everything was utterly charming after three bottles of something that burned the throat and turned vision blurry.

Nami tried and failed to distract herself from Firth. Sitting just out of reach, he was engrossed in conversation with Lynnette and a mermaid on his other side. She focused on Dan's words instead, and yet Firth's presence seared like the pakalot that now hung loosely on her wrist.

"How did they get you in?" she asked. Her mind jumped to this morning's headlines. The newssheets had been plastered with it: thirty-nine fathomfolk found dead at the depot, victims of people-trafficking. From Atlitya, escaping the haven's civil war. They'd spent their life savings for some hope of a better future. On the settlement vessel it had never occurred to Nami that she was one of the lucky few.

Dan coughed and rubbed his eyes, still adjusting to the acidic waters of Tiankawi. He hesitated. "You don't want to know. But I meant what I said – Hong-Gi is safe. I made sure of that."

It was a strange way to word things, and yet Nami barely noticed, wanting to get something off her chest before she lost her nerve. She looked down at her lap, words blurting out in a rush. "I'm not here out of choice. I made a deal with my mother. To come here as an exile, to find out answers about the Onseon Engine in return for your freedom. But I wasn't fast enough. I wasn't—"

Dan barked, a caustic laugh interrupting her blethering apology.

"We are here now. And we'll see if our hands remain clean." His mood was more sombre than Nami was used to. Whatever had happened, he was changed from the kappa she knew.

She tried to galvanise him. "Who would've thought, both of us here in Tiankawi!"

"Living among mudskippers." He spat the last word like a foul taste in his mouth, then snapped his beak. "They're every bit as disgusting as we suspected. I don't know how folk do it. Live among them, befriend them, choose partners from them."

Nami was silent, refilling their cups slowly. She'd not heard that slur in so long, it took a moment to process. They'd used it all the time in the Anemone Club, scattering it like seasoning. On Dan's lips it sounded more crass than it had previously. She felt the need to defend. "They aren't all bad."

He looked at her quizzically, head cocked to one side.

"I mean, most of them are scum. But a couple are ... okay." How could she explain it? She could barely sort out her own thoughts, never mind articulate them. It wasn't that everything she'd heard was untrue. Some of it was exactly as expected. Some even worse. But slivers of gold existed. Embedded deep.

"Nami, you do know what the Drawbacks stand for, right? This isn't just a group for shouting slogans and painting strongly worded banners." The kappa put his webbed hands together, pressing his fingers against each other. A reflex Nami had seen him use when debating with fools back at the Academy. He was giving her that look. The one her mother, Kai, Mira had all given her. It built a wall between them, one that had not existed before. She ignored his remark, instead asking him how things were back home in Yonakuni haven.

"The reefs are still dying, bleached white as bones. Even the bottom-feeders go hungry. People are flooding in from Atlitya. More and more each day. There've been fights, nasty ones too. Folk worried there's no room," Dan said.

Nami bit her lower lip. The sentiments echoed what she had heard in Tiankawi. *We're full. We need to look after our own.* The similarities made her uncomfortable. The havens should be better than that. Everything had repercussions. If Atlitya fell, where would folk go? Only two havens would remain. "Our people are dying."

"They've always been dying. It's whether we choose to ignore the pleas for help." Dan splayed one hand on the table, letting it stick and peeling it back with a look of deep ire on his brow. He would not be further drawn on the subject.

They drank into the small hours. Nami had to drag Dan through the water to catch the last tram, certain they would miss it. Her lungs burned as she took the stairs two by two, breathless words of encouragement shouted back to the kappa. From behind, a grunt of surprise, and then Lynnette was bouncing past her, Dan over one shoulder. The Drawback leader deposited him into the carriage and still had energy to spare, holding the protesting doors opened so the water dragon could squeeze in.

The mohawked kelpie nodded in satisfaction, winking to Nami as the doors finally slid shut. She'd been different to what Nami expected. At the rally, her words were a beacon during a starless night. Her actions a bloodied knife with a singular purpose. Tonight she had been softer. Mellow. Just one of the group rather than a charismatic force that demanded all attention.

The juddering movement in the carriage made Dan stumble forward. Swaying drunkenly, he went down on all fours and shook the water from his amphibious skin. The other passengers called out in protest. The human woman closest had been fast enough to shield herself with a bag, but her partner wrinkled his nose as he wiped the water from his face with the back of his sleeve. "Seriously?"

Dan stood and bowed mockingly, his hands out at his sides to keep his balance. His arms were riddled with scars; mostly older ones, but there were fresh cuts too. Dark green in raised welts. Despite her own merriment, Nami realised the whole carriage was looking. And that was not what they needed when Dan was here illegally. No pakalot in sight. It was easy enough to jump the ticket barrier, but if someone reported them ... She pushed him down to sit as the tram rumbled slowly into the night. Threw her jacket around his shoulders and buttoned it. He muttered drunkenly.

"Keep your head down," she hissed.

"I didn't want to ... I didn't. I'm sorry, Nami." Incoherent ramblings. He tried to say more but Nami stopped him. She was the one who should be apologising. The words jumbled in her brain, but she grabbed at them, pulling them into some semblance of order. Just as she was about to speak, Dan's head drooped forward with a loud snore.

"By the seas, are you a siren?" a voice asked. Three human girls had approached her. Despite the fishnet tights, expensive flowing dresses and artfully waved hair, their faces betrayed their youth. Too young to be out this late, but probably too well-off to be stopped. The girl speaking had swirls of blue painted around her eyes and down her cheeks. Her arms jingled with dozens of silver bracelets, and a brown henna octopus snaked up one of her pale arms.

"No, I—"

One of her companions squealed, startling Nami out of her words. "Don't tell me you're a naga; we've not met a naga yet." This one had piercings down both ears: dangling silver fish, starfish and shells that shimmered as she moved.

Nami stood up slowly, not really understanding what was going on. "I'm not a naga either." She was conscious of Dan asleep at her side. Inched a few steps in front of him so he was hidden.

"Please," said the first girl, her palm out flat to Nami's face, "don't tell us, let us guess."

They all took a step back, looking at her like they were studying a rare artefact at a museum. One had started taking notes on a pad with a pen shaped like a piece of spiny coral. Nami made eye contact with the third girl, wondering if she could clarify what her friends couldn't. She wore one of the masks humans used to breathe underwater, but it was strapped to the back of her head, decoratively covered in small gems and pieces of fringed sea-weed. Her hair was coiled up and through the straps, completely impractical however pretty the effect. These girls had clearly not been underwater tonight.

"Maybe tianchi," the first said.

"I didn't even consider tianchi!" said her friend.

Nami interrupted, her foot tapping on the floor. "What are you doing?"

"We're Lakelanders. I mean, the name is only starting to catch on, so you might not have heard of us. But we're with you," said the first girl. She spoke the last words with emphasis, as if it explained everything. The air was pregnant with anticipation of Nami's response.

"With . . . me?" Nami faltered.

"With fathomfolk. You're amazing. And it's, like, really not cool how you're being treated. We're inspired by you!" The girl splayed out her skirts with both hands and Nami realised there had been a deliberate attempt to patchwork the opulent fabric. Like the threadbare garments of the poorer humans and folk in the city.

"All fathomfolk," her friend agreed. The quiet third girl nodded.

"So you want to help us by going around guessing what we are?" Nami said slowly. She hoped the girls would realise how offensive the whole set-up was, but they nodded earnestly, the message washing clean over their heads.

"Well, unless you're a dragon! In which case we'd ask for your pearl," the first girl answered, laughing to herself.

"Where do they even hide the pearl?" the second one interrupted. The quieter friend whispered in her ear and the three of them shrieked, covering their mouths between blushing and laughing.

Nami wanted to slap their stupid faces and tear the jewellery from their ear lobes. It was just a big joke to them. If you had a pearl, all your troubles were solved. She'd even seen cleaning products promoted as being better than dragon pearls at removing dirt. Like she was a fucking laundry detergent. That her life, Kai's, that of their unborn sibling in the Peace Tower, were of no consequence. All these idiots could think of was favours and how to accessorise.

"So tell us, what are you?" The second girl brought the conversation back round.

"I'm ..." Nami could feel the heat of her ire seeping out through her skin. Her pakalot pulsed a warning. Luckily the tram pulled into a station, the brakes sending them all stumbling. More people rushed into the carriage, separating the girls from where Nami stood. An unfortunate trio of kun pengs were positioned right next to them, water droplets rolling off their waxy feathered fins.

"Kun pengs! Oh my gosh, can I practise my kungo with you?" she heard the first girl ask. Her bangles jangled loudly, and only now did it click: stylised pakalots.

Nami pushed her nails into her arm to stop herself from shoving through the other passengers and shouting at the fools to go home. Children messing with something they didn't understand.

The words sounded familiar.

Sobekki had scolded her similarly back in the Peace Tower. Telling her she had much growing up to do. Nami couldn't help but stare down the carriage at the flamboyantly dressed girls.

No. She was different.

She was certain of it.

Chapter Thirty-Seven

Flanked by her two giant squid guards, Cordelia stalked across the sea floor. Fathomfolk scattered before her. People were not foolish enough to get in the way of an angry sea-witch. With her limbs pure white and spread to their full extent, it was clear what mood she was in.

The agreed meeting point was aboard a shipwrecked carcass. All the metal and usable furniture had been long since scavenged. Both human and folk saw it as a place of ill fortune, leaving it well alone. It was one of the Drawbacks' safe houses, although they had dozens she'd yet to figure out.

Cordelia was early, but Lynnette was already there, arms folded firmly. Each wanted to put the other on the back foot. She slowed right down, making the kelpie wait, even though she was in clear sight now. They'd chosen the wrong seawitch to mess with. Firth was by Lynnette's side, a limpet on her surface. He was everywhere, folk drawn to him like moths flickering around a naked flame. And there was another fellow, the diminutive kappa again. Her informants had been remiss in finding out much on that one.

"Cordelia," Lynnette said, her fist-palm salute so stiff she looked like an anxious new recruit meeting her captain. A vein in her neck pulsed.

"Give me one reason why I shouldn't shrivel your head and stamp on it right now," the seawitch retorted. They had kidnapped her daughter, wanting to use her to blackmail Cordelia into doing their bidding. Threatened to reveal her identity and destroy her whole family. Everything she had worked so hard to achieve. It had been pure luck that Mira had intervened, rescuing Qiuyue before any real harm had been done. Now Lynnette had reached out for a parley, promising a mutually beneficial deal.

"Because I can make Samnang the Fenghuang." Lynnette finally let go of the knuckled salute, flexing her stiff fingers. For someone who held all the cards, she was surprisingly anxious. Cordelia filed that away for later. "Don't take it personally. This is purely business."

"You brought my family into it."

"Says the person who uses blackmail like a dipping sauce," interjected Firth, scorn lining his chiselled features. "A clever stunt you pulled there with the curfew. Really ties up the city guard checking everyone's gill lines. Keeps them busy."

Cordelia bared her sharp teeth at the kelpies, inches from throttling them with her suckered limbs. They were trying to rile her. Waiting for a slip-up.

"Such a tragedy what happened to those people. Thirty-nine dead, was it? You must've lost a lot of business." Firth spoke casually, as though remarking on the weather. Picked at the dirt under his nails. But such tragedies were fortunate for a cause like the Drawbacks. Innocent lives lost made for better headlines. The horror of it kept the story in the press for weeks. Carefully leaked details about the lives and hopes of the victims, hungry ghosts beyond the grave. Made folk angrier, more inclined to rally to their cause. Tied up the border guards and made them ineffectual.

It also weakened Cordelia. After all, it was her bargains they were testing. Fucking with her smuggling business was bad for business, for her reputation, but it was also bad for her health. Her black ink already looked more like sugar syrup than before: the effect of her unfulfilled bargains, even if it was not her fault. She kept her mouth closed, though, unwilling to give the Drawbacks anything more.

Lynnette looked at Firth but remained silent. Unrestrained, he went on. "Desperate Atlityans who thought humans could solve all their problems. Fools every one."

Cordelia couldn't help herself. "Those were fathomfolk – kelpies included. Were you not in the same situation years ago?"

"Death would've been better than the Nurseries!" he said scornfully.

Lynnette finally took a step forward, hand touching Firth's forearm. He shrugged it off like a bug against his skin. The Drawback leader looked back at him, caught between the two. Reflexively made the sign of the sand gods across her chest as she cleared her throat.

Cordelia slipped across the rotting wood of the decking, her limbs making short work of the distance. "Kidnap and blackmail? Reveal all my secrets. This is your plan?" She let out an exaggerated yawn, through both her mouth and the siphons near her collarbones.

The whites of Lynnette's eyes showed, and she half turned as if to pull Firth back into the fray. Despite her large frame, she was hunched over trying to be as small as the kappa at her side. She swallowed and revealed her trump card. "I've not even mentioned your stolen siren song."

Cordelia steeled her features into blank indifference. Beneath the surface, a storm broiled in her blood. How the abyss did they know? Her every movement, her every important deal and disguise. They tried to close a net around her no matter how her body contorted out of reach. And it was clear their ambitions went further than pakalots and people-smuggling.

"Serena, Serena, Serena. Who would've thought such a lovely and thoroughly human wife was actually an odious seawitch? Her children half-saltie mongrels. Entrenched in the upper echelons, manipulating Tiankawian society with stolen siren song. What a scandal! What a terrible, career-ending shame! Can't trust anyone these days." Lynnette's voice lilted like she'd rehearsed this little speech. Practised the condescending little digs before a mirror. "I hear the bargain you made for the song is due to end soon."

"My children are half of nothing." Cordelia had to focus to stop her colours flaring along her skin. "You think I know nothing of your secrets? Of what you did in the Nurseries?"

"We all do what we have to in order to survive." Lynnette's tone was light, but the hesitation was back again. Her hand rubbing her sand god amulet. Another mouthy leader. Cordelia relaxed a little. She'd seen many come and go. Politicians, revolutionaries, religious leaders. They all faded in time while water levels continued to rise.

"Get to your point."

"Two things. Easy enough for you. A potion, and a lock."

Cordelia raised an eyebrow. Her nails had crept to the crook of her elbow, but she forced them to stop scratching. "Not just any old potion and any old lock, I take it?"

"Astute, aren't you? Say I needed to make a pod of whales sleep. Permanently. And say I need to unlock a door warded by two seawitches."

The seawitch whistled low. Pondered aloud even though she'd already figured out what they were after. "A whole pod of whales using one potion? Peculiar request, isn't it? I mean, Tiankawi hardly has many pods of whales, unless someone is keeping them well hidden."

"Humour me."

"I could make this poison – I mean potion. Theoretically. Most of the ingredients are difficult to procure." She placed a finger beneath her chin as if struggling to recall items needed, muttered under her breath and raised fingers to count them. Lynnette squirmed a little and it was worth every second. "Not impossible. Apart from one. And I suspect you know this."

"Yes, that we can acquire for you." Lynnette glanced back at Firth, who nodded his assent.

"It's rare to find seawitches working with the competition to make those sorts of wards. Rather went out of fashion about a decade ago. Too time-consuming. Too expensive. The only buildings that still have that sort of lock ... why, they're government buildings." Cordelia shot a glance at Lynnette as if the thought had just occurred. "My, my, what are you up to?"

The kelpie chose to ignore the dangling bait. "One lock, one potion and I'll not breathe a word about your identity for the rest of my life."

Cordelia knew before she finished her sentence what the lure would be. It had probably been the plan when they took Qiuyue. But no one outsmarted a witch at bargains. Her squid guards slipped under the crack of the door and crept forward in full camouflage. Lynnette barely noticed. The kappa fellow, on the other hand, narrowed his eyes but said nothing, beak pursed tight.

"You'll not be allowed to speak, write or sign any communication pertaining to my identity and that of my children," Cordelia clarified. Lynnette gave a grimace but nodded curtly. "And the other Drawbacks?"

"They don't know your secret," Firth called from the shadows, as if this would convince her of their ignorance.

"You'll swear, on contract, that anyone who knows of my dual identity will also be bound." She drew out the bamboo scroll she wrote her bargains on. The bottle of ink was sealed with wax, the precious drops only used for such occasions. It had to be her ink – drained from her own body like blood – to ensure the bargain was ironclad on both parties. She had dyed it, turned it black as it should be rather than letting them see how weak she had become.

Lynnette conferred with Firth before answering. "Fine, fine. Any Drawbacks who know about Serena are sworn to secrecy."

"Associates. Drawback members and non-members also." Cordelia's eyes flickered to the undernourished kappa. "On pain of . . . well, excruciating pain and death. Naturally."

"Naturally." Lynnette shifted her weight onto her other foot, glancing once more at her second in command.

"And just for fun, let's say a visible scar across their face. Just so I know which of you insurrectionists tried to rat me out."

"We prefer the term revolutionary."

Cordelia ignored Lynnette's interjection. "In return, one potion that will *permanently* take out a pod of whales, *sans* the special ingredient; and a single-use double-ward-breaking key," she said, careful with her wording.

"You'll speak to no one about this bargain."

"No humans."

"No fathomfolk either." Firth put his hand on the scroll, preventing Cordelia from etching the sentence until she acknowledged him. She wrinkled her nose, annoyed that she'd not been able to wiggle that one past them.

Lynnette checked the wording and they both put their signature to the document, the ink hissing as it tattooed itself deep within the grain. As she swam away, Cordelia petted her squid guards absent-mindedly, wondering how quickly the Drawbacks would double-cross her. It was an inevitability really.

As was the fact she would do it first.

Chapter Thirty-Eight

The pipa player took a long drag on his cigarette and exhaled as he strummed the instrument. His fingers curled, raindrops on the strings, as the sound filled the small room and pulled the audience closer. And then the singer started. His crooning voice wafted high against the pockmarked ceiling, seeking the sky through the cracks in the plaster.

Siren. Hands tucked nonchalantly in pockets, rocking on his heels. Intoxicating.

It wasn't until the end of the set that Mira took a breath. She ached to join the song, add a harmony to the wordless melody. Others had done so, raising voices on an uneven keel. Lusty and enthusiastic. But she refrained. Kai touched her hand across the table, his face flickering in the candlelight.

"How did you find this place?" Mira caressed the palm of his hand.

"A Tiankawi secret you don't know!" Kai had refused to take no for an answer, almost dragging her here. They needed a break. Mira nearly refused him, except he was right. They had barely had a minute to themselves. To breathe and remember the world outside of riots and people-smugglers. And Kai, as always, had a plan.

The next group started, the drums like thunder in the distance, pounding through her ribcage as if they would shake secrets from her heart. The drummers moved their whole bodies into each beat, the sticks like oars paddling through muddy waters. People were dancing, jumping and swaying in the audience. Mira was on her feet, pulling Kai up with her. His eyes glittered as he followed her into the centre of the crowd. She let the music take hold of her head, closing her eyes and moving with it, carried along in the stream. Dimly she felt others around her, packed sweating bodies, shoulders and table edges against her as she moved, Kai next to her, clapping, jumping. But it was only at the periphery. The music was everything.

Her eyes snapped open as the drummers stopped. Her clothes clung to her back, her feet throbbed through her shoes, but mostly she felt expansive. Joy unfurling from within her. It had been a long time since she had experienced it.

"That was ... unlike anything!" Kai wiped his brow with a wide sleeve. He smiled at the other people with that easy charm she loved. Bantered with the couple next to them, helped another find the shoes they'd kicked to the floor. He approached the stage and thanked the stagehands for their efforts, admired one of the huge drums at a respectful distance. All of this in the time it took Mira to get drinks from the bar.

"What are you smiling at?" he said as he came back to her.

"You. Even sweat-drenched and on your day off, you're still ... you." She kissed his forehead. He tasted of salt. Kai didn't answer, just pulled her into his arms, slow-dancing her across the empty floor to an off-key melody hummed under his breath. She basked in the glow like sunlight kissing her cheeks. This was how it could be. Inside this tiny bar, humans and folk interacted like it was nothing at all. Like their differences did not matter.

But eventually they had to leave.

They walked back arm in arm, taking the long way round the walkways while the sky was clear. The tinny noise of the hastily erected loudspeakers crackled. A voice announced in Tiankawian, then multiple folk languages, that there was one hour until fathomfolk curfew. Even though she and Kai were exempt, Mira still felt the urgency tingling on her skin like a rash. The ticking of her pocket watch louder than their footfall.

"I've lost you," Kai said. Mira looked up, trying to recall what he'd been talking about. A moment ago she'd been completely at ease, thinking of nothing more than the music. But the loudspeaker had been a reminder: of the jobs mounting up, the mental tick lists and the guilt that threatened to drown her. It was never enough.

A wheezing cough from the darkness put her on high alert. Some of the shadows were more than just closed street stalls and debris. She stilled, pulling Kai to a stop as her eyes adjusted. There. Four levels down, propped against a wall. A hunched figure. Track marks and blackened fingers. The fugu dealers were getting more and more fearless. It was no longer the drug of the entertainment district and the submerged city far from kumiho eyes. It was everywhere. And more often than not laced with cheaper squid ink, ground-up mussel shell or boiled hair.

Finding the nearest stairs down, she kneeled by the stranger, checking his pulse and shouting until he flickered open rheumy eyes. Human. Addiction didn't care about the salt in your veins.

"Piss off, bottom-feeder!" His speech was sloppy, dripping from the corner of his mouth along with the line of saliva. Spit flecked Mira's cheek and the stench from his mouth forced her to stifle a gag.

"Hold your tongue, we're trying to help," Kai said. His voice was flustered.

"Didn't ask for no help. Not from fish fuckers."

Mira put a hand on Kai's shoulder. Just a little squeeze of reassurance. Not that Kai was the type to fly off the handle, but the remarks clearly bothered him. He'd been cushioned up there in his Jingsha penthouse.

The man was as safe as he could be without Mira finding a

telephone box and calling round the shelters. Upright enough not to choke on his vomit, a warm enough night for him not to freeze in his sleep.

"Can I do anything?" Kai said. He looked hesitantly at the drifter.

Mira smoothed down the crinkles in her dress. Noted with chagrin that the hem was mud- and algae-stained. "We can call it in at the nearest guard kiosk. You mind if we do a circuit?"

"It will add to the ambience of our stroll."

They had walked for a while before she registered Kai's remark. She'd marched on ahead, leaving him quite far behind. Mind in full work mode as she looked down each alleyway, sniffed the air for the telltale scent of the burning fugu, added more jobs to her list. She'd neglected the north-east. It was so damned close to Jingsha, not to mention the Peak. An area of growing affluence she hadn't even thought to check. Despite the lights of the stilted mansion houses at the lower slopes of the mountain, she spotted the shanty town. An anomalous bank of ramshackle rafts and scavenged material. Old wooden doors and patched tarpaulins propped at angles. She spied the hull of a rowing boat tipped upside down as a shelter. Bamboo scaffolding had been lashed together as makeshift walkways and to prop up faltering walls. A couple of witchlights glowed from exposed cracks, but most people had already headed home, not wanting to risk the wrath of the heavy-handed city guards.

"Ah, that's what the junior construction official was harping on about," Kai said. "Quite a rant about stolen scaffolding at the Council meeting!" He made a low noise, pleased with himself. Beside the jumble of the floating shacks, his finery looked out of place. Not a single darning stitch on him.

Mira rubbed the hem of her coat. She had sewn up the frayed edge with old fishing net, and the lining was a patchwork quilt. Skills her mother had taught her when they lived somewhere not dissimilar to this. "Who cares about some bamboo poles? Do you want to take them back?" She heard the anger in her voice. It surprised both of them, appearing like a flash flood. Kai held his hands out, made soothing noises. That just infuriated her more.

"I wasn't suggesting that," he said, his voice slow and steady. It reminded her of the teachers at school. How they talked down to her, always checking that she understood. She told them time and time again: Tiankawian was her first and only language.

He watched her, attempting to read her mood before finally speaking again. "Did you . . . want to check for anything?"

What did he expect – that she would haul people from their beds and interrogate them? "Like addicts? You presuming they're all addicts just because this is where they live? They're people! Humans and folk stuck in the river of shit that surrounds Jingsha. No one's going to pay for their meals in rotating restaurants." She threw the words at him, not caring where they landed.

Former boyfriends would have thrown the rage back at her, quarrelled until words could not be unspoken. Not Kai. He knew she wasn't really angry. At least not at him. He took her hand, unruffled by her outburst. "My place doesn't suit you, does it? Tell me what you need."

Mira's heart squeezed tight. He'd cut through every layer. Peeled them back and found her centre. She wanted to deny it. Demand to know why he was changing the subject. But he wasn't. It lay beneath their every recent conversation, a brine lake she concealed in the darkest corner of her worries. She couldn't trust herself to speak.

"A place to live. Our place," he said.

She looked at him, looked past him at the shanty town behind. How preposterous to talk about this now. Her eyes lingered on a rusted corrugated-iron roof, and she could recall the exact sensation of the metal yielding beneath her feet as she ran across it. The hollow sound and the yells that followed. The moment of doubt that it would warp and she would go flying. The constant struggle to scrub the black mould from their clothes and furniture. The bowls and buckets used to catch the leaks in monsoon season. An orchestra of drips and splashes that would lull her to sleep.

"I can't switch it off," she said finally. "Everywhere I look, I see it. I know – it's my day off, but my brain doesn't work that way. A moment sleeping, or dancing, or having dinner – it's another moment wasted." Her words hung there like a spider's web, gossamer thin and easy to break, and yet she was caught.

"I'm not asking you to. But I can't change where I'm from. What my life has been up until now. All I can do is build a future you'd be happy in. Isn't that enough?" Kai offered his arms again and she let herself fall into them.

"It's enough." She closed her eyes, screwing them tight to make her words true.

Chapter Thirty-Nine

Nami had expected codewords, blueprints for secret plans, and covert identities in the Drawbacks. Instead she got a shellycoat playing wunlan, his hands darting out from his matted rattling shell hide to move the pieces on the board. Ikan keli catfish twins, Trieu and Bien, who taught non-contact martial arts and sold fish sauce like it was moonshine. And an elder dugong called Ibhar, who turned rags into wearable clothing. It was like one of Mira and Kai's projects rather than the revolutionaries she'd anticipated.

She spent the mornings with Ibhar and Dan sorting material. Worn clothing, ripped sails and filthy bed sheets. The dugong's tough grey skin was plump and hairless, giving her a youthful appearance despite the gravel in her voice. Even in human form her hands kept a semblance of flippers, making her stitchwork meanderingly slow. Nami and Dan washed, and Ibhar mended what she could. Nami itched, and not just because the tub of water was shit brown and filled with dead mites. She bit her tongue and rolled up her sleeves.

Ibhar explained that the Drawbacks had been a community group. Took in donations, helped new arrivals with housing and visas. Tea mornings and toddler sessions. Clothing was expensive. Hemp, cotton, silk – all needed land to grow. The prices were beyond most folk. Nami looked down at her own clothes: the yellow and blue top now an extravagance, whereas she'd thought it plain when Mira had purchased it. The Drawbacks had gathered threadbare clothes – scraps really – worn soft and fragile from the salty water. Patched them together with white thread in beautiful sashiko patterns like the rings of a tree trunk.

Nami stabbed her finger sewing and bled several times before Ibhar sent her to hang out the material to dry instead. It turned out Dan had excellent mending skills from helping out at home. Ibhar was quite taken with him already. She was the only Drawback Dan warmed to, the kappa subdued in the presence of the others.

They revealed a little more after a few weeks. Lynnette brandished a slingshot at her. Like a silent beacon, the others rose, grinning with a singular purpose. Only Ibhar stayed behind, waving them off with the resident black cat purring in her lap.

Nami's questions were ignored and a flask of laver rum was liberally passed around. They stepped onto the tram, ten minutes before curfew, Lynnette stomping up and down until one by one the other passengers vacated the carriage.

They didn't care who saw, swaggering into the business district. Trieu took the first go with the slingshot. His long barbel whiskers wiggled as he waterweaved an ice rock as large as his fist and let it fly. It smashed upon the steps of an innocuous building. Bien heckled his twin before giving it a go himself. His shot flew high, knocking a couple of the tiles loose. One by one they took a turn, some better than others. Finally the slingshot was put into Nami's hands. She looked for an explanation. The Drawbacks grinned at her; folk she barely knew, and yet she felt a kinship. Echoes of the student meetings back in Yonakuni, the dedication and defiance that united them as one.

"Our mutual friend from the Webisu fire. His office is in there," Firth said. He'd handed her a gift. The outraged man who'd accused them of letting his houseboat burn. Who'd called the kumiho to arrest her. Nami's cheeks hurt from grinning now she understood. They were a family. She took a drag on the flask, the spiced alcohol burning her palate and bring her sharp clarity. Kai would've told her to let it go; Mira would have given her a lecture on going through the correct channels. Only the Drawbacks got her.

She teased a stream of water from between the boards, weaving it into a sphere. Glancing at Lynnette's hair, she added spikes to the icy outer layer. Bien showed her how to swing the sling by her side, letting it sail at just the right moment. They could've pelted the building with direct waterweaving, but that wasn't the point. This took effort. Enacting their petty vengeance together. On the first three attempts her projectile smashed into the ground. But on the fourth it sailed straight through a window with a crystal smash. They laughed as they ran, curfew ignored, the city alive in their hands.

No one could stop them.

Firth liked to remind them, at every subsequent rally and underwater protest. "We didn't have the status. To work, to rent houses, to go to school. They put a manacle on our wrists and said it was for our own good! Because we hadn't waited for the right documents. Because we fled with only the possessions on our backs. My brother died on the way to Tiankawi. But not any more. Together, no one can stop the tidal wave."

The story changed from the one he'd told Nami. Changed with every iteration. Yet it worked. People fell over themselves to join. As she became more and more involved with the Drawbacks – ducking questions from Kai, staying out all night – Nami barely had two minutes alone with Firth, time to snatch a few furtive kisses but nothing more. She thought about him endlessly, twisted up in her bed sheets during sleepless nights. She even tried to ambush him at the end of meetings. Always apologetic, he had many excuses. She couldn't blame the Drawbacks for using his pleasing face to charm, but her stomach jerked when she saw him laughing with other women.

It's just a subterfuge, Ibhar promised. All shadow, no heart. But Nami was unsure who she was referring to any more. Another fish chasing lights in the darkest oceans. It was for the best. Don't get enamoured. She would prove her allegiance through action.

In time, Lynnette took her to a different safe house. Seagrass woven mats lined the floors and the catfish twins were warming up against the wall. Their training ground. Finally.

She watched, at first with elation, then trepidation, then a slow slide into mild horror as the hours ticked by. She'd earned the Drawback leader's trust to be here, watching her weak points as they practised. The kelpie had many. She was strong, as tall as Firth, muscle-bound and taut. But she moved slowly, as if unaccustomed to her own body. Fighting the drag of the water even though they were topside. Even stooping to brush two fingers across the sand god shrine in the corner of the room before each round she was awkward and ungainly. The brothers danced around her. Bien, with his three-part staff twirling over and under his arms, hit her as he passed. Trieu had a long spear, sweeping it under her legs and tapping at her feet as she took too long to move out of the way. Lynnette sweated heavily, her hair drooping into her eyes as the session went on. Nami desperately wanted to call out, to jump in and even the match up. She shifted uncomfortably on her stool.

She offered to spar, deliberately losing a few rounds to boost the Drawback leader's ego. Lynnette was silent, powering through Nami's light touch with a barrage of blows in the first five minutes. But she didn't know how to pace herself, tiring quickly. Nami chose her words carefully, talking about holding back and waiting for opportunities, but the kelpie did not listen, face contorted. "Go *spar* with Firth!" she snapped at the end of the session, words biting and insinuating.

Firth came to practise now and then, reaching for Nami's hand as if leading her in a dance. Ignoring Bien's taunts as he circled her with an arched eyebrow and a beckoning gesture. Waiting for her to make the first move, eyes roving like a famished beast. Nami pushed back her hair, intensely aware of the humidity as her clothes clung to her. Watching the bead of sweat in the hollow of Firth's neck. He fought in no style she recognised. Moments of feigning elegance followed by a ruthless twist of her arm behind her back. She gasped with the sharpness of it as he leaned over her exposed neck, breathing deeply. "Admit defeat."

Swivelling out of his grasp, she flipped forward and rolled to a crouch near where Lynnette and the others watched. Caught the brunt of Lynnette's glare like a hammer to the chest. It made her stumble, forget that Firth was behind her until she felt the dagger point at her back.

"You're always a useful distraction, Lynnette," Firth gloated as he put the knife away, wiping the moisture from his brow. He'd used an unfair advantage. In an honourable fight, Nami would've won. She swallowed the complaint. But more than that, Lynnette's expression imprinted on her. A look so venomous that Nami wanted to follow the Drawback leader as she stalked off. Trieu caught her arm, shaking his head without explaining further.

She was determined to make a difference. Threw herself into training. Instead of instructing Lynnette, fearful of the woman's ego, she gave the catfish twins pointers on using their latent weapons: their serrated fins, which could be summoned in human form, a protective barbed edge running up their forearms. Or the mucus they could excrete from their scaleless skin. Trieu instinctively knew to release it during a fight, making weapons and hands glance off him, but Bien needed more practice.

They started practising set forms early in the morning and before the sun set. Lynnette shadowed them from a distance, always turning to look indifferent when she caught Nami's eye. After a few weeks she lost her slouch and openly joined in. Demanded to be kept informed on new training strategies, as the leader of the group and all. Nami taught her to coat her fists in ice, shield herself, make the most of her strength and size. The water dragon didn't expect to be a good teacher. She'd always been the student who switched off. But the practical aspect, the ideas that burrowed into her head overnight, the clear differences she saw in Lynnette's stance and confidence, made her reconsider. Perhaps, outside of turgid books and monotone lectures, this was something she could be good at.

Chapter Forty

Mira didn't have time for this. She needed to fund funerals for those who'd died on the smuggler vessel. The Drawbacks were demanding a monument and the kumiho were putting the blame squarely at her feet. As if that wasn't enough, the settlement ship was due in from Atlitya haven this week, and she'd already heard about trouble aboard. Guards had reported finding stowaways, threatened to turn back to the border. She ordered a flotilla of chinthe boats to escort the vessel, hoping it would calm frayed nerves. It would not be another Nursery. If Atlitya fell, its people wouldn't be detained in disease-ridden hovels while officials argued about cost. Never again.

So she really didn't have the time for this appointment. But Cordelia had insisted.

Graffiti was sprayed over the windows of the tram, racist slurs in letters that wept. Mira swept her eyes over the carriage as she helped her ama in. Trish could now move with the aid of crutches and was determined it wouldn't stop her. Mira's gaze jumped from passenger to passenger, assessing the risk, looking at their bags, at the paper umbrellas and long coats that could conceal weapons. Trish chattered oblivious as she inched them towards seats at the carriage end. A clear vantage point. Not to mention a straight path to the door.

Her ama had asked a question. Mira shrugged, hoping it would suffice, but the act wouldn't work this time.

"Were you even listening?" Trish sat gingerly, placing her crutches to one side as she continued to talk, her face turned upwards towards her still standing daughter. Mira declined the seat next to her, too pent up. Drummed her fingers against the pole. Kai's name was mentioned and immediately Mira's mind went blank. They'd not quite argued lately, but the tension was palpable. No, she could not, would not think about him. Had too many other things to worry about. More important things.

Even though Trish was still talking, all Mira could hear was her own pulse in her ears, the loudest thing in the whole tram. She opened her mouth. "What?" she asked, and her voice was distant. Shouting through thick glass.

The tram juddered to a stop and she stumbled forward. Trish caught her hand. Forced the issue. "What's going on with the two of you?"

"Tickets and identification!" a deep voice demanded. Four kumiho guards had entered the tram, walking in pairs down either end of the carriage.

"You've got to be kidding me," Mira muttered under her breath. One of the city guards heard her, striding decisively towards her with hackles raised.

"You have a problem?" he said, folding his arms.

"Since when did we have to travel with identification papers?" she said, holding his gaze. He looked down on her, but she was used to it. Intimidation with height and size.

"Don't question, just show."

"You can only ask for identification papers for a suspected crime. Even then the accused has two days. That was agreed in Marine Laws, and curfew or not, those still stand."

She was aware of his flaring nostrils, of the fist curled at the side of his body. Of Trish's look of marvel, of the other guards turning, hands on their sticks. Knew he was waiting to be provoked. Had worked with the likes of him before. People who joined to pick on those smaller. Just what she needed today.

She sighed, flipping open her coat where her badge was pinned on the lining. The guard yelled. Slammed her to the ground. Her mother screeched over and over, crutches clattering to the ground, "She's chinthe, you idiot, she's the chinthe captain!" He was shouting about a weapon, a weapon! In the cacophony, chaos ensued. With her cheek against the cold metal, Mira could see food remnants under the chairs. Salt crusting the edges of the windows. Smears of dirt by the doors. The kumiho guard pulled her arm hard behind her back. More force than was needed for someone half his size. There was a knee in the small of her back, slowly crushing her. Her gills heaved ineffectually, because her lungs could not.

Her ama was still shouting, voice crackling as she tried to be heard above the din, but all Mira could see were faces. The faces of other passengers: people staring through the windows, peering in through the open doors. She heard her name in whispers. Mira. That's Mira. The captain. The siren. What's she done? A weapon? Well, she must have done something.

Let her up, an older voice said. The tight hold on her loosened and Mira coughed. She rubbed her wrist and shoulder, the strain still aching through her. There would be a behemoth of a bruise tomorrow, but feeling at her ribs, they didn't seem to be broken. She rose to her feet, taking her sweet time.

"Captain," the woman said, fist-palm saluting her. A kumiho lieutenant she did not know, but with a little more sense than the others. "Apologies for the inconvenience."

"Inconvenience?" Trish yelled before Mira could respond. "You beat her up for talking. Is that what you're doing to folk these days?"

The woman glared but answered with restraint. "My colleague detected a weapon."

Already the others had bundled the offending guard away. Concocting a cover story should Mira take this above their pay grade. And yes, she was most definitely doing that.

She flipped her coat open again. The gold stripes of her captain's badge glinted in the daylight. And inside a patchwork pocket, there was a glass tube, a scroll she'd shoved there and long forgotten about. The toughened glass had cracked and she cut her finger as she extracted the scroll. "Is it illegal to read now as well?"

"If you'd not questioned the guard and simply showed your documentation as requested . . ."

"I asked him – and I will ask you – on what law is this based? Why were we questioned, and everyone else in the carriage was not?" She gestured at the humans around them, who'd been watching with slack jaws.

"It is highly irregular for fathomfolk to be . . ." The guard trailed off into babbling incoherence. Through the window, the imposing glass-fronted buildings of Jingsha filled the view.

To be above water. To be in the more affluent areas of the city. Mira had put up with the confused looks, the outright hostility her whole life, especially when Kai took her to opulent restaurants and music halls in the north. The arched eyebrows when they found her name on the guest list after all. But it had been years since they'd dared say it to her face.

When the tram doors finally slid shut, she sat down on one of the seats. Exhausted. She had taken the guards' names, ranks and badge numbers. Doubted anything would come of it, but she planned to file a complaint anyway. Even Trish was quiet, staring out of the window as it started to rain. The scroll Mira had pulled from her pocket was still in her hands, dotted with spots of blood. She unfurled it, seeing Kai's handwriting and regretting it immediately. It was the certificate he'd made on her promotion. She crumpled it up into a ball.

Mother and daughter were still subdued when they reached Cordelia's apothecary. The seawitch raised an eyebrow but made no comment, getting to work on Trish's regular massage as her assistant tended to herbal medicine brewing on the counter. The liquid Cordelia drew from the elder siren's lungs was thick as tar. Mira felt the knots in her chest tighten further. She'd been too busy, and Trish had missed many sessions. The sickness was progressing faster. The very thought of losing her mother . . . No. Her vision dimmed at the periphery and she turned away. Paced the shop and looked at the peculiar jars on high shelves as she took long, deep breaths. Pushed the fear back down, cramming a lid on and screwing it tight. She couldn't let it overwhelm her.

Trish caught her eye as she sat up after the massage. Her robe sagged over her slight frame, her veins almost translucent in her thin skin. "You needn't look at me as if I will keel over tomorrow. But one day you'll have to do without me."

"No," Mira snapped. She dared not go on. Her voice betrayed her.

Cordelia's limbs stilled from their busy work. One smoothed itself against the counter, slowly peeling off rows of suckers as she spoke. "Even I have my limits. But a decade of gill rot hasn't killed her yet; who knows what the future holds."

"See, tougher than you all give me credit for," Trish said, patting her daughter's knee. She shuffled behind the screen to dress.

"You didn't call us here for a sudden act of kindness. What do you want?" Mira spoke in low tones, one eye on the rice paper screen.

"Nahla, go see if Trish needs help." Cordelia waited until the mermaid was out of earshot. "Tell me something, Captain. Would you call yourself human or fathomfolk?"

"I've said this before," Mira said exasperated. "I'm estuary."

Cordelia grinned, her smile so wide and uncharacteristic Mira thought there was something wrong with her face. "Well, do I have some interesting information for you."

Chapter Forty-One

Nami hadn't expected the long-promised trip to the Onseon Engine to include crawling through the sewers. The bulk of the building was like an iceberg under water. Beneath the water level, beneath the crumpling old city roads, a disused sewage system still existed, linking the older buildings together. The authorities hadn't thought anyone could use them: submerged, filled with detritus and inhabited by moray eels. It was surprising how much rubble had been excavated, hidden beneath a hawker's food cart over the course of a few months.

They swam in near darkness – Firth, Lynnette, Dan and Nami – the only light source an eerie glow from the witchlight, the glass sphere pulsing through its rope netting. Nami was surprised at Dan's presence; he'd been distant with her since they reunited.

As they neared the end of the sewers, Lynnette withdrew a gold key from around her neck. She twisted it in the lock; a mesh of blue light flashed across the door, then a second of green. They shimmered like dew on cobwebs before dissolving. A satisfying click and the door swung open.

"The witch didn't screw us over," she said, incredulity tingeing her words.

"Yet." Firth's response wiped the glee from the other kelpie's face. Whatever else Lynnette was going to say was lost as they all turned towards the magnetic draw. Waterweaving. Strong, pulsing waterweaving like a hidden spring. The hum of power called out from up ahead. Clamoured and coaxed, demanding all their attention. Lynnette reached out with both hands, her voice awestruck. "I've missed this."

And while Nami laughed at the words, she understood the sentiment. Felt herself drawn too, prey dazzled by the light of an anglerfish. It was nothing but power, a raw waterwoven barrier placed on the door in front of them, on the ceilings, to stop the water from seeping up through basement level. And yet she wanted to throw herself at it, roll in it and fall to the floor. Once the oceans were filled with this – ripe and common as low-hanging fruit. But pollution, gill rot numbed the extremities. Power – and waterweaving – was diminishing across the oceans, had been for decades.

It reminded her of the scent of her father's hair when he carried her on his back, a smell she had never had reason to recall until now. Warmth rippled through her, conjuring memories of fishing trips, sleeping on sandy beaches and whittling driftwood. Memories she'd been unaware she had even buried.

"My father," she said aloud. The others looked at her expectantly. "It's ... no, it's nothing." Nothing more than a flight of fancy. Saying it aloud would give it more weight. She had to be imagining it. Nostalgia mixed with longing, that was all. There was no way she could sense her father's waterweaving in the mix.

"Can you open it?" Firth asked, hand brushing her arm. She leaned into the touch, a wilting flower turning its head. Delicate hands would be needed here, to unlock the barrier without all the water bursting through the dam. At the Academy they would've studied it, made careful plans on how to peel open the layers. Would practise for a whole term on a construct as difficult as this one. Prepare like musicians until the power flowed without thought. Muscle memory in patterns. They'd have support as well, classmates willing to assist if needed.

Firth held her eyes with his own, drinking them in. Despite her pounding heart, Nami realised this casual trip to the Onseon Engine was not just about answering her questions. They'd gone to too much effort for that. The barrier she was about to break – the one the Drawbacks had not even bothered to warn her about – was clearly beyond their skills. This was a well-defended building.

"What exactly are we doing here?" She searched Firth's face for a clue, but he held her gaze steadily, giving nothing away. Lynnette had turned away with a snort, poking at the waterwoven barrier with the toe of her shoe.

"Just a little bit of mischief." He winked, and his fingers laced with hers. His familiar touch eased the tension in her shoulders.

It was Dan who finally convinced her though. "We need you," the kappa said quietly. The visible scars on his limbs reminded her what he had been through. For her. Some of the bruising looked fresh, swollen on his skin. The flat of his head, usually dampened with a shallow pool of water, was dry. Green skin peeling and patchy. Had it been like this since his arrival in the city? Nami couldn't recall. Before she could voice the question, Lynnette cleared her throat impatiently.

There was time for that later.

Voices sang to her – six, no, seven of the waterweavers who'd created the net. A crisp hand of ice, the down of fur, the feel of scales brushing across her face. For a second she could discern the individual strands, but then they came together again, a tight harmony. She took the lightest touch of her own weaving, no more than a single thread, to bob alongside. Following the natural curves and dips, acclimatising to the stream. The barrier pulled away from her at first, mistrusting, but as she became one of the voices, it fell back into place. That was when she moulded it, funnelling more of her own waterweaving through the gap and wedging it open. Strands dropped down, knitting together as quickly as she could break them. Her focus was erratic and distracted, the power slipping between her fingers and pooling all around her. She forced herself to breathe deeply, dredging up the lessons drilled into her.

Water will always flow. We can only change the direction. Her old teacher's voice was ever calm in her memory. The dance steps they used to anchor each movement. Everything Nami did was effortful: whole body movements just to raise one geyser, a monumental focus to push waves in the opposite direction.

And now the familiar movements ran through her body. She didn't have to dance any more, but she could spin off a wave from her shoulders and flick it on her wrist. She drew the barrier back, sewing the edges into themselves. With it, the water made a pocket, a bubble of air in a sharp wedge. Firth grinned and ducked through, the others following. Nami was last, the barrier slamming back down behind her. A deep breath of air hissed from her gills. Relief.

They stood waiting as their bodies shifted to land forms, Nami feeling her heart beating all the way through to the soles of her feet. Water dripped from her skin, but she was too tired to dry herself off. The battering of the sea made the door frame protest in a long moan before the barrier settled back in place.

Firth beamed, his hand on her arm squeezing so tight that she winced. He was oblivious, running up the stairs two at a time. Fatigue lay like a weighted blanket but Nami shrugged it off. Up they went through the bowels of the building. Past crates of cleaning supplies, wires and components. Corridors lined with windows gave glimpses into tidy, well-used offices: fabric armchairs, metal tables and hanging glass lamps, free of the black speckled mould that was prevalent throughout Tiankawi.

Lynnette beckoned to Firth at a set of double metal doors, the handles large spoked wheels. She turned one, the door inching open with a begrudging exhale. Nami helped Firth with the other.

"What is this?" Dan said, peering into the darkness with the witchlight swinging from his hand.

Reclining chairs were set out in three semicircles, all facing a plain white wall. From the ceiling dangled wires like jellyfish tentacles, seemingly floating in all directions. Dan tugged at one of them, craning his neck upwards where they converged into a funnel-like apparatus. It reminded Nami of the stinging curtain protecting the Peace Tower. Human tech. Complicated and obscure. None of the books she'd read since her arrival had mentioned this. Like someone had simply omitted the relevant chapters.

As she examined one of the chairs, queasiness filled her. Her skin prickled, screaming that something was not right. She forced her shaking hand to touch a wire, flimsy as she followed it to the end. Three clear plates splayed out at the end like a budding flower, each no larger than the tip of her finger. She touched one, the membrane sticky and tingling. The plate puckered and pulled her skin with it. Nipped as it reluctantly came loose, leaving a red mark like a leech. Her skin was numb where it had made contact.

"What is this?" She echoed Dan's words.

Firth and Lynnette were wrestling with a control panel. "You wanted a tour, well here it is. In all its glory!" Lynnette said, her voice dripping with simmering rage. The Drawback leader turned her back, pulling a package from her knapsack.

Explosives. Nami remembered Firth's face that day on the Peak. The plans ticking over in his head.

She stumbled after them into the next few rooms, her head reeling too much to protest. Some rooms had low stools and straight-backed chairs like a tram platform. Others had more reclining chairs. One room was filled with narrow cots, wicker frames layered with plain blankets. The wires were ubiquitous, hanging like tentacles above their heads, the three innocuous buds at their terminals. In each room, Lynnette and Firth wired explosives into a panel, handling the wire strippers with deft ease.

Something was missing. Something so obvious that no one talked about it. "Why would you want to blow the place up?" Nami said, not expecting them to answer.

Lynnette grinned, uncharacteristically chatty. "Why wouldn't you? It all goes down! It will take them weeks – months if we're lucky – to fix. Freeing our own."

Firth said nothing, but looked sharply up at his fellow kelpie. Lynnette clamped her mouth shut, her body vibrating with excitement. Nami searched her history lessons. The other power sources had been failing for decades. Oil and gas were running out, despite humanity's desire to defile the oceans in its search for more energy. They were developing heliacal sailmills and eddy farms, but both were yet in their infancy.

Human technology continued to be unrivalled, far surpassing anything they could achieve in the underwater havens. Humanity had made up for their lack of waterweaving through invention. Knowledge and machinery.

Lynnette cocked her head, a pitying look flickering across her face as she registered Nami's blank expression. Despite biting her tongue earlier, she couldn't help herself. "You really have no idea? Why d'you think they took in so many refugees?"

Replicate their methods or destroy them? Her mother's parting question. Fathomfolk weren't workers at the Onseon Engine.

They were the power source.

Her hands shook as the realisation flooded over her. It was so obvious now. She looked down, trying to steady herself. The pakalot shook on her wrist and she noticed for the first time that three of the small indents upon the mesh surface were larger. Circular. The size and shape of the dendrite ends of the wires. Her legs crumpled under her.

Her mother had known. What would she do? Yonakuni could never match human technology because it involved the aberrant practice of siphoning waterweaving. Something rendered illegal centuries ago in the havens. Yes, fathomfolk could generate more, given time, but take too much and that way lay death. Nami's insides convulsed in wave after wave of nausea. Dry-heaving when her empty stomach could eject nothing but bile.

"I'm sorry." Firth kneeled beside her. Wrapped his strong arms around her shoulders and pulled her into an embrace. "I didn't think you were ready to hear the truth."

The shock faded away, and red tinged Nami's vision. Furious heat that melted all coherent words in her head. Words that could lance the wound, snap at him for treating her like a child. And yet . . . was he not right? Was she not now falling apart? His hand stroked down her back. She was shaking. She drew comfort from his presence and yet hated him all the same.

He hadn't told her.

Kai hadn't told her.

They had left her like a fool going through the archives when it was so obvious. No wonder the folk had ignored her questions as she accosted them before a shift. They were selling themselves, their waterweaving, the raw power taken like blood from their veins. Shortening their lives to pay the rent, put food on the table. She just hadn't taken a step back to look at the whole picture.

Between deep gulping breaths, she finally managed to push out two words. "How long?"

"Bartering waterweaving for goods has been around for as long as fathomfolk in Tiankawi. But the humans really figured it out when Iyoness fell. It made quite a few political careers," Firth said.

Nami had no response, her mind filled with raking nails scraping at the inside of her skull. How many times had she taken the tram? Enjoyed hot water straight from the taps, the buzzing lights in Kai's penthouse, the lift that glided between floors? The pressure pulsed around her temples and eyes. She pushed herself to her feet. Shook off Firth's hold. Dan stood beside her, his presence reassuringly familiar amid everything she had just heard.

"If we close this place down, the city loses power. But it also forces them to talk about it – the Council, the people on the streets who've ignored the truth for so long," Lynnette said. She slammed one fist against an unopened door. "They pretend folk have a choice. Just a job, right? You can walk away from a job. Except you can't. Because there's nothing else, nowhere else that will pay so regularly, so well. Because who are they shitting kidding; it was the only reason they closed the Nurseries. The only reason they issue visas to so many folk. We have to finish it before they finish us."

Firth took Nami's hand again, and this time she didn't resist. "I thought it'd be easier if you saw for yourself." His face was close to hers, breath hot on her cheek. She remembered how that had made her feel, only a short while ago. Thought back to the day on the Peak, and how her whole body flushed with heat at his touch. Now she simply felt confused. He should've told her earlier. But it sounded whiny and inconsequential now.

"Do you have what it takes to finish it?" Lynnette pushed.

Replicate their methods or destroy them? That was the true lesson her mother wanted her to learn? "I'll end it."

Another wave of sickness wafted through her, the taste coating her dry tongue. Firth's arm around her was the only thing keeping her going as she stumbled through the rooms, her vision inexplicably blurry. He let her go abruptly, the drop so sudden that she took a half-step forward. They'd reached a control room, two panels of displays against the walls. Buttons and switches like pebbles on a beach, lights flashing or dark. Hundreds of them. Firth stood before the controls, hand on his chin pensively.

"Well?" Lynnette said. "Are we doing this?" She turned dials haphazardly on the complicated panels until Firth tapped her wrist with a frown.

"We need to overload the system," he said.

Lynnette looked confused at his explanation. Clearly even she did not know the whole plan.

Nami could see the panels were clustered and demarcated by thin lines. The rooms. Most of the lights were off, the empty chambers they had passed through. A scattering, all in one area, blinked amber and green. "What's that?"

"The night shift." Firth did not expand.

Nami was suddenly ice cold, her fingers white from lack of circulation. The final piece clicked into place. "Those are fathomfolk. People!" She shoved her hands under her armpits but couldn't stop herself from shaking. Trish had once worked in Onseon, the only job she could get.

"We'll wake them up and get them out," Firth said, not unkindly. "Come on, just down this corridor." Nami kept glancing back, aware that Lynnette hadn't moved. Her mouth a grim line as the amber lights illuminated one side of her face.

The corridors were black as night, the glow from the single witchlight more of a firefly glimmer. The room was a million miles away, their steps echoing down the hallways for an eternity. The chamber at first seemed like all the ones before. Except people lay in the narrow cots. Shadowed figures barely breathing, the air like rotting fruit.

"Help me wake them," Firth said from the darkness. Nami took the witchlight from Dan, hovered the blue-red globe over the nearest person. A gaunt selkie lay on his back, the wires latched onto his pakalot, bracer tight around his wrist. It cut like a noose against inflamed skin. A fish caught in the nets. In human form, the selkie's silver hair was like down, cropped close to his scalp. Nami tapped him on the shoulder tentatively. Then a little harder. Harder still. Grabbed him and shook so hard his head drooped back and forward. She yelled in his ear, tried to pull the socket from his wrist. He was as if dead, skin waxen and cool to the touch, a sourness about his person. Only when she stopped did she detect the shallow movement of his chest.

The silence was deeper than the abyss.

"It's the night shift," Lynnette said from behind them. The hairs on the back of Nami's neck lifted sharply. "They're under for days, sometimes weeks; they'll take hours to rouse, but we can—"

The alarm went off.

It wailed down the corridors like the echo of a ghost and the lights of the building flickered on with a flashing red brilliance. Nami winced at the blood-coloured haze that surrounded them.

Firth cursed loudly. "The witch double-crossed us!"

"Of course she did," said Dan. He snapped his beak at the kelpie.

For once Lynnette looked horrified. She took a step towards Firth, eyes wide. "But we don't have time to wake them!"

"We don't have time to wake them," Firth repeated. Firmly. No question in his tone. Deep in a wordless debate with the Drawback leader. Lynnette tore her gaze away, eyes falling to the unconscious sleepers. She took a deep breath and straightened her shoulders.

"I'll stall the guards," Firth said, halfway out of the door before Nami realised what was happening.

She was sick of only half understanding. She turned back to Lynnette. "You're going to leave them?"

"No." The kelpie looked at the clock on the wall. "There's only one way we can set off the explosives. Reverse the direction of the power."

"You'll kill them."

"No, *you* will." Neither kelpie was precise enough for the water-weaving they needed. That was why Nami had been brought along. She was beginning to understand what choices the Drawbacks meant when they talked about what was best for the city.

She gulped suddenly, hiccuping breaths that didn't give her the air she needed. Her gills opened too, but it was not enough. Her heart pounded like a dying bird in her ribcage, vision blackening at the edges. She forced long, slow breaths through her nose, back out through her gills. "I won't do it."

"Half a dozen lives, if you can even call it that!" Lynnette said, gesturing at the shadows on the beds. She sneered. "What do they matter? You don't even know them."

"You're insane." Nami shook her head, starting towards the door, towards where Firth had gone, taking with him the common sense. The flashing overhead light was giving her a headache, but this was a line she would not cross.

She felt the thrown water before it touched her, deflecting it with the witchlight still in her hands and crouching instinctively into a low-centred position.

"What are—" The words caught in her mouth as Lynnette shot another burst of water at her. She threw the globe at it, watching as the glass smashed against the wall, the lights darting pinpricks in her vision before she thought to close her eyes. She formed gauntlets of ice around her arms and ran forward, deflecting the attacks against the walls, the floor, kicking one high into the ceiling. The wires glowed in recognition, sucking the waterweaving like starving cleaner fish.

Lynnette barrelled into her, knocking her to the ground. She was saying something, desperately screaming Firth's name, but none of it was coherent. Nami could only let herself fall, trying to roll upright before being grappled. She swept an arc of water under the kelpie's feet.

"Enough!" she said.

"My thoughts exactly," Lynnette replied. She held Dan by the neck. The kappa's webbed feet dangled off the ground. He looked at Nami, beak gaping, although the only sound was a rasping gasp. Nami's eyes were inexplicably drawn to his thin legs. Meat hanging from a butcher's hook. "Enough."

"You don't mean this. He's one of us. We want the same things," Nami said, taking a step forward.

Lynnette shook her head, lifting Dan fractionally higher. The kappa's green skin was grey-tinged around his flat crown. His mouth opened and closed uselessly. She was strangling him. Nami remembered the drunk at the rally, the way the Drawback leader had stood in the exact same pose. Everything repeated itself. Dan once again being punished for her mistakes. "Do it or I kill him."

"Firth would ... Firth wouldn't want this," Nami said. Mumbling any words to stall, desperate for the other kelpie to return and talk reason into his friend. He would know what to say. Calm her with plaintive soft tones. Lynnette's gaze flickered briefly to the corridor, her jaw clenched tight as the steel spokes on the doors they had opened.

Nami let her shoulders fall, beaten. "Put him down first," she said, one hand mollifying. The other was held behind her back, the water dart already formed in her palm. She manipulated it between her fingers into the right position. "Put him down and we'll talk."

Lynnette looked through her, pausing for so long Nami thought she'd turned to stone. Finally she started to lower the kappa to the ground. Dan's webbed feet were grazing the floor when Nami flicked the improvised weapon out in front of her. The dart aimed true, but Lynnette reacted fast enough for it only to nick her cheek. She'd absorbed Nami's training.

The water dragon ran forward, throwing arrows of water recklessly. They pierced Lynnette's shoulder, tore through the lobe of one ear. But the water softened with Nami's hesitation. She wasn't a killer. Lynnette walked through her barrage like it was a spring shower. Thrust Dan right against Nami's hands. His eyes were closed. Body already limp. Her oldest friend, who'd always believed in her, who'd been imprisoned for her, who'd joined the Drawbacks for her.

Nami dropped her waterweaving, the half-formed arrows falling as harmless rain. "Please, please . . ." she whispered, reaching for Dan's lifeless form. "I'll do it, okay. I'll do it. Just let him go." She felt the weight of the kappa, lighter than she was expecting, fall against her. Gently put him on the ground. He was breathing. Just about. No more than the fathomfolk workers who'd remained slumbering throughout.

Lynnette's hand came down on her shoulder, gripping it. The adrenaline coursed through Nami's body, a tidal wave of strength despite herself. Her hands shook as she glanced back, only once, into the blood-red shadows. The alarm continued to wail, a death keen overhead. Firth was not coming to rescue her. If she half lidded her eyes, she could pretend the fathomfolk were merely sculptures. Porcelain and unfeeling.

"Do it," Lynnette's voice threatened.

And yes, it would be so easy. It was the only thing she could do with this nebula of power building tight in her chest. The anger she had no outlet for. Release it. Let it ground itself. Fall. It was just a game, a test. Soon Firth would laugh and pull her to her feet. Mira and Kai, her mother perhaps, would emerge from where they'd been hiding, and what a lark, they'd say. How she fell for it! But the seconds ticked by and nothing changed.

The Drawback leader made a muttering sound and kneeled by the kappa's unconscious body. She pulled a blade from her belt and held it over Dan's heart. No, no, no, stop, Nami heard herself say, her voice thick and distant. Then do it. Lynnette's voice. Had she even opened her mouth? She was pushing the blade, just a little, into Dan's chest. Blood welled up, staining his shirt with a growing bloom. A deep rhythm pounding in Nami's head, blocking everything else out.

"Now!" Lynnette said, her grip changing to twist the knife further in.

Nami plugged her pakalot into the system. It leeched from

her almost immediately, pulling hard like a thirsty viper at her veins. She had to fight with it, pull back until a sort of balance had been created.

It was like turning a giant sand timer. The power was heavy, pooling on one side. But once she managed to tip it over, it would be impossible to stop. A broken dam. She coaxed it, carved shallow trails up towards the panels. Trickles became streams, streams became torrents, and then she couldn't control it. The energy ripped through the system and back out into the empty rooms. The wires melted with the surge and triggered the explosives. She was with it, flowing through the ceiling, down the walls to another room, and another.

But before it returned in a full circle to where she stood, she tore the wires from her arm. It burned. White-hot pain ripping up her arm. Focus! She only had a few seconds. It would be enough.

It had to be enough.

Screaming to force herself forward, she waterweaved a blade of water and sliced crudely through the overhead wires. The tip of the blade cut one loose. The person closest to her gasped and coughed, their body seizing up for a moment. She could break the connection before the backlash reached the room. It wasn't pretty, but better than being dead. She kept slashing, as fast as she could. Four left. Three. Two more, then—

The surge of power jolted through the room. The overhead lights came on, brighter and brighter, then the bulbs smashed one after another. The wave of power rippled out like a shock wave, sending them all to their knees.

Too late.

The closest sleeper, the selkie, still connected, jerked. Angled knees and elbows twitched out. A smothered groan, the creak of grinding teeth, and he was still. Nami crawled over to him, wailing despite herself. Grabbed the limp hand that swung from the cot and squeezed it. No, no, wake up, damn you, wake up! Thin trails of blood dripped tap, tap, tap onto the floor. Her hand was red with it. How many, how many had she missed? How many more rooms like this? And still the explosives went off. One after another, like a fireworks display in the distance. Each burst of sound made her quiver as she lay on the floor, head curled by Dan's, letting the water flow out.

"Nami?" Mira's voice. A small group of guards stood at the door. The chinthe captain looked at her, horror on her worn features. "What have you done?"

Chapter Forty-Two

Mira coughed and spluttered, shielding her face with the collar of her coat as Lynnette threw a smoke bomb to the ground. Eyes streaming with tears, she stumbled after the Drawbacks escaping through the exit at the opposite side of the room. The ground shook violently and she fell sprawling to the floor. Cracks tore up the walls and plaster dust rained down from overhead. The lights flickered and went out. She swallowed hard. The Drawbacks – Nami with them – would wait. Right now, the safety of her people was more important.

They regrouped above the waterline. Gede had finally arrived with the kumiho guards. Late, of course, despite her pleas to Samnang. She ignored him for a moment, staring across Tiankawi's skyline. Plumes of smoke billowed into the night sky. Flickers of copper lit the underbelly of the looming clouds. Guards cried out in fear, the wordless sound echoing far into the distance as the street lights blinked off, one after another. The power was going out. People would be in trouble. Humans and fathomfolk. Ordinary people. The ones who couldn't afford private boats and penthouse apartments. Not Samnang's people. Hers.

"My father's orders were to bring you back. Immediately." Gede gaped at the sight before him, unable to tear his gaze away.

"Not yet." Mira pointed at the devastation unfolding. "Let me do my job."

He hesitated, finger loosening his collar. "They'll blame you. You had some knowledge of it. That's why you got here so fast. That's why you didn't stop it."

Mira closed her eyes for a moment, composing herself. It was a peace offering of sorts. He meant to warn her. By not reporting to the Council, she was as good as admitting her own guilt. "I'm still going."

He moved out of her way, the other kumiho taking his lead. She was thankful for that at least. Another problem to deal with later. She fired off orders to her chinthe. Then Kai was there, running towards her.

"Thank the sand gods!" he said. He looked out of breath, pale with worry.

"What're you doing here?" Despite being flustered, Mira was comforted by his presence. She felt stronger already.

"Trish told me." Of course her mother had listened in to the conversation in Cordelia's apothecary. Her ama worried. Just as Kai worried about his little sister. Treating her like she was still the kid he'd left behind in the havens, when in fact she was a radical, up to her neck in this shit. Mira couldn't tell him. Couldn't destroy that sibling relationship without getting Nami's side of the story first.

"Go home and—" An unworldly screech made everyone look up. One of the trams, nothing more than a silhouette curving around a soaring Jingsha column in the distance, groaned with a metallic cacophony. An irate beast stirring in the night. Too far and too high for them to reach without the power on.

"Get on," Kai said.

It took Mira a second to understand, but yes, it was the fastest way. She jumped onto his back as he transformed, elongating fully to dragon form. His scales were cool and she buried her head against his bristling spines as he galloped towards Jingsha, his shoulder blades jostling under her arms until she found her

balance. He raced up the stairs towards the nearest tram platform, then, without missing a beat, pushed forward, sure-footed
on the sleepers as they ascended. But they were on the wrong line,
the track curving away from the now dangling distant tram.

"Hold on!" The wind pressed at Mira's face as he leapt. The
curse word was snatched from her mouth, fingers clutching Kai's
spines with all her might. He landed heavily on the tram tracks
below, knocking the breath from her chest. One of his rear legs
slipped but he regained his footing. Mira made the mistake of
looking down. Despite having ridden the tram countless times,
the sheer drop to the water level was like a punch to the gut. The
walkways like washing lines, the houses mere driftwood. She
wrenched her head back up, squeezing her eyes shut for a moment.

Kai had to cross over to an adjacent line, running through the
crowded tram platform. A stream of faces and hands reached out
to touch his sides. Without hesitation, he wove between them,
curving his body when they would not give way. No time. A baby
gave a colicky cry.

Mira looked back, Kai's tail moving side to side like an oar
in the water, keeping his balance. She scanned the faces, the
darkened platform. But no, they weren't in danger. Just afraid.
They all were.

"The Drawbacks want another riot," Kai said as he found
his rhythm.

"No. A revolution." The knowledge of Nami's involvement dangled on her lips, but she bit it back.

Kai's breathing laboured under the pace. They neared the
derailed tram. The rear carriage tilted precariously to one side.
The metal wheels were only connected to the rail on one side
and the trolley pole swung loose from the overhead wire. A few
people were clambering out of the windows, but there were no
walkways here, no station. Only a slim track hundreds of feet
in the air. If the carriage didn't tilt any more; if the people were

careful and calm; if they could walk a mile or more to the nearest station without losing their balance; then they might be able to get everyone out the rear windows. If.

The passengers called out as they approached, banging on the windows, screaming so all Mira could see was the inside of their mouths. Faces pressed up against the glass. She dismounted, standing between Kai and the carriage. "Can you push it back onto the track?"

Kai nodded. His agile form twisted half under the track as he leaned against the tilted side, pushing with the length of his body. It was not an easy move. His claws were curled round the steel struts at an awkward angle and there was no real leverage. He lost purchase, slipping. Taking a deep breath, he tried again, straining against the carriage doors. It had no effect. Like trying to move a mountain. The carriage groaned, leaning a little more.

Glass cracked.

Mira lunged forward, thinking at first the carriage was breaking apart. It was a fist, then an oxygen canister being launched at the window. Passengers broke the glass, clambering over each other to get to Kai. One thrust her child in his snout, screaming at him. *Take him. Take him!* Another pulled at his whiskers. Kai withdrew, his body arching with an involuntary hiss. They dug fingers under his scales. Swarming on him, pressing against the precariously tilting carriage in their desperation. One man had climbed out completely, holding onto Kai's spines and kicking him in the side like he was a steed.

"You're making it worse!" Mira's voice was drowned out, submerged in the noise. Dozens of hands grabbed and scraped and lunged. She saw scales come loose in their hands. Kai's calls of pain cut through her. And beneath their panicked pleas, the carriage leaned even more.

She felt her vision go hazy. Screwed her eyes shut. There was nothing, nothing she could do. With a siren song she could have placated them. With waterweaving she could help Kai right the carriage. But she had nothing. Useless. Her hands shook as she looked down at them. She saw the brass buttons on her formal coat, the one she'd put on to remind herself. Remembered every damn military school exam. She'd been better at the book work and faster at the physical tasks than the other trainees. Still they said her rise through the ranks was because she was folk. She fastened the buttons, touched the captaincy badge with her thumb.

The whistle blow was long and shrill. She held it for as long as she could, until the piercing sound cut through the commotion, until all eyes were on her. "Stand down!" She picked on one man, a large fellow with an oxygen canister raised above his head. Held his gaze until his hands faltered. The crowd quietened, taking note of her uniform, her firm voice. She just had to keep up the act. The glass was already broken, so she climbed into the rear of the carriage as if it was the easiest, safest thing in the world. Ignoring the creak and the dizzying impact of the world at an angle.

"Step away from the window. Slowly."

Two or three people started moving, but the effect of authority seemed to be wearing off. Now she was closer, they could see her small stature. Her young age. Her credibility flaking off. If they all rushed to the back of the carriage at once, it would topple over, pulling the whole tram down with it.

Whispered questions were slung from the back of the crowd. *Who the heck is she? Where are the kumiho? Are we going to die?* "One more insubordination and I'll have you arrested," she said. Channelled Samnang's sneering disdain. Put her hands into her coat pockets like she had something there to threaten them with. It worked, temporarily silencing further questions. "Now move!" As they shuffled, she strolled up the carriage, pretending nonchalance. Tried not to stare at Kai outside as she stepped forward. He blinked the blood from his eye. Shook his head at her unvoiced question. He could not hold on much longer.

The carriages were not connected, but the passengers could climb across. It had to be organised. Mira pretended it was a military drill: the fittest at the front and rear to support the rest across. They emptied out, not a single complaint as they handed over toddlers and infants, an old gentleman who could not stand. A bridge of hands, of voices working together. This side, he's slipping. Pull him forward now. That's it. Have you got her? She's safe. Send the next one. No more space, crouch on the roof. There. Hold them so they won't fall.

They had halfway emptied when the carriage lurched again with a protesting shriek. The remaining passengers tumbled to the floor, Mira included. She gripped a bench, willing the movement to stabilise. If there wasn't some way of uncoupling the carriages, all would be for naught. The rear would pull the rest off the tracks.

She scanned faces, shouted across to those in the next carriage. "I need fathomfolk."

The silence was uncomfortable. People turned and looked at each other's necks, hands. She yanked aside her own collar, showing her gill lines. "Please!"

A lanky youth on the roof raised his hand. Then, after a pause, a nudge in the ribs, the older woman beside him followed suit. The family resemblance was clear. Their grey eyes did not quite meet hers. Wary.

Her face upturned, Mira took a deep breath. "Sever the coupling."

"But then—" the lad said. Before he could continue, the rear carriage tipped more. Mira had only a split second to reach out for the handrail, hugging her body tight to it as the whole carriage swung out. Someone fell, screaming past her, smashing through the broken window at the rear of the carriage, tumbling into the darkness beyond.

"Do it," she said. Her voice was firmer than her emotions. She was no fool. Kai was so tightly wrapped around the dangling carriage that he might not be able to move clear of it. Sever the coupling to save the passengers. Cut loose the tons of steel and the dragon desperately trying to hold it up. It was a choice he would approve of.

She slithered carefully down the now vertical carriage towards the broken rear window. Caught a glimpse of Kai near the doors. He had transformed to human form to stop his weight dragging them down. But something was wrong. His hands were still scaled claws, mid transformation. Out of energy, waterweaving at its limit.

"Take my hand!" she called.

He looked at her like she was the most wondrous thing in the world. Gave her a goofy smile. "I like you in work mode." Distraction. He did it when he was stressed.

"Shut up and take my hand," she repeated. He reached for her, but they both realised too late that his talons would cut her to shreds. He swung away from her, hanging by only one limb now. Mira leaned precariously out to pull him up by the forearms, but there was nothing to hold on to. Her sweaty hands slipped on his scales and she cut herself on his dewclaw.

Kai looked up at her with an almost delirious grin. Idiot was going to let go. She could see it in his eyes. Her hand patted subconsciously at her coat, as though once again she had the solution there. A weapon to solve every problem. But it was just a coat. She shrugged it off and swung one of the arms down, twisted the other around her wrist. It batted his face, but he didn't react at first. "Grab hold!"

As soon as he gripped onto it, she pulled. Hard as she could, her arms burning. The material puckered at the seams, tearing on the sharp glass edges. He was too heavy. The inane grin had finally gone from his features. The seams of the sleeve began to separate. He wasn't going to make it. Mira grimaced and ignored the pain in her limbs. She swayed her body from side to side, setting a rhythm to it.

"On three, jump," she said between swings. It was easy enough. Get some momentum, then let go. Like heaving a sack of rice onto a boat. She'd done it before. One of her many jobs. Nothing to it. Nothing at all. "Did you hear me? One, two—"

The sleeve ripped.

She shouted his name in a panic, unable to see him out of any window, ignoring the pain in her shoulder.

"It's going!" A warning from the next carriage.

A metallic groan like a whale breaching the surface. Mira had no time to think. Vaulted up the almost vertical carriage, hauling herself over the seats. Her right arm protested with an audible pop and the pain radiated down her side. She screamed. The arm flopped uselessly at her side, but she had another. She had legs, and she had the fastest bloody time in training. Hands waved at her from the next carriage, encouraging her, yelling.

She focused every ounce of attention on them as she jumped. Dozens of hands grabbed her. Pulled her by the arm, then around her chest and waist. Heaved her up and in as they watched the decoupled carriage fall. It crashed through the lower rail lines, the walkways, taking chunks of masonry with it. Finally it hit the water, wedging itself up against one of the high-rise buildings and slowly scraping into the depths below.

"Kai," Mira said. More of an exhale than a word. No response. Louder this time, more desperate. "Kai!"

"I'm here."

And he was. The swing had worked, giving him enough momentum to grab onto the tracks as the coat had torn. Mira couldn't tell if she was laughing or crying.

Chapter Forty-Three

Cordelia slid the teacup across the table, letting Ayumu take her time. As she lifted her hand from the porcelain surface, it visibly shook, rattling the gold bangles on her wrists. "And to think what would've happened if someone had been in the elevator," she said with a shudder.

Two days after the explosion at the Onseon Engine, and more than half of Tiankawi still had no power. The Council were scrabbling, hampered by the impact on the trams and cable cars also. While they sent emergency support out where possible, looting had been reported in some areas in full blackout. Even the Council chambers were inaccessible, as power had not been restored there. Serendipitous foresight meant Serena had insisted their house was powered by the eddy tide farms to the north-east. The eccentric whim of a new wife. Now Samnang was congratulating himself. As one of the few households with full power, he magnanimously offered to host Council meetings. A stroke of good luck, he kept saying, never thinking to ask his wife what her issue was with the fathomfolk-operated Onseon in the first place.

Serena - or rather Cordelia - genially conducted her hosting duties for the partners and children of the ministers, one eye trained on the sliding wooden door. It was frustrating to be stuck here when crucial decisions were being made on the other side.

"An absolute travesty that they still haven't caught those

responsible," Ayumu continued. "Pyanis said these Drawbacks are diehard radicals. No reasoning with them."

"The Boat Race riots must've impacted on your warehouses near the dockyards?" Cordelia said, voice neutral.

Ayumu stiffened, glancing to where Finnol and Qiuyue were playing by the fireplace. Her stepdaughter, Eun, sat with them, legs tucked under her, scrutinising some mouldy lotus leaf papers like they were fine jewels. She had secured a seat beneath the brightest lamp in the room, not even attempting to make small talk or excuses for her dishevelled appearance.

"We lost a lot of stock. Raw ore from deep-sea mining. And now the little we have left will have to be used on repairs, reappropriated for city use at cost." Ayumu shook her head sadly.

"A terrible shame. To think you could've auctioned them for two, perhaps three times the usual price. If only the Minister of Finance hadn't already sent his officials round to tally up numbers." Cordelia dangled the peace offering, waiting patiently to see if the hook would embed.

"If . . . only," Ayumu responded. Her eyes flickered up to catch Cordelia's and she gave a very slight inclination of her head. "Pyanis and I are so grateful for the friendship Qiuyue has offered our son. Please do tell us if there's anything she might need. No request is too great."

"They'll be voting on the new Minister of Justice; can't justify putting it off given the circumstances," said Eun, squeezing between chairs to snatch a handful of candied lotus root. The young woman had not an ounce of tact. She flipped her long hair behind her ear, not noticing that crumbs scattered into the strands as she did so. She barely looked up as she retreated to her documents, munching her pilfered snacks. Other conversations in the room quietened. Cups were put down on the marble table, eyes drawn upwards.

Cordelia cursed her internally. An educated fool who could

read five languages but not the room in which she sat. The sea-witch had been trying to steer the conversation away from the voting for now. Ayumu was a wounded kitten after the fire and now the power cuts. But she still had claws. Cordelia perched on the edge of her stool, adding hot water to the teapot. A few of the leaves floated to the top, separating from the crowd.

"For the good of Tiankawi, the Council must act in agreement rather than letting individual egos insist on misjudged curfews and escalate riots." Ayumu clasped her hands on her knee. The slightest shimmer ran through the room, a communal in-breath as the first shot was fired. They looked to Cordelia for her riposte.

"Hindsight is easy. Especially for those who simply wait and watch, shielded behind comfortable desks." Cordelia picked up the teapot and refilled people's cups. A few of the junior officials nodded and took a sip. Most did not even reach for their cups, the tendrils of steam curling up between them. She felt an iron hand tighten around her throat. She swallowed, pushing the discomfort and anger away. She had sacrificed too much trying to win over these preening fools.

She touched her seasilk pouch, the one she'd bargained for long ago. Putting a lilt in her voice, she continued. "What we need is a person of action. Someone to restore order; who can mobilise the city guards to protect our property, our families." The siren song worked the room, gentle as a warming fire. Just enough to ease the knots. Of course Samnang was the best person for the job. Cordelia let her gaze linger where the servants were occupying Qiuyue, Finnol and the other children at the far end of the room with fragile shadow puppets.

"I quite agree, family is so important," Ayumu said. "I can't begin to imagine how distressing it must've been when Qiuyue went missing. The city guards, so well trained, so faithful, and yet his own daughter taken. I mean, it could happen to any of us." Her hand was on her chest, eyes glistening with moisture as she spoke. She cleared her throat, blinked back the tears before they ruined carefully applied make-up. Cordelia would applaud her acting skills if she weren't so incensed.

Ayumu did not even wait for a response. She strolled across the room to put a hand on Finnol's hair, kiss his head as if she had just exchanged pleasantries about the weather. Around her, Cordelia felt the seeds of doubt germinate. Her subtle song lost beneath Ayumu's comments. She could push them harder, force her point, but many of them wore charms against such compulsion effects; would sense folk skills had been used. Her hand trembled over the seasilk pouch. Hesitating.

It was all slipping away.

Cordelia stood up to portion out the steamed fish at the dinner table. The oval platter took up the centre of the turntable, with the meats, vegetables and stews dotted to the sides. After her altercation with Ayumu, she had gone to the kitchen to vent her anger. Thrown out two perfectly good dishes, shouting at the cook about oversalting, and sent one of the new maids away in tears. She did not care. Mincing meat with a cleaver, she pulverised the pink flesh. Her rage still had not dissipated by dinner.

"How did the Council meeting go?" she asked Samnang. She heaped a spoonful of stewed water chestnuts onto Qiuyue's rice bowl, silencing the start of a protest with a glare. Her daughter sensed the mood and dipped her head, wrestling with her chopsticks. Gede looked between his parents, eating noisily with an open mouth. An idiotic goldfish.

Samnang sighed, putting down his own chopsticks to pinch at the bridge of his nose. "Not well."

"Did you fire the chinthe captain?" Gede interjected. Cordelia pursed her lips and scraped back the ginger and spring onions from the top of the fish, the white eye glaring at her. She would upbraid her son, except she wanted to hear the answer too.

"If you'd passed the officials' exam rather than flunking it three times, you would know that I have no such authority. The border guards are a separate division of the military."

"Aren't you the Minister of Defence?" Gede was unable to keep his mouth shut.

"I am one voice. It would need a Council majority to vote her out. Something complicated by the fact that she and Kai are considered heroes for the tram incident."

"You need to get rid of them both," Cordelia said. Here was a situation she still had control over. Mira had her uses, but the most valuable of all was the bargain she had made a decade ago. Making the situation hopeless enough that the siren would renew the deal was key to Cordelia's ongoing plans. "She was first to get to the Onseon Engine – a tip-off she still refuses to tell you about. Clearly she knew. Waited long enough to take credit. Rustled up that little tram stunt to win public favour. She is getting far too popular, too powerful. You won't be able to control her for ever."

"My dear—"

"And who knows how she is influencing the Council, using her siren song to stay on top. Leaving her in post is showing your own weakness."

"Serena!" Samnang's voice was raised and Cordelia finally stopped. She had shredded the fish to pieces with the spoon and chopsticks, tearing at it as she spoke. Both of her children looked at her with alarm. Gede scraped his chair back, enticing his sister to look for glutinous rice cakes. Qiuyue bounced along beside him, glancing back with a confused expression at her mother. Cordelia managed a reassuring smile, a little wave before she sat back down.

"What's got into you," Samnang said once the door had closed.

"My apologies, dearest. The afternoon tea didn't exactly go as planned."

"I heard that the Minister of Ceremonies' wife got you in quite a fluster. You do know these things don't matter." Her husband patted her on the hand indulgently. Samnang, who thought he had risen through the ranks due to competence and talent. That his wife indulged in parlour games.

Cordelia whipped her hand out from under his grasp. Longed to take off the mask she had worn for so long and let him peer into her horizontal pupils. Then she would see if his patronising tones remained. Or would he scream in horror like the rest? "I'm just concerned we're missing an opportunity. Decisive action will get you votes."

"*I* am not missing anything. The Onseon incident is the biggest attack on Tiankawian waters in living memory. Push too hard and the Council will see me as some militant fool rather than a candidate for Minister of Justice. It needs a softer touch." Although his voice was steady, Cordelia knew by his quiet demeanour that Samnang was seething. Usually she gave him time to nurse his wounded ego, letting her advice sink in so he believed it was his own. But she couldn't help herself. Couldn't hold her tongue any longer. Too much was off plan already. Too many variations. Her own thwarted schemes made her push harder.

"If you were less of a coward, the Ministry of Justice would already be yours," she said, voice a furious vibrato. "Who'll bear the brunt for this blunder? You? Our family?" She clutched at the pouch at her waist. Samnang's pupils dilated and he blinked rapidly as if intoxicated. He tried to shake away the fugue, but Cordelia bore down. Finally his shoulders stooped.

"So be it. In the morning, I'll motion to have Mira fired. Are you happy now?"

Cordelia barely noticed as he left the room. The remains of the family meal were scattered around the table, unfinished. She upended the pouch to look at the stone within. It had cracked in two. A thin line of blood on her palm showed where the jagged edge had dug in. The last of the siren song. A decade of power, eked out carefully to plan each move. She had hoped it would last a little longer. The other contracts would have to suffice in the meantime. A week here, a few hours there. But this song had become familiar to her – a favourite pair of well-worn shoes. The others would be less effective, difficult to use without detection. No matter. Mira would be desperate after she was fired. And desperation was the best time for making – or renewing – bargains.

With renewed vigour, Cordelia picked up her chopsticks and finished her meal alone.

Chapter Forty-Four

Nami ran. Her feet were slower than her head, and she tumbled into the sand. She could hear someone behind her, her brother, catching up despite the head start he always gave her. Before her was the sea. The lapping aquamarine a treacle trail on the beach. Kai called her name, called and waved until she turned. Now he was on the shoulders of their mother, just a boy, a little taller, a little older than Nami. That's cheating, she told them, before she was swept up too, squealing in delight as Jiang-Li swung her by the arms and plunged them all into the water.

Their bodies lengthened, scales forming. Her mother lay on her back, her tail a rudder, waving as the two children gave chase in the shallows. Nami trod water and gulped mouthfuls of brine in her attempts. It was hard to float. To be halfway between the water and the land.

She held their hands, her mother and brother on either side, imagining they were on the back of a giant turtle. She said it aloud and Jiang-Li smiled indulgently, touching her daughter's cheek and saying that would be a grand adventure. If only those turtles were still around. If only humans had not killed them to make soup from their flesh and boats from their shells.

The sky bled. Crimson tears and bitter ash in her mouth. Her lips were dry: salt-licked and blistered. She raised her head from the watery cushion, her hands now empty. Rubbed her fingers together and wondered where everyone had gone. The beach's golden sands had been replaced by stone. Barren rock pools. Sharp edges underfoot. Someone was on the shore. The tide pushed her out. Nothing more than lapping and yet she was further out than when she had started. She walked forward, every step cutting her feet to shreds.

Looked up.

Further still.

The figure was just a dot on the horizon. Her father. Waiting for her, just beyond the next wave. She swam forward, flicking her tail, strong and steady. He would tell her now, finally, what he had done, what humans had done, why he had left them, why he'd died.

Now he was closer. The figure motionless against the now orange-hued sky. Waiting for her. Nami closed the distance, pulling herself upright. Hobbling as the rocks cut into the soles of her feet. Water poured from her, dragging heavily on every step. It was okay. It was her father. He would know what to do.

She reached the figure. Saw the face.

The selkie from the Onseon Engine night shift.

Blood trailing from his nose, his eyes, his ears. No. But no words sounded. No screams. His skin crumpled loose under her touch. A bloodied pelt in her hands.

No.

No.

No.

Nami picked the algae layer from the safe house walls. Scratched it with her nails to feel the peeling paper behind. She'd worked away at a small circular patch by the stairs, her legs hooked around the metal railing so she wouldn't float away. If she kept at it, she might clear the wall in a few weeks. A fresh start.

She'd not slept in days. Never knew if she was awake or asleep as they moved underwater, one safe house to another. A whisper. A thrown glance. An apology she did not understand. A tray of food by her hand. One time she turned and Ibhar was there, the Drawback elder chattering away with her mending drifting in the water. The algae was especially thick, carpeting the rotting stairs where the dugong sat. Nami pushed her away. Noticed with indifference the heavy lock and chain that bound her in place. It mattered not. She had work to do.

Firth was there, long auburn hair falling into his eyes. He took both her hands, kissing the broken green-tinged nails. Her hands blistered and inflamed. His words floated like dead fish in a stagnant pond. No one was meant to get hurt. Lynnette had gone too far.

Nami blinked the film from her eyes, trying to articulate words that slipped like sand through her fingers. Firth promised. He hadn't known. There was a plan. He touched her face, held her hand to his chest as if she could see the heart of him. But all Nami could see was bodies.

"What was the plan?" she asked.

The kelpie never answered. Pressed her head to his shoulder, cupped her small hand in both of his like an oyster clamped around a pearl. Nami did not know how long he sat there with her. Hours or days had no meaning. Only when he tilted her chin up and kissed her, chaste and tender on the lips, did the world regain a little colour. "Lynnette locked you up. Not me. Afraid you will go to your brother, to the authorities. But you'll never trust us if we treat you like they've treated us."

His amber eyes were still for once, without the glint they'd once had. He searched her face, pushing back her hair. The lock clicked open and the heavy chains that bound her fell loose. He rubbed her wrists with finger and thumb. "I will not bind you. You'll come back to us. To me. I know you."

He kissed her again, more insistent this time. He tasted of the kelp forests of home. His arms the sponge corals she had slept among. She drifted in his hold, floating wherever the tide chose to take her.

Dan was next to her. Called her name, distant and muffled like shouting down a tunnel. Nami looked at him, perplexed, then continued her work. Important work. A job someone had given her. A task to complete. He reappeared some time later with a flat piece of metal. Used it to scrape the wall. The rasping sound caught her by surprise. The algae, paint and paper all flaked off together, leaving a small pit. She could see brick. A glimpse of terracotta.

"What am I doing?" she asked, dropping her arms to her sides. Her wrists were inflamed from the rub of heavy chains that now lay on the floor by her feet. Her tongue moved heavy in her mouth, speech coming slow with lack of use. Her hands ached as she let them relax, a slow burn in each joint.

"Whatever you need to," Dan said. Out of the corner of her eye, she saw her pakalot, and it all flashed back. The wires, the sleepers. What she'd done. Ibhar, Firth, others calling to her through the fugue. Dan's voice twisted, caught on the edges when he spoke. "I never thanked you."

"Don't. Not for that," she said. She wanted to compress the memory into a ball. Throw it as far as she could and let it sink to the bottom of the ocean.

"I honestly didn't think you'd choose me," Dan said. He plucked a hair from his head, twisting it in his mouth. Nami focused on that instead of the discomfort pushing from her ribcage. She didn't want to examine her choices. Look too closely and she'd unravel.

"You used to do that in Yonakuni," she said.

He looked down at his hand, surprised. A smile formed. "I was nervous. The first scholarship student. The weight of expectations upon my shoulders."

"You always worked harder than any of us. Stayed behind. Asked extra questions." Nami remembered the earnest kappa Dan had been. First to lessons and last to leave. Wary of social gatherings, always assuming praise was mockery. It took months for her to break past his shell. For him to finally realise she wanted to be friends.

"I needed to," he said. The marks on his arms looked like they were multiplying. He caught her eye and covered them with his sleeves.

She had first noticed him while studying in the common chamber. Late, when the others were socialising, she had to revise the day's work again. She learned the hard way that while others absorbed knowledge effortlessly, picked up skills with one example, she wasn't one of them. Sheer willpower and practice got her through. Going back over the lessons once, twice, three times before they solidified in her brain. The reading rooms would empty gradually, people swimming home until it was just the two of them under the witchlight. She and Dan. He was smart. Effortlessly intelligent. But he needed to be better than them all. Faultless exams, word-perfect recitations, a knowledge of history that allowed him to correct their teachers at times. The best student they had, all the teachers agreed. Yet while others had jobs lined up for them – opportunities aplenty – Dan had none.

It was the injustice of it that led them both to the protest meetings. Dan was never afraid, and Nami admired that in him. He might be the smallest, the least affluent in the group, but he had a sensible head. He was as likely to tell her all her faults as to back her up. She appreciated that. Not someone pandering to her because of who she was.

"I thought studying would get me everything. That if I proved myself, nothing else would matter," he said.

Nami never realised how prejudiced Yonakuni was until she became friends with Dan. That they placed shape-shifters – human-passing folk – above those like him who looked different. That she subconsciously did the same. She had assumptions about his family, his home that were etched into her grain. She wished she could take a blade and shave away the rot, but the deeper she dug, the more she realised the veins ran right through her. All she could do was acknowledge them. Try to change them.

He rubbed his neck, the marks from Lynnette's hands as clear as though painted on. It made Nami wince just to look, to remember how he had dangled off the ground like a ragdoll. "I . . . I know why people take work like that. Like Onseon. Because if it keeps their family safe, there's no price too high. Even if they hate themselves," he said. His words were slow and considered. The coil tightened around her chest.

"What're you saying? Lynnette is unhinged. A monster."

"What would you've done? If you'd a real choice?"

Nami's tongue stuck to the roof of her mouth, refusing to move. She realised she'd never apologised for pulling him down, for getting him involved. All because of her idiotic stunt with the Peace Stone. She didn't think. That was the problem. Not through to the consequences. It was easier to pick holes than find solutions. All she knew for certain was that murder – of folk or humans – wasn't the solution. There had to be another way.

"Idiot," Dan said into the over-long pause. The word stopped her internalised panic. He was scowling at her, the face he used when she was being foolish. "Princess," he continued. "Pampered toddler."

"Sceptic," Nami retorted. "Aggravating, foul-mouthed arse." The words burst forward before she could stop them, her hands too late to cover her mouth.

It worked. The long-unspoken words were cathartic. She felt rejuvenated. Chuckled. Soon they were both laughing, rocking in the water as they let full-bellied sounds float them up to the ceiling and back down. She could feel the rust flaking from her like the wall. She let the merriment subside but kept hold of the warm glow. Swept her hand through the water, touching the exposed bricks.

She knew what she had to do.

After days of lethargy, the Drawbacks assigned to watch her had grown lax. It was easy enough to prise loose the rotten planks from an upstairs window. Nami swam as fast as her legs would kick, Dan not far behind.

Above water, the trams were still on their rails. Stopped in stations, halfway up their spiralling ascent, and in one case, crumpled and broken where a carriage had fallen. Twisted onto its side, metal collapsing like it was nothing more than paper. Nami stared for a long while. She'd not considered a city in motion when they'd switched off the power. Hadn't thought of the after-effects at all.

Her stomach lurched, heaving, although she had eaten so little in the past few days there was nothing to bring up. Her heart thudded loudly in her chest, confessing to every stranger within earshot. Guilty, guilty, guilty, it said with each painful squeeze. Tearing at the bars of her ribcage, desperate to be let out, to be free of her skin.

Dan crouched on the walkway, watching her. He gave her the moment, standing slowly as she uncurled herself. His beak tapped a few times as if hesitant to say something. To disown her. Disavow his previous support. Nami dug her claws into her fleshy palm. Pushed so hard that the crescent moons imprinted on her skin, giving her something to focus on.

It was nearing midday by the time they reached Webisu, the lack of transport making the journey arduous. They slipped into the water, keeping their heads bobbing on the surface as they swam across to the sampans. Nami imagined the warm interior of Trish's home. The kindness the siren had shown her. She wanted to pull herself onboard and let Trish stroke her hair like her own mother never did. Say it was okay. That she'd make it better. But it was self-indulgent even to be here. She just needed to contact Mira discreetly. Get a message to Kai without bringing the authorities down on all of them. They had done so much for her, and she'd given nothing back.

It was clear something was happening. People were moving around the sampan flotilla with haste. Supplies had been stacked on the decks, bundles lashed to the curved roofs. They were preparing for a long journey. Lotus-leaf-wrapped parcels were being handed out as the baking sun sent everyone into the slivers of shade. It was a rare dry day, the monsoon rains having finally settled in the morning. A couple of children were coiling rope, their legs dangling from the sides of vessels.

A flash of limp feet on the cots of the Onseon Engine. Nami pushed it back.

She pointed out Trish's sampan to Dan and they swam silently around, trying to keep away from the other vessels. A human man was cleaning out his breathing apparatus, wiping the seal diligently and holding it up to the light. Trish emerged from the curved shelter of her boat, a plate of filled flatbreads in one hand, leaning on her walking stick with the other. The smell of fish curry wafted behind her.

"I can't believe we're really doing this," the man said, helping her with the plate.

"Me neither. My whole life is here," the elder siren said. Her fingers were unsteady, the joints swollen like bulbs under her skin, making it hard for her to be dexterous. She tore a piece of the oily flatbread clumsily. "If Mira is to be believed ..."

"She's never steered us wrong. I trust your daughter; we all trust her more than the Council."

Trish harrumphed. "We're collateral to the rest of them. Best we're out of the way. Far, far out of the way before the real fighting begins."

They looked together into the distance, companionable silence filled only by the sound of sipping tea. A handful of terns flew above them, one swooping down to grab at the stack of flatbread. It blustered away in a flurry as Trish yelled. Waved her stick overhead. Then indulgently she threw the scraps off the side of the boat, watching the birds swoop and swerve.

Nami felt wings smack into the side of her head and dipped back below the waterline. *We're collateral.* The tone had been matter-of-fact. The elder siren had fought this battle over and over. The thrashing seabirds dived in and out around her, their black heads like darts in the water as they vied for food. And then a huge bird, a cormorant, landed among them. Snapped with superiority until the smaller terns screamed annoyance but flipped their wings down. Accepted the order of things.

The cormorant fished up all the soggy scraps, alone with its feast. The terns were one flock. They might have lost the battle, but nevertheless, they persisted.

"I'm going to talk to her," Nami whispered.

Dan shook his head, hand on her shoulder. "Mira's mother? She's friends with humans! She'll have us arrested."

"Trust me." She heard a gulp of water as Dan submerged himself in her wake.

Trish was waiting by the prow, head on her arms. "Was wondering how long it would take you."

Nami didn't have a response. She ducked her nose under the water, letting the salt fill her mouth. She was glad Trish was far enough away that she couldn't see the shame written across her face.

"I really hoped you weren't involved . . . I prayed you weren't."

"I—"

"Don't tell me."

The sun beat down on Nami's scalp and shoulders. Salty tears fell from her eyes, hot and fast, blurring her vision. *What should I do?* The words clamoured in her head, rolling around in her internal storm while outside the seas were calm. They mocked her, whining and childish, until she bit them back. Afraid of the answers she didn't want to hear. She needed to set things right. Only one person in Tiankawi would know what to do. "I need Mira," she admitted finally.

Trish stood, leaning heavily on her cane. The sun lit her from behind, her silhouette tinged with light as Nami squinted up. Her face was humourless, no longer filled with the mirth from her earlier interaction. "You're too late."

Chapter Forty-Five

Of course they fired her. The highest-profile fathomfolk in the realm. Captain of the border guard. She'd disobeyed orders: at the Boat Race riots and again at Onseon. First on the scene and yet apparently had no clear description of the perpetrators.

Of course they fired her. Who else did they have to blame? They congratulated themselves for the decisive action as they talked in circles about which district to supply emergency power to. The financial sector of Jingsha, where nearly all of the Council members had second homes and offices, or the southern districts, where crime had exponentially increased because no one was there to police it?

Of course they fired her. She had fulfilled her duty as a diversity project and had deviated from the plan. Actually pushing for reforms and standing her ground. That wasn't the deal. Now they could say they'd tried, but folk just weren't suited to the role.

They would've taken her coat except it was in pieces littering the water after the tram incident. Samnang relished slapping a pakalot back on her wrist. No more exceptions. Just another saltie. The manacle was heavier than she remembered, periodically pulsing to remind her of its existence. As if she would forget. Thinking of violence against humans? She was barely thinking at all.

The port was dark. The street lights both above and below the water were off, nothing more than statue sentries. An otter ran up the walkway, silhouetted only by the wan moonlight. Glanced back at Mira thoughtfully before slipping into the inky depths.

She took a drag on her cigarette, the curling tobacco filling her mouth with smoky bitterness. It'd been years since she'd quit smoking, but after everything that had happened in the last few months . . . Fuck it, she deserved to smoke the whole pack, even if it made her sick afterwards.

She ran through the chinthe code under her breath. The litany of rules had a mesmerising effect. Soothing. Not that she needed them any more. She should erase them to free up space in her overcrowded head. She paced the platform, avoiding the broken glass. The tram shelter was cracked, some pieces of glass still in place, but fragile, bending inwards like a gut punch.

The platform, the whole port was empty. Only the shadows made ghosts in her mind. Anyone with a modicum of sense was at home, doors and windows barred. Between the fathomfolk curfew and the power outage, the streets were not safe. The sail-mills and eddy farms were providing some power. Enough for essential services. Mira scowled. She disagreed with the decision to class Manshu district's luxury condos as essential services. But she forgot herself. There were no more Council meetings. No more officials to cajole. She was as voiceless as the other folk now.

She lit another cigarette, the red light brightening as she brought it to her lips. Her eyes adjusted to the flare. A shape moved. "Mira?"

"Shit." She stubbed it out hastily, coughing as the smoke caught in her throat.

Kai said nothing. His expression was enough. Mira pulled her coat tighter around her. The beige jacket had felt wrong when she'd shrugged it on, but it was the only one that wasn't chinthe green. She was accustomed to living in her uniform – a protective shell; felt exposed without it.

"Isn't that bad for your voice?" he asked, gesturing at the cigarette. Mira shrugged. Kai had never heard her sing a siren's song, never asked why the topic made her uncomfortable. Too polite to push. He hesitated, standing a couple of metres away. The wounded look on his face said he'd noticed she was avoiding him. Had been since the power outage, if not before. "How's your shoulder?" he asked.

She rotated her arm carefully, the bruising tender to the touch but no longer aching. "It will heal."

"A record of your experience," Kai said with a twitching smile on his lips. A mockery of the formal teaching he'd had in Yonakuni. Mira had found it endearing before; tonight it rubbed like gravel in a wound.

"Not all experiences are worth having." Everything had been handed to Kai. He hadn't had to swim through polluted waters, climb broken ladders and knock on doors with chapped raw knuckles. He didn't have a pakalot slapped on his wrist after the tram incident. He didn't have to bargain away half his identity to pay for his ama's gill rot treatments. No, he was Yonakuni-born. Dragon-born. Not some bottom-feeder from the Seong slums.

He took a few paces towards her, reaching out with both hands. "You can come back from this."

"Can I? All the training, the extra shifts, for what?" Her anger burned the cold from her skin, setting her ablaze.

"We're not talking about your shoulder, are we?" Kai said. His empty hands fell back to his sides. "Come home with me."

Great. Like Samnang's simpering other half. Making tea and buying expensive jewellery. Mira laughed. A sound ringing into the night, harsh as a mockingbird in one of Jingsha's rooftop restaurants. Kai flinched, a pained expression darting across his face. "I'll not be your caged bird."

"That's not what I meant."

"I also know what others will think. What *I* will think."

"For once in your damn life can you not accept a little help? I'm not trying to stifle you. I want to support you. Isn't that the whole point?" Raindrops had started to fall, plastering loose strands of his hair against his cheeks and the nape of his neck. Mira longed to reach out and wipe them away, to let him fold her under his coat and go home to his apartment.

If she took a moment, it would calm her. Hadn't she taken so many of them in the past? Long, deep breaths to dissipate the rage after every snub, every backhanded compliment, every time they ignored her.

But she couldn't accept that. She was tired of the broken system. Of trying to grow around a tangled fishing net that was strangling her. Her heart was breaking, and if that was the case, better to rip the bloody thing right out of her ribcage. "I'm bored of this rich boy, poor girl charade. I'm done with it."

Kai's eyes widened, but he shook his head. "No, no you're not. You're hurt and lashing out. I know you."

"You know fuck all. A tour of Qilin and a couple of stories about my past." The words were spat out, the shame of her secret debts weighing heavily. She had put off the meeting with Cordelia for too long now. There were only days left on the old bargain, not weeks. She was dragging her feet for a solution that refused to rise to the surface. She had thought things would be different a decade on. That she would've finally confessed the truth to her mother, figured out an alternative with her help. But instead everything had fallen apart.

Mira looked up at Kai through wet lashes, his face blurring in the rain. There was no question he would not answer, nothing he shirked from. No matter how bad the argument was tonight, he'd patiently wait for her to come around. He always did. He was devoted in a way that scared her. His faith so complete that Mira was certain she'd break it. She was waiting for the disaster to happen.

Why not just end it? Then she wouldn't have to hold her breath any longer. Wouldn't have to wait for him to realise how flawed and broken she truly was. Rip off the bandage. She licked her lips, hesitating for a moment before she said the words that would hurt him to the bone. "Nami was at Onseon."

Kai blanched, mouth overfilled with unanswered questions. Finally, "She ... got caught up in a bad crowd."

"They killed people. Fathomfolk."

He stuffed his hands into his pockets. "I mean – there must be an explanation."

"You're the same, you dragonkin. Entitled, selfish, arrogant. You've sacrificed nothing, and still you get everything." Would she have kept her job if she'd turned Nami in? She suspected so. Samnang would delight at reeling in bigger fish. But for better or worse, she had kept her mouth shut. Protected Kai's little sister. The rhythmic tapping of rain on broken glass lent a dreamlike quality to the exchange. It didn't really feel like she was talking. An unfamiliar voice spat the serrated words. Mira was merely pushing him back to shore. Away from the floating junk pile of her life. But Kai wouldn't give up so easily. She had to twist the knife deeper. "You'd be more use as a pearl."

His eyes snapped up, holding hers. His nostrils flared just a little, and for a flash, his spines prickled down the length of his back. The first time she'd seen him truly angered. His pain was palpable, and it was all she could do to stop herself from immediately apologising. She steeled herself, face like stone.

"You don't mean that." The certainty of earlier had gone from his voice. He looked defeated.

"Just go home. Your Yonakuni home. You don't belong here."

Their shoulders brushed as Mira walked past him. Her feet were heavy, dragging as though stones filled her boots. Kai reached for her hand, her name etched on his lips. She recoiled sharply, shunning his touch. If he reached one more time, her resolve would break. The act would crumble like castles in the sand. Kai stopped. Crestfallen face dropping towards the ground.

She had exactly what she wanted. But all she felt was hollow. The cold water soaked up through her. The rain hid the rivers that ran down her cheeks.

Chapter Forty-Six

The buildings were older than the glass facades in Jingsha, and half the height. Cutting edge a century ago, perhaps, but now nothing more than fading brick monoliths. The Old Town. But this was where Kai's secretary was adamant he was, running up a tab for days.

A stone gate marked the entrance to the Old Town, decorated with stylised carp, tails pointing toward the skies. The grey stone buildings were ornately carved with mythical land creatures: chin-the lion dogs, kumiho nine-tailed foxes and kancil mouse-deer. Once a tableau of remarkable intricacy, now they were pockmarked by erosion. The worn hand of time softening their edges.

The singing wailed into the communal corridor and the dim oil lamps made Nami's head hurt. Dan had both hands on his ears, not caring if it appeared impolite. He peered in a few of the doorways, smiling to himself.

"What is this place?" she said. She didn't want to shout, but it was hard to be heard over the cacophony.

"You've never . . . ?" Her friend couldn't keep the grin off his face. He tapped a webbed foot on the floor, almost dancing with delight. "Of course you've never."

"Gonna let me in on the secret?"

"You'll find out soon enough." He pointed at the door. Off-key singing assailed Nami's ears; Kai's off-key singing.

The onlookers – two female and one male – sat on a curved sofa throwing apologetic glances at newcomers. One was lackadaisically plucking a zither. In the centre, swaying on his feet and waving his bamboo flute in one hand, was Nami's brother. Stained robes spilled free of his loosely tied sash, revealing smatterings of scales on his chest. His antlers were showing through stringy hair and his bare feet were dragon claws. It was as if he'd given up halfway through shape-shifting. He locked eyes with her and took one step closer. The siren with the zither strummed a new melody and Kai lurched back again. Brought the flute to his lips.

"How much has he had?" Nami shouted over the din. One of them gestured at the many empty glasses on the marble table. She took a few steps closer and a wave of pleasure swept over her. Involuntarily her hand wandered to touch the stranger's shoulder, to kiss her soft lips and press their bodies together. Anything to spill the sweet ecstasy she could feel brimming over.

The stranger winked, lips so close they brushed Nami's as she spoke. "Teahouse rules, if your wards are down, consent is assumed. I'm more than happy to . . . be your guide."

Nami's dilated eyes narrowed as she pulled back and tried to shake off the haze. She used a touch of her power to ward her mind against the compulsion effects of the sirens' charms. Her hand was pressed into a fist over the rapid-fire beating of her chest. She glared at Dan, but her friend had doubled over in silent laughter, rocking on the chair he had plonked himself into.

Nami had only been to one siren teahouse back in Yonakuni. A famed siren had charmed the room, her voice bouncing off the coral to make a chorus. They'd applauded so hard Nami's hands ached for a week. It'd been an act of defiance, going with her Academy friends when her mother had always told her it was a place of ill repute. She'd been surprisingly disappointed at how tame it was: poetry readings and sweet-sounding voices. It wasn't until the siren had started that she sat up. By the end of the set she'd laid her head down in the performer's lap and begged to kiss her. She'd known, of course, the allure of a siren's song. But she'd wanted, just once, to be tempted.

"Has he ... ?" she ventured tentatively.

"Believe me, if a seduction could shut him up, I would've done it days ago." The male siren rolled his eyes.

Kai's fingers fumbled over the holes of the bamboo flute and failed miserably. He threw the offending instrument across the room with a curse. "My murderous little sister, what else are you here to destroy?"

The sirens hastily made excuses to go, closing the door firmly behind them. Luckily for Nami, family feuds were not included in the package Kai had paid for.

"Who's this? Another revolutionary?" Kai said, pointing at Dan.

The kappa scratched his flat crown. Awkwardly made a fist-palm salute. "Tamsui, but call me Dan."

Kai cocked his head. Despite intoxication, he still had his wits. "One of the Academy graduates who helped in that Peace Stone stunt? No offence, but shouldn't you be in a Yonakunish jail?"

"None taken, and yes, I should." Dan tucked both hands behind his back. His voice was level, confident despite the difference in stature and status between the two. Kai shrugged, falling into a chair and grabbing the nearest bottle of rice wine. Shook the remaining drips into his mouth before tossing it onto the sofa.

"Where's Mira? We need you – *I* need you!" Nami said. Her brother picked up another bottle and peered at the dregs.

"Managing fine all by myself – isn't that what you always say?"

She deserved that. For every offer of help she'd thrown back in his face. "Kai, the Onseon Engine ... why didn't you tell me? Why did no one tell me?"

He coughed with a mouthful of warm swill. Took a long

moment before responding. "Had to find out for yourself. Mother made me promise."

"You knew? All along you knew?" Fissures opened up in Nami's chest, raw edges infused with grief. A wilful daughter who needed to see uncomfortable truths for herself. She should be distraught, or angry at least at the subterfuge, but all she felt was numb. Battered driftwood floating on the surface of the water.

"I have never been. The one place in Tiankawi I could not bring myself to visit. Was afraid of what I would see, what I would do if I saw them. Pretending it wasn't really happening seemed easier. Pretending our parents didn't play their part." Kai spoke soberly.

Nami saw clearly now the guilt weighing him down. The paka-lot bill made so much sense. A small change for the better in the face of the immovable mountain that was the Onseon Engine. He did not berate her for her involvement. Perhaps, deep down, he had always known it would come to this. Hoped for it. Someone had to break the bones before they could reset.

In between the discarded bottles and glasses, Nami saw a familiar collection of pebbles: one dappled grey, another the colour of stirred molasses, a white teardrop. She held them in her hand, warming them against her palm. They clacked together pleasantly. Kai had collected them as a boy, pockets forever full of stones worn smooth by his touch. She saw now that boy, knees pulled close to his chest. Alone on the sofa.

She stacked one stone on top of another until, five high, they toppled over. Again. And again. On her third attempt, Kai added a pebble atop hers. When they were little, whenever she got in trouble with their parents, he took her to the surface. Let her skim stones alongside caustic declarations. Once, twice, three times the stones would skip over the water's surface then sink down, until Kai's pockets were empty. He'd shrug when she apologised for his lost collection. Build it anew.

"Mira's left me." The pebble tower tumbled over, stones

clattering onto the floor. He retrieved a smooth white stone, rubbing it between finger and thumb. "Some nonsense about being from two different worlds."

"So you drank yourself stupid." Nami expected a retort. Not the red-rimmed eyes he turned on her then. As he leaned forward, head in his hands, his long hair fell over his face.

"This time was different."

Once Nami would've said good riddance to her. That the siren was using him. Nothing more than a common estuary girl. Now she wasn't so sure. "She lost her job, was just lashing out."

Kai said nothing.

"She ... might have her mind on other things." Dan fidgeted as he spoke, pressing his webbed hand into the water rings on the table. Nami had all but forgotten he was there. The kappa held both their attention and he squirmed under the scrutiny.

"What do you mean?"

"I heard the Drawbacks talking about it. They ... she ... No, forget it. I probably misunderstood." He folded his arms, curling to make himself even smaller.

"Dan!"

He sat up straight, neck bobbing before he finally answered. "They said Mira made a bargain. With the seawitch."

"Cordelia," Kai and Nami said simultaneously. They looked at each other with sudden clarity. Like a break in the rain.

Kai said it aloud first. "She sold her voice."

Mira had never exerted influence over Nami, not the way she'd felt walking into the teahouse. The estuary girl was so determined to prove herself, she'd fought tooth and nail for everything. Always picking the harder option.

"Her ama," Kai said, open-mouthed with realisation. He jumped up from the chair, gesticulating wildly. "Trish has all the signs of gill rot, has done the whole time I've known her. And yet she isn't declining as fast as others. I never questioned it."

"She sold her voice to save her mother?" As Nami said it, she knew it was true. Mira would do anything for the people she loved. Sacrificing part of herself or pushing them away.

"But why now? What hold would Cordelia have over her now?" Kai said. He loomed over the kappa in his dragon-scaled skin, his curving antlers almost sweeping the ceiling. Reflections of their mother's poise echoed through him. His dark eyes held Dan's, making him shift with discomfort. Her friend looked like a dying fish caught in a net. Shaking like he would bolt for the door at any second.

She put a hand on her brother's shoulder. "Kai, stop. You're scaring him. Dan's a friend – trust him." The kappa glanced up at her, swallowing hard. The tension in the room did not ease, but Kai took a step back, opening his hands in placation. The wail of singing from other rooms penetrated through the walls in the silence. The turquoise sea glass decorating the room appeared to undulate under Nami's tired eyes.

"There's an expiry date on the bargain. It's . . . soon."

Nami recalled the look on Mira's face after the Boat Race riots, holding Trish in her arms. The way they joked together with an affection Nami didn't have with her own mother. And the pervasive image, the face of the selkie from Onseon. It could've been Trish. Another folk scraping a living, trying to support their family.

"Renew the deal or let Trish die." Kai's voice was mournful. It melted something in him and he sat back down, body pooling softly. All the edges gone.

Nami pointed at the pitcher of water. Dan obliged, bringing it over. As Kai reached for a glass, Nami upended the whole jug over his head. Her brother gasped, spluttering as the cold water drenched him. His skin took on a silver coating for a few seconds as he waved his hands at her for explanation.

She smiled wickedly, enjoying his response far more than was warranted. "You're no good to anyone drunk. Now, what are we going to do?"

It was a few days before Nami could find time away from both Dan and Kai. Days in which letters from Firth had made their way into her hands; passed over from couriers, left in her bag or on a table when she wasn't looking. The Drawback network was more extensive than she'd realised. She ignored them at first, not even bothering to read past the first sentence. But curiosity buried like a worm into her core. She couldn't sleep for thinking about the familiar sloped handwriting and the scent of the curling paper. It smelled like him.

The Barreleye Club looked closed from the outside. The recent unrest had all but destroyed the business, and it was only through a back door and multiple assurances of discretion that they let Nami in. Those who dared risk the curfew were here for the night, the door bolted shut behind her. The atmosphere had completely altered. If it'd been a merry simmer before, now it was tepid. Cold currents ran through the water and people kept to their own niches, hidden shadows in booths lining the cavernous club. The witchlights had been dimmed, so that Nami could barely see her hands in front of her face. She remembered dancing here with Firth and the other kelpies, the joy of that night. Wondered if she was here to say goodbye, or something else. She glanced up as the now familiar wail of the curfew warning echoed dully through the water. No going back.

He was waiting in the private room, just as his messages had said. Some sort of meeting with other folk that he quickly dismissed as his eyes met Nami's. She barely even saw them leave, the merrow and naga both giving her a peculiar look before the door closed behind them.

All the words she'd planned to say, the questions she wasn't going to let him avoid, washed away in the tide as the kelpie swam towards her. Firth had that effect. One that transformed her from wilfully stubborn to a gibbering wreck. She loathed it. She loved it. Her heartbeat throbbed with a distracting intensity. She forced words out, her voice jarringly loud in the silence. "I came."

He said nothing. Cocked his head and gave a faint smile, letting her run on.

"I don't know why I came, but I did. It doesn't mean I believe you. Or forgive you. Or trust you. But I came." She wanted to start over. Hold a knife to Firth's throat and demand answers. Instead she was like a frantic mouse skittering across a kitchen floor.

"We want the same thing, you and I. A better world for fathomfolk." Firth took a step closer, reaching for her hands. Nami shook, desperate to cling to him but forcing herself to pull away. Hold her hands behind her back until she had answers.

"At what cost? You're close to Lynnette, you must've known what she planned." She closed her eyes, unwilling to witness his pained expression.

"I knew of her fury, the same as any of us. I knew what each of us vowed when we joined the cause. It's not how I would've done it. I pleaded with her after the incident at the meeting. But change is ugly. Anything else is simply a lie."

Nami said the words she'd not yet said aloud. A confession that was tied around her neck in a noose. "There are deaths on my hands. Fathomfolk deaths."

"If I'd been there ..." Firth turned away, voice breaking. His pain was palpable and it gave Nami the kinship that she desperately needed. Her eyes flicked open as she reached a hand against his cheek. He leaned into it, the stubble on his jawline brushing against her, kissing her palm with the lightest touch. "I would've taken that burden from you. Let me carry it – the anguish, the worry."

"I just don't know if we're doing the right thing." Her voice was a whisper that rattled around the room. A betrayal of the inner circle of Drawbacks where she'd started to feel she belonged.

"I'll go to the kumiho, say it was me." He nodded to himself as if it was settled.

Lying for her was not the outcome Nami wanted. Another friend incarcerated on her behalf. She rejected the notion, refusing the offer inarticulately.

"Then what can I do? How can I earn back your trust? I want to protect you, Nami. Make those decisions that are filling you with doubt. I would be your guiding light."

"My lighthouse?" she said with a sobbing laugh. A rough-edged sound veering into hysterics. She was tired. More tired than she'd ever been in her life. Her head was bursting at the seams with threads that she dared not tug at. She was merely treading water, putting one foot in front of the other. Firth's proposal was appealing. She longed to lay her head in his lap and stop worrying about the poor choices she'd made.

To stop her head from spinning, to stop her mouth from running, to stop his forlorn eyes from staring, she kissed him. Her head tilted up and she pressed her lips against his. Opened her mouth to taste him. Her hands slipped down from his face to his shoulders and her fingers combed through his wavy hair. He overwhelmed her. Heady from the touch of his skin against hers, the press of his thigh between her legs. He responded in kind, butterfly kisses on her cheeks and running down her neck. She gasped when he bit her ear. His head delved down between her collarbones, unravelling the fastenings of her top.

Nami closed her eyes and wondered at this feeling. She'd taken lovers before. With casual curiosity she'd experimented with a range of genders, finding it a pleasant enough distraction. But she'd never felt it consume her entirely. Stepping onto the lit pyre and watching the flames lick at her feet. Her whole core burned with want of him. Scarcely noticed the moans that escaped her lips as he tentatively cupped the curve of one breast. Her hands were clumsy and slow, too slow for the need that thrummed in her midriff as she tugged at his loose trousers.

Abruptly she stopped. Swam backwards out of his grasp. Firth growled with hunger, pupils dilated as he followed, legs kicking to wind his body around hers. Nami reached for the door as they spiralled in the water, and flicked the lock closed.

Firth smiled with understanding. Not the lopsided half-smile he usually gave. One that possessed her without touch. Owned the very breath from her gills. She closed the distance between them.

No more interruptions.

Chapter Forty-Seven

By the time she reached the surface, Cordelia's colours were under control. Neutral brown-spotted. She had to play her cards close to her chest. Peak too early and she'd lose this opportunity. Nonchalance. Calm. That was what she needed to exude.

Mira's long hair was loose and whipping curls into her face as she stood on the end of the pier. She did not carry an umbrella, despite the heavy days of monsoon rain. There were no taxi boats this evening, none for days. The empty taraibune boats knocked together like buckets, spinning slowly around their docking ropes.

Cordelia's lower limbs wrapped around the wooden posts and she pulled herself above the water. Motioned for her squid guards to stay hidden. A gecko slithered in the fading light, outstretched limbs clinging to rotten wood. The air was clammy up here, stifling despite the recent downpour. The seawitch flicked the excess water from her forehead, taking her damn time. "Dear Mira, how is your mother? She's missed her last couple of appointments."

The siren met her eyes steadily. Her voice betrayed nothing. "I thought it was best she move further out."

"Indeed. Terrible affair, terrible," Cordelia said. She knew Mira was stalling. Despite her own impatience, the seawitch indulged her. After all, the chase was more enjoyable than the meal. She did love it when all pretences broke down at the end, leaving only the fermenting sweetness of desperation. One of these days she'd learn to bottle that also.

"You've kept your end of the bargain, Cordelia. For that I suppose I owe you thanks."

"But let me guess – you've realised that your siren song might be useful after all?" Cordelia waved a limb, a pitying expression on her otherwise delighted face.

Mira folded her arms tightly around herself. A fine drizzle plastered curls around her forehead. "I don't regret it. Who I was back then. I hated myself, thought I had to be more human. I've changed, but I've had ten more years with my ama."

"You've changed *because* you had ten more years with your ama." Cordelia had not meant to be sympathetic, but the words spilled from her nonetheless. She was certain her own children would never understand the decisions she'd made. She brushed away the discomfort as if it were a fly buzzing over food. "This is all very profound, but what'll it be?"

"We could change things. An alliance."

A few months ago, she might actually have considered it. Had proposed an arrangement the day Mira got her captaincy. But she needed that siren song now, before Samnang got any more bright ideas. "Oh, how tempting, saltlick. An alliance with the captain of the chinthe, partner of the ambassador. No, wait, my apologies, how could I forget? An alliance with a nobody with no friends, no job, and very soon, no mother." She gestured to her hidden squid guards in case Mira was in need of more forceful coercing. "I'll not offer it again. Sign, or don't sign. It's only your ama's life."

Mira was silenced. She had nothing. No hidden blade up her sleeve or guards to arrest the seawitch. Alone and broken, just as Cordelia had intended. They needed to be surrounded by water for the transfer of power. As she turned towards the moored boats, Cordelia caught sight of a sheathed dagger at Mira's waist. Her chinthe ceremonial weapon. They hadn't bothered to ask for it back after they put a pakalot on her wrist. Muzzled as the rest of the folk. Cordelia's limbs curled around the sides of the taraibune boat, wondering if the freshwater fool had brought it to break the bargain the old-fashioned way. A knife at her throat.

Mira twisted the oar, the awkward little bathtub boat spinning at first before making its zigzag path across the darkening waters. It looked hard work in the growing rain, but Cordelia was not about to offer help.

Flashes of light came from above, the cloud illuminated briefly. A rumble of thunder sounded in the distance. The downpour got heavier as darker clouds rolled in. Fat droplets now, faster and faster, like pellet drums. A deluge filling the round boat until they were ankle deep. They watched in silence as forks of lightning jumped between heavy storm clouds. The thunder roared, a purring bassline. This Cordelia could work with, her skin refreshed by the tapping on her shoulders and back.

"It's time." She had to shout over the storm. She removed the stone from her drawstring pouch: a cracked trapiche emerald shaped like a waterwheel. Dull now, the colour almost brown without the siphoned siren song. Ten years. Cordelia had leaned – just a little – on *so* many people. Opened doors for her blunder-headed son. When Qiuyue was older, she would help her too. Teach her the ways of bargains and deals or any other profession her daughter wanted to pursue. She needed more for that. More influence, more power in this sinking city.

"What will you offer?" The ceremonial words to start the binding. They still had power even in Tiankawi's foul waters.

Mira's face lit up with a flash from above. Over the last couple of days, her siren charms would've returned to her. But here, surrounded by water, everything was magnified. Cheeks flushed, she opened and closed her hands, the tinge of energy coursing through her body. She might think to use her charm on the seawitch. Or her blade. Cordelia had the scars to remind her. Her lower limbs could regenerate but she still felt pain when they were severed. At a gesture, her squid guards slid up the sides of the boat, putting themselves on either side of Mira. Taking no risks tonight. The siren breathed out, the glow diminishing as it suffused her skin. Sense shrinking her back down to size.

Cordelia held the bamboo scroll in her hands, letting it unfurl in a rattling ladder. The rain drenched the cramped handwriting, but no elements could fade the unbreakable terms of the contract. Characters written in Cordelia's own ink and signed with Mira's scratched signature a decade ago. "What will you give for another ten years?"

"I've fought for *us*, for folk, for the disenfranchised," Mira said. Her words were acerbic as she continued. "For the voiceless! She's my mother. She's all I have left."

It was a shame. If things had been different, if Mira had more to bargain with, Cordelia might've considered it. No matter. "Business is business."

Mira was more broken than she had ever been. "Then all I have to offer you is the same. My voice. Take it. You might as well."

The seawitch shrugged as if indifferent. The smug satisfaction nestled between her three hearts. She unstoppered the vial of ink, dipping the pen in and watching Mira scrawl on the renewal line. The ink in Cordelia's body thrummed in response, the taste of it like rich umami behind her gills. Ten more years. Elation puffed out her body, relief that something had gone to plan. "Sing for me then, saltlick." Another streak of lightning, and another, like eagle claws raking at the sky. The thunder was nearly overhead now and the downpour continued.

Mira's dark hair whipped up around her head like a halo of curls and she sang. Soft at first, her voice uncertain and wavering. It slipped a little, sliding in the water before steadying itself in the choppy seas. Stronger now, matched to the drumming of the rain, the knocking of the thunder above. A pure melody without lyrics, soaring above the din. Her outline glowed in phosphorescence, pinprick lights darting like fireflies into the air. Lightning lit up the boat and the siren song rose like the aurora borealis from her skin. Cordelia wondered if this was the first time Mira had dared use her power since their return. She did not seem the kind to wield it lightly. Squeamish. Unable to do what needed to be done.

Despite shielding, the seawitch was swept into the intensity of the song. The siren power in its rawest form battered against her defences. She pushed her limbs reluctantly off the decking, untying the gossamer fishing net at her side. She needed to keep focus, get the contract renewed, bound. Around her, Mira's song wafted upwards, like a paintbrush swirled across the air, coated in soft feathers of white and lilac. Cordelia threw the net, gathering the edges together, and pulled it together. Tighter. Tighter. Constricted it into a dense ball. It pulsed luminescent. Once she had gathered it all – hauled in her catch – she would distil it as before into a stone.

Mira was clutching at her throat, gagging without sound. Cordelia had taken some liberties this time to ensure she had every last note; dragged the siren's whole voice from her throat, not just her song. The fool hadn't even read the terms of the agreement. Mira looked at her with horrified realisation.

Something lurched behind the seawitch. She turned in time to see his face. A dragon. Kai. He tore the captured song from her fingers, throwing the net and its contents into the waves. A flurry of blows and her squid guards were knocked into the water also. Then there was only human-shaped Kai standing beside Mira.

"Mine!" Cordelia said, looking over the side. She motioned urgently to the giant squid, heard them slip under the waves to chase the voice. The orb lit the darkened waters on its descent.

"You have no right," Kai said, his own voice husky as he touched Mira's throat. She reached up to his shoulder, as if uncertain it was real. Opened her mouth to speak, but only a reedy sound emanated from her lips.

"I have every right. She agreed on a binding contract. A bargain's a bargain." Cordelia had seen it all before. Family, friends, pleading, wheedling their way out.

Kai took the bamboo scroll, looking at the script as if he were in his office rather than out at sea on a bathtub boat slowly filling with rainwater. It sat low in the choppy seas now; Cordelia was submerged up to her calves. With Kai's added weight, the taraibune would not last much longer. And while she and Kai could swim to safety, she was not so sure the half-human Mira could. The seawitch's smile masked the questions in her mind. Kai's appearance was a surprise. A deviation from the plan. Who had tipped him off? She would have noticed if she had been followed. Maybe Mira would not, in the state she was in.

"Revisions can still be made within the hour of signing," Kai pointed out. Mira had schooled him well in the Marine Laws. "I'll duel you for it."

"A challenge?" Cordelia laughed so hard her sides ached and she had to clutch her waist with her lower limbs. "People don't duel! Not in Tiankawi. You can lodge a complaint, see if the Marine Court will give you the time of day. She chose. It's this world you have a quarrel with, not me."

"And you do it from a place of philanthropy?"

"We all need to survive."

Mira reached up and took Kai by the collar to get his attention. Shook her head at him and tried to push him away. Honestly, Cordelia was a little touched. It was playing out nicely, all things considering. Perhaps she could squeeze something from the dragon after all.

"An amendment then, a substitution," he said, and reached out his hand. The sky flashed with crackled light. One ragged line hit the water in the distance, and another. The skies groaned. The

noise thrummed through Cordelia's body, turning her skin mark-
ings into black and white flashing waves. Kai said something else,
but his voice was lost in the noise, the rainwater sliding down her
forehead and blurring her vision.

Chapter Forty-Eight

Nami chased the swirling light of Mira's voice in the depths. The water was black, so obscured that she lost it in the darkness, could barely see her hands in front of her face as she dived deeper and deeper. She tasted it on her tongue. Ink. Overhead, something thrashed like a beached whale, and she spun in the water, looking for the cephalopod guard who was clearly stalking her. A dim light glowed in the distance. She swam towards it, blindly seeking with her hands as the spherical shape grew in diameter. That must be it: Mira's voice. One orb . . . two, dancing. Two? She was near enough to touch them, near enough to—

The light blinked. A pair of glowing eyes - no, make that two pairs. Tentacles loomed towards her face.

Shit.

She ducked and kicked backwards as the two squid separated to flank her. A beak snapped down. She pushed away with cuts of her waterweaving. Propelled herself to the surface. The water was clearer here, giving her a small chance.

She glanced behind, but one of the squid was still on her tail, tentacles ballooned out like a cage. She grasped at driftwood and flotsam, launching it at the squid's head. The beast pulsed red and white, dancing out of the way with ease. The second had disappeared.

What else did she have? She wished to the black abyss she'd brought a weapon. It had not been difficult in the end to find where Mira was. They'd asked a couple of stallholders at Qilin and word got around. Within hours they had news of sightings. Kai had to decline multiple offers of support, such was Mira's reputation. Violence isn't the way, he said. We'll negotiate with Cordelia. Well that plan was working out well. Try talking to the pet cephalopods who were about to cut Nami to shreds. The squid was bigger than her, with a longer reach. She could not outrun it, but she could outsmart it.

She redirected the energy from the churning water above her head and pushed it down. A jet stream slammed into the squid's arms, twisting them back. Nami swallowed her fear and dived towards her pursuer, pushing the water all the while with her hands. Up and over, churning the momentum. The squid chittered, trying to break her hold, but she held on, turning it faster and faster in a tight whirlpool.

The water slipped at the sides, escaping her control. She knew she couldn't hold it much longer. One more push, directing the whole mass down to the seabed. Driving behind it with both palms. She uttered a visceral yell. The squid slammed into the broken back of a rusted tram carriage. It'd been lucky. The seabed was littered with twisted iron girders, frames and scaffolding in a sunken wasteland. It lay splayed for a moment, twitching, before one dilated eye looked up at her.

Nami gulped, feeling the fatigue on her limbs despite the adrenaline rush. She'd depleted most of her waterweaving reserves. The squid made another noise, a yammering squeal, and then streaked past her to disappear into the distance.

Kai and Mira were dimly silhouetted by the witchlight above the water. But where was the orb with Mira's siren song? There! The swirl of colours drifted as it rolled on the rocky seabed. Nami swam down and picked it up by the netting. The voice was warm to the touch, humming like a lullaby. It was ... easy. Suspiciously calm. Then the algae beneath her moved. Arms wrapped up and around her like a snare. The skin of the second giant squid shimmered as it broke camouflage and peeled itself from the algae-covered girders. Bright white as it wrapped tentacles around her feet. It was bigger than the one that had fled. Scars riddled its flesh, the battle-scarred arms now splashed vibrant orange. The suckers had teeth, biting down hard. Nami yelled, throwing her hands up to toss the orb upwards before she was pulled in.

Black ink and churning water obscured Cordelia's visibility as the boat finally capsized and they fell. She saw a dragon tail flash and the tentacles of her oldest guard release for a moment before she turned her attention back to Kai and Mira, a tableau under water. The dragon was holding Mira, rubbing at her neck where the gills should open. She gasped, bubbles of water rising to the surface from her mouth, shaking her head. Then the song light was propelled up towards them, drawn to the siren. She held it in her hands for a moment, trembling. Brought it to her chest in an embrace. An acceptance. The glow disappeared as her gills gasped open.

Mira floated there, treading water. The look on her face was incredulous as she gazed around her in wonder: at the occasional fish that loitered nearby, down at the endless blue. The water churned, but it was relatively calm compared to the storm overhead.

"You came for me." Mira's hand reached out, faltering until Kai re-anchored it in his own.

"Always," he said, and kissed her palm.

Her eyes unfocused as she looked behind him. "Your sister!"

Cordelia blocked the way, waving a finger in warning. "We're not done here, saltlick."

"I offered you a deal already. Like for like," Kai said, pushing the siren behind him. Mira was singing, a low melody wafting through the water. Cordelia ignored it. Only a fool would think such blatant tricks would work.

Mira was not even looking at her, instead staring down to where the flashing orange body of the squid was lashing out. Slicing across the dragon girl with serrated suckers. Blood darkened the water. A shame really. Nami could have been useful. But if she couldn't even handle herself in a skirmish . . .

The squid wrapped its tentacles around her: curling round her neck and arms in a lovers' embrace. Smothering her gills closed. Pulling her closer and closer to the beak within its folds, to crush and dismember her bit by bit. The idiot barely struggled, barely moved. It was as if—

Cordelia snapped her head to look at Mira. The gentle lullaby was focused entirely on the fight beneath them. Then the siren pulled her dagger from its sheath, met Cordelia's gaze with a steely stare and dropped the weapon.

The illusion Mira had created with her song disappeared as soon as the squid brought its beak down to break the fake Nami in two. It squealed in frustration as its catch disintegrated to nothing. Nami rose behind it. Scales covered her throat and arms, spines prickled down her back. She'd tried and failed to transform into her lithe dragon form. Waterweaving exhausted, all she had left were her wits. So she did what it least expected: swam straight towards its head, gouging with her thorn-like spines as she collided with it.

Black ink burst into the water as the squid writhed, clouding her vision. It smacked her hard on the side with its movements, but the damage was done. Her spines had torn into one eye, blinding it on that side. The incensed guard clicked and shrieked as it lumbered towards her.

Nami feigned, first to one side, then the other. The squid's limbs missed her by inches, its vision clearly affected by the injury. But it was adjusting, each movement a little closer now, and Nami a little more out of breath. Something glinted in the water, an object falling heavy like metal. A dagger. She lunged between grasping squid limbs, fingers outstretched to catch it. The squid followed, wrapping a tentacle around her outstretched arm. Wringing it with a grip that burned all the way up to her shoulder. Twist hard enough and it could shatter her bones. The dagger slipped out of her fingers.

The triumphant squid guard carried her down towards the seabed, nowhere to escape. If only she could raise the broken wrecks as a barrier against it. Stubbornly she tried anyway, water-weaving splutteringly weakly. Drained. Even at full strength she would have struggled to raise them. Blood ebbed from dozens of wide slashes on her chest and legs. She kicked up gravel to buy herself time, but the squid used its other tentacle to pin her down. The hooks in the suckers dug beneath her skin. Its arms inched over her face, pressing her gills closed.

Terror drained into her stomach as though a sluice gate had been yanked open. Stubborn to a fault, she refused to believe this was how things ended. Here among the debris that littered Tiankawi's seabed, asphyxiated and cut to ribbons. Refused to believe she had nothing left to give. This was not how things went down. Wrenching one hand loose, she screamed through her lungs, through her gills, through the very pores in her skin. Reached with the trickle of waterweaving she had left.

The squid looked warily around with its good eye, but the girders remained unmoving. Nami was grasping for something smaller. The dagger. It limped through the water towards her, dragging along the seabed like a scuttling crab. Too insignificant to attract the squid guard's attention. The hilt fitted snuggly into her palm, and she stabbed upwards, plunging the blade between its giant eyes..

Its arms spasmed. Released their choke hold on her. Its longer tentacles flexed straight out, a long, lamenting cry. The orange pulsing across its skin turned pure white, giving one last shudder as it died.

Lightning struck the water's surface. Cordelia felt it, the tingle running down her back. She was sandwiched here between Nami below; Mira and Kai swimming above. Had just seen her strongest squid guard eliminated. They had the upper hand. No bargain was worth losing her life over.

"Like for like." Kai held out his hand to her. He said something else, his voice lost in the thunder that rumbled overhead.

"Agreed," Cordelia said, eyeing Nami, who was slowly swimming her way up to them. Better to take a consolation prize than none at all. She extended her hand and shook Kai's. Felt her power arc over to the water dragon and encircle his body. New characters appeared on the contract she held, a revision to the bargain concerning Trish and Mira, carved into the bamboo with her own ink. Kai added his signature to Mira's at the bottom.

"What did you give her? What?!" Nami said, swimming closer. The younger water dragon was bleeding from long gashes up her arm, stemming a wound on her stomach with one hand. Her skin was pallid, as if she would faint at any second, and her spines like shrivelled leaves. Cordelia was crestfallen. She had acted too hastily.

At least she had like for like. The equivalent of a siren's voice, which for a dragon would mean ... a dragon's pearl? His life? What she could do with that power. Gede would need quite a bit of it, but there would be enough for both children. Invest in their futures.

A single note sounded, low and off-key. It was coming from Kai. He was ... singing. Terrible. Little fish darted away from him. Cordelia covered her ears. What was that? *Why* was that?

A shimmer rippled around his body and a dusting of colour rose from his lips. Nami's mouth fell open.

"No," Cordelia said in horrified realisation. *Like for like.* The bastard. He'd said something as the thunder sounded, added his own footnote. And she'd shaken his hand anyway, too excited to let the big fish get away. The colour poured from his mouth towards her. She held it in her hands. A small orb. A lotus seed really. Clear, with a slick of green, another of grey, swirled inside it. The most useless part of a dragon.

"I don't want your voice!" the seawitch said. A decade of healing Trish. Of ensuring the old dear didn't die of gill rot lest the ink-bound bargain turned the sacs in Cordelia's body into poison. It would've been worth it for siren song: the influence and illusions that came with the magnetising voice. But instead all she'd got was the off-key dronings of a water dragon. Her body seethed with rage, but the other three barely noticed, wrapped up in their little reunion.

Cordelia was incredulous. This wasn't possible. Her brain scrambled to replay the interaction, to see where she'd gone wrong. It simply was not possible! She'd been planning this for weeks. Everything had gone according to plan. Everything *always* went according to plan.

But the script on the contract confirmed it.

She held the orb of Kai's voice up to her eye, resisting the urge to throw it far away. Then she pocketed it, a heavy weight despite its minuscule size. The resentment at being outmanoeuvred would prey on her for weeks. Fucking dragons ruining everything.

Kai made signs with his hands towards Mira. The siren shook her head. "I don't know what you're saying, I never learned to sign!"

Nami swam next to her brother and Mira. Translating the hand signs between them. "He says it's okay."

"Why? I didn't want you to be dragged into this!"

A long pause as Nami waited. "We promised to fight for each other, not with each other. Always."

There was a silence as Cordelia departed. Let them enjoy their little moment. She would win out in the end. She heard the siren's voice, more sure of herself this time. "Teach me how to sign *I love you.*"

Chapter Forty-Nine

Despite Mira's misgivings, the healer was happy with Nami's progress. Her fever broke after three days and her wounds were free from infection. Still she slept. Fifteen, eighteen hours at a time, waking only briefly to take a sip of water, a mouthful of rice porridge. Her body needed to recuperate, that's all, they said. There was only so long Mira could sit, foot tapping, making endless cups of seaweed tea she never finished. It was with a guilty gratitude that she accepted Lieutenant Mikayil's request to meet. Nami's kappa friend, Dan, promised to remain behind.

There was no easy way from Kai's apartment to the Qilin district now that the trams and cable car were down. The line for water tuk-tuks was long and Mira was about to start walking when she realised she could swim. Everything had been restored: her siren song, her gills functional for the first time in a decade. The water was opaque from where she stood, shivering with indecision. She ought to. She'd done it during the stand-off with Cordelia, hadn't she? Face her demons, see the submerged world she'd only imagined for the last decade. Things must've changed, the landscape shifting in the tides. Yet her feet wouldn't move. Her toes wiggled inside her worn boots. She'd lived topside for too long. In the end, she joined the boat queue.

Qilin, the boxy complex of co-dependent buildings, was still. No lights, nor smoke from the crooked chimneys, and the criss-crossed washing lines were bare. The signs that had flashed in gaudy witchlight were dark, softly creaking in an unseen breeze. A wall of fallen bamboo scaffolding blocked her way, bent over like broken corrals across the front of the building.

Mira knew what to expect. After the power cut, she'd passed the message on for the residents to barricade themselves in; certain that things would get ugly. But the devastation still shocked her. She kicked pieces of masonry off the walkway and shouldered the bamboo until she could wedge a gap open with broken crates. Glass crunched underfoot. She made a path through it, awkwardly stepping over tangled debris and crawling on her hands and knees at times.

At the main entrance, planks of wood had been nailed across the doors and windows. Mira peered through the rough slats, leaning on the crude barrier. Her hands came away wet, and not with the ceaseless rain. Crimson stained her palms. Backing up, she read the jagged letters, paint dripping tears.

FISH FUCKERS

She blinked to refocus. After a detour, she managed to find a discreet side entrance. Most of the shops were shuttered. A kappa boy ran across her path, stopping to look at her before dashing home. A small tremor shook the building, but it barely registered. Figures in the distant shadows turned from her, footsteps and flippers hastening away.

The central open area was subdued. Hawkers' stalls eerie in their silence, without the hum of conversation and cooking. Wooden stools stacked up on round tables, apart from at one stall at the far end. The patrons sat like ghosts as she approached, apprehension treading up the back of her neck. A thin wisp of smoke directed her further, as did the familiar faces emerging from the shadows: Mikayil, Tam, her ama and Kai.

Mira forced an awkward smile onto her face as she looked at

each of them in turn. Jokingly filled the silence. "Did I forget someone's birthday? Or is this an intervention or something?"

"Something. Sit." Trish patted the stool next to her.

"Didn't we agree you'd sail out to the border?"

"Yes, but that was before I was informed about the bargain my daughter made."

Thoroughly chastened, Mira sat meekly as indicated. Trish's eyes shone at her, guaranteeing there would be words later.

"We found a loophole." Lieutenant Mikayil sat stiffly, his large frame swamping the small table. Rainwater splashed on his chinthe coat, and Mira had to resist the urge to brush off the droplets. The sight of his uniform filled made her yearn for her old coat.

Kai reverently handed over a paper scroll with both hands. She scanned his face for clues, but he nodded towards the text and waited. Ever since the night he lost his voice, the dragon had been characteristically optimistic. The little time not spent nursing Nami was used to teach Mira more signs, write her love poems and act out anything he could not otherwise explain. Together they had found joy in it: more united, more attentive to each other now they had to slow down and listen. She'd laughed more in the last few days than she had in the preceding year.

You're the strongest person I know, she read. *You turned the chinthe around in a few short months. But it was never a level playing field. They were always going to scapegoat you. That doesn't mean the fight ends here. What it means is that it's time to bend the rules.*

"I'll not do as the Drawbacks are doing – destroy all we've strived to create." Mira glanced up, but all four pointed at the scroll. She turned it over to continue reading.

Mikayil called us here because he found a by-law. In the event that the fathomfolk ambassador is incapacitated, his legal partner may hold their place on the Council until a new ambassador can be appointed.

Kai was the Yonakunish ambassador: the Minister of

Fathomfolk. But Mira had no legal status as his partner. To enact this law, well, that would mean they'd have to be . . .

He slid a lacquered box across the table and opened the lid. Inside were two bangles. One bore the image of a serpentine water dragon curled around it. The other was engraved with the likeness of a siren, musical notes forming the cuff. Betrothal gifts. Beneath her shock and confusion, Mira was aware that these were not items that could be hastily purchased. He had commissioned them. Had them ready long before today.

"Well?" Trish said. Despite the nonchalance of her comment, Mira's mother had slipped right off her stool, a taut string on a zither. Her expression a hopeful question with only one correct answer. Tam nodded vehemently beside her, looking as if he might burst.

"Wait, you want me to – But no. I mean, that's not – it's absurd . . ." Mira's voice spluttered, words tumbling over each other. Her body reacted, chest sweaty with heat but fingers shaking and like slivers of ice. She couldn't help but reach out and stroke the curve of the dragon bangle. Different hues played on the surface: matt grey and warm copper, glittering flecks and streaks of midnight. Scrap metal. It wasn't done to save money – she knew Kai could afford gold and silver if he wished; he'd done it for her. In honour of where she had started in life; of the threadbare coat she refused to throw out; of the differences she tried to bridge. Mira wanted this. In other circumstances she'd have blurted out yes already. But for a seat on the Council, it was so transactional. Cold.

She blinked, her vision oddly obscured. Tears swam in her eyes. She pushed them back by gulping down air. Kai took her hand, swivelled her so she was properly facing him. Signed earnestly as Trish interpreted for her. *Our first?*

"Our first meeting? I took you here! Wanted to shock you." Right here, Mira belatedly realised, to this beaten-up stall that only served spicy prawns. Kai ate them until his face was red and beaded with sweat but did not complain. Instead he bought dishes from other stalls, offered them to neighbouring tables when he realised he'd over-ordered.

He signed clumsily and slowly as he mouthed the words. *You give everything. Everything to change the city. For fathomfolk. For us.*

She'd given one of her speeches, a lecture about how he knew nothing, being Yonakunish, being a dragon. And she'd expected him to storm off, take offence and demand a better guide. Titans knew, that was half the reason she'd provoked him: because she didn't want a job babysitting the new ambassador. But instead he'd listened. Had started taking notes.

Together.

Mira shook her head, but her mother interrupted. "That's enough of that. I can't take back what you did, what you sacrificed a decade ago, but you aren't the only one who cares. You aren't the only one willing to make sacrifices. It's plain rude to refuse help." She raised an eyebrow across the table at Mira, as if she'd been impolite at an auntie's house, then rubbed at the handle of her walking stick, the wood worn away to a polished shine.

"It's not the way I do things."

"We tried it your way, Captain. We watched you struggle. The system is rigged. You know they've appointed Gede as the temporary chinthe captain?" Mikayil added.

"He's not even—" Mira broke off her sentence to give a strangled half-scream. Her blood boiled at the notion of the blustering bully leading the border guards. The fact that they chose him over Mikayil and Tam and the other incredibly competent chinthe within the ranks.

"You played fair – it didn't work. Time to make the rules work for us," Tam said, speaking solemnly for once.

Mira looked back at Kai, at the betrothal bangles on the

table. "This is not how I wanted it. To trap you in a marriage of convenience."

Kai laughed wordlessly, rubbing his thumbs on her palms. He let go to reach into his wide sleeves. One more scroll. Of course he had one more scroll.

I wanted to marry you since the first prawn. Since you first paced up and down in a rage. Since you convinced me to change the world and not just live in it. We can wed today for a political reason, but the rest of our lives will be for us.

For once she had no argument. "Yes," she said finally. It was hard to ignore Mikayil's polite applause, Tam's whistles and her ama's joyful shouts and claps, but she did it all the same, lost in Kai's embrace. In the kiss that connected more than just their lips, like coming home.

It was only as he fastened the bangles around her wrists that the last detail clicked. "Wait, *today?*"

Behind them, the metal shutter of the hawker stall rolled up. The peculiar quiet she had noticed earlier was more subterfuge. Dozens of people stood there, clapping and cheering. Qilin residents and shopkeepers she knew tumbled out, bestowing gift after gift. Wedding robes, dishes of food, even musicians. They'd thought of everything.

Mira didn't know if she was laughing or crying. She was light-headed, as if in a dream. People moved around her, fist-palm salutes, back-slaps, congratulating the couple. Tables and chairs were noisily rearranged. She should say something, do something to help. But she couldn't articulate the myriad of emotions running through her. Her stomach alternated between nausea and giddiness, the latter swelling until it pushed all other feelings aside. A sudden thought entered her mind. "But we need an official to marry us. Who would dare—"

"I found someone," Mikayil said. "Lucia's uncle is a junior official." Mira spotted him now, a nervous-looking man loitering at the back.

He came forward to greet them. "Lucia talked about you, about the difference you were going to make. I'll marry the two of you today, in honour of her."

They waited, all of them. Belatedly Mira realised they were waiting for her. Her cheeks flushed pink and her hesitant smile broadened. "Let's get married!" The three little words, spoken aloud, were both outrageous and also too simple to convey the depths of how she felt. But when she took Kai's hands and looked across at him, she knew, regardless of circumstances, that it was the best decision she'd ever made.

Chapter Fifty

It had been a bad week. Cordelia had gone to her apothecary; to the locked and warded chest in her back room. Her nest egg. Her best contracts.

It was empty.

Nahla, that idiot assistant with a crush on Firth, had stolen them all. Clearly she'd been the one to give away the seawitch's secrets also. Every last siren song to tide Cordelia over. Waterbull strength, misfortune siphoned from malicious hantu air spirits, even the bargains a few eminent humans had made. Her rainy-day fund ransacked. Firth's chiselled cheekbones could clearly cut through granite. The Drawbacks' allure was mostly firebrand politics, but the swagger of a charismatic hustler could not be denied. Cordelia didn't see the appeal – didn't on a general level understand the fools who were led by their loins – but Lynnette used it judiciously.

Nevertheless, she couldn't have Nahla swimming around saying she'd got the better of her. Luckily, not all of her contracts were stored at the shop. Nahla's mother was in agreement, of course. It wasn't pleasant delivering bad news, but the elder mermaid had signed a contract as a guarantor. The girl would get used to her legs eventually. She'd have to.

The whole thing – Mira, Nahla, the lot of them – had put Cordelia in a foul mood. She nursed her headache, inhaling the mint tea in her study to mask the dark cloud hovering over her. She needed a new plan.

Qiuyue burst into the room suddenly, her pigtails bouncing behind her as she brought a drawing for her mother's attention.

"I'm sorry, madam," the governess said breathlessly from the doorway. "She rather insisted."

Cordelia let her daughter climb into her lap, stroking her hair and adjusting the misaligned buttons on her silk jacket. "It'll cheer you up," Qiuyue stated with the confidence only children have. She brandished the sheet of paper, ink still wet and blotchy from where it had run. Two people holding up a tram carriage. She beamed, clearly pleased with herself. "When I'm older, I want to be a siren."

Cordelia stood abruptly, her daughter yelping as she scrambled down to avoid falling. She glared at Qiuyue, her hand tingling to hit her confused little face. The girl's bottom lip quivered as she realised her mother was upset. "I thought you'd like it," she said in a stage whisper.

The governess wrapped her arms around her, slowly shuffling them both back towards the door. "Your mother is busy, let's return to our lessons. My apologies, madam."

Cordelia barely heard the door close, the sound of her own rage crashing like waves against the shore. All her hard work, years of planning and pandering to Samnang's ego, only for an upstart and her upstart partner to sweep the public's imagination. To rub salt in the wound, they'd got married in Qilin a few days ago. The newssheets had gone wild, desperate for a good-news story to counter the endless gloom of rolling blackouts and yet more violence. No matter what she did, a seawitch could never garner that sort of positive press. They might come to her for help, but their fear and disgust was always poorly concealed. She'd never be loved.

She grabbed at the nearest object and flung it across the room.

The ornament smashed against the wall, cracking into pieces against a silk painting. Heavy footsteps thudded down the corridor and Samnang threw the door open. "What in the blazes...?" He looked at his wife and the broken shards. Stooped to pick up a piece, the body of a titan manta ray. The sandy island that had perched on its back lay broken on the floor. "Serena?"

She recalled herself then, the moniker reminding her of who she was supposed to be. Gentle Serena. Loyal Serena. Softly spoken, never flustered fucking Serena. She hated it. Loathed the prison she'd built around herself.

"I just ... It slipped." The lie was entirely unconvincing, but Samnang didn't argue, crossing the room and tilting her chin up. He would say something comforting. A kind word and an embrace for his helpmeet. She anticipated it, willing herself to accept the awkward attempts to console her.

"I don't have time to babysit you," he told her, his fingers breaking contact, and Cordelia felt her head slump forward. She looked at the golden-brown skin of her arms, the petite frame of her masquerade, and tried not to let her visceral response show on the outside. What would he do – the Minister of Defence, the fourth-generation kumiho captain who could trace his lineage back to Tiankawi's founders – if he knew what she really was?

He paced over to the bookcase, hand running down the spines of books at random. "What a meeting! Not only did she attend, she thought she had the authority – her! – to speak as the temporary Minister of Fathomfolk." Samnang's voice was laced with sarcasm as he waved a book in one hand. Threw it on the table and yanked out another. "Quoting the law as if I don't know it. Blocking my attempts to bring order to the city. Ridiculous!" The book was a casualty of his temper, pages tearing as it ended up spine down on the floor. Four or five books along and he would trigger the mechanism to the concealed door. Cordelia scratched at the inside of her elbow as she nodded along with his tirade.

"I should never have listened to you in the first place. If Mira was still the chinthe captain, she wouldn't have an official place on the Council. Too busy chasing after petty vandals. Firing her just made things worse. Much worse." His fist slammed against the wall, and the hollow sound echoed in Cordelia's ears. She moved quickly.

"She only has the authority for as long as Ambassador Kai is incapacitated. They haven't even disclosed what the matter is with him. Have probably been lying about the whole thing. Most certainly. Demand that he attends a public appearance – the next press conference – and explains himself!" She was thinking on her feet, barely aware of what she was saying. All she wanted was for Samnang to move away from the bookcase.

Her husband nodded silently. His bruised knuckles rapped one more time on the wood, as if for luck, then he turned to face her.

"An excellent idea. It's a relief to say things out loud, have your ears listen, even if you don't understand it all." His rage was gone. Vanishing as quickly as it had come. Cordelia's was not so easily extinguished.

Chapter Fifty-One

Nami drifted in and out of feverish dreams. The wires from the Onseon Engine rooms were wrapped around her head and the bud endings loomed towards her temples. She stumbled backwards to evade them, falling over an unseen obstacle. The gaunt selkie, still lying in the chair. Dan, cracking a joke as if nothing was wrong as he lay in a pile of arms and tails, his small face swamped by the dismembered limbs. Nami grabbed at him, holding onto a hand and wrenching it up. But it was not him, it was Kai, neck broken and face ashen. Staring at her through dead eyes, his voice no more than a hoarse croak. A shadow eclipsed him, the figure of a horse looming above them. Rearing onto hind legs, hooves aiming straight for her skull.

Nami screamed and struggled upright. Dan was by her side, patting her forearm ineffectually. The room was warm and familiar despite the dull aches from her legs and torso. Kai's place.

The kappa squeezed her, hand damp in hers. "How d'you feel?"

Nami did not respond. Touched the bandaged wounds, the lightest contact making her flinch. The pieces of fabric were damp with a foul-smelling pus. Of course squid ink was poisonous as well. "Like I got beaten up by a pissed-off cephalopod."

"You should see the other guy." Dan's voice was mild, but he gave her the slightest of smiles.

"How long have I been out?"

"Nearly a week. A lot has happened." He looked like he would say more, his beak opening and closing without making any sound. He hopped off his chair to ensure the door was closed, his back to it as he closed his eyes and came to some sort of decision. "Nami, I've not told you everything. You need to know they gave me no choice. I—"

The door slid open despite Dan's weight against it and he yelped as he moved out of the way.

Firth. His presence, here in Kai's apartment, made Nami's heart race and her stomach turn. Queasy from fear her brother would find out, elated at knowing Firth cared enough to visit. She couldn't look at him without recalling his touch that night at the Barreleye Club. She blushed crimson and looked out of the window to regain her composure. Before she could speak, the kelpie turned to Dan, curt with his words. "Watch at the door."

Dan did not respond. Did not fire back the caustic retort Nami was expecting. If she'd treated him like that, her friend would've told her to piss off. Called her a princess. But there was something between the two kelpies and the kappa. Something beyond the fading bruises around Dan's neck. He glanced back only once as he stepped outside the room.

Firth closed the distance in three steps, leaned over and kissed her. Nami had not expected it. Dizzy, she slipped back against the pillow, unable to put up any form of protest.

"You made me worry." He loomed over her still, pinning her against the bed.

"I'm sorry." She blurted the words, although she was unsure what she was apologising for.

"We promised no secrets." Firth waited, the pause expectant and awkward. The ache in her side was dull but lingering enough that the unnatural position she lay in caused her pain. The kelpie's usual smile had fled, replaced by a deep furrow between his brows. Nami had let him down, that was clear. She reached a hand to his face, but he flinched, as if her touch was toxic. She had no idea what was wrong. When she'd left him, in the early morning of the Barreleye Club, they'd parted as new lovers did. Embarrassed and delighted. Taking turns to trace every curve of skin, to laugh and talk and make plans together.

Mira. Nami realised she had said nothing of Mira's bargain with the seawitch, nothing of the plans she'd made with Kai. It hadn't seemed right to share.

"It was Mira's personal matter ... not for the Drawbacks to get involved," she explained gently. She tried to wriggle into a seated position, but Firth didn't respond to her movements, didn't give her the space she needed.

"You got involved," he countered. "Your injuries ..."

"Mira's like a sister." The truth of her words lingered like a curious taste in Nami's mouth. Their relationship had bloomed over the months, evolving in ways she hadn't expected.

"And what am I to you?" Firth sat back, the mattress shifting under his weight. Rather than explaining, Nami's words had only made things worse. Heaping kindling to the fire in his eyes.

She rubbed at the bridge of her nose. Her mind remained in a stupor despite her attempts to find words. To explain in the way Mira would, the way Kai would, that the kelpie was overreacting. But the mist remained. Her eyes ached like she'd never closed them, despite days of bedrest. She had nothing to offer other than the same trite words. "I'm sorry."

"How can we move forward if you keep things from me?"

The apology leapt to Nami's lips once more, but this time she bit down on it. She hadn't even put her feet on the floor and he was jabbing her like a pincushion, one of Ibhar's projects to be darned up and tacked in place. Like she'd brought ruin upon the city through this one omission. Her own hackles rose to match.

Firth's hand was on hers suddenly. A tender movement that made her start. His eyes glistened. "I'm to blame also. I know. I asked too much of you, too soon. I just . . . thought we understood each other."

"We do," Nami responded. The reversal of his mood made her remorseful over her earlier annoyance. He cared, that was all. She bowed her head towards his until their foreheads touched. Hoping that everything she sought to say would become clearer now. Hoping to hold onto the one thing that was going well.

Much later, after Dan had helped Firth to sneak out undetected, Nami sat alone in the armchair looking out of the window. She no longer felt the nausea of vertigo, just a sadness that the once bustling city seemed asleep. Afraid and locked away behind their doors. The broken tram carriage still wedged precariously between the Jingsha towers mirrored the shipwrecks below the waterline. The Drawbacks had made an impact. She just wasn't certain to what end.

"You're up then." Mira's hair hung loose, and even though she was not wearing her ubiquitous green, the formal grey robes gave her an air of authority. "What happened at Onseon? No half-truths."

Nami's tongue stuck to the roof of her mouth. She wet her lips. Mira deserved the truth; they all did. But saying it aloud was different; letting the words breathe would make them real. She could no longer deny the nightmares pushing in at her edges. Her bones ached as she stretched out her legs, joints creaking. Placed her bare feet gingerly on the cool floor. "The plan was to evacuate, then blow it up. Send a message to the Council. But everything went wrong."

She wiggled her toes, looking at them so intensely they felt like someone else's. Someone else had done it. A shadow, a double. She could pretend for a few moments longer. Her throat tightened like a hand about her neck. She'd been a part of this. The Drawbacks couldn't have done it without her. She needed to accept it; tell the story before her nerves took over.

She spoke. Stumbled over the words but said them anyway. Thorns cutting at her soft lips and tongue, ulcering the inside of her mouth. Excuses rose, bobbing on the surface, but she pushed them away. Yes, Lynnette had played her, played her for a fool, and now she was a murderer. It was not a silly stunt her mother could bail her from.

She sucked in air, but it wasn't enough. Short, shallow breaths were all she could manage, her shoulders heaving and vision spinning. Mira put hands on her head and spoke in melodic phrases. Nami couldn't hear the words, but the siren song penetrated through the haze. Enough to bring her out of the wheezing breaths, until her shaking hands no longer felt as though they belonged to someone else. She was dimly aware that whatever fears she'd had about Mira using her siren song previously, it was never like this. That her own prejudices made her suspicious. The coaxing hand of suggestion had never actually been there.

"The guilt is yours to bear. But Nami, you were used. We both were."

Nami let the silence linger between them, not wanting to ask the question. As much as it would pain her to hear, the dead deserved to be remembered. "How many?" She barely knew if she'd said it aloud or simply in her head.

"Four on the night, two more couldn't be saved by the healers. But you saved five. The connection was cut in time."

She barely registered the second remark. Six deaths by her hand.

"We need to know her endgame." Mira looked hopeful.

Nami gingerly tested her legs. Her limbs were swollen from lack of use and the cool marble floor was like ice under her feet. Her abdomen wound ached in protest as she took shuffling steps, but she did not fall apart. At least not on the outside.

"I – I know their next move." She shrank down. Firth's smell lingered on the collar of her shirt, and yet she spoke the words of betrayal.

Mira tapped her foot, waiting for more. More patient than Nami could ever be. The water dragon was reluctant to continue, not meeting Mira's eye. Her omission regarding Mira's bargain was one thing, but now she was actively defying the Drawbacks. "The Minister of Defence has called a press conference."

"The one they've demanded Kai and I attend," Mira mused. "Most of the Council will be there, the press as well. Maximum impact and coverage." She started to pace the room, up and down as the perfectly tuned gears in her brain turned. "Gede will have to listen to a threat warning. Have the chinthe prepped."

"You were right, by the way," Nami said. As the siren raised an eyebrow, she hastily amended her statement. "About some things. Not everything. But I'm beginning to see the merit."

"In what?" Mira insisted.

"In that . . . it's more complicated than I thought. After this, I'll turn myself in. I'll answer for Onseon, even if no one else will." The silence was broken only by the sound of the bamboo wind chime by the window, hollow knocks like ghosts at the door.

Mira slid her sheathed dagger across the bed. Her chinthe blade, the one Nami had plunged into the squid guard's head. "You're also right, Nami. Sometimes we need to break the rules."

The dagger was made of obsidian, the hilt embedded with frosted sea glass in blue and green. Nami ran her thumb over the irregular surface. She hated sea glass. Ubiquitous as the trash that drifted off from human settlements. Others thought it was decorative, using the pebbles as jewellery or embedding them in the wet clay of their homes. And yet this blade didn't bother her. She'd seen the power of it. A tool grasped in a moment of desperation. It cut, and that was all that mattered.

Dan had listened without response when Nami had explained. Nodded at her intention to spy on the Drawbacks, to undermine whatever they planned. That should have been a clue. He was not one to hold his opinion back, certainly not when a scheme was as idiotic and flawed as this.

The kappa was silent in the elevator from Kai's penthouse apartment. Nami recalled her first few weeks in Tiankawi and how the vertigo had been unbearable. It seemed so long ago now. Dan looked up at her, skin sticky with perspiration. Wrung his hands together but kept silent. Nami left it. The pressure was getting to all of them. After all, they were double-crossing a nest of vipers.

At the sea-level entrance, everything took longer. Nami didn't want to risk her recently healed injuries. The water smarted as they finally plunged in. The acrid taste not just in her mouth but tingling around the edges of her stomach wound. She pressed her hand against it, swimming gingerly as her gills slowly opened. It used to be the other way round. Coming onto land felt like wearing thick gloves. Her senses dulled, her movements clumsy. Now the water had the same effect. Like revisiting a childhood home to find she had outgrown it, her antlers too tall to fit beneath the door frame.

"You didn't ask," Dan said. He kicked his webbed feet so he swam at her head height, but his gaze remained pinned to the middle distance. "I waited. I told myself, if she just asks."

His sudden comment caught Nami off guard. But before she could reply, it came to her unprompted. The sisters he always talked about. The mother who worked two jobs. His family. It slotted into place now. Dan would never abandon them. His commitment to any protests, any political causes took second place to his family. It always had.

And yet here he was.

"Dan." She exhaled his name. She had hoped to protect him,

but he was already in too deep. "What did they do? What did they do to your family?"

A boat drifted overhead as she waited for the answer. The shadows it cast covered Dan's face. His hand closed into a fist and reopened again. His eyes drew up to meet hers. Distracted, Nami felt a sharp nip in her arm. A stingray barb jutted from where he had jabbed it, the tranquillising effect already flowing through her body.

"I'm sorry, Nami. I really am."

Chapter Fifty-Two

Cordelia smoothed the fabric of her gown again, frowning as the creases re-formed. She smoothed over her expression also. The attentive wife of the kumiho captain was genial. Tranquil. Her hand lightly resting on Samnang's elbow as they greeted the others. Gede had listened to her advice at least, turning out in his full formal uniform. The chinthe green looked odd on him, and his captaincy badge was pinned upside down. He whispered hurried messages to the border guards, shifting his weight from one leg to the other like an excited little boy at a festival. After drifting for far too long, his interest was finally piqued. Responsibility had changed him. Cordelia had not exactly confided in him since his last screw-up, but out from under her wing he stood taller, more assured than before. Perhaps she should've pushed him out the nest a long time ago.

The other ministers watched from one side, waiting like circling sharks for Samnang to make a mistake. Ayumu spoke some sharp words to her stepdaughter, Eun. The young woman blew her loose fringe out of her eyes in exasperation as she reluctantly tucked the scroll she was reading back into her bag. A smarter woman, Cordelia thought with sudden clarity, would use that bookishness. Ayumu should send her among the journalists, or to ruffle feathers in the judiciary.

Qiuyue picked at the loose thread of her embroidered tunic

until Cordelia was drawn back to her own offspring. She tutted at her daughter, shaking her head slightly. That one would not be kept out of trouble for long. Banned from the water, Qiuyue had taken to climbing instead, scaling lamp posts and drainpipes like a lizard. She had her father's dark brooding eyebrows, and Cordelia wouldn't be surprised if she'd inherited his temperament.

Another round of camera bulbs flashed as the waiting press fired questions. What would happen now? Would the kumiho take decisive action regarding the power outages? Would Samnang personally ensure the safety of all humans? He waved his hands to lower the din. Of course it was terrible, for normal people, for normal businesses. But the Council hadn't thrown all their lot in with Onseon. Grants for heliacal sailmills and eddy tide farms would be improved. Two emergency short-term measures. Restart the deep-sea drilling. And mandatory shifts at Onseon for fathomfolk. Everyone had to play their part.

A ripple ran through the journalists. Mandatory? Could they be trusted? Could they be coerced? Could they . . .

Cordelia flinched internally with each question. These people. These demands. Querulous. Suspicious. They had not changed over the years. Wanting rid of fathomfolk but wanting something from them as well. The privileged ilk who made bargains with her whilst simultaneously spitting in her eye. She wasn't forcing their hand, not most of them anyway. If anything, she was risking herself, risking the backfire if a deal went wrong. This is why she would always put loyalty to her own family first. To her own interests. She'd been born in Tiankawi. A third-generation citizen of the city. And yet she'd always be an outsider. Her Serena mask hid all of this from the clicking cameras, the genial smile firmly pasted across her features.

As they walked off the stage, Cordelia took Qiuyue's hand, almost crushing it. Her daughter smelled of soap and the morning's rice porridge, washing away some of the bitterness. Samnang touched his wife's waist. Reassuring himself more than her. "Are you certain the saltie got the invite?"

It'd not taken much, a few coins, a favour returned, to detour Kai and Mira's boat at the other side of the city state. Stall them for long enough that her ruse would be undetected. "Patience, my dear."

She handed Qiuyue over to the governess, excusing herself. Hidden away, she transformed. Humans and fathomfolk alike did not trust seawitches. Duplicitous. Sly. Two-faced. She had heard it all. She had more than two faces. More than other fathomfolk, who shifted only between human and true form. She could be the boy next door or the old auntie in the market. A strapping young boatswain or a crippled merman. But today, she was a dragon.

The hand mirror showed Kai's face: his full human appearance, with ebony locks pulled into a topknot and neat facial hair. She adjusted the colour of the robes, maroon and white, to match other clothes she'd seen him in. The eyes were still Serena's, though, light amber irises. She needed a good few seconds to turn them to darkest liquid brown. The more she changed, the easier it was. But she didn't often impersonate real people. Things weren't quite right. She could hold an appearance but not how they moved and spoke. She much preferred to be her own invention. Besides, the one thing she couldn't change was her voice.

It was a risky plan, but she was beyond caring. Her rage simmered at all hours and she would have her revenge. At any cost. She pulled out the slick pebble that swirled with Kai's voice. They sought to outmanoeuvre her, but she would always have the last word. And if this crushed the ambassador's popularity, had him sent back to Yonakuni, then all the better.

She walked back towards the crowd. *It's the ambassador – finally. Kai is here.* Never slouched, never timid, that one. Born into a family that were told they were superior, revered across the seas. She nodded, straightening her shoulders, smiled, fist-palm-saluted people, never letting her feet deviate from their path towards the stage. The whole crowd had swivelled to face her. No wonder the lad was so confident. She could get used to this. All she had to do was smile and the official surrendered the microphone. Camera clicks followed her. She spoke and the voice was Kai's.

"People of Tiankawi, several weeks ago, the city was thrown into turmoil. In an act of needless violence, a group of fathomfolk calling themselves the Drawbacks sabotaged the main generating station. The consequence was devastating. Repairs will take weeks, possibly months."

The upturned faces were sombre but nodding, agreeing with every word. It was so easy with this visage. The same people turned from her true self with horror and fear. As Serena they didn't even see her; she was nothing more than decoration. The power she could yield with this voice was tempting. It was a terrible shame she was about to destroy it.

"The thing is . . . I'm a dragon. I've better things to do with my time. More important things." She wrinkled her nose, letting the silence drag like a trawler in deep waters. "It was amusing for a while. A bit of fun." She paused again, licking her lips as a single camera shutter clicked. She hadn't had time to study Kai's mannerisms, but no one seemed bothered. The voice, the look was enough. She let out an exasperated sigh. "I mean, fuck it – I don't really care!"

A moment of silence as people processed the words. Then an eruption of noise pressed from all sides. A veritable wave of condemnation. Cameras like a murmuration of birds sweeping down upon her. Samnang calling for Kai's immediate deportation, the press heckling with questions, the officials fussing and shouting, and all through it Cordelia cackled. Roared with laughter, enjoying the chaos: she had said aloud what she had always thought about their petty manoeuvres, and destroyed Kai's reputation in the same move.

The kumiho city guards were easy to dodge, knowing as she did exactly how many and where Samnang had positioned them. One of them grabbed her arm, tearing at the fabric. Too close! Cordelia swivelled and sprinted towards the water. They could not follow her. Cool water embraced her as she dived down, the silhouettes above blurring through the ripples.

That ought to be enough to satisfy Samnang. Even he was smart enough to use the opportunity. A few more minutes and she could emerge as Serena again. Claim she'd had a headache.

A sharp pain cracked into her shoulder and she lost all control of her semblance, reverting to her true form as the pain lanced across her chest. She stared in shock at the harpoon head piercing through to her front. It yanked back, pulling her up through the water with it. Her blood spilled, bursting in thin dark clouds around her. No, no, no.

This was not part of the plan.

She thrashed against it, yanking with all her lower limbs until the rope was taut, but the harpoon merely wiggled in the wounds, tearing into new flesh. It pulled her closer and closer to the surface, the pain threatening to make her pass out. She grew weaker, unable to struggle now. Nothing more than a fish on the line.

Hands grabbed under her arms and dragged her onto the decking. Cordelia sprawled there, her limbs splayed. Hissed at them with her sharp teeth, puffing up as large as she could get. Agony pierced her again and she collapsed into a soft puddle. Her skin flashed through different colours instinctively: brightest of white, rippling black stripes, orange and purple blooms bursting like pulses.

They were on one of the chinthe patrol boats, not far from where the press were standing, but far enough. "That's not the dragon," a guard said. His eyes tracked her suckered arms to their ends, horror turning his skin grey.

"Captain said something would be up. We should bring her in anyway," another responded.

Captain? Mira had been waylaid; that part of the plan had gone perfectly. Cordelia groaned in realisation. Her fool of a son was captain now. Finally making decisions for himself. Absurd, dunderhead decisions like harpooning an ambassador because he swore at a press conference.

Gede stepped from behind the two guards, his face a picture of shock as he looked down on her. "Am—" He hastily coughed to cover his mistake. "Where's the ambassador?"

She shook her head. The cogs in Gede's head were turning, but he looked at the border guard, clearly unsure. Never the fastest of thinkers.

"Move aside!" She heard a second familiar voice. Perfect timing. Samnang had come over in a smaller boat with his kumiho. The chinthe guards reluctantly stepped back. Gede gnawed at his bottom lip, but then made a decision. Stood in front of his mother, blocking the way. "This is chinthe jurisdiction, sir. Let me handle it."

"Get out of my way, Gede," Samnang said. His voice was bloody murder. Gede closed his eyes, bracing for some sort of blow. Despite everything, Cordelia felt an immense pride for her idiot of a son. His father merely shoved him aside.

"Witch, where's the ambassador?" Samnang said, his voice carrying.

"You'll get nothing from me," Cordelia spat. Kai's smooth baritone came from her throat. Shit.

A flicker crossed Samnang's face. Cordelia flicked the small orb out of her fingers behind her. It clattered as it rolled across the decking and plopped into the water. His head swivelled to follow it, eyes narrowed.

"You might as well kill me," she said, to distract him. It was mostly bravado, but she meant it. Better it be swift at his hands than the drawn-out torture that she feared. Better her children were not implicated.

"What're you still doing here?" Samnang shouted. Cordelia blinked in confusion, but the words weren't directed at her. He was glaring at the kumiho who'd accompanied him. "Clearly the dragon isn't here. Take the patrol boat back out, or would you rather swim?"

The guards scarpered. Only Cordelia, Gede and Samnang were left at this end of the vessel. The seawitch felt hollow. A surreal lack of fear as her blood stained the grain of the wood. Perhaps it was the shock from the injury, but for the first time in a long while, she was as serene as her namesake. At peace with it all.

She recalled her husband holding Gede – their firstborn – as a babe. Voice wavering, disbelieving. A side of him she'd rarely seen before or since. Now he unsheathed his kumiho sword with a keen inhale. Cordelia closed her eyes. His familiar smell filled her nose nonetheless. She felt him lean over her, waited for the cold steel to slide against her throat. She had planned and manipulated most of their relationship, but he was, she grudgingly admitted, a decent man. One she had grown accustomed to over the years. A familiar piece of furniture that had moulded to her shape. Had things gone differently, perhaps she would have grown to love him one day.

It was too late now.

"You're smarter than this," he said. Cordelia's eyes flew open. Samnang had cut through the harpoon rope. She flexed her hands in disbelief. "You think I didn't know?"

She could not look at him. Watched as her skin turned waves of blue and white beyond her control. Once, she had held all the cards in her hands, and now they were floating away. Carried on the tide.

"I'm going to pull the harpoon through. You need to hit me and Gede. Hard – make it convincing. Then run. Swim. Whatever it is you do. We'll talk later."

"Samnang, I—"

"Don't. Not now. Don't make me regret this."

Before she could say another word, he tugged the bloody harpoon through her shoulder wound. She howled in wretched pain, body protesting at the movement. But she was free. He nodded at her, waiting for her to strike him, but Cordelia could not do it, could not comply with anything other than the reeling in her head. Samnang looked exasperated, like when she fussed over Qiuyue. He threw himself backwards. Clutched at his leg in a performance that would make her laugh under other circumstances. Gede, who had watched the exchange stupefied, belatedly stumbled to the decking as well.

Go.

Don't make this for nothing.

Her limbs retreated across the boat, her eyes trained on Samnang. She could not read him, could not tell what he was thinking. In all her calculations, she had never suspected.

Chapter Fifty-Three

Nami opened her bleary eyes and the ground moved, shaking like a strong earthquake. It took her a long moment to realise it was not the floor moving at all, but her. She was slung over someone's shoulder and they were walking at a relentless pace through a dimly lit tunnel. She craned her neck to see Dan's face a few steps behind. Her friend gasped, stumbling on some loose rock. "She's awake."

"About bloody time," Lynnette said. Nami was thrown to the ground. Her eyes adjusted to the dim light of the long cave tunnel. The walls were slick with algae, and rock pools spotted the ground, but they were above water. Lynnette stretched out her back and cricked her neck. "Well, what're you waiting for. Walk."

Nami's body responded to the rough kick hefted towards her, and she hastily got to her feet. She'd taken a few disorientated steps before she stumbled, limbs still weak. "Oh for titan's sake," Lynnette cursed, heaving her up. Nami took the moment to absorb everything that had happened. Dan had ... Dan had betrayed her. Had been working for the Drawbacks all along. Her insides tore like someone had gouged at their walls. Carved into the green wood to find rot.

The Drawbacks were definitely not going to the press conference, then. A ruse to occupy the chinthe and Mira? But where were they? She'd been in plenty of submerged caves, but to be above water, the entrance had to be higher. The only natural structure in Tiankawi above sea level was the Peak. But why would Lynnette want to come here?

Her questions were quelled as the tunnel opened up into a huge chamber. The walls and roof were wide enough to house a blue whale. Chinks of light shone down like arrows, illuminating patches where lush green foliage and spindly saplings had tentatively made a foothold. Small birds, bats too, flitted between the stalactites, nesting high up beyond her sight in the long shadows. In the centre of the cavern was a wide lake. Firth kneeled on a rocky surface, his hands cupping the water.

"Glad you could make it." He stood as they approached, walking towards them as if Nami had come for a visit, not been drugged and dragged here. He reached out a hand to her. "Lynnette has a job she needs our help with."

If the lake was saltwater, Nami could escape. In true form she'd be faster and more manoeuvrable than the others. At least she hoped that was the case. The edges of her vision were still blurry from the soporific Dan had stung her with and her stomach injury had started to weep through its dressing. Still, it was a chance she was willing to take.

She ignored Firth's outstretched hand, unravelling herself from Lynnette. Took a few stumbling steps left and right as she scanned for an escape route. Firth cleared his throat and gestured to the water's edge. "There's someone I'd like you to meet."

Nami made her way over, taking her time. Moss grew in odd shapes by the walls. The echoes of previous visitors were visible: long-handled pickaxes and woven baskets, roughly carved drinking gourds and a little sand god shrine. Abandoned. Forming peculiar lumps and mounds half hidden under mossy coverings. The old quarrying mines, long since forgotten.

She reached the edge of the lake and leaned forward to peer in. The water was crystal clear. A microcosm of life thrived: crabs and fern-gilled axolotls made their way across the smooth rocks; fingers of water ferns and wide anubias leaves lined the edges; small fish swam along the shallow mottled bed, picking and feeding. Nami blinked and looked again. They were cleaner wrasses, symbiotic fish that lived on the dead skin and parasites of larger species. Her eyes scanned the clear waters. There were no fish there that were any bigger than the wrasses. What were they . . . ?

A tremor ran up through her feet, shaking them significantly. She placed her hands on the ground to steady herself. Simultaneously, the bed of the lake rippled and the water level rose momentarily before dropping again. Nothing in the ecosystem seemed bothered by the movement, as if it was an everyday occurrence. A memory just beyond her recollection stirred from its slumber. She took a few steps back, squinting at the whole lake. The bed was neither sand nor rock; a peculiar shade of grey dotted with irregular white spots.

The spots were familiar, and not from a hazy distant memory – she'd seen them recently. She glanced around, eyes sliding to the moss-covered relics. The sand god shrine was a carved whale shark, its spots and lines like ancient writing. She looked back at the lake bed.

They matched.

"A titan. A sand god right beneath our feet." Firth grinned like a kid, waving both hands in an exaggerated motion. "Surprise!"

A titan whale shark. Underneath them! *Bodies as long as islands. A village could live on one fin.* The giants of the sea: the dragon turtle, the colossal nautilus, the gargantuan manta ray. Titans. The Academy, the history lessons back in Yonakuni haven had taught her they were real enough. But Nami had never worshipped them, never believed in their elevation into deities. She didn't know where to begin. What to think. Her mind spun in circles, trying to recall every tiny detail from the bedtime stories her father had told her. From the performances and artworks she had seen.

Children's stories. No more than tales. If the legends were true, then ... then this was only a small part of the sand god. The being was submerged under the city.

She looked up in realisation.

The sand god *was* the city. After all, it'd never quite made sense how Tiankawi was spared from the devastation of the Great Bathyal War, the war between humanity and the folk, as the flood-waters rose. How most havens had been rebuilt from scratch but the bare bones of humanity still stood.

Lynnette's spear was pointed towards her. The obsidian blade was brittle, black glass cut as sharp as teeth. "Now, we need a little something from you."

"You can't have it." Nami's words tumbled over each other. This much she recalled from the stories. Water dragons could do it. Could kill a sand god. "A pearl can only be given freely. And I won't do it!" It was a truth she rarely let herself think about. Since she had been old enough to transform between true and human shape, her parents had drilled into her the great honour and responsibility. Dragons had a choice: to experience life and guide others through accumulated knowledge and wisdom; or to give up their pearl so others could benefit in a more material way. The older a dragon got, the more their pearl diminished. Spent.

She recalled the Peace Tower, and the unhatched sibling who'd never experienced what she and Kai had. A hostage to the peace terms. So much had changed since that small act of defiance. "What would you do with it anyhow? Turn the Drawbacks into an army?"

Firth burst into laughter. Belly laughs that had him holding his sides and wiping merry tears from his eyes. Nami's conviction faltered, flimsy as tissue paper. Before she could think what else they meant, he pulled her to her feet, his familiar hands reassuring in hers. Fingers rubbed her scabbed knuckles with a care that made her ache. "My love, you're worrying about nothing. There's no ruse to steal your pearl. You're one of us, remember. Trust me."

The hairs on the back of her neck quivered at his words. It was the first time he'd used that term of endearment. He continued, his calm words working reason through her aching bones. "Change is not easy. You think a banner ever changed someone's mind? Or a hard-working half-breed did anything other than make the Council look good? I wish it could, honestly I do."

"We aren't playing games any more, princess. The sand gods betrayed us. Sold themselves to humans," Lynnette interrupted. Her face was a thunderhead, barely holding back a storm. She hadn't lowered the spear. "Spill some blood or I'll do it for you."

"Lynnette!" Firth shot in warning. The Drawback leader shrugged but responded to his admonishment, taking a step back.

Her words sat on the surface like oil on water. If Lynnette didn't want the pearl, then why ...? Dragon blood. Her mother had warned Nami to be careful of shed scales, broken claws or spilled blood. In the wrong hands they were ingredients. Poison. It was a preposterous plan, but it might work. Maim the titan. Level the city regardless of who lived in it. Or more likely because of. Lynnette had twisted herself in so much anger that thorns grew into her own skin and she no longer felt them.

"I never said it would be easy," Firth said, hand cupping Nami's face. "But it's the right thing to do."

Nami's body vibrated with coursing blood and the noise of her own breathing. She tried to look away from him, but his face filled her line of vision. The world began and ended with him.

"We don't have time for this," Lynnette interjected with exasperation. "Indulge your little project all you want, but I—"

"Lynnette!" Firth repeated. His tone had a keen edge. The Drawback leader stared back, her chin tilted defiantly. Nami only half understood her incandescent rage, but the heat of it crackled throughout the cave.

"Fathomfolk will die too," she said, her voice barely a whisper. Her eyes flickered between the two Drawbacks for any sign of support. The catfish twins, Ibhar and the others had all mentioned family in the city. Siblings, parents, children. The sort of devastation they planned wouldn't distinguish friend from foe. "You can't mean it."

She felt as though she was at the Onseon again. Why did this keep happening to her? The Drawbacks had told her that violence was necessary. That all change required it. And she had bought into it at first. Believing the rhetoric to be aimed at humanity and humanity alone. The mudskippers had it coming to them.

"Humans turned the titans against us. They were our gods, were supposed to protect *us*!" Lynnette's face was contorted, knuckles white as they gripped the spear. She blamed the freshwater folk too. Did not distinguish those just living their lives. Surviving. Conforming. Adapting to life in the submerged city. They were collateral because they were already compromised. This was where Nami's opinion differed. She would not, could not, have another Onseon incident on her hands.

"You said you were willing to do anything," Firth added.

"I didn't mean this!" Nami chewed her bottom lip.

"Sometimes we need to make sacrifices. For the greater good. It's not about them; not even about us. It's about a future beyond all of this." Firth was so self-assured. Knew exactly what he wanted and followed it through with unwavering conviction. He was disappointed that her ambitions were so limited. Afraid. Nami could not deny the twisted logic of what he said, and yet dread filled her entirely. She could not articulate it with his poise, she just knew that every scale on her body screamed that this was wrong.

"I'm sorry. I can't."

He turned away, his grip on her loosening. Her skin was ice cold where he had once touched, lost without his guidance. He walked towards the cavern entrance, his words bitter hail raining down. "Make the kappa bleed her. See how she feels when someone *she* loves betrays her."

Lynnette shoved the spear into Dan's hands. Folded her arms and watched.

"I ... I've never ... I don't know how ..." Dan said, throat bobbing as his hands flapped weakly. He let the spear roll onto the ground.

"Cut her or I will cut off your sisters' fingers, toes, tongues and beaks and serve them to you in their own shells," Lynnette said, gesturing to each body part as she mentioned them.

Dan hastened to pick up the fallen weapon, clutching it across his chest. His family was the world to him. Nami longed to reach out, tell him it would be okay. A platitude she didn't have the right to utter. As he approached her, he squeezed both eyes shut. The spear shook in his hands. He looked preposterous with it.

"She'll never let you go," Nami cautioned.

"What choice do I have?" Dan barely whispered. Shrunken beyond recognition. She should've seen it earlier, noticed the warning signs, but she'd been wrapped up in her own problems. A poor excuse for a friend.

"I'll stop her, Dan, I promise. No matter what it takes. But you can't keep them safe like this, you know that." She wasn't sure if the words were meant for him or for her own ears.

She looked around desperately. Backed into a corner, seeing her friend broken, all her own doubts quelled. It lit a fire within her, one that flickered with tiny sparks. This was not Dan's fight. It never had been. They were using him, just as she once had. She hadn't meant to, but the result was the same. She glanced up one more time, taking into account the height of the cave ceiling, the flitting swallows overhead. Then she rubbed her fingers together, clasping and unclasping them. Filigrees of water shimmered between her hands like dew on a spider's webs.

"I could throw you?" she murmured.

Dan hesitated, opening his eyes a fraction. Cocked his head to one side. Slow realisation dawned on him. His face contorted through a myriad of emotions before he finally responded. "Like a ruddy slingshot pebble."

"Whirlpool," she corrected. "It's your best chance."

He went to glance up, but stopped himself just in time. He gave one nod of agreement and a crooked smile. "You aren't a very good shot." The remark was enough to make Nami's eyes shine. Her friend was still in there.

"I'm also out of practice." Before he could say anything more, before Lynnette could get any closer, she acted. It took barely any effort for her to knock the spear out of his hands with her weaving, flipping it towards where Lynnette stood. The move was ineffectual, easily diverted by Lynnette's instant wall of water. But it was distraction enough.

Nami threw her water net over Dan and spun him round, once, twice, three times, then launched him towards the ceiling. The kappa had tucked his limbs into his shell, streamlining himself as much as possible as he shot upwards. She scooped great arcs of water from the lake, angling them to boost him towards one of the shafts of light. If her calculations were correct, the gap was just big enough for someone of his side to squeeze through. Higher and higher he flew, the birds and bats scattering with flapping wings and noisy chatter.

A wordless sound of wrath curled behind her and a spear of ice whistled through the air. Nami changed the trajectory of her last boosting arc of water to smash the spear in two. Dan started to fall and she yelled out in warning. He sprang out of his shell, reaching for a nearby stalactite. Arms stretched, he hit hard but his webbed hands held on. No time to catch his breath. Lynnette launched more crude ice spears at him and Dan scrambled across the formations towards his freedom. Some collapsed under him, plunging down with great crashes. Nami ducked her head and rolled out of the way, but she was laughing, elated sobs, as she slammed her fist on the ground. Yes. Dan had got out. Alive. She hadn't saved him in Yonakuni. Perhaps she could do so here.

She barely resisted as Lynnette grabbed her by the legs. Kicked half-heartedly as she was thrown in the water. Freshwater, she realised with shock as her gills flapped open. She'd not tasted it since she was little. She hadn't thought there was any left. It was like potent alcohol, tingling on her skin, leaving her light-headed with giddiness.

"The kappa . . ." Lynnette said, as Firth waded into the depths.

"Leave him, he's nothing." Firth's tawny hair had turned green like fronds and strong hooves had replaced his feet.

Nami darted away from them both, her movements neat and precise as she turned and kicked. There were only so many places she could swim in the small lake. She was unused to claustrophobic spaces, and the edges snuck up on her like they were closing in. The kelpies worked together, driving her down towards the mottled skin of the titan below. Nami laid her hand on the thick hide. A ripple of recognition ran through her.

She pulled her hand away in shock, flipping over to swim elsewhere. But there was nowhere. Lynnette's eyes narrowed on her, and Nami chose to take the titan over the Drawback leader. She thrust her palm back down on the lake bed. A wordless presence shook awake, the contact between them creating a link. Something pressed at her skull and she consented, letting the sand god blink through her eyes, speak directly into her head.

Who?

"Great titan whale shark, most venerable ancestor, we've come to beg a boon." Firth spoke, prostrating himself suddenly. He gestured frantically for Lynnette to do the same. The Drawback leader merely floated, her face filled with pure awe, her hands making the sign of blessing across her chest. They could all hear the words of the sand god then. Firth's assured reasoning continued. "Humans befouled the lands and seas. This city is a monstrosity. They used you! They built houses on your sleeping body. We seek vengeance. It is time they paid."

Paid?

We chose this.

We offered sanctuary. A place where humanity and fathomfolk could thrive.

Together.

"You did this? Willingly? After all humanity have done?" Lynnette's former reverence was lost, the disgust curing in her mouth.

What point is there in retribution? What would it take to satisfy all the hate? We sought a way forward. So I ask you . . . did it work?

Did it work? The bruises on Trish's body; her treatment on the settlement ship; the "no salties" signs in windows. The Drawbacks and more peaceful protesters. Mira's defiance, Cordelia's machinations, the Qilin workers. The girls on the tram. The healer who'd looked after Nami; the librarian at the Nurseries; Trish's neighbours laughing with her.

Nami answered before Firth could. Before Lynnette. Blurted, "It isn't that simple."

It was never simple. But you are still trying. That's enough.

She felt the presence fade, drifting back into a dormant sleep. It filled her with the tranquillity of calm waters. Of . . .

Pain. She looked down, surprised to see blood in the palms of her hands. She'd barely noticed Firth cut her, but the tendrils of red bloomed in the water like unfurling flowers. The kelpie held a glass vial to the cut, crushing Nami's hand open so that blood spluttered out crimson and hot. It mixed with the milky fluid within the bottle, settling to the bottom. The whole vial turned deepest purple. The agony Nami continued to feel was far beyond the small wound. It did not explain the deep lacerations like hot iron in her skull. It pushed further and deeper into her, tearing through layers of tired flesh, shattering bones that were centuries old. She felt her chest and torso. She was whole, no new injuries in sight.

Only then did she see the spear Lynnette had plunged into the titan whale shark's opened gills. The twisted blade was keeping them open, and the Drawback leader upended the vial, the poison made of Nami's blood, into them. The viscous liquid was slow to pour as Nami struggled against Firth's grasp in vain. He looked at her with pity in his amber eyes. Surely not. A few drops of her blood couldn't . . .

The cave rocked with an earthquake. Birds and bats shrieked and fled in thick, suffocating waves through the gaps in the roof. The surface of the water grew murky as rocks fell from the impact of the tremors. A quake far bigger than any Nami had experienced since arriving in Tiankawi. Firth swam to Lynnette's side.

"That must be enough now?" Lynnette sounded uncertain.

He did not answer at first, batting her away like a petty annoyance. "It's too late to turn back."

That was what they'd always wanted, Nami realised. No change was enough. Death was always the plan.

Chapter Fifty-Four

In all fairness, Mira wouldn't have been able to recall the face of the skipper in a line-up. Nor for that matter the name, type or colour of the boat that was supposed to bring them to the press conference. Fingers interlaced with Kai's, she hardly took her eyes off him, only glancing for brief moments in surprise at the betrothal bangles round both her wrists, giggling like a youth when he kissed her neck. She traced the veins up his arms, dancing her fingers between the occasional scale that shone from his skin. They lowered their heads and Kai signed, big, exaggerated movements so she could copy the hand shape and direction. Mira was a fast learner, but it was vastly more enjoyable to falter so her husband reached round to straighten her fingers. Her husband! The word was sweet on her tongue even without saying it aloud.

It was not a surprise in hindsight that the motorboat had driven in the wrong direction for quite some time before they finally noticed. The radio was suddenly cranked up to full volume, and as they stood to investigate, Mira saw the skipper jump off the side of the boat and swim a short distance to another waiting vessel. Her unvoiced question was answered when Kai pulled at the control levers and attempted to restart the engine. A guttural sound spluttered beneath them, and all they could hear was the static from the wireless.

"Someone really doesn't want us there," Mira said. Her hand was on the controls, about to flick channels on the wireless to call for help, when they heard Kai's voice. Crackling and thin over the radio waves, it was nonetheless him. She turned to her husband, squeezing his hand. She had seen him touch his throat, mouthing words into his cupped hands when he thought she wasn't listening.

"I mean, fuck it – I don't really care!" Pandemonium broke out over at the press conference, raised voices drowning each other out. Moments later, the broadcast was silenced.

Mira sat back down on the bench. "Bloody Cordelia." Kai sat beside her, echoing the sentiment with emphatic signs.

They could see the tall sailmills from here, like white cranes with one leg tucked up against their bodies. Kai looked down at the choppy water and signed. He was right, they had to take the long way back. It was the only logical thing to do, and yet Mira still hadn't faced the water.

"What if I've forgotten how?"

He mimicked singing, and she nodded. "I know my song has come back, but that's different. I hated the water when I was younger. I swear it hated me back." So many assumptions had plagued her childhood. She could swim, but it never felt graceful like the mermaids and baiji that lived around them. Left her feeling exposed, highlighting every way she didn't belong. She would wear scarves around her neck, so tight her gills couldn't open properly underwater. She cringed now at the memories, of what she thought she was achieving by it. But despite the insight, the discomfort remained. Like a pebble in her shoe that she could never be bothered to shake out. Over time, it hobbled her all the same.

Kai patted his shoulders, and finally Mira laughed, tension breaking. There was always the option of a dragon-back ride. If she had to be marooned out here with anyone, she was glad it was him.

He slipped into the water and held out his hands, waiting for her. Mira sat on the edge of the boat for a long moment, the water lapping at her ankles. Now or never. She slid in, her eyes screwed shut. The cold pressed her on all sides with clammy, cloying hands. Her gills flapped at first, overworking and exhausting her. She scrabbled, paddling and sinking, spluttering mouthfuls of salt and drowning in the darkness, until she felt Kai touch her cheek.

She opened her eyes, and despite the frantic beating of her heart, she saw. The way her hands moved through the water. Smooth and slow. The buoying tide pushing and pulling. And the dragon – her husband – at her side. Only in the water could he be his true shape. Long equine face, whiskers that trailed like wisps of smoke, scales that shimmered iridescent even in the dim light, and emerald spines finer than the Fenghuang's embroidered silk sails. His serpentine body turned to face her, and he nuzzled her cheek and chin. He did not need words to tell her how he felt, nor did she need them to respond. She kissed the space between his nostrils, her worries momentarily forgotten.

They both felt it simultaneously. The earth twisting its spine with a low, aching snarl. The water above pushed down as the seabed rose, and for a moment Mira was crushed between the two.

After the third tremor, they knew this was no normal earthquake. Shoals of fish started to move inwards toward the city's heart. Moray eels slithered up from the seabed, groupers with their wide lower jaws loomed from behind, and all manner of catfish streamed by. Single-minded, darting and frenzied, sniffing something in the water. Mira indicated upwards and Kai obliged, breaking the surface so they could see.

A crimson tide was moving towards them. Blooming like cumulus clouds in the water, turning everything red. This was what the fish were responding to. Blood. Kai gave a single mournful cry and Mira grabbed his antlers as he dived under. He swam faster now, sleek muscles moving beneath her. The water was foul, with both blood and the frenetic fish. The panicked shoals made it difficult to move quickly. Kai burst through the surface of the water and dived back down, undulating with the waves.

Mira crooned, a low, rasping sound at the back of her throat. She drew in more water through her gills and strengthened the siren song, adding layers as her confidence grew. The fish parted before them, responding to her compulsion, drawn aside like sliding paper doors. The clenched fist of fear she hadn't known she was holding loosened its grasp. Her gills, her song still worked. But there was no time to celebrate, and certainly no time to ease herself back in.

Chapter Fifty-Five

"Ama?" Qiuyue said, rubbing her eyes with the back of her hand. She sat up in her bed as her mother pulled clothes out of the wardrobe.

"Get dressed. Quietly now. We're going on a trip."

"A trip? Where?" Qiuyue's voice was furry with sleep, but she obediently started to get changed, pulling on the thick padded jacket and fiddling with the embroidered buttons. She padded towards her mother for help, but stopped short. "You're bleeding!"

Cordelia pressed a hand against her shoulder, pushing the makeshift bandage back into place. She'd taken pain-numbing herbs but didn't want to waste any more time. It would take hours to clean and stitch her shoulder. She needed to get the children out before—

The light flicked on. Samnang stood in the doorway.

"Aba, we're going on a trip," Qiuyue announced, tugging at her father's sleeve. "But I think Ama needs the healer first."

"No healer. Qiuyue, get your shoes - not the fancy seasilk ones, the boots you wore hiking." Cordelia kept her voice level, trying to read her husband. She ensured the lilt stayed out of her tone, no question or hesitation in her command. She was not asking his permission. Samnang was dressed. Fully dressed. Had been waiting for her. Good. They had things to talk about.

He met her eyes steadily as Qiuyue prattled on. "Those shoes pinch my feet."

"Qiuyue!" Her daughter bit back any further complaints. Once the child had left the room, Cordelia knotted the drawstring of the bag tightly, fiddling with the loops so they were even.

"Serena, where do you think you're going?" Samnang said. His voice was tinged with disappointment.

"Serena?" Cordelia said, unable to keep the hard note from her words. Yes, that was who he saw. She caught her reflection in the bedroom mirror, wavy hair pulled into a side bun and lace-trimmed skirts. The unobtrusive wife who complemented his outfits like a polished medal.

The facade did not matter any longer. He knew her ruse. Had known it for some time. Cordelia was tired. She let the glamour – Serena's form – fall like shedding snakeskin. Her body extended itself from the uncomfortable illusion; her broad shoulders stretching, her lower limbs unfurling. She exhaled, loosening a belt cinched too tight. Her true eyes with their horizontal pupils blinked at him, catching the slight shift in his weight. He moved into an offensive stance, hand at the sarong tied about his waist.

"My true name is Cordelia, but I think you knew that already."

"No. I married a woman. A human woman called Serena. The mother of my children." The furrow in his brow deepened. Cordelia could make a map of his wrinkles. The way his eyelashes fluttered when she slipped out of bed at night. He never moved. Always with his left cheek on the pillow, face turned towards her when she departed or returned.

She put her hand back on her injured shoulder. It came away blue with blood and she showed him her palm. "You knew, though. You knew and you chose to let me go."

"I let you go so my *wife* could return to her family. Serena. Her duty is to remain here. I know nothing of *this*." He gestured towards her suckered limbs, only looking out of the corner of his eye. Afraid of the rumours that seawitches could turn people to stone. Tear out hearts and devour them whole. Sell your soul if you blinked.

Fury filled Cordelia, flowing through her like a burst dam. "Look at me, you damned coward!" Her cracked words screamed across the short distance as she loomed tall on her eight limbs, head brushing the ceiling light.

Samnang looked away.

"I got you into the Council. I would've made you Fenghuang! You were willing to let me. But now? Now you complain?"

He had pulled the sarong out entirely, winding it around his hands. He was a fool if he thought she would be hindered by a slip of cloth. By any of his so-called techniques. "Cordelia is a wanted criminal. The seawitch and the ambassador are working with the rebels to sabotage our city."

It was no surprise that he had fed this story to the public. It was the easiest way to explain her presence at the press conference. "Tell me something I don't know."

"The house is surrounded. I suspected the seawitch would target my daughter again. If you try to leave with Qiuyue, the guards will take you. You'll never see her again."

"You bastard, you wouldn't—"

"But if you stay – as Serena, as my wife – live a quiet life, give up these *hobbies* of yours, then who am I to deny a mother and daughter their time together? In the safety of their own home." He offered it up as a reasonable alternative, a substitute from the drinks cabinet.

Cordelia parsed his speech. "Confines, you mean?"

"A prison to one is a shelter to another." He was bluffing. After all, she'd got into the house without remark. But she had been in a hurry, had not truly taken note. There had been several boats moored alongside the family vessel. Groups of people milling on the walkways near the house. "Come back to me, Serena. We can put this whole sorry affair behind us." He spoke of it like a minor inconvenience.

If his condescension had not crowded out every other emotion, Cordelia might have applauded him. Praised his plan. A hard-edged bargain with little room for negotiation. Except he was fucking with her and their family. Everything she had done had been for him, for them. He had known. Had taken it. This was her thanks.

"Qiuyue. QIUYUE!" She didn't care who heard her. The servants, the kumiho be damned, she needed her daughter. She slid across the floor, splaying her limbs wide as she bore down on Samnang. Kept shouting her daughter's name, cutting through her husband's feeble retorts. He half-heartedly made a move towards one of her arms, but she slipped free. Pulled the furniture towards her with her many limbs: a chair leg, a claw-footed chest, a four-panelled screen. Pushed them towards Samnang as he scrabbled back into the corridor. It was quick work: wedging the furniture up against her husband, trapping him.

"Aba?" Qiuyue's voice said from behind her. Cordelia turned with relief to be met with her daughter's ear-piercing scream. It cleaved through her rage. "A monster, a monster!"

Of course. The child didn't know her true shape. All she saw was a beast attacking her father. "Qiuyue, it's me, it's Ama," she said softly. The girl's eyes widened as she saw Cordelia's sharp teeth, and the screaming – the weeping – intensified. There was no way she would be able to camouflage or move with a frightened girl in her grasp.

Gede burst out of his room, dishevelled and half-robed. Qiuyue bounded towards him, burying her face in his side. "Tell her, tell her it's me!" Cordelia said, stretching out her hand. Her skin was ash grey, pulsing with subdued hues. Gede looked at her, then over at Samnang. His father, pushing desperately at the heavy furniture pinning him in place, shook his head.

Gede picked up his sister, caressing the back of her head comfortingly. He paused for half a moment. In the end, his words of betrayal were muted. "I don't know who that is."

A raw shriek ripped through Cordelia's throat, but she swallowed it hard. Her lower limbs coiled into twisted knots, skin pulsing vivid blue rings. Bitterness filled her mouth, her own venom mixing with saliva.

"Come now. Enough is enough." Samnang looked at her as if she were a child having a meltdown. He had turned them against her. Weaponised her family to keep her in a cage. He had it all figured out. But he did not know her.

He did not know her at all.

"This isn't over," she vowed.

She snaked to her study as Samnang called for the guards. As their feet pounded down the corridor, she slipped through the secret door and the passageway beyond. Spaces too narrow for human shoulders to fit through were easy enough for her. If only she could block out the sound of her daughter's crying echoing after her.

Chapter Fifty-Six

"We sang songs about the sand gods." Another quake shook the cavern. Nami let herself drift down to the lake bed, trailing one hand across the titan whale shark's hide. They'd been here for hours, Lynnette determined to silence the ancestor beneath their feet. And while the initial tremors had shaken the cave to the core, sending waves of pain through them all, it'd now settled into a throbbing headache.

She'd tried attacking Lynnette from behind, but Firth had stood staunchly in her way, a stony wall of defence. Regretful and contrite as he held her back. She counted to ten, taking long, slow breaths despite the thudding palpitations in her ribcage and temples. Keep talking. That was what Kai and Mira always advised. There was a solution, she just couldn't see it. Closing her eyes, she pushed back the fears. "They say our great-great-grand-uncle met a titan leatherback turtle when he was a child."

"Shut up," Lynnette said. Her heart wasn't in it, though. Not like the first three dozen times she'd retorted. Directionless, unsure of what to do next, she flicked at stones underfoot with her wide tail, the sand puffing in little plumes. Nami watched it resettle and continued.

"Do you recall the Tale of the Dark Lake? That was my favourite. One wayfinder in a boat sailing the open seas. Finding the titan whale shark and pleading for help to heal a polluted lake. The orca pod, the narrow straits, the whalers and the winter freeze – the titan whale shark overcomes it all. Filters the contaminated water until it runs clear. The people celebrate, name a festival after it. Their children are called shark kin."

"Whale kin," Lynnette corrected.

Nami pretended not to notice. Touched her stomach wound tentatively. It'd stopped bleeding but felt like embers sewn under her skin, glowing hot as she prodded them. She touched the same hand to the whale's body beneath her. She was not the only one hurting. "When it's done, when the titan is a corpse, will you stop? Will it be enough? Will anything be enough?" Her words pounded at Lynnette's chest and the kelpie closed her eyes to block them out. The roles had reversed. Nami was her own mother, trying to talk sense into a wayward but well-meaning fool. Jiang-Li would laugh to see her now.

The sand god remained silent. But the Drawback leader's right eyelid twitched. She made a sign of blessing across her chest before swimming back to where they'd poured in the poison. Pulled out the spear and thrust it back in. It went no deeper than previously, a splinter under the skin.

Nami changed her tactics, turning to Firth. "She won't stop until it's dead, you know that, right? The old gods, the ones who brought us out of the silt."

Firth glanced back at his companion for a long moment. His hard exterior was being chipped away. Nami pushed further. "Onseon wasn't an accident – she wanted to murder those folk. Make *us* murder them!"

"Sacrifices have to be made," Firth said. His lips were pursed in a grim line. "You of all people must understand that."

She propelled herself forward, holding his mournful gaze. Reached out a tentative hand until it came to rest against his chest. The kelpie covered it with his own. "I do, Firth. I understand why you're doing this. But I cannot believe it's the only way. Help me. Stop this madness."

His heartbeat was fast under her palm. He laced his fingers with hers. "We've gone too far to stop."

Cracks had appeared in his confident demeanour. Doubts that would germinate in crevices. Nami prodded at them. "There must be a way."

Firth took a deep breath. "Only one. Your pearl."

She snatched her hand away, fingers burned by the heat. The kelpie continued, tone low and insistent. "Let me use it. Lynnette trusts me. I can get close and—"

"Firth?" Lynnette had swum over without either of them noticing. Despite her formidable size, she looked lost. Hurt by the words she'd overheard. "This was not what we discussed."

"Plans change." He didn't even turn to look at her.

"You would betray me? After everything I—" Her hand reached up instinctively to make the sand god sign across her body again, stopping midway as she realised what she was doing. Her nostrils flared and her eyelid twitched. "No."

"What?"

"I promised to lead you, but I did not promise this." She launched herself with a strong thrust of her tail, pinning Firth beneath her, arm against his neck. They grappled for a moment, muscles taut. They were evenly matched, or would've been if not for the hidden blade Firth rammed into Lynnette's side. She roared, blood blooming from the wound. Headbutted him with a crack before swimming back to yank the spearhead out of the sand god's gills.

Nami did not wait to see what would happen. She would never have a better opportunity to escape. She swam up like a dart, breaking the surface. Blinking the water from her eyes. The ground shook and she swerved as rubble fell towards her. On hands and knees she scrambled across the cave floor, looking for the narrow passageway they'd entered from.

She glanced back only once, wondering if there was more she could've done for the titan whale shark. If she should have stayed to help Firth. She was in no state to rescue anyone. Could barely save herself. She would come back, with Mira and Kai; yes, they'd know what to do. The lie was easier to swallow.

Feeling her way in the dark, she kept her waterweaving in reserve. Behind her there was a sudden rush of air. It funnelled her forward and she ran with it, barely on tiptoes. A rumble. A long, deep note like the ocean itself was mourning. It was the titan, a pained lament that lingered long after the tunnel started collapsing around her.

Nami ran. Everything moved too quickly for her waterweaving to have any effect. She slammed into something hard, a barrier of sorts, a door. With her remaining energy, she drove a wedge of water against it. Stumbled out the other side, nearly falling off the narrow ledge in her haste. The cry finally died, floating off with the rustling dead leaves underfoot. Nami crouched in a huddle, gasping for air. Her vision was blurry with endless inexplicable tears. Her ears rang with the force of the song.

And in the distance, she heard an echo.

"A call to one is a call to all. Sand moves with the tides," she said, the verse she'd once been made to memorise rising to the surface of her mind unbidden. The words were ripped into the wind, heard by no one but the whirling gulls.

Titans were pairs.

And something had answered.

Chapter Fifty-Seven

Mira had no authority any more. Even if she could find a working telephone exchange, they wouldn't necessarily patch her through. As they hit the city's walkways, tremors still shuddering underfoot, she directed Kai towards the one person who'd know. Who knew everything.

Cordelia was stuffing glass cylinders into a bag as Mira rudely shoved open the apothecary door. The seawitch looked up with dead eyes. "Not today."

A flick of water slammed the door back in Mira's face. Only her foot stopped it from closing. She kicked it open again. "What did you do?"

"Me, saltlick? Try the Drawbacks." Cordelia didn't even bother to look up this time. Mira's eyes narrowed, but she didn't argue. As much as she wanted Cordelia to pay for the press conference stunt, for the irreparable damage she'd done to Kai's image, now wasn't the time. Neither was it the time for subtlety.

She sang one crystal note, holding it until the cylinder in Cordelia's hand shattered. The seawitch flinched, jumping back as the pieces smashed on the ground. "Tell me." Mira put compulsion into her reverberating siren song. The power flowed through her more easily this time, muscle memory stirring like the tides. Too easy.

"The sand gods," Cordelia said. Her neck strained, red-rimmed eyes bulging. That she only said three words was a testament to her strength of will. Then again, Mira was surprised the sea-witch didn't have her shields up already. Her mind was clearly elsewhere.

"Folk bedtime stories. What's that got to do with anything?"

Cordelia turned and touched her finger to the forehead of her sand god pair: a small soapstone turtle and a manta ray. Mira had barely noticed them sitting on a shelf amid claypots and shisha pipes. "Legends have grains of truth. From before the Great Bathyal War, from before the city was racked by earthquakes."

"Are you telling me the Drawbacks found a sand god?"

"They didn't just find it. They're killing it."

Mira heard her own shocked gasp before she could conceal it. Of all the things she'd been expecting, this was not one of them. "How can you kill a god?"

"Not everything about sand gods is true. Nothing is truly immortal. You and I, of all people, know fables are often embellished." Mira disliked being put in the same category as Cordelia. Yet she had a point. Sirens and seawitches were infamous, for different reasons. Stories blown out of proportion. She couldn't make men stop breathing with a glance, nor hold someone charmed their whole lives. Lies and inventions.

The comment reminded her of the compulsion effect still tightening around the seawitch's body. The unseen song was tangled in Cordelia's limbs, wrapped around her mouth, nose and siphon. The strength of it was beguiling, even as Mira's mind told her it was not the just way to do things. One more question, she promised herself. Just one. "What will happen when it dies?"

"I don't plan to be around to find out," Cordelia said. She'd said enough to push back against the compulsion, resuming her haphazard packing.

Mira let the song ripple and fade. She looked over at Kai, but the same shocked expression that must be gracing her face was plastered across his. He had no plan for this. Words, then. She always had words. "This isn't the time to run!"

The seawitch peered down her slim nose, her mouth a sneer of disgust. "Can you not be a little less . . . It's giving me a migraine." She readjusted her robes, bandages striping her shoulder and chest. It looked like a nasty new wound.

She noticed Mira staring. Glared defiantly as if taunting her to ask at her own risk. Turned her back to open various small drawers behind the counter, revealing vials, pendants, figures made of obsidian. She brought each to her face, some slipped into a bag, others dropped to the ground.

A sudden low cry shook the whole building. Mira ducked, dragging Kai with her under the counter as the quake swayed the room. The ceiling joists creaked and the cacophony of objects smashing on the ground was a discordant orchestra. Mira had experienced earthquakes her whole life, but none had come with a death song slipping down her back. A choking sensation strangled her throat and tears sprang to her eyes without warning. A lament, even though she knew not how she knew.

"It's dead . . . isn't it?" she said. Kai could only nod in affirmation through wet eyes. They all felt it.

As the quake subdued, Mira rose gingerly to her feet. Cordelia looked just as shaken, surrounded by the detritus of her shop. Her voice was incredulous. "Well. They actually managed it."

Before Mira could respond, an answer echoed. A roar like a savage beast howling from the clouds. Cordelia redoubled her packing efforts, frantic now. "There isn't time," Mira said, her hand grasping the mouth of the bag, folding it closed so she had to listen. "Don't you remember the tales? That was an answering call. We have about an hour, maybe two, before the impact."

"Impact?"

"The biggest tidal wave this city has ever seen." Mira had never believed in the sand gods, but she knew the signs of tsunami. In an earthquake-heavy city, it was part of their jobs as chinthe to do withdrawal drills, sound the warning bells, watch for shifts in the ocean. She swallowed her fears, pummelling them back, and let the training, the reflexive knowledge, float to the surface like oil on water. "Evacuate. To the Peak."

"The Peak is compromised. You'd be better off in Jingsha," Cordelia said despite herself.

"You have the resources to save humanity. And everyone along with it." Mira chose her words deliberately. Humans were the only ones who would drown, but without them, without Tiankawi, freshwater folk couldn't survive. After her experiences coordinating the rescue effort at the Boat Races, she knew the city's telephone lines could not handle this. Only one person had a network extensive enough among the folk and outcasts of the city, those who would be hardest hit. A network fast enough to pass urgent messages, get boats and people to the right place quickly.

"Why should I?"

Time was being wasted because Cordelia still cared more about her own skin than others. "If everyone's dead, who will do business with you? Isn't there anyone you care about here? Help us and I'll—"

"Yes?" Cordelia couldn't help it. The mere hint of a proposition, a deal in the making. Meanwhile Kai had put his hand on Mira's shoulder, shaking his head emphatically. No more bargains. But the risk was hers to take.

She gritted her teeth. "I'll be in your debt."

The seawitch smiled. Her severe face broke for once, the wrinkles around her often pursed lips now soft laughter lines. She covered Mira's hand with her own. "Deal."

Sharp needles pierced the skin of Mira's palm. She flinched back, the circle of dots welling up with pinpricks of blood. Cordelia had palmed her octopus ink pendant, the edges like teeth sealing the makeshift bargain with the contact. The implication of her poorly chosen words.

The seawitch picked up something that had fallen in the quake, a gong like a full moon. She hooked it precariously on the broken edge of a shelf and hit the tempered surface. The sound shimmered out, soft as distant thunder, then louder, crashing like waves through Mira's bones. Only a few moments later, footfalls rushed to the doorway. A pair of elder mermaids in human form, racing to Cordelia's side regardless of the chaos around her. They waited silently for further instruction. The seawitch nodded her head towards Mira. "Whatever she needs."

Mira paused, the weight of the authority both comforting and frightening. They assumed she'd have a plan. A way to lead them out of this. She licked her cracked lips and stood straighter.

"Evacuate the city. Fathomfolk and human alike. Head for the highest buildings, head for Jingsha. A tsunami is coming." They nodded without question, darting out before Mira had finished the last word. No wonder Cordelia could manage her affairs so well. Mira turned to Kai. "I need to get to a telephone exchange, get hold of Mikayil. Sirens as well, sirens can carry the warning if the power is down. Ama knows how to get the word out. Can you . . . ?"

She did not need to finish. Kai nodded. He could get to the siren teahouses quickly, persuade them to lend their support. *Always*, he signed back as his eyes wrinkled at the corners. There was no time for anything else.

"Cordelia." Mira spun back, but the seawitch had vanished. In her wake she'd left a cellar trapdoor open. Kneeling to peer down, Mira saw dozens of cylinders lashed together with rope. The air cylinders humans needed to breathe underwater. And now she realised that among the debris that littered the ground was a pile of breathing masks.

"One more thing," Cordelia said.

Mira jumped back but couldn't find the source of the voice. Out of the corner of her eye, she caught something moving. A box warped and a stool rippled for a moment, but as soon as she focused, it was solid again.

"Tell anyone I helped, and I'll break every bone in your body."

The door slammed shut. Mira was certain Cordelia had left. Or as certain as she could be.

Chapter Fifty-Eight

Nami heard the wailing of the emergency beacon first, the flashing orange light sending her heart into palpitations. It was so much like the Peace Tower in Yonakuni that for a moment she forgot where she was, waiting to be marched to her mother for a slap on the wrist. Then the warm breeze blew through her, shaking the fugue, reminding her she was topside now and the emergency beacon was in fact a tsunami warning.

She heard the siren song next. Hundreds of voices taking up the call as she skidded down the treacherous mountainside. Like birds passing on a new song, they echoed, warbling in tune. *Go to Jingsha, the central district. The tallest buildings, the strongest structures. Go. Run. Swim.* A litany in her head as she slid on her backside, scraped her hands and knees before reaching flatter ground. Then a new melody started, a counter-harmony to the first. *Help needed. Help in Palang. In Samaga and Seong districts. Help.*

She was still not at sea level. The water below frothed white with foam, the dark backs of rocks like turtle shells. She bit her lip, hesitating for only a moment before she took a running leap. Mid-air, her spines unfolded down the back of her head and silver scales coated her elongated body. Her whiskers tasted the salt spray and the wind whipped past her angular jaw.

She hit the water hard, only her scales protecting her face from being cut to ribbons. Her body curved instinctively, darting past the jagged rocks, her belly scraping one she couldn't avoid as her tail fanned out as a rudder. The change in temperature shocked her, leaving her spluttering as her gills adjusted. It had been weeks, perhaps months since she'd been in full dragon form. She didn't have time to enjoy it. She swam for Seong district. For the port where she'd arrived in the city half a year ago.

The larger vessels had headed out to open waters. All that was left were the rowing boats, the sampans and taraibune like drift-wood in the spreading storm. Oars were helpless against the waves, and the capsized undersides of boats bobbed wherever she looked, scraping up against buildings. Countless people struggled in the choppy water. Those fortunate enough to still be in undamaged vessels were being dragged down by the sheer number of desperate hands clinging to the sides. The air thick with pleas for help.

Nami swam forward to cushion the struggling bodies, flatten-ing her spines against her back as she felt people grab on. One pair of arms clung so desperately to her sides that they clamped down over her gills. She shook lightly but the vice tightened. She broke the surface of the water, gasping through her mouth.

"I can't breathe!" she said, writhing her neck. But the people barely heard her, faces white with shock, gripping on for dear life. Somehow she swam through it, water like molasses with bodies that stifled every stroke. When she reached the pier, she rested her head on the mildewed planks. Firm, commanding voices took charge and the load was lighter, the grip on her gills gone.

"You'd think these fools have never read a book in their lives. Everyone knows gills are essential to folk ability to breathe underwater, and causing any damage would simply hinder rescue attempts." A hand stroked down Nami's snout. Her wet hair was plastered against her face and her gold-rimmed glasses were bent, but Nami recognised Eun from the smell of old books and the mumbled speech. Despite everything, she was warmed through to know that the librarian's ramblings would continue even as the city crumbled around them. The sound of two vessels colliding in the harbour distracted her, and when she turned back, Eun was gone.

It was like staunching a dam with sand. No sooner had Nami deposited one group, than she spotted another, and another. People called out: from the water, from overfilled boats, from makeshift floats that were nothing more than broken planks of wood. She turned this way and that, frozen by indecision. There was no time. Who should she rescue? Whose voice shouted the loudest?

A body brushed against hers, scaled skin like cherry blossom against a pale spring day. Kai. She twined herself with him, an underwater hug of relief as they nuzzled each other for a moment of reprieve. They broke the surface. "There's too many, Kai. It's too late."

She felt the tiny bubble of hope burst without so much as a sound. Nothing more than soap and water. She'd said the words aloud, hoping Kai would correct her. Waiting for the answer she'd not thought of. He merely looked back with mournful eyes, his whiskers heavy with water droplets. Shook his head.

The water behind him started to churn. Like vibrato on a string, the sea hummed. Between the boats, the stilt legs of the houses and the swimmers, the water frothed with activity. Nami could not make sense of it. Heads emerged from the waterline: kappa and chang-bi, kun peng and jangjamari, naga and baiji. Fathomfolk. Some carrying masks and air cylinders to aid the humans.

She'd not been the only one to answer the call. The bubble reformed inside her chest, molten hot as spun sugar. She needed to keep it turning.

With the extra aid in the water, they pulled people onto the walkways. But now there was a different problem. Throngs of people shuffling and shoving to get to higher ground. Like insects crawling over each other to reach the top. It was not certain the stilted structures would continue to bear their weight. What good was it to rescue people from the water only for them to be trapped in the platforms between narrow buildings when the water crashed down?

They needed a way up. Fast. Nami shrank back into her human form as she peered up at the cityscape, catching her breath. This was what Tiankawi had been built for: surviving the waterline. The tram line was still unusable, repairs unfinished. Another stab of guilt at that. She shoved it to one side. Guilt could come when there was the luxury of time. A single cable car swung like a pendulum in a growing gale. They'd been powered down as well. But they still worked.

"We can use the ropeway," she said, looking at the dark cabin abandoned in the station at the far end of the walkway. She'd not been able to face it; the swinging cable car made her sick to the stomach just to watch. But it would get them up there. After all, that was what they'd been doing for years: using fathomfolk to power the city. There would be a way.

"We can do it," she repeated. No one was listening. She climbed the bottom few rungs of an exterior ladder, swinging herself out to one side so the crowd could see her. "We can power the cable cars back up!" She'd not expected her voice to carry. Not expected a sea of upturned faces. Listening. She gulped before pushing on. "The ropeway was undamaged. It's a short straight trip to Jingsha if we pool our waterweaving."

"Aren't you one of them?" someone asked. "A Drawback?"

There were no good words with which to answer. No justification she could give. The desire to explain, to stack sandbags around herself was overwhelming. "I was wrong. Each of your lives is important. And if you let me, I'll protect them as best I can."

She jumped down and ushered the nearest humans towards the cable car. "Get in!" she urged. A small boy yelled in fear as she reached for his arm, and cowered behind his father. "Please, trust me!" she said to the man. He met her eyes briefly, then turned away. "I don't know you."

It was true. They didn't. She hadn't taken the time.

"You know me," a familiar voice said. It was Mira, jumping across from a small vessel. She landed on one knee, taking a moment to straighten out her clothes, her wavy hair damp with spray. The crowd parted for her without question. "Nami's made mistakes, but she's a friend of the city, a friend of mine. I trust her."

The siren walked confidently toward the cabin, manually overriding the sliding doors and yanking them open. A beat, and then someone followed her. It was Eun, her lips pushed together as if stopping herself from spewing forth a lecture on ropeway history. Nami was elated to see her. Knowing that they were keeping Eun safe made her feel lighter somehow, a load lifted from her shoulders. The librarian wiped her glasses on a dirty elbow as she took Mira's outstretched hand and stepped into the carriage. Others slowly followed suit. Humans and fathomfolk alike crowded in. Kai, shifted back into his antlered human form, shut the doors behind them.

Now she just had to move the damn thing. Nami stared at the control room in the station with mounting dread. Beneath a layer of crumpled newssheets, tea-stained cups and cigarette butts was a complex panel. Dials and switches marked with indecipherable symbols. She prodded at the buttons, pumped at the lever to one side. She smiled up at the cabin full of anxious faces, giving them an inanely self-assured wave before crouching to look under the panel. Maybe if she just . . . yanked out some wires?

She would focus her waterweaving. It would find a way – like a river across an open plain. Simple. The image of the pallid selkie, his shaved head, sprang to the forefront of her mind. She didn't push it away. Stared into the memory and what she could recall.

The water streamed towards her, a jet snaking between the planks and dripping from the windows into her hand. How exactly she would convert it to make the ropeway move was another matter. There was a rumble in the distance. Masonry fell into the water. Timbers. Broken homes collapsing under the onslaught.

A tall black man came to the control room door. "The panel under the lever," he said without preamble. "Open it. There's a backup connector." Nami stared without comprehending. "I work here," he added.

She didn't bother to argue. Prising the panel open, she found a wiring kit with the familiar three buds. She connected it to her pakalot and hoped for the best. It felt like someone tugging on her arm, although not in any specific direction. Tightening until her hand turned white with the constriction and she felt sick to the bone. Her stomach flipped, churning in protest, and she dry-heaved. A hand touched hers, the man, a look of concern across his face. *Breathe*, he mouthed, but she couldn't hear him beneath the blaring in her mind. Then Kai was there. He moved his hand to her elbow and she felt him channelling his waterweaving, seconding her just enough to stop the sickness. He reached out his other hand, beckoning the other folk still on the walkway.

The power coursed through her, warm as a bellyful of food. She sparked with the strength of it: a chain of waterweaving connecting them. There were disparate voices at the edges of her awareness: young and old, freshwater and estuary alike. Fathomfolk with even a modicum of waterweaving had lent their strength. Even a few humans had linked in, for fellowship more than anything, but slivers of power were eked out all the same. The sum total threatened to overwhelm her, knock her out with the unexpected abundance.

The lights dazzled bright in the carriage and the ropeway mechanism whirred to life. A ragged cheer lifted, and the man who'd given her advice pulled a lever. The cable car lurched forward. Nami remained at her post as they filled a second carriage, then a third. With each cabin gone, however, there were fewer people to power the ropeway, and the burden of it burned at the small of her back like coals eating through layers of skin and tissue.

She and Kai got into the final cabin, the cable car operator showing them how to power the mechanism directly from the car. It sped up, staggering into a lopsided sway as it lifted off the ground. Only the steel rope above their head held things taut. Nami trained her eyes on her pakalot bracer as the water and buildings pulled away, trying to ignore the rocking sensation. She could barely comprehend those with their noses pressed against the glass. Were they not concerned about plummeting to the ground? Kai kept his hand on her shoulder, steadfast, a constant stream of power and calm exuding from him. If they kept the pace, if they took turns, they could get there. They could all get to the top. The first cabin would already be unloading by now. There were twenty or so cars behind it. A few precious seconds of peace. The promised safety of Jingsha's spires up ahead. She would just close her eyes for a moment and—

Something slammed into the side of the car. Everyone fell to the floor. Nami rolled across the swaying cabin, hitting legs and bodies as the power connection was yanked abruptly from her wrist. The ropeway jerked to a stop. The car swung sharply. People screamed, pointing at the cracked window, at the door that was being prised open from the outside.

Lynnette. Nami had left the two Drawbacks fighting, but had the kelpie followed her here? She wondered if Firth had made it out, wondered at her conflicted feelings if he hadn't.

The door was open. Lynnette's familiar face looked at her with murderous intent, but before Nami could react, Kai kicked out, sending the kelpie flying back. With a luck she did not deserve, the Drawback leader landed on scaffolding, rather than plummeting to the ground below. She had waterweaved a gangplank of solid ice to reach them, spanning from the bamboo scaffolding of the unfinished tower to here where the ropeway came close to the buildings. Kai did not hesitate, leaping straight across the gap and continuing to spar with her.

In a fair fight, he was the better of the two. Years of training to hone his waterweaving, tuition in replicating martial weapons and his natural height gave him the advantage. He had made a curved blade, the water rippling on each swing but hardening to ice on contact, and he moved quickly, on the offensive, thrusting and slicing in a blur. Each cut was precise, cutting into the kelpie's legs. It was water, but not the way he handled it. Nami felt a swelling of pride and confidence in her brother.

But as the two continued to fight, she noticed something else. He was tired. Reflexes dull from the rescue effort, from shapeshifting and giving his waterweaving to the ropeway. Lynnette, on the other hand, had gained a second wind. She barely dodged Kai's strikes, taking the blows in her stride like they were nothing. Her muscles bulged taut, veins dark and popping abnormally on her exposed skin. Her eyes were bloodshot, pupils dilated like she'd not slept in weeks. Since Nami had left her on the Peak, the Drawback leader had grown inexplicably stronger.

"Give me a boost!" Nami shouted to the people behind her. Almost immediately a stream of water punched up on her, and she ran with it, using the momentum to clear the gap between the carriage and the ice gangplank. She crouched on landing, sliding precariously across the smooth surface, then pulled on her scales and let adrenaline take over.

She shouldered into Lynnette as her brother moved aside, and they both tumbled onto the ice. It was wet now, water pooling in pockmarked holes. Lynnette transformed into full horse form, her shoulders broadening, her hooves edged like ice picks. "You ruined everything!" she snarled, pawing the ground. The ice protested under her weight.

"Likewise." Nami siphoned water from their feet to make a thin rope, weighting the end with ice and swinging it in a large circle to either side of her body. Giving her brother the space to catch his breath. She couldn't beat Lynnette's strength, but she could keep the kelpie at arm's length. Lynnette reared onto her hind legs, eyeing the swinging rope for a way through, but Nami changed the pattern erratically. Pushed her back, step by step, away from the cable car, away from the people she might hurt. Lynnette sensed it, taking her chance to lunge forward.

Nami barely slipped her headlong charge, ducking out of the way at the last second. "It doesn't matter," Lynnette goaded between laboured breaths. She turned slowly back to face Nami. "As long as I'm in the way, you've lost."

She was right. When the great wave came, everyone would be destroyed. Without Nami and Kai to move them, the static cabins would be swept away, dooming the people they'd hoped to save.

In desperation, Nami transformed, growing to full dragon height, her back pressed up against the scaffolding carcass of the unfinished building. As her body lengthened, though, something felt wrong. Scales flaked away, and one of her antlers was stuck beneath the skin. Only one of her claws had formed, the other still a soft human hand, as Lynnette reached her, hooves kicking her in the abdomen. Nami fell back towards the building, bamboo poles splintering and breaking her fall. Blood filled her mouth, drops of red dripping towards the white foam far beneath her.

Lynnette grabbed her, biting at her shoulder. Nami kicked and kicked futilely at her knees; desperate and exhausted. And then, from the shadows of the construction site, someone hit the Drawback leader hard on the head.

Nami stood, words on her lips to thank Kai. But it was not her brother. He was still kneeling at the far end of the ice shelf near the cable car, exhausted.

Firth.

Lynnette's eyes widened as the other kelpie loomed over her. Tears froze as they dripped down her ruddy cheeks, forming hard crystals. "I did it. Everything that was asked. More."

"You did," Firth acknowledged. "But plans change."

Lynnette turned to lock eyes with Nami. "I was you once. He's not who you—" Her eyes glazed silver and her head slumped forward. Firth had his hand on her neck, a grip that looked like a soft caress, and yet Nami knew enough to realise he'd snapped it.

"Now do you trust me?" His question lingered between them, clinging to her like morning dew.

Distantly she heard her name being called. There was no time to consider what Firth had said. What he'd done. All she could do was put one foot in front of the other. *Run*, she told herself. From Firth. From Lynnette's crumpled body at his feet.

"I did it for you," he said. His words fell on barren ground, the thin cracking of ice underfoot ringing in Nami's ears as she withdrew, leaping back across the gap to the cabin.

Hands caught her and pulled her in. Kai followed. Firth did not pursue her, watching with glassy indifference as the last of the ice melted. The bridge between them collapsed, a downpour of water drumming on the walkways and roofs below.

The cabin pulled away. Firth's shadow was still there, loitering in the skeleton of the unfinished building. A small movement and Lynnette's body fell. She hit the walkway on the way down, bouncing off it like a ragdoll. Onlookers in the carriage let out horrified screams, mouths covered as they watched the grisly display. They had not seen what had happened in the dark. Had not realised the Drawback leader was already dead.

Chapter Fifty-Nine

They'd just unloaded the final cabin at Jingsha station when a huge earthquake hit. The tremor ran through Mira's marrow. The world swayed, the tall buildings like saplings in a breeze. The fractured sound of glass breaking around her. Smaller buildings yielded to the quake, crumpled like mere sandcastles on a beach. A discordant song of fear and panic rose from the people around them.

Her home was falling apart. It was not perfect, but it was the only one she had. A place she believed in, for all its faults. She moved through the station as if in slow motion, her feet weighed down with lead. A pair of shaking hands clung to a nearby lamp post. Her hands. She wiggled each finger in detachment, noticing how they responded. When the quake finally stopped, she felt the absence like a part of her had been cut off. Not a limb or a finger. The pain wasn't tangible that way. A change in the damp air. She hadn't even realised the titan whale shark existed until a few hours ago, and yet its death was undeniable.

Kai slumped in her arms as she reached him. Where he'd been ported into the ropeway cabin after the fight with Lynnette, the copper wires had fused under his red-raw skin. Her mother had done this once: sold her power to send Mira to school. To let her daughter live her dreams. She could only fervently hope that

Ama had headed for higher ground after sounding the warning. Knowing Trish though, the siren would still be in the water helping human stragglers. The thought pierced Mira's conscience dimly, like someone banging on a neighbour's door. She could not think about it right now.

She tore the wires from the panel. They dangled like aerial roots from her husband's skin. Wincing for him as the motion opened fresh wounds, blood trickling in a delta between his fingers, she shouldered him inside the building.

The first day she'd met him had been here at Jingsha station. Furious that she'd been assigned minding duties over the new ambassador; a job they'd surely given her because no one else wanted it, because they thought it would somehow suit her better – being a saltie and all. She'd positively scowled from under her hat as she'd greeted him. He'd been charming, intelligent, slightly awkward, craning his head this way and that. Exciting, marvellous, wonderful: everything was a delight. His optimism smoothed out her edges, curved them upwards to match his own. She became impatient for their next meeting. Extending the city tours to strolls before breakfast and boat trips after dark. She kept infinitesimal stories, bawdy songs, sticky rice cakes in waxy leaves – tucked them into her sleeves to share with him. And at some point, she'd stopped scowling.

Now the same reception area was almost unrecognisable, filled with people grouped like sea urchins in spiky huddles. The grand chandelier had fallen to the ground, glass and shell ornaments like spilled tears.

"Is it over?" Nami said. Her voice sounded dazed. Her body had also given up mid transformation, with one scaled and clawed hand, the other half the size. Her short hair was flecked blue-silver and her branched antlers were broken.

Kai shook his head. Signed: *Drawback*.

"They've gone," Nami said, whispered it again under her breath as if to check it was for real. She had collapsed into herself, staring at the cracks in the tiled floor. "Lynnette is dead."

"No," Mira explained. The younger dragon looked up in shock, like she had somehow forgotten the warning beacons still blaring around them. "The drawback before a tsunami."

Nami punched at the wall. Mira understood the sentiment, but they didn't have time. All eyes were watching, waiting for leadership. Move forward. Always move forward. The next job, the next checklist, one foot in front of the other. It was the only way to outrun the despair. To keep going despite the quicksand at her feet. The numbness like a cavernous abyss hollowing her out. She forced out the words. "Higher ground. Now. Everyone!" She urged the crowd up the station stairs, making for the roof as fast as they could.

It was already too late. Mira gripped onto the high roof walls, hair obscuring half her vision as the howling winds buffeted her. The water had started to pull back. It was morbidly fascinating, seeing the hitherto concealed roofs of submerged buildings, the seaweed-clagged pillars. How different must Tiankawi have been a century or two ago. When they'd walked on dry land like it was of no consequence. Taking it all for granted.

"I don't know where Ama is," she said aloud. Or the others. Tam and Mikayil, who had stepped up against Gede's orders. Her favourite shopkeepers in Qilin. Even Cordelia . . .

Kai's warm arms wrapped around her, folding her against his chest as she shook. His chin was on the top of her head and his steady heart beat against her ear. He smelled of lemongrass and mellow loose-leaf tea. As safe as hiding under the covers against a day she didn't want to face. She could stay in the circle of his embrace and pretend it wasn't happening.

But she couldn't shield herself from today. They had to stand in the cutting wind and face the consequences. She moved away. Kai wouldn't let go, not at first, until she kissed him on the lips with a weary smile.

Nami stood apart from them, hands clutching the edge of the roof. Her short hair flicked around her forehead in the wind, and for all her immaturity, she looked older now. The softness about her jaw had gone and the time above water had sun-kissed her nose and arms. "I know what I have to do," she said.

Kai immediately stepped to her side, shaking his head.

"I can do it. It's the right thing. I see that now." Her voice rambled, trailing into a whisper as she turned. She was shaking, her whole body quivering as she tried to control it, grasping her own forearms with a determined look on her stubborn features.

She elongated herself, starting the transformation into true form. Rather than sinking to all fours, she stood upright, her body extending upwards like a column. Mira had never seen anything like it. There was something exquisite about the sight. Like a pillar of light. But then she faltered, dropping abruptly back into human form, doubling over and collapsing to her knees. She banged her fist on the floor in frustration. "I can't, I can't. Titans help me, why can't I do it?"

Kai signed at her frantically, pushing his long hair out of his eyes. Mira could not keep up. She didn't understand what they were arguing about, what they could possibly do as a tidal wave was about to crash down. What skills did they have to—

It clicked, just as Kai signed: *I'll do it.* Part of her had known since their visit to Cordelia, since Kai had taken her place in the contract, taken up her fight in the Council, believing in everything she believed in.

"Your dragon pearl," she said.

"It's my idea, not yours. My sacrifice to make," Nami said. Her breath quickened, eyes locked in a fierce battle with her brother. "You have Mira, you have each other. It doesn't ..." Her gaze darted around and she gestured wildly. "I'll do it. I can do it."

"You couldn't even weave a drop of rain right now," Mira said. She hated herself for saying it, and yet she couldn't help herself.

Inside, her body screamed, pounding on her chest to fight for him, to make him change his mind. But her eyes were trained on the horizon and the white line that was making its way towards them.

"Neither can he, look at him!" Nami said. She touched Kai's elbow. "You're the better one. The good one. This city needs you. Mira needs you!" She waved over at the siren, wanting backup in her plea. But as much as Mira's heart cried, she couldn't let it show. If she faltered, he would too. And she loved him too much to stop him.

She parted her lips, trying to hold back the pain from her voice. Forced out the words she knew she had to say. Words that drove a knife through her anyway. "It's your choice."

Kai took her hand and squeezed it. She remembered now that it was she who'd made the first move in the end. He'd been too polite, afraid of misreading the signals. Lingering at the edges without a modicum of his usual confidence. She had taken his hand during a walk together, held it until he'd finally asked the question.

"There must be another way," Nami said.

I trust you both. Protect the city. Kai turned to Mira one last time, kissed her hand the way he had when she'd finally nodded. When she'd tilted her face up to kiss him as she'd been longing to for all the weeks and months in each other's company. One last sign: the first they had mastered together.

He let go.

Before they could say another word, another protest, he stretched himself tall. Taller. Reaching up towards the grey sky, unfolding into the serpentine body of his true dragon form. Then, just as his sister had done, he faltered, worn down and out of power. Falling back to earth. No, Mira thought. No. She put her hand against his scales and lent him her strength. Tears flooded her eyes as she gave him every ounce of power so that he could save them all. A coy smile played about his lips, and it was still him. The person she'd fallen in love with.

He continued to elongate but his eyes remained the same, locking on Mira's one last time. He was the most beautiful thing she'd ever seen. He was the most beautiful person she had ever known. Then he flew up into the air, her hand left empty and cold.

He snaked upwards, hitting his rhythm, relaxing into the wind as he turned, curving into bends and loops. His long body knotted into a swirling sphere. Pulsed with pure power. White light seeped from between his scales, illuminating each crescent moon down his length. The brilliance grew, brightened to encapsulate Mira. She closed her eyes, not that it stopped the tears rolling down her cheeks. The warmth of the light touched her face in a gossamer goodbye.

When she opened them again, he was gone. A single pearl spun in the air above her head. It drifted down, and she cradled it in her arms like a babe. It was opalescent and warm, not yet firm.

The line of the tsunami stretched out on either side as far as the eye could see. The thunderhead of foam increased in height as it moved towards the city. It sounded like the whole population screaming at once, roaring at the tops of their voices. The wave was taller than most of the buildings outside Jingsha. And still it grew.

Mira passed the pearl to Nami. "You need to use it."

"I don't know how. What to do with it, with him." Nami faltered.

"Protect the city," Mira said, echoing Kai's last message. She'd just watched the person she loved sacrifice himself. Turn himself into a pure mass of energy. A dragon pearl. She should have said something more. Given Nami an idea. But she could barely keep herself from tearing her nails down her face. He'd done it for them. For her. Because he believed in making Tiankawi better. Because he wanted to protect her, her family, her friends. Because long before he'd made this sacrifice, he'd magnified love like no one else she knew.

And she had just lost him.

All of this filled her mind as the tsunami washed closer. The world would end in minutes, but for Mira it was already over.

Chapter Sixty

Nami felt the warmth from the pearl. *Brother, tell me what to do.* He was gone. She could never ask him for advice again. It was not enough that he was better at waterweaving, studying, martial skills, he had to be better at sacrificing himself too. She heaved a dry sob. She had one chance to ensure his sacrifice was worth it. One wish. Expand and intensify what was already there.

The tsunami raced towards them, a hundred thousand white horses pounding their feet on the surf. Trails of white like wings behind them.

What could she ask for? Bigger vessels? Taller buildings? Raise the seabed? Time was running out. Her fingers sank into the soft outer casing of the pearl and she closed her eyes. She talked to its heart. Whispered what she thought was best, for them, for everyone. For a moment, she heard Kai laugh. The good-natured sound of an indulgent older brother. The pearl sang, a single high note, and a blue light burst from it, spreading like a ripple across the city. Then it disintegrated in her hands.

The white line of the tidal wave was on them now. The roar of the water was deafening, battering Nami's eardrums. It pushed over the surface of the smaller buildings, sweeping them away like the brush of a hand. Masonry collapsed with a low-bellied growl. She saw the ships in the water turn, facing the waves straight on;

their best chance, although it looked like a fool's errand. They had run out of time.

The wave crashed over Jingsha, cresting like a wall. Pushing, crushing as it went. Everything below the tallest buildings was covered. The rolling mist pushed past them. Boats and buildings swirled and rammed into crevices, wedged between towers and under bridges. Those on the roof instinctively fell to their knees, the gale buffeting them, dragging them towards the far side of the building. Nami grabbed onto Mira, holding the siren close. Their foreheads touched as they hunkered down. Despite the noise, she could hear Mira's cries, the wetness of her tears mixing with the ocean spray. But all Nami felt was numb.

Like a howling beast beating its chest, the crest finally passed. Nami ventured a glance, the wind still cutting into her skin. Shielded her eyes against the grit and sand, every muscle protesting as she stood.

Wave after wave slapped against the buildings, churning the filthy soup. People bobbed in the water, fathomfolk ducking their heads under and popping back to the surface. Humans on other rooftops stared in horrified fascination. The waves went on and on, but their power was fading now, each one weaker than the last, until finally the sea was exhausted, its rage reduced to sullen brooding.

Hours passed, although it seemed to be little more than minutes. The silence that followed the tsunami was peculiar. The whole world had been washed clean. Nothing stirred. Just the lapping of the waves, knocking capsized boats together. Seabirds flying overhead swooped back down, perching on roof ledges and bobbing on the rippling surface of the water as if nothing had happened at all.

"Let's go," Nami said, feigning confidence. Mira nodded but couldn't speak. Nami linked her arm, lacking the words to articulate how they both felt. Signs of damage were everywhere in the building. Water had poured through the windows and everything was drenched, dragged through the rooms as the wave passed. Bodies too, ones Nami didn't want to examine closely. A few fathomfolk were up and about. Dazed.

It hadn't worked.

She felt herself turn cold, shaking as her tongue stuck dry to the roof of her mouth. She had wasted Kai's sacrifice. For nothing. She kneeled down next to a body, checking for signs of life. The woman spluttered and coughed wetly. She was okay. Nami moved on to a family huddled together. Bedraggled but fine. The mother was patting down her children, disbelief written all over her face. "We were submerged, completely submerged ... I felt myself drowning," she said softly.

The next floor was the same.

And the next.

They reached the surface level. Nami's feet moved on automatic, one in front of the other. The waves lapped into the reception area, the tiled floors still ankle deep in muddy water. By the front door, the wooden walkway had splintered away to nothing. The upper bridges looked like they might be repairable, but the crop walls didn't look great. Chunks had been ripped clean away. A chinthe vessel chugged its way towards their position.

"Captain!" called one of the men on board, waving at Mira. She looked around, perplexed as to what she should do with the mooring rope they threw her. All the cleats had been ripped clean off. Then the guard laughed and just jumped off the side of the boat into the water. Another one followed, and another.

"Be careful, the water's deep here. The debris—" Mira began. Her warning stopped sharply as she saw the same thing Nami did.

The officer brought his hands to the sides of his neck, displaying what looked like a collar of delicate flesh-coloured ferns. "We grew gills!"

Almost simultaneously, a woman screamed. Rubbing at her

son's neck, at the newly formed gills as if they were dirt stains to be removed. She ran her hands down her own neck, eyes widening in horror at what she found.

Mira looked at the chinthe officer, stunned, then to Nami, then back at him. Nami no longer remembered the frantic words she had whispered to Kai's pearl as the tsunami crashed around them. She recalled the sentiment though. To extend their similarities. To help them find a way, as Kai always had, to bring protection and kindness and understanding to Tiankawi. She had hoped for something her brother would approve of, something that would make a difference.

It had worked.

They had saved people. Prevented them from drowning. But looking at the elation, the palpable fear, the blank faces of pure shock, she realised that this changed everything.

Nami sat forgotten on a capsized taxi boat as Mira was reunited with her people. The muted hustle of the clean-up had already started behind her, but she needed a moment to herself. She rubbed self-consciously at her crown, where the broken antlers had since smoothed back under her short hair. She had not been able to do it. Had not been able to sacrifice herself when the crucial moment arose.

"Nami," said a now familiar voice. She'd been waiting for him. Firth was a survivor, after all. "Thank the titans, you're still alive."

His choice of words made her wince. The titan. Lynnette. How could she ever trust him again? But then she looked down. Firth was badly bruised, a deep cut running up one cheek that puckered in the saltwater. Despite herself, she slipped into the water, running her hands over his face. Her fingers trembled, her whole body shaking as the shock of what had happened burst within her.

Kai was gone. Because of the Drawbacks. Because of her.

She knew this was wrong. But the grief was a swirling maelstrom. Ravenous, it tore at her raw edges, dragging her entire being with it. She was adrift. A choked sob escaped her lips, one she dared not express in front of Mira.

Firth gripped her by the wrists. His hand clamped over her pakalot, making it bite against her skin. "Look at me." His voice was deep. Intense as the eddies in his eyes. "I love you."

In that moment, Nami did not care if it was true. Did not care if she trusted him or not. He was a compass point in the storm. She kissed him. He tasted of salt and iron. She screwed her eyes shut and let herself drown.

Epilogue

The harsh sun beat down on the docks, sending most people under the shade of the partially erected shelters or pulling wide-brimmed hats low over their brows. Cordelia wrapped a damp towel about her neck. No one concealed their gills these days. The landscape continued to slip and slide, but the preponderance of gills since the tsunami meant they didn't mark people as different any more. Eyes no longer slid over necklines. All hands were needed to rebuild the city, and those left were thankful to be alive. Things were quiet. Subdued.

Temporarily.

She shouldered the sack of seeds towards the small vessel, on her left side since her wound still had not healed. They desperately needed to replant the crop walls before winter came. Casual work was easy to pick up, especially for a strong-limbed water bull. Cordelia maintained a moody persona in her current tarbh uisge guise. It stopped people from chit-chatting, allowed her to plan her next steps. One day at a time. But she would rebuild.

Tiankawi was changed, for now and ever more. Too early to say whether for better or worse. The clean-up after the tsunami was slow and still ongoing. It was exactly the time when they needed new blood, new settlers in the community. The reasons to take in more fathomfolk were insurmountable. What did being folk even mean now? Especially with a strong voice on the Council.

Familiar figures stood on the docks. "Nami!" Mira, newly confirmed Minister of Fathomfolk, strolled decisively towards the dragon. She waved to the workers, nodding and complimenting as she went. Even Cordelia had to admit that she looked good in her green uniform, reappointed as captain of the chinthe. Rumour had it she might go for Samnang's job. The captain of the kumiho had inexplicably resigned, citing family reasons, and withdrawn almost entirely from public life. Mira styled her hair differently now too, wrapping her long hair into a bun. It made her look older. That or perhaps the way she glanced into the middle distance from time to time, forgetting herself as she spun the betrothal bangles on her wrists, her fingers tracing their delicate design.

Cordelia grabbed another sack from the pallet, her feet wandering closer to the pair to eavesdrop as she passed.

Nami and Mira hugged tightly. "It's been weeks," Nami remarked.

"Your fault for turning down the position as minister," Mira said.

Nami shrugged, and Cordelia observed her indifference to be real. The change she cared for was not the kind that could be effected in meetings. She had neither the patience nor the interest for that sort of world. "I still need to answer for Onseon. The inquest, the punishment . . . Besides, they found the best person for the job."

Mira arched an eyebrow but nodded all the same. Then she turned to look out at the settlement vessel slowly making its way towards them. "It's become a bit of a ritual, this. Being here when they arrive. A welcoming face for a fresh start."

"I needed that when I arrived."

"Planning to go back?"

"To Yonakuni?" Nami looked at her in surprise. "For a visit, perhaps. But this is home now."

Mira punched her lightly on the shoulder and then linked arms with her. "Dinner tonight?"

"You have time? Rumour has it you've started a gill adjustment programme."

Mira shrugged, not denying it. "Ama is making dhaal and dulse cakes."

"Arm twisted." Nami grinned. They stood together in easy companionship as around them people bustled.

"Titans, I miss him," Mira said, so quietly Cordelia almost didn't catch it. She leaned her head on Nami's shoulder. "Sometimes I swear I hear his laugh, expect to see his face in the crowd."

Nami did not respond, looking towards the flapping flag on the settlement vessel. The gangplank was slowly lowered. "I see him too. In every new pair of gills. He's still here." She squeezed Mira's hand in her own.

Mira cleared her throat, rubbing her cheeks and straightening up. She turned, suddenly looking Cordelia in the eye. The sea-witch had been staring with a ferocity she hadn't intended. She pretended the sack had slipped, stopped to adjust it and whistled as she moved on.

They'd all forgotten – or at least wanted to forget – that *something* had answered the titan's dying call. Something was coming to Tiankawi, and Cordelia was the only one preparing for its arrival.

Below the waterline, at the far edges of Tiankawi's waters – beyond the tuk-tuk drivers and the water market; the spindle-legged stilts and iron struts; further than the carcasses of shipwrecks and rusted tram carriages – lay a burgeoning kelp forest. The vertical columns of seaweed billowed in the currents as sea otters spiralled through the fronds chasing fish. Nestled there on the seabed, unremarkable in the gravel, was a curious stone unlike the others.

A figure reached a hand down, plucking the stone like a ripe berry from a tree. Held it up to the dim light piercing the kelp.

Swirls of green and grey coated its surface and a burst of off-pitch singing slid through the squeaks and coos of the otters' play, frightening them away.

A fist closed around the stone. The muffled sound carried anyway. Rippled in the current to lap up against Tiankawi's broken walkways and boats. Further out, beyond the city boundaries, another wave was set in motion.

The story continues in...

Tideborn

Book TWO of the Drowned World

Acknowledgements

I always love to read the acknowledgement pages in books. It helped me understand books don't exist in isolation, no matter how films portray a real author™ as a chain-smoking, whisky-drinking loner in log cabin with an old typewriter. So hello, fellow inquisitive reader. These are the fine individuals who helped keep Fathomfolk afloat.

Thanks to my stalwart agent Alex Cochran for championing this novel and holding my hand during the whole process, before, after and during. Also for continuing to tolerate my unsolicited toddler photos in your inbox. My UK editor Jenni Hill, who egged me on to put cabbage man references in the novel: thank you for pushing and polishing and asking the questions I hoped I got away with not answering. You helped plug all the holes in this leaky boat! To Nazia Khatun, my publicist and fellow Studio Ghibli enthusiast – so glad I enthused about magical balls all those years ago at Fantasycon. Brit Hvide, my US editor, thank you for bringing this novel across the pond and seeing the modern East and South East Asia that Tiankawi is based on. I'd like to thank EVERYONE but apparently there are simply too many hard-working people involved in bringing a book to publication. This is an incomplete list of some amazing individuals who inputted, but I know there will be others who worked damn hard as well: cover designer Ella

Garrett, cover artist Kelly Chong, project editor Zakirah Alam, copy editor Jane Selley, Rose Ferrao, Serena Savini, Madeleine Hall, Jessica Dryburgh, Angelica Chong, Bryn McDonald, Ellen Wright, Angela Man, Natassja Haught, Rachel Hairston, Lauren Panepinto, Alexia Mazis, Dorcas Rogers, Tracy England, Louise Emslie-Smith and Camilla Smallwood.

To my beta readers who read the broken early draft of this novel, Ashley Deng and Tobi Ogundiran. I'm sorry your eyes had to endure that mess. Thank you for pointing out its flaws to make it shine. My cottagecore writing besties, G.V. Anderson and Jess Hyslop. For the crit swaps, prosecco, the gifs and rambling late night messages: I didn't understand the appeal of cons and networking until I found the two of you. Social media is in fact good for something, and you are both evidence of this!

To my many mentors over the years, whether they knew it or not. Beth Dickson, the only English teacher who didn't stick their nose up at my fantasy stories. Neil Williamson, for the gentle but insistent cajoling to keep writing, no matter the miles and years between our infrequent meetings. To Maisie Chan, without whom I would never have dragged the first draft kicking and screaming from my brain. Thank you for mentoring me, for the Bubble Tea Writers group and for all you have done for East and South East Asian representation in the UK.

To my Northern boardgame and RPG geeks, Tom Lean, Gareth Morgan, Emily Jones and most especially Steph Edwards and Ali Lean: for reading; for listening; for forwarding every article about creepy deep sea creatures and obscure folktales; for brainstorming fishy curses and using every water-based emojis you could find. Thank you. Books brought us together all those years ago and I could never ask for a better bunch of miscreants to hang out with. Pathfinder on Tuesday?

To my parents, who have always been baffled by my "hobby" but eventually realised it was not just a phase. Thank you for the roof over my head, the food on the table and for encouraging a love of reading, even if this was just free childcare to leave me in the public library whilst you went to the supermarket. My father passed away before this book was published, but sharing my book deal news was the one bright spark in an otherwise difficult year: 爹哋,一百千 and more. P.S. I would've been an atrocious doctor! To my sisters Teresa and Melissa, thanks for existing. Read more books please. Yes, I mean this one specifically. To my in-laws Claudia and in memory of John, thank you for your support and answering my obscure questions about Chinese culture.

To my son, who confidently understands that mummy's job is "drinking a cup of tea". Thank you for not hitting delete on my manuscript when you've wanted to play with the ABCs. May you find fantasies of your own as you grow.

And last, but never least, to my husband Ken. For acting out action scenes in the kitchen, for bouncing ideas together during long car journeys, for gifting me with seawitch and water dragon jewellery, for being my biggest fan and best friend. I regret to inform you, you can't retire and live off my millions yet, but together, let's keep pursuing that dream.

extras

orbit

meet the author

Sandi Hodkinson

ELIZA CHAN is a Scottish-born Chinese-diaspora author who writes about East Asian mythology, British folklore, and mad-women in the attic, but preferably all three at once. Eliza's work has been published in *The Dark*, *PodCastle*, *Fantasy Magazine*, and *The Best of British Fantasy 2019*. *Fathomfolk* is her first novel.

Find out more about Eliza Chan and other Orbit authors by registering for the free monthly newsletter at orbitbooks.net.

if you enjoyed
FATHOMFOLK

look out for

THE JASAD HEIR
The Scorched Throne: Book One

by

Sara Hashem

A fugitive queen strikes a bargain with her greatest enemy that could resurrect her scorched kingdom or leave it in ashes forever in this unmissable Egyptian-inspired epic fantasy debut.

Ten years ago, the kingdom of Jasad burned. Its magic was outlawed. Its royal family murdered. At least, that's what Sylvia wants people to believe. The Heir of Jasad escaped the massacre, and she intends to stay hidden, especially from the armies of Nizahl that continue to hunt her people.

But a moment of anger changes everything. When Arin, the Nizahl Heir, tracks a group of Jasadi rebels to her village, Sylvia accidentally reveals her magic—and captures his attention. Now Sylvia's forced to make a deal with her greatest enemy: Help him hunt the rebels in exchange for her life.

A deadly game begins. Sylvia can't let Arin discover her identity, even as hatred shifts into something more between the Heirs. And as the tides change around her, Sylvia will have to choose between the life she wants and the one she abandoned.

The scorched kingdom is rising, and it needs a queen.

CHAPTER ONE

Two things stood between me and a good night's sleep, and I was allowed to kill only one of them.

I tromped through Hirun River's mossy banks, squinting for movement. The grime, the late hours—I had expected those. Every apprentice in the village dealt with them. I just hadn't expected the frogs.

"Say your farewells, you pointless pests," I called. The frogs had developed a defensive strategy they put into action any time I came close. First, the watch guard belched an alarm. The others would fling themselves into the river. Finally, the brave watch guard hopped for his life. An effort as admirable as it was futile.

Dirt was caked deep beneath my fingernails. Moonlight filtered through a canopy of skeletal trees, and for a moment, my hand looked like a different one. A hand much more manicured, a little weaker. Niphran's hands. Hands that could wield an axe alongside the burliest woodcutter, weave a storm of curls into delicate braids, drive spears into the maws of monsters. For the first few years of my life, before grief over my father's assassination spread through Niphran like rot, before her sanity collapsed on itself, there wasn't anything my mother's hands could not do.

Oh, if she could see me now. Covered in filth and outwitted by croaking river roaches.

Hirun exhaled its opaque mist, breathing life into the winter bones of Essam Woods. I cleaned my hands in the river and firmly cast aside thoughts of the dead.

A frenzied croak sounded behind a tree root. I darted forward, scooping up the kicking watch guard. Ah, but it was never the brave who escaped. I brought him close to my face. "Your friends are chasing crickets, and you're here. Were they worth it?"

I dropped the limp frog into the bucket and sighed. Ten more to go, which meant another round of running in circles and hoping mud wouldn't spill through the hole in my right boot. The fact that Rory was a renowned chemist didn't impress me, nor did this coveted apprenticeship. What kept me from tossing the bucket and going to Raya's keep, where a warm meal and a comfortable bed awaited me, was a debt of convenience.

Rory didn't ask questions. When I appeared on his doorstep five years ago, drenched in blood and shaking, Rory had tended to my wounds and taken me to Raya's. He rescued a fifteen-year-old orphan with no history or background from a life of vagrancy.

The sudden snap of a branch drew my muscles tight. I reached into my pocket and wrapped my fingers around the hilt of my dagger. Given the Nizahl soldiers' predilection for randomly searching us, I usually carried my blade strapped in my boot, but I'd used it to cut my foot out of a family of tangled ferns and left it in my pocket.

A quick scan of the shivering branches revealed nothing. I tried not to let my eyes linger in the empty pockets of black between the trees. I had seen too much horror manifest out of the dark to ever trust its stillness.

My gaze moved to the place it dreaded most—the row of trees behind me, each scored with identical, chillingly precise black marks. The symbol of a raven spreading its wings had been carved into the trees circling Mahair's border. In the muck of the woods, these ravens remained pristine. Crossing the raven-marked trees without permission was an offense punishable by imprisonment or worse. In the lower villages, where the kingdom's leaders were already primed to turn a blind eye to the liberties taken by Nizahl soldiers, worse was usually just the beginning.

I tucked my dagger into my pocket and walked right to the edge of the perimeter. I traced one raven's outstretched wing with my thumbnail. I would have traded all the frogs in my bucket to be brave enough to scrape my nails over the symbol, to gouge it off. Maybe that same burst of bravery would see my dagger cutting a line in the bark, disfiguring the symbols of Nizahl's power. It wasn't walls or swords keeping us penned in like animals, but a simple carving. Another kingdom's power billowing over us like poisoned air, controlling everything it touched.

I glanced at the watch guard in my bucket and lowered my hand. Bravery wasn't worth the cost. Or the splinters.

A thick layer of frost coated the road leading back to Mahair. I pulled my hood nearly to my nose as soon as I crossed the wall separating Mahair from Essam Woods. I veered into an alley, winding my way to Rory's shop instead of risking the exposed—and regularly patrolled—main road. Darkness cloaked me as soon as I stepped into the alley. I placed a stabilizing hand on the wall and let the pungent odor of manure guide my feet forward. A cat hissed from beneath a stack of crates, hunching protectively over the half-eaten carcass of a rat.

"I already had supper, but thank you for the offer," I whispered, leaping out of reach of her claws.

Twenty minutes later, I clunked the full bucket at Rory's feet. "I demand a renegotiation of my wages."

Rory didn't look up from his list. "Demand away. I'll be over there."

He disappeared into the back room. I scowled, contemplating following him past the curtain and maiming him with frog corpses. The smell of mud and mildew had permanently seeped into my skin. The least he could do was pay extra for the soap I needed to mask it.

I arranged the poultices, sealing each jar carefully before placing it inside the basket. One of the rare times I'd found myself on the wrong side of Rory's temper was after I had forgotten to seal the ointments before sending them off with Yuli's boy. I learned as much about the spread of disease that day as I did about Rory's staunch ethics.

Rory returned. "Off with you already. Get some sleep. I do not want the sight of your face to scare off my patrons tomorrow." He prodded in the bucket, turning over a few of the frogs. Age weathered

Rory's narrow brown face. His long fingers were constantly stained in the color of his latest tonic, and a permanent groove sat between his bushy brows. I called it his "rage stage," because I could always gauge his level of fury by the number of furrows forming above his nose. Despite an old injury to his hip, his slenderness was not a sign of fragility. On the rare occasions when Rory smiled, it was clear he had been handsome in his youth. "If I find that you've layered the bottom with dirt again, I'm poisoning your tea."

He pushed a haphazardly wrapped bundle into my arms. "Here."

Bewildered, I turned the package over. "For me?"

He waved his cane around the empty shop. "Are you touched in the head, child?"

I carefully peeled the fabric back, half expecting it to explode in my face, and exposed a pair of beautiful golden gloves. Softer than a dove's wing, they probably cost more than anything I could buy for myself. I lifted one reverently. "Rory, this is too much."

I only barely stopped myself from putting them on. I laid them gingerly on the counter and hurried to scrub off my stained hands. There were no clean cloths left, so I wiped my hands on Rory's tunic and earned a swat to the ear.

The fit of the gloves was perfect. Soft and supple, yielding with the flex of my fingers.

I lifted my hands to the lantern for closer inspection. These would certainly fetch a pretty price at market. Not that I'd sell them right away, of course. Rory liked pretending he had the emotional depth of a spoon, but he would be hurt if I bartered his gift a mere day later. Markets weren't hard to find in Omal. The lower villages were always in need of food and supplies. Trading among themselves was easier than begging for scraps from the palace.

The old man smiled briefly. "Happy birthday, Sylvia."

Sylvia. My first and favorite lie. I pressed my hands together. "A consolation gift for the spinster?" Not once in five years had Rory failed to remember my fabricated birth date.

"I should hardly think spinsterhood's threshold as low as twenty years."

In truth, I was halfway to twenty-one. Another lie.

"You are as old as time itself. The ages below one hundred must all look the same to you."

He jabbed me with his cane. "It is past the hour for spinsters to be about."

I left the shop in higher spirits. I pulled my cloak tight around my shoulders, knotting the hood beneath my chin. I had one more task to complete before I could finally reunite with my bed, and it meant delving deeper into the silent village. These were the hours when the mind ran free, when hollow masonry became the whispers of hungry shaiateen and the scratch of scuttling vermin the sounds of the restless dead.

I knew how sinuously fear cobbled shadows into gruesome shapes. I hadn't slept a full night's length in long years, and there were days when I trusted nothing beyond the breath in my chest and the earth beneath my feet. The difference between the villagers and me was that I knew the names of my monsters. I knew what they would look like if they found me, and I didn't have to imagine what kind of fate I would meet.

if you enjoyed
FATHOMFOLK
look out for

THE PHOENIX KING
The Ravence Trilogy:
Book One

by

Aparna Verma

From a stunning new voice in fantasy comes an Indian-inspired, action-packed debut of fire magic and ancient prophecy, in which the fate of a kingdom rests in the hands of a princess desperate for power and an assassin with a dark secret.

The Ravani kingdom was born of a prophecy, carved from unforgiving desert sands and ruled by the Ravence bloodline: those with the power to command the Eternal Fire.

Elena Aadya is the heir to the throne—and the only Ravence who cannot wield her family's legendary magic. As her coronation approaches, she will do whatever it takes to prove herself a worthy successor to her revered father.

But she doesn't anticipate the arrival of Yassen Knight, the notorious assassin who now claims fealty to the throne. Elena's father might trust Yassen to be a member of her royal guard, but she is certain he is hiding something.

As the threat of war looms like a storm on the horizon, the two begin a dangerous dance of intrigue and betrayal. And the choices they make could burn down the world.

CHAPTER 1

Yassen

The king said to his people, "We are the chosen."
And the people responded, "Chosen by whom?"

—from chapter 37 of *The Great History of Sayon*

To be forgiven, one must be burned. That's what the Ravani said. They were fanatics and fire worshippers, but they were his people. And he would finally be returning home.

Yassen held on to the railing of the hoverboat as it skimmed over the waves. He held on with his left arm, his right limp by his side. Around him, the world was dark, but the horizon began to purple with the faint glimmers of dawn. Soon, the sun would rise, and the twin moons of Sayon would lie down to rest. Soon, he would arrive at Rysanti, the Brass City. And soon, he would find his way back to the desert that had forsaken him.

Yassen withdrew a holopod from his jacket and pressed it open with his thumb. A small holo materialized with a message:

Look for the bull.

He closed the holo, the smell of salt and brine filling his lungs.

The bull. It was nothing close to the Phoenix of Ravence, but then again, Samson liked to be subtle. Yassen wondered if he would be at the port to greet him.

A large wave tossed the boat, but Yassen did not lose his balance. Weeks at sea and suns of combat had taught him how to keep his ground. A cool wind licked his sleeve, and he felt a whisper of pain skitter down his right wrist. He grimaced. His skin was already beginning to redden.

After the Arohassin had pulled him half-conscious from the sea, Yassen had thought, in the delirium of pain, that he would be free. If not in this life, then in death. But the Arohassin had yanked him back from the brink. Treated his burns and saved his arm. Said that he was lucky to be alive while whispering among themselves when they thought he could not hear: "Yassen Knight is no longer of use."

Yassen pulled down his sleeve. It was no matter. He was used to running.

As the hoverboat neared the harbor, the fog along the coastline began to evaporate. Slowly, Yassen saw the tall spires of the Brass City cut through the grey heavens. Skyscrapers of slate and steel from the mines of Sona glimmered in the early dawn as hover-trains weaved through the air, carrying the day laborers. Neon lights flickered within the metal jungle, and a silver bridge snaked through the entire city, connecting the outer rings to the wealthy, affluent center. Yassen squinted as the sun crested the horizon. Suddenly, its light hit the harbor, and the Brass City shone with a blinding intensity.

Yassen quickly clipped on his visor, a fiber sheath that covered his entire face. He closed his eyes for a moment, allowing them to readjust before opening them again. The city stared back at him in subdued colors.

Queen Rydia, one of the first queens of Jantar, had wanted to ward off Enuu, the evil eye, so she had fashioned her port city out of unforgiving metal. If Yassen wasn't careful, the brass could blind him.

The other passengers came up on deck, pulling on half visors that covered their eyes. Yassen tightened his visor and wrapped a scarf around his neck. Most people could not recognize him—none of the passengers even knew of his name—but he could not take any chances. Samson had made it clear that he wanted no one to know of this meeting.

The hoverboat came to rest beside the platform, and Yassen disembarked with the rest of the passengers. Even in the early hours, the port was busy. On the other dock, soldiers barked out orders as fresh immigrants stumbled off a colony boat. Judging from the coiled silver bracelets on their wrists, Yassen guessed they were Sesharian refugees. They shuffled forward on the adjoining dock toward military buses. Some carried luggage; others had nothing save the clothes they wore. They all donned half visors and walked with the resigned grace of people weary of their fate.

Native Jantari, in their lightning suits and golden bracelets, kept a healthy distance from the immigrants. They stayed on the brass homeland and receiving docks where merchants stationed their carts. Unlike most of the city, the carts were made of pale drift-wood, but the vendors still wore half visors as they handled their wares. Yassen could already hear a merchant hawking satchels of vermilion tea while another shouted about a new delivery of mirrors from Cyleon that had a 90 percent accuracy of predicting one's romantic future. Yassen shook his head. Only in Jantar.

Floating lanterns guided Yassen and the passengers to the glass-encased immigration office. Yassen slid his holopod into the port while a grim-faced attendant flicked something from his purple nails.

"Name?" he intoned.

"Cassian Newman," Yassen said.

"Country of residence?"

"Nbru."

The attendant waved his hand. "Take off your visor, please."

Yassen unclipped his visor and saw shock register across the attendant's face as he took in Yassen's white, colorless eyes.

"Are you Jantari?" the attendant asked, surprised.

"No," Yassen responded gruffly and clipped his visor back on. "My father was."

"Hmph." The attendant looked at his holopod and then back at him. "Purpose of your visit?"

Yassen paused. The attendant peered at him, and for one wild moment, Yassen wondered if he should turn away, jump back on the boat, and go wherever the sea pushed him. But then a coldness slithered down his right elbow, and he gripped his arm.

"To visit some old friends," Yassen said.

The attendant snorted, but when the holopod slid back out, Yassen saw the burning insignia of a mohanti, a winged ox, on its surface.

"Welcome to the Kingdom of Jantar," the attendant said and waved him through.

Yassen stepped through the glass immigration office and into Rysanti. He breathed in the sharp salt air, intermingled with spices both foreign and familiar. A storm had passed through recently, leaving puddles in its wake. A woman ahead of Yassen slipped on a wet plank and a merchant reached out to steady her. Yassen pushed past them, keeping his head down. Out of the corner of his eye, he saw the merchant swipe the woman's holopod and hide it in his jacket. Yassen smothered a laugh.

As he wandered toward the homeland dock, he scanned the faces in the crowd. The time was nearly two past the sun's breath. Samson and his men should have been here by now.

He came to the bridge connecting the receiving and homeland docks. At the other end of the bridge was a lonely tea stall, held together by worn planks—but the large holosign snagged his attention.

WARM YOUR TIRED BONES FROM YOUR PASSAGE AT SEA! FRESH HOT LEMON CAKES AND RAVANI TEA SERVED DAILY! it read.

It was the word *Ravani* that sent a jolt through Yassen. Home—the one he longed for but knew he was no longer welcome in.

Yassen drew up to the tea stall. Three large hourglasses hissed and steamed. Tea leaves floated along their bottoms, slowly steeping, as a heavyset Sesharian woman flipped them in timed intervals. On her hand, Yassen spotted a tattoo of a bull.

The same mark Samson had asked him to look for.

When the woman met Yassen's eyes, she twirled the hourglass once more before drying her hands on the towel around her wide waist.

"Whatcha want?" she asked in a river-hoarse voice.

"One tea and cake, please," Yassen said.

"You're lucky. I just got a fresh batch of leaves from my connect. Straight from the canyons of Ravence."

"Exactly why I want one," he said and placed his holopod in the counter insert. Yassen tapped it twice.

"Keep the change," he added.

She nodded and turned back to the giant hourglasses.

The brass beneath Yassen's feet grew warmer in the yawning day. Across the docks, more boats pulled in, carrying immigrant laborers and tourists. Yassen adjusted his visor, making sure it was fully in place, as the woman simultaneously flipped the hourglass and slid off its cap. In one fluid motion, the hot tea arced through the air and fell into the cup in her hand. She slid it across the counter.

"Mind the sleeve, the tea's hot," she said. "And here's your cake."

Yassen grabbed the cake box and lifted his cup in thanks. As he moved away from the stall, he scratched the plastic sleeve around the cup.

Slowly, a message burned through:

Look underneath the dock of fortunes.

He almost smiled. Clearly, Samson had not forgotten Yassen's love of tea.

Yassen looked within the box and saw that there was no cake but something sharp, metallic. He reached inside and held it up. Made of silver, the insignia was smaller than his palm and etched in what seemed to be the shape of a teardrop. Yassen held it closer. No, it was more feather than teardrop.

He threw the sleeve and box into a bin, slid the silver into his pocket, and continued down the dock. The commerce section stretched on, a mile of storefronts welcoming him into the great nation of Jantar. Yassen sipped his tea, watching. A few paces down was a stall marketing tales of ruin and fortune. Like the tea stall, it too was old and decrepit, with a painting of a woman reading palms painted across its front. He was beginning to recognize a pattern—and patterns were dangerous. Samson was getting lazy in his mansion.

Three guards stood along the edge of the platform beside the stall. One was dressed in a captain's royal blue, the other two in the plain black of officers. All three wore helmet visors, their pulse guns strapped to their sides. They were laughing at some joke when the captain looked up and frowned at Yassen.

"You there," he said imperiously.

Yassen slowly lowered his cup. The dock was full of carts and merchants. If he ran now, the guards could catch him.

"Yes, you, with the full face," the captain called out, tapping his visor. "Come here!"

"Is there a problem?" Yassen asked as he approached.

"No full visors allowed on the dock, except for the guard," the captain said.

"I didn't know it was a crime to wear a full visor," Yassen said. His voice was cool, perhaps a bit too nonchalant because the captain slapped the cup out of Yassen's hand. The spilled tea hissed against the metal planks.

"New rules," the captain said. "Only guards can wear full visors. Everybody else has to go half."

His subordinates snickered. "Looks like he's fresh off the boat, Cap. You got to cut it up for him," one said.

Behind his visor, Yassen frowned. He glanced at the merchant leaning against the fortunes stall. The man wore a bored expression, as if the interaction before him was nothing new. But then the merchant bent forward, pressing his hands to the counter, and Yassen saw the sign of the bull tattooed there.

Samson's men were watching.

"All right," Yassen said. He would give them a show.

orbit

Follow us:

f /orbitbooksUS

X /orbitbooks

▶ /orbitbooks

Join our mailing list
to receive alerts on our
latest releases and deals.

orbitbooks.net

Enter our monthly
giveaway for the chance
to win some epic prizes.

orbitloot.com